SHADOWRUN

HOUSE OF THE SUN

Nigel D. Findley

A ROC BOOK

ROC
Published by the Penguin Group
Penguin Books USA Inc., 375 Hudson Street,
New York, New York 10014, U.S.A.
Penguin Books Ltd, 27 Wrights Lane,
London W8 5TZ, England
Penguin Books Australia Ltd, Ringwood,
Victoria, Australia
Penguin Books Canada Ltd, 10 Alcorn Avenue,
Toronto, Ontario, Canada M4V 3B2
Penguin Books (N.Z.) Ltd, 182–190 Wairau Road,
Auckland 10, New Zealand

Penguin Books Ltd, Registered Offices:
Harmondsworth, Middlesex, England

First published by Roc, an imprint of Dutton Signet,
a division of Penguin Books USA Inc.

First Printing, July, 1995
10 9 8 7 6 5 4 3 2 1

Series Editor: Donna Ippolito
Cover: Jim Thiesen

 REGISTERED TRADEMARK—MARCA REGISTRADA

In memory of Nigel Findley
(July 22, 1959–February 19, 1995)

Nigel was in the final stages of proofing this novel when he passed away on February 19, 1995. This novel, like all the others he wrote, exhibits his incredible creative ability to take the unknown and transform it into something believable and enjoyable. *House of the Sun* has special significance to the life of Nigel because Dirk Montgomery was his favorite character and Hawaii was his favorite place. To put Dirk in turmoil again was a challenge Nigel embraced with his usual flair, wild imagination and pursuit of excellence. As I know the pleasure he derived in writing this novel, I dedicate it to Nigel's incredible gift of writing, to his enthusiasm for living and to the wonderful man that he was.

—Holly Langland
Friend and Partner

1

Her name—the one she gave me, at least—was Sharon Young. Not beautiful by any means, but attractive. A strong face, with a good, full mouth. Sharp eyes, the kind that don't miss much, a rather striking shade of green. Long, straight black hair. And, despite what looked to me like a deep-water tan, she was a shadowrunner.

She didn't tell me that, of course. It's hardly something you admit to someone, not unless you trust him with your life. But the good ones don't have to tell you—there's something about the way they move, the way they watch everything that's going on around them—and she was one of the good ones. She wore a loose-fitting jacket, possibly armored, that hung open, and I found myself playing the old game of "find the heat." I gave it up quickly, though: there were enough places under that jacket to stash anything from a hold-out to a chopped-down SMG. I watched her take a sip of the beer she'd just bought, saw the slight frown of distaste. That raised her one notch on the Montgomery Scale of Aesthetic Appreciation. The only thing that kept the draft at The Buffalo Jump from looking green was the unhealthy brew of preservatives, artificial colors, and flavors it contained.

She set the glass down. Time for biz, I thought. "Mr. Montgomery," she began.

"Derek," I corrected. "Or Dirk."

She inclined her head, flashed me a quick half smile. "Dirk." Then she paused again, apparently getting her thoughts in order, deciding just how much she needed to tell me, and how best to go about it.

I glanced away while she did so—a touch of courtesy that also gave me a moment to indulge my own paranoia. A quick look around the room reassured me that nobody in the bar was paying us any undue attention. It was about fifteen hundred hours—midafternoon, between the lunch crowd and the afterwork rush. When I'd arrived in Cheyenne a year ago, I'd been mildly surprised that the Sioux Nation worked on the same nine-to-seventeen schedule as Seattle. I don't know quite what I'd expected to be different ... but I *had* expected some differences. Now, though, I understood that cities were cities—*sararimen* were *sararimen,* whether they were Nihonese, UCASan, or Amerind.

The salad show was in full swing on the small stage, two pieces of blond jailbait, surgically modified to look like identical twins, contributing to the delinquency of a vegetable in an impressively desultory manner. Nobody seemed to care much, even the occupants of "gynecology row" down front. The soundtrack—second-tier glam rock, ten years out of date—could just as well have been white noise for all anyone seemed to care, the DAT recording so overused and abused that digital dropout made the songs virtually unrecognizable. I felt one of those momentary flashes of *déjà vu.* For an instant I wasn't in The Buffalo Jump, but an almost identical place a thousand klicks away—Superdad's, in the Redmond Barrens ...

I shook off the memories, forcing them back into the black mire of my subconscious where they belonged. I wasn't ready to think about Seattle, not yet. With an effort, I refocused my attention on Sharon Young.

By now the attractive shadowrunner had figured out how she was going to make her pitch. With elaborate slowness—obviously to ease the suspicions of a twitchy contact—she reached into a pocket and drew out two small objects, which she placed on the table before me. One was an optical memory chip in a protective casing, the other a silver certified credstick. Again she paused, as if waiting for me to make a move for the chip and certstick—a test to see if I'd breach street etiquette. I kept my hands stationary on the scarred tabletop and waited.

She smiled then, a momentary thing like the single flash of a strobe. I knew it was a test, she knew I knew, I knew she knew I knew, and all that. "I need a background check," she said quietly. "A *confidential* background check."

"An employment issue?"

"If you like."

"Then I assume current information is of most interest."

Again that flash of a smile, accompanied by a millimetric nod.

We understood each other. She wanted a line on someone—present whereabouts, current activities, all that kind of drek. And she didn't want the subject to know I was doing any digging. A standard trace contract, the kind of low-risk, low-exposure backdoor stuff I'd been taking since I drifted into Cheyenne.

"You have a name, I presume."

Her green eyes were unreadable. "Then you'll take the contract?"

Another test—she was being careful. "Contingent on reasonable disclosure," I shot back.

"You'll have minimum exposure," she said calmly. "The subject's out of the country at the moment."

I raised an eyebrow at that. If she knew the subject wasn't in Cheyenne, what kind of paydata was she looking for? I tried to cover my surprise by running my forefinger lightly around the rim of my beer glass.

My *left* forefinger. It was a concentration exercise. I was gratified to see there was no tremble, no instability in the finger. Maybe the glitches in my cyberarm were really behind me.

"It really is a background check," she continued after a few seconds. "Any buzz you can get on current activities will be valuable, don't get me wrong—motivation, connections, exposure ... But I'm really looking for deep background—the whys and the hows, how he got to where he is."

Okay, that made more sense. She knew the subject was out of the country, but she wanted me to learn what he was doing, and presumably what led up to the trip. I nodded. "You're the principal?" I asked, a little test of my own.

She just flashed me another grin—passed with flying colors. "The subject is Jonathan Bridge," she told me at last. "Ork. Sioux citizen. Born and raised in Cheyenne."

"Personal background?"

She tapped the datachip with a fingernail. "Standard rates," she said, with a glance at the certstick. "Half on acceptance, balance on delivery. Deadline ninety-six hours, ten percent on twenty-four, twenty on twelve." That meant a ten percent bonus for each full day by which I beat the deadline, and a twenty percent penalty for each twelve hours I was late. "Standard expenses."

"Extraordinary disbursements?"

"We'll talk."

I nodded. As she'd said, the conditions were standard. I'd done enough of this kind of work in Cheyenne to know the going rates. Just one more thing ... "Any direct exposure, and I bail," I said flatly.

Her turn to nod. "I understand," she replied ... and I couldn't shake the feeling that she really did. How much did she know about me, beyond the "brag-sheet" I'd circulated through the shadow networks?

"Contact information's on the chip," she said, rising smoothly to her feet.

I stood too—didn't offer my hand, just as she didn't offer hers. "I'll be in touch."

"I know you will," she said quietly. She turned and was gone. I waited for her to leave the bar before scooping up the chip and the certstick—etiquette, again and always. I sat once more, turning my gaze on the pseudo-twins, while using my peripheral vision to look for any response to her departure. Nothing, no "trailer" making his or her way to the exit—not that I'd expected anything. Pro is pro, and you get a sense for it ... if you want to stay in this biz, you do, at least.

2

I parked my American beside the Dumpster in an alley just off Randall Avenue, swiped my keycard through the maglock on the back door, and climbed the narrow staircase to the second floor. I approached the door to number 5 and looked for the telltales I'd put in place when I'd left. All were where they were supposed to be. Again I waved my keycard, then thumbed the secondary maglock I'd installed the day after I'd moved in (*right* thumb, of course). The circuitry hummed for an instant as it decided whether I was me. Then the bolt snapped back and the door swung open.

As soon as the door was shut behind me, I peeled off my duster and tossed it toward the nearest chair. Midsummer in Cheyenne is hotter than hell (but it's a *dry* heat, yeah right)—much too hot to warrant anything more than shirtsleeves, let alone an armored coat. But I'd rather be slick with sweat than drenched with blood; call it a character flaw. Since I'd left Seattle, I'd made it a point—bordering on an obsession—never to leave my doss without at least some armor between me and any high-velocity ordnance that might be directed my way.

I crossed to my "office"—a small desk wedged into one corner of the tiny, two-room apartment—and slumped down in a swivel chair that was probably older than I was. I flipped my telecom out of standby mode, and waited while the drek-kicked flatpanel got the idea.

Finally the ancient system came grudgingly online. I slotted the certstick Sharon Young had given me and checked the balance—more from a sense of completeness than because I expected any jiggery-pokery; there's no percentage in stiffing someone on an advance. The numbers came up just the way I'd expected them to: 4,000 nuyen in certified funds. I hit a couple of keys, and my telecom happily transferred the cred from the stick's microchip to my account in

the Cheyenne Interface Bank. That made my account ...
well, pretty close to 4,000 nuyen, if you wanted to be picky
about it. Of that, I earmarked 800¥ for rent, to be siphoned
out of my account whenever my landlord got around to it.
(I'd already made the mistake of bouncing one transaction
off him. *Big* mistake. My landlord was a big, bad, bald ork
with a sunburned pate, creased as though someone had wrinkled it up and then tried to flatten it out again. Everyone
called him "Mother" and left it at that—probably because
anyone who tried to go any further was too busy spitting
teeth to finish.)

Banking duties finished, I pressed the keys to display my
mail. One message in my default mailbox, the one I use for
biz. I thought I knew what that one would be, particularly
when I saw that the Matrix code was Cheyenne. Two messages in my private inbox. Since only three people have the
passcode, it wasn't tough to guess about those either.

Business before pleasure, unfortunately. Another couple
of keystrokes, and the biz message flashed up on the screen.
I recognized the digitized image at once. Jenny was her
name, troll and proud of it, Amerind and even prouder of
that. She wasn't quite a fixer, but she did occasionally bro-
ker "consulting" contracts for people she liked. For some
reason I had yet to fully understand, she *really* liked me.

I kicked the replay up to double speed, and let my mind
drift while Jenny yammered through her message. I knew
what it was about, a contract she'd tossed my way a week
back as a favor, to help me make my rent. Everything had
come out the way the contractor wanted, and Jenny was
gushing with overspeed praise. I slipped the replay back to
standard speed when it seemed that Jenny was winding
down.

"... And if you want to talk about it some more, why
don't you come visit some time?" she was saying, with a
bedroom smile that would frighten small children. "Our
friends will be putting the credit transfer through tomorrow."
Her smile grew broader until I thought she'd swallow her
ears. "Catch ya later, Bernard." And the screen went blank.

I couldn't help but chuckle. "Bernard." I don't know
where it had come from, but the term had swept its way
through the shadow underground of the Sioux Nation over
the last couple of weeks, a kind of trendy substitute for
"chummer" or the Japanese "*omae*." So far it wasn't in com-

mon parlance—not yet—but the local shadowrunners and
wannabes had cottoned onto it as a kind of lodge recognition
signal.

Shadowrunner. It was to laugh. Jenny would drek her
drawers if she ever met a *real* shadowrunner. (Christ, *I* almost did my first time.) The kind of biz she brokered might
be considered "shadow contracts" if you really stretched the
definition of the term, solely because they were mildly illegal, or perhaps extra-legal. All of them were a far cry from
the media-fed vision of balls-to-the-wall shadowrunners,
tweaking the noses of the megacops while dodging a fusillade of bullets. Been there; done that; too rough; pave it.

Let me tell you about the "run" I'd just completed for
Jenny. There was a midrent co-op apartment block on the
edge of Cheyenne's downtown core—the Avalon—that had
been having problems with chip dealers running their business out of one of the penthouses. Activity all round the
clock, disreputable types coming and going, chipheads in the
lobby, and all that drek. The renters' council had tried to
evict the suspected chipmeisters . . . and had been told, in no
uncertain terms, that if they filed the necessary papers, their
knees, elbows, and other body parts would come into conflict with blunt objects in the hands of hired bone-breakers.
The cops couldn't move against the dealers because there
was simply no proof. The residents *knew* what was going on,
but they couldn't bridge the gulf between knowing and prov-
ing.

Enter Dirk Montgomery, stage left, riding a white charger.
My contract—my "shadowrun," if you will—was to roust
the chipmeisters and get them out of the building. No con-
straints on how I was to go about it, no questions asked, results being the only things that mattered.

Jenny, I think, expected me to confront the chipmeisters
directly, possibly over the iron sights of a big fragging gun.
(God knows where she'd built up her exaggerated, romanti-
cized image of me . . .) In the old days, maybe she'd have
been right; maybe I *would* have taken the direct route. But
things have changed. These days, I prefer "social engineering" to hanging my hoop out in the wind.

So how did I handle the chipmeisters? Simple. I staked
out the apartment building and identified the dealers' major
clients—secondary distributors, mainly, rather than the
guttertrash users. Once I had lines on most of them, I sent

each one a personal message by registered e-mail, politely informing them that I had reason to suspect that the person they were visiting so regularly at The Avalon was involved in the illegal chip trade—all "for their own good," of course. The kicker was that I CC'd each letter *to the Cheyenne vice department*!

The upshot? The secondary distributors stopped visiting, and within a couple of days the chipmeisters had moved on. "Shadowrun" complete, zero exposure—just the way I liked it these days.

What? No gunplay? No hashing it out with corp secguards? No exchanging friendly volleys of small-arms fire with Lone Star troopers?

Well ... *no*. By choice. You could say I'm getting old, slowing down. I'd say I'm getting *smart*, wising up. There's a lot to be said for subtlety.

I'd never had any desire to prove I was the baddest, steel-hooped motherfragger ever to walk the streets. Not only did an acquaintance of mine—maybe a friend, depending on your definition—have a lock on the title, in my biased opinion, but experience told me too many people got themselves rather dead trying to go that route. Better a live rat than a dead juggernaut, I'd always figured.

And anyway, you needed edge to get out there on the street. Juice, jam, fire, whatever you wanted to call it. You had to have the moves and the instincts ... and when the drek came down, you had to *trust* those instincts. Did I still have the instincts? Over the last year, I hadn't trusted them enough to find out. And, out there in the shadows, that would have made me a walking target.

All right, granted: there was the sheer adrenaline rush of putting your ass on the line, the transcendent joy you couldn't get any other way without feeding BTL signals into your forebrain. But everything came with a cost, and I always had a reminder of that to hand—my *left* hand.

So let Jenny think what she wanted; let her play her shadowrunner games. Let her pretend that she was operating on the periphery of the shadow "major league." Everyone to her own illusions and delusions. I'd played in that major league once—just once, just one night—and I knew I didn't have what it took to survive a second exposure.

I felt the rush of memories, but I headed them off at the mental pass. That was then, this was now—to (mis)quote

Gautama ... or was it Michael Nesmith? I deleted Jenny's congratulations, and brought up the messages from my personal mailbox.

I didn't recognize the originator address of the first message, but when the image came up on the screen, I knew it had to be a guest account on a remote system somewhere. A shock of dirty-blond hair, cut short and subtly spiked. Slender, slightly elongated face—attractive rather than classically beautiful. Brown eyes in a pale, slightly freckled complexion.

"Hoi, bro," my sister Theresa said.

I flicked a key to freeze the playback while I scrutinized her image. There were dark circles under her eyes. Those eyes had once seemed to flash with the sheer joy of being alive. Now they reminded me of documentary footage I'd seen of soldiers shipped back from the insanity of the EuroWars. Her cheeks were slightly hollow, and I guessed that she was still almost ten kilos undermass.

But there were also noticeable improvements. Her eyes were still shell-shocked, but at least they didn't look quite so *wounded.* Her lips were quirked in a tentative half smile—a long way from the old days, when her smile would have brightened up the whole of my dark, dingy doss, but still a vast improvement from just a few months ago. The pain was still there—the pain that had prompted the choices that, in turn, had directed the course of her life. And the pain that those choices had caused her. That pain would probably *always* be there, I realized sadly. But there was a major change for the better. Now she felt pain; before, she had *been* pain ... and there's one frag of a big difference. These days, I could look into her eyes without wincing.

She was bouncing back—finally I could perceive it, and trust that perception. It had taken almost four years—eighteen solid months of detox, analysis, psycho-rehab, chemo- and electro-therapy, followed by twenty-eight months learning how to relate to the real world again. But it was finally starting to pay off. I shook my head. It was absolutely staggering what the human body—and, more important, the human *mind*—could endure without collapsing.

I backed up the replay a couple of seconds and keyed Play.

"Hoi, bro," my sister Theresa said. "Greetings from the

Front Range Free Zone. Sorry I missed you, but I'll try again in a couple of days.

"Denver's a wiz place, even more schizo than Seattle, if you can believe it. Have you ever made it down here? I can't remember.

"Anyway, next stop's San Fran, I think, if I can get the datawork cleared. Then maybe I'll swing back through Cheyenne and you can take me out for dinner."

Her tentative smile broadened, and for a moment I could see the old Theresa Montgomery. My mind filled with echoes of sudden enthusiasms and innocent laughter. "I'm still having a blast out here, bro," she continued. "It's a big, wonderful world. Oh, and in case you're wondering ..." With a slender hand, she brushed back a blond bang to display her datajack. The jackstopper plug was still firmly in place, the polymer seal unbroken and showing the logo of the detox hospital.

"Still clean," she boasted. "Forty-plus months and counting.

"Catcha ya, Derek." Her image reached toward the screen to break the connection.

Again I paused the playback. I reached out with my left hand, and touched my sister's face—synthetic flesh touching synthesized image.

She was making it, she was really making that long trek back. When the therapists at the medical center had told me she'd been talking about taking a *wanderjahr*—a protracted traveling vacation—I'd been drek-scared. She was too vulnerable, I'd worried, not yet far enough from the precipice of drugs and chips (and worse!) that had almost claimed her. She wouldn't have the strength to resist the thousands of temptations that the real world represented.

They'd known what they were doing, those therapists—I had to admit that now. They'd known what my reaction would be to the news. Instead of letting me have it out with my sister, instead of letting me browbeat her into abandoning the plan, they hadn't even let me speak to her until *I'd* undergone a little therapy of my own. I hadn't been an easy subject, but I'd eventually come to understand. I *couldn't* have stopped Theresa from going on her *wanderjahr,* if that was what she wanted. Sure, it represented a risk—the therapists and detox doctors recognized that. But the damage to her self-esteem if I, or they, had forbidden her to follow her own truth would have been much more devastating, and absolutely certain. It had been a hard sell, but I'd finally accepted that this was the final therapy for Theresa: final confirmation that she had *control* over her own life, and her own direction.

It had been a gamble, but the wager was won. Forty-some months clean and sober. Coming up on four years of experiencing the world as it was, without the anodyne of simsense, BTL, or 2XS. My sister was on her way back from the brink.

And I couldn't put off viewing the second message any longer. I cleared Theresa's image from the screen and pulled up the other entry in my inbox.

Another woman's face, almost as familiar as my sister's. Short, straight, coppery hair. Gray eyes. Class and refinement by the bucketload. Jocasta Yzerman, sister to the dead Lolita Yzerman—I'd known her as Lolly—and a major player in the . . . the *events* . . . that had precipitated my relocation to Cheyenne. Beautiful Jocasta. There was a pain in the middle of my chest that I wished I could write off as indigestion.

Sometimes you want to experience emotional pain in all its fullness; other times you want it over with as fast as humanly possible. I flipped the telecom into double-speed playback.

Even overspeed, her voice was the perfectly modulated velvet of a trained professional. (I wondered momentarily if she still had her trid show on Seattle's KCPS?) I blotted out the words she was speaking—not difficult; the message wasn't anything but a verbal postcard, "long time, how's it rolling," that sort of thing—and I concentrated on that voice. I remembered the first time I'd met her those four years ago, wound up as tight as the string of a compound bow in her tailored smoke gray leathers, a tall and slender figure with a pistol aimed steadily between my eyes . . .

The message played out, ending with the usual empty benedictions and wishes for my good health, and Jocasta was gone. I stared at the blank telecom screen for a long moment. She'd weathered the storm incredibly well, had Ms. Jocasta Yzerman—no, Mrs. Jocasta Brock, wasn't it, these days? No physical scars, and if there were any emotional ones she kept them well hidden. Was she really that strong, that resilient? Or had she learned something from me during our brief time together—the skill of lying to herself, of totally suppressing emotional pain—ironically, at the same time that I was *un*-learning the same thing? What were her dreams like, in those lonely hours of the night when one's defenses are at low ebb? I supposed I'd never know, not now.

For a few moments I considered sending her a reply—right now, spontaneously, without mentally scripting it all out beforehand. It didn't take me long to flag that as a bad idea. Not now, when I was emotionally open and vulnerable after thinking about Theresa. Hell, I might go so far as to actually talk about what I was really feeling, and who knew where *that* might lead . . . ?

My left arm started to hum softly. I hated when it did that, dropping into some kind of self-diagnostic routine when its central processor figured it had the time. (The spirits alone knew what it did while I was asleep at night.) The sound was very soft, probably inaudible from two meters away, but I always reacted to it the way I would to an alarm clock going off next to my ear. I clenched my left fist strongly a couple of times, and the whirring sound shut itself off.

Silently, I gave thanks to the fine people at Wiremaster Incorporated. That whirring sound from my arm—they might call it a diagnostic routine; *I* called it a wake-up call, a reminder that I was living in the real world. I sighed.

Well, since I had the telecom all powered up, I might as well get some work done. I pulled out the datachip Sharon Young had given me in The Buffalo Jump, slipped it into the telecom's socket, and pulled up the data.

Lots of data, I realized, as it scrolled rapidly off the top of the screen. I cut off the flow of text, specified a more reasonable scroll rate, and repunched the display command.

Jonathan Bridge, this is your life. Almost instantly, I got a better understanding of just why Sharon Young was hiring me. She had a lot of background info here—date of birth, family history, Sioux passport number, partial match of his SIN, even summaries of his transcripts from elementary school. Spot checks of his financial picture, dating back more than ten years—almost a third of the slag's life. The full trip. Obviously, somebody had seriously had their way with the poor, trusting computer in the Sioux's central citizenship registry. I scanned the data again. Pro work, no doubt about it. Working for a solid week, popping wake-ups like candy, I might—*barely,* if the Great Spirits of data processing smiled down on me—be able to rape the system for this kind of personal data.

But that's *all* it was, just data. Numbers, facts, bits and bytes. You'd think that people would understand it, in this computer-driven world of ours, but not many do. Data isn't *information;* data is facts. Information resides in the interconnections, the *interrelations* between facts. Like, putting together the *fact* that water boils at 100 degrees Celsius, and the *fact* that sodium melts at 98 degrees, to extract the *information* that sodium isn't a good material for making teakettles.

What Young wanted from me, obviously, was to take the *facts* that some other researcher—much better at the brute-level stuff than me—had generated, and turn them into some overall sense of friend Jonathan Bridge. That involved sorting through the reams of facts on the datachip, looking for correlations—in time, in space, and in many other more theoretical "axes" (like "financial solvency")—and contradictions. In other words, the interconnections between the numbers. Take an example: Mr. Bridge was flat busted in June 2050, left Cheyenne, and returned in August to pay off a rather large bank loan with a single credit transfer. Conclusion? His business trip out of town had obviously paid off big-time. That sort of thing.

Back in the Bad Old Days, I'd have had to do most of the grunt work myself . . . or, if I wanted to stay true to the hard-boiled-gumshoe archetype, hire a leggy brunette with a sharp tongue and soft heart to do it for me. Today, smartframes and search demons can get the job done faster than any brash-talking secretary, making up in efficiency what they lack in sex appeal. A change for the better? You tell me.

I sat back and stretched. My shoulders were knotted, and a throbbing headache had taken up residence in my left eye. I pushed my chair back from the telecom and checked my finger-watch.

Twenty-three hundred hours, give or take. That meant I'd put in about four solid hours on the machine, whipping up the smartframes and search routines I'd soon be letting loose on Jonathan Bridge. I shook my head—stopped when the headache made its displeasure known.

I wondered what my father would think if he could see the use to which I was putting my aborted university education? Nothing good, I was sure. I sighed. A lot had changed since I'd bailed out of the computer science program at U-Dub—the state of the art waits for no man—but at least I understood some of the basics, a thorough enough grounding on which I could build.

And build I had since I'd left Seattle. I was no "slicer"—one of those bleeding-edge console cowboys who shave black ice for the pure quivering thrill of it—but I'd turned myself into a pretty fair code-jockey. I didn't chase down data as such; let the slicers beat their neurons against corporate glaciers if that was their idea of fun. In contrast, though, I was starting to build a reasonable rep for turning the raw paydata that others collected into usable information. I'd learned just what kind of resources were available out there on the Matrix—open to all comers, or with minimal security—and just how to make best use of them. It was just another extension of the rule by which I'd been living my life since arriving in Cheyenne: No Exposure.

A lot of the learning had been on my own, downloading texts, digital magazines, and even academic papers from the Matrix. When hypertext hadn't been enough, I'd sought out a couple of the *éminences grises* of Cheyenne's "virtual tribes"—aging deckers who didn't have the reflexes to shave ice anymore, but who kept up with the theory because it was all that was left for them. I guess some of my "professors" had seen some potential in me for the trade, because they'd tried to pressure me into going under the laser for a datajack. Okay, granted, I could see their point: Even for the kind of code-slinging I was doing tonight, a datajack would have made the job so much quicker. Fingers on a keyboard are no match for direct neural connections.

I couldn't do it, though. It wasn't weak-kneed queasiness over surgery, which I'm sure was their interpretation. My reservations were far more concrete, though I couldn't tell anyone about them: I simply didn't trust myself enough. Even though I'd tried to keep myself isolated from that facet of the shadows, I'd learned early on that some Cheyenne chipmeisters were dealing in 2XS chips. A source of 2XS, plus a direct feed into my brain? I've always prided myself on strong will, chummer, but I'm not *that* strong . . .

Again I shook my head, and to hell with the headache.

This seemed to be my evening for morbid thoughts. I scanned my code creation one last time, pointed it toward the greater Matrix, and keyed in the electronic equivalent of "Fetch!"

And that was the first part of my contract for Sharon Young, complete. There wasn't much for me to do until my smartframe—mentally I'd dubbed it Naomi, for various personal reasons—returned with the correlations it had generated. That would be maybe an hour, I figured—which would probably sound ridiculous to nonprogrammers: spend four hours writing a program that runs for one hour, and that I'll never use again. Normally I'd agree; I've always considered any meal that takes longer to prepare than it does to eat to be a bad allocation of resources. This time, though, it was the only route that made sense. Doing the same sort of search manually would have taken several times the five hours—four coding, one waiting—I was investing in the smartframe. Don't work harder, as one of my old U-Dub profs had screamed at me, work *smarter.*

Good advice. I went to bed.

3

Goddamn it, it was *The Dream* again—"lucid dreaming," I think that's the right term, where you actually *know* you're dreaming, but still can't do squat about it.

I thought I'd finally left The Dream behind me; I thought I'd finally moved on enough that my subconscious didn't feel the need to dredge up old fears and pains anymore. Fat chance. Granted, The Dream *had* become much less frequent than it had been in the Bad Old Days. During the first few months after I'd gotten my cyberarm, The Dream was a regular visitor to my nighttime landscape. *Every fragging night,* it came back like a ghost to haunt me.

Maybe it would have been easier to deal with if it had always been the same—if repetition had numbed my responses—but it wasn't. The overall flow was the same every night, the general shape of events. The details changed, though—largely superficial things, like the order in which people were killed, or exactly when certain events occurred—so that I never knew what to expect.

Over time, as the level of chronic stress in my system started to fade, The Dream grew less and less frequent: once every three nights, once a week, a couple times a month . . . Then even longer periods between incidents. Tonight, it had been nearly three months since The Dream had put in an appearance, and I'd started to hope that my shattered psyche had finally healed itself. Like I said, fat chance.

The setting was just as it always was: the secret lab complex underneath building E of Yamatetsu's Integrated Systems Products facility in Fort Lewis. Hawk had driven off the two hellhounds guarding the site, Toshi had dealt with the maglock on the main door, and Rodney was beside me as we made our slow way along the wide, helical rampway leading down into the bowels of the facility. The sadness was a dull ache in my chest and throat as I looked at the silent figures moving through the dreamscape. Dead, all of them: Hawk the shaman, Toshi the samurai, Rodney Greybriar the mage ... Dead because I'd dragged them into something I didn't understand, something that was way too big for me. I'd hired "irregular assets," I'd become the Johnson to a team of shadowrunners. I'd thought I had it all chipped, I thought I knew what we'd be up against. My overconfidence cost me my left arm, but it cost Hawk, Toshi, and Rodney much more.

Silent as the ghosts they were, the figures around me descended the spiral ramp. I could smell that strange, vaguely biological smell—something like yeast, but not quite—that would become so familiar later. We moved on through the soft, sourceless light—about the intensity of dusk, but redder than sunlight.

I knew what was waiting for us at the bottom of the ramp, I *knew* it ... That was what made The Dream into a nightmare. I *knew*, but I couldn't tell anyone of my knowledge. Hawk, Toshi, and Greybriar had agreed to join me on this job, thinking they'd find a connection between Yamatetsu's Integrated Systems Products division and the new dreamchip scourge on the street, 2XS. At worst, they expected to face corporate sec-guards and *sarariman* chipmeisters. I knew better.

We reached the bottom of the ramp, saw before us the door that I knew had to be there. I knew all too well what we'd find on the other side of that door, and I couldn't face it again. I tried to speak, to warn Hawk and the others away, but I couldn't force the words out. As Toshi started to hotwire the maglock, all I could do was turn away.

I couldn't go through it again. Even after all this time—even after seeing my sister, Theresa, alive, clean and sober—I couldn't face it. It would rip me apart, tear open all the emotional wounds that had *almost* healed in my psyche. I couldn't look into that curved-walled room and see Theresa lying there, a sickly yellow umbilicus connecting her comatose body with the wall of the chamber ...

The Dream hit me with a jump cut, and with no sense of transition I found myself walking point along the familiar curving tunnel that would lead Toshi and the others to their deaths. Again, no matter how I tried, I couldn't croak out a warning. And, even worse, I couldn't control my own body. I *knew* what was waiting for me around one of these corners, but like a passenger in my own skull, I couldn't stop myself from walking on. I felt my hands cradling my Remington Roomsweeper almost as if it were a baby. A lot of good it would do me.

Around the corner we went, and there she was as I knew she would be: the Wasp spirit Queen. The insect spirit summoned by the insane shaman, Adrian Skyhill. She lay there in the darkness ahead of us, a massive, distorted shape the unclean white of a maggot. Her huge lower body was segmented, her upper body the emaciated torso of the human woman she'd once been. Her long blond hair was missing in patches; her skin was bloated and blistered. Thin lips drew back from yellowed teeth in what could almost have been a smile.

I tried to throw myself aside as the magical bolt arced from her hand, but I was too late as I always was. The blue–white fire lashed over the left side of my body, engulfing my arm, and I *screamed*. Even in The Dream, the pain was overwhelming, all-encompassing. I collapsed to the soft, yeast-smelling ground, as Hawk and the others rushed at the Queen, weapons spitting.

Hawk was the first to go this time, turned into a flaming, twitching firebrand. Then Toshi, transfixed by a torrent of fire, and dancing in death like a dervish. I heard a scream from behind me, a shrill, piercing shriek that went on and on . . .

And suddenly I was awake, my pulse pounding an insane tattoo in my ears, my chest laboring like a bellows. My body tingled, from the tips of my toes to the crown of my head, as though someone had tried using me as a resistor in a low-voltage electric circuit. I rolled my eyes wildly for a moment as reality reassembled itself around me.

Yes. I was lying on the bed in my Randall Avenue doss, staring at the shifting patterns that the lights of passing cars painted across my ceiling. I was still fully dressed, and my clothes were wringing wet with chill sweat. Very comfortable indeed. I tried to slow my breathing as I let comforting normality seep into my body and flush out the fear poisons.

It took me a moment to realize that the high-pitched shriek was still in my ears, as if the scream had followed me out of sleep. I blinked and shook my head, and—almost like a digital sound effect—the sound morphed from a semihuman squeal into a more familiar electronic tone. With a muffled curse, I swung into a sitting position and glared at my telecom.

An incoming call, that's all it was. The alert tone had penetrated my sleep, and my unconscious had gleefully taken it and woven it into the fabric of my dream. Just what I needed.

The tone cut off as the telecom software decided I wasn't going to pick up the call myself, and went into auto-answer mode. According to the data display in the corner of the screen, the call was directed to my default, rather than my private, mailbox, so I had little incentive to shake myself out of the rack to answer it in-the-meat. While the ancient telecom was chugging through the initial handshaking, I checked my finger-watch. Nigh on oh-three-thirty. Looked like I'd overslept on my intended one-hour nap. Idly, I wondered if Naomi the smartframe had made it back with the correlations already, or whether she'd been waylaid by some electronic diversions along her path.

The telecom screen blinked and an image appeared . . . and my thoughts were suddenly anything *but* idle. I recognized the face at once. A middle-aged man: a strong face, a commanding, aquiline nose, and cold eyes. His hair was still cut short, subtly spiked, showing the chrome-lipped datajack in his right temple. When I'd last seen him, that hair had been salt-and-pepper, with the pepper predominant. Now it was almost pure gray–white, with only a few streaks of black left near the crown. His face looked older than it had only four years ago, too—a good decade older. The skin looked sallow and slightly loose, and there were dark bags under his eyes. I remembered the last time we'd spoken. He'd been working his guts out on an Ultra-Gym machine, running the computerized system at a setting of eighteen on a scale of twenty. Yet he'd still been able to carry on a conversation without gasping or yarfing up his lunch. Would he be able to handle even level *one* these days? I doubted it.

Jacques Barnard, his name was. When I'd last done business with him—if that's the right phrase—he'd been a senior vice president of Yamatetsu Corporation, in charge of the megacorp's Seattle operations. If my bookie would lay odds on that kind of thing, I'd have considered him a sure bet for senior management, the ultimate corporate warrior, undeterred by the obstacles in his way.

Now? I'd have tried to buy back that hypothetical bet. He looked like an old man, did Mr. Barnard, worn and ravaged.

Not by time, so much, as by *knowledge*. The eyes that burned out of my telecom screen looked like those of a man who'd learned things he simply didn't want to know. (And the fact of the matter was, I thought I could make a damn good guess as to what some of those "things" were . . .)

"Mr. Montgomery, good day." Barnard's voice hadn't lost any of its resonance or its somewhat daunting self-confidence. "Or perhaps 'good evening' is more appropriate. It's unfortunate that I missed you, but"—he shrugged with a wry smile—"I don't imagine our daily schedules follow the same lines.

"I have some matters I wish to discuss with you, Mr. Montgomery," Barnard went on smoothly. "I assure you that the discussion will be mutually beneficial.

"I'm appending a secure switching code—a 'cold relay,' I think is the current term on the streets." A Receive icon blinked in the corner of the screen, and the telecom chuckled softly to itself as it stored a digital data string in its nonvolatile memory. "Please contact me as soon as practical," Barnard concluded. "I look forward to the chance of talking with you again." With a faint musical *bink*, the call terminated.

I don't know how long I stared at the blank screen. When I finally shook myself out of my self-absorbed funk, my eyes were so dry they felt gritty.

It's funny how things work out . . . or it *might* be funny, if those things don't involve you personally. From my side, I failed to see the humor. That faint musical tone had signified more than the end of Barnard's call, hadn't it? It had also sounded the death knell of the life I'd been living. One simple *bink*, and everything changes.

I shook my head and sighed. What were the odds of *The Dream* and Barnard's call coming together like that? Quite a coincidence.

Of course, some people wouldn't see it that way. That friend of Jocasta Yzerman's, for example, the one she'd taught with back in the sprawl. What was his name? Harold Move-in-Shadows, or something like that. Old Harold, he'd have told me in that sententious way of his that there's no such thing as coincidence, and that everything happens because it's the will of the Great Spirits. Yeah, right. If that's the case, then the Great Spirits have a pretty fragging twisted sense of humor.

The call . . . I sighed again, a deep, heartfelt sound. It had to happen—I'd known that from the outset. When things had gone to hell in a handcart that night underneath Fort Lewis—when Hawk and Rodney and the others had been slaughtered—it was Jacques Barnard's cred that had put things back together again. He'd paid off the "Wrecking Crew"—the shadow team I'd hired—including death bonuses for Toshi and Hawk. He'd arranged for me to "die," at least as far as the people at Lone Star who might want to track me down were concerned. And, most important, he'd paid for the cybernetic replacement of the arm that the Queen spirit had burned away.

He'd never even discussed the matter with me. When I'd woken up in the hospital—an exorbitantly expensive private room, again courtesy of Mr. Barnard—it had all been handled. He'd never put any strings on the payments, never demanded any concessions from me.

He hadn't needed to, of course. We both knew the way things work. Corps and corporators don't give gifts; they make investments. Barnard had invested in me, and we both understood that some time down the road he'd come looking for a return on that investment. Over the intervening four years, he'd never mentioned the matter; hell, I'd never had *anything* to do with Yamatetsu during that time, and that was just the way I liked it. But again, he hadn't needed to mention it, or remind me. Megacorporations the world over have integrated a lot of ideas from the old Japanese world-view. When someone is in your debt, it's *his* responsibility to remember the fact, not yours to remind him.

So now it was time to call in the marker. That's what the call meant. I owed him for my arm, and my livelihood—frag, for my *life*, if you got right down to it—and he was going to collect.

Dully, I walked over to the telecom and idly pressed a few keys. The smartframe *had* made it back, filling temporary files with a couple of megapulses of data on Jonathan Bridge. Those files probably contained what I needed to discharge my contract with Sharon Young, and net myself some much-needed cred.

Yet I couldn't work up the enthusiasm to open them. What did it matter anyway? I couldn't guess what Barnard would want from me. Similarly, though, I couldn't imagine that paying off my debt would leave my life unaffected.

I didn't call Barnard back right away.

I couldn't drag it out *too* long, though. He'd tracked down my LTG number in Cheyenne, so it was a safe bet he knew I was in town. If I didn't return his call within some reasonable span of time, he might start wondering whether I'd forgotten my obligation or—worse—that I was considering shirking it. How would a high muckamuck corporator like Barnard respond to that kind of irresponsibility on my part? I remembered the two business-suited knee-breakers who'd escorted me to Barnard's enclave in Madison Park four years ago, and I had no desire to meet them again on less genteel terms.

Still, I pushed it as long as I figured was politically wise . . . and then a bit longer. After all, up until the moment I actually placed that call, I could still lie to myself that I was a free agent.

I spent some of my time running a quick research scan on Jacques Barnard (know thine enemies in case your friends turn out to be a bunch of bastards, and all that). I'd assumed that Barnard was still part of Yamatetsu's Seattle operations—the fact that the "cold relay" number he'd given me was a local node just reinforced the idea—but that turned out to be off the beam. Y-Seattle was now the purview of some slitch by the name of Mary Luce, while Barnard had been bumped upstairs to become executive vice president of Yamatetsu North America. With the promotion had come a transfer to the bright heart of the Yamatetsu world—the city of Kyoto, in Nihon.

So Jacques Barnard had shaken the mud and grime of the sprawl from his thousand-nuyen shoes, had he? What would that mean for me?

Putting off the inevitable is a mug's game. Finally I bit the bullet, and placed the call: seventeen hundred hours my time, oh-nine-hundred in Kyoto. I watched the icons flicker and flash along the bottom of the screen as my telecom dialed the LTG number Barnard had given me, and made the connection. My system synched up and shook hands with the Seattle node, then the call was suspended—put on hold, basically—by the remote station. I watched as my screen echoed a call to Denver . . . and was put on hold again. The process happened three more times—when Barnard said a relay was cold, I decided, he meant you could use it for cryogenic research—before I finally saw the standard Ringing symbol blink.

I frowned as the telecom waited for an answer. What the frag was I going to get pulled into, here? If Barnard figured he needed a five-node relay to talk to me, I had the nasty feeling that we wouldn't be chatting about the weather . . .

The telecom whined for an instant, then an image of Barnard himself filled the screen. He was sitting at a desk, as I'd expected, but not in an office. Or, at least, not an office like any I'd ever seen before. The background was slightly out of focus, but I could still make out white marble walls, broad windows, and an open door leading out under a portico, and beyond into an ornamental garden. Life-sized, classical-style statues stood in uncomfortable-looking poses among the flowering shrubs.

Barnard looked up from what he was doing—something that was outside his telecom's field of view—and smiled when he saw my face. "Mr. Montgomery." There was real warmth—or an impressive simulation of it, at least—in his voice. "I'm glad I was able to reach you."

It was funny, but in that instant, I was glad, too. I hadn't known it until now, but this moment had been haunting me for four years. Just as you can get so used to pain like a toothache that you forget it's there, I'd become accustomed to the chronic, low-grade stress of wondering when the call would come, when the other shoe would drop. But that didn't mean the stress hadn't been there, hadn't been real. Now, as Barnard smiled at me out of the screen, I felt a strange, twisty sensation in my gut . . . and I realized, with a shock, that it was four years' worth of tension finally being relieved.

"Mr. Barnard," I said noncommittally. "Long time."

His smile—more genuine than I'd have given his acting ability credit for—grew broader, and he leaned back in his chair. His telecom's video pickup adjusted focus, and I got a better view of the statues beyond the portico. "How are you enjoying the sunshine in Cheyenne, Mr. Montgomery?" he asked lightly. "A pleasant change from Seattle, I would imagine."

I shook my head, momentarily dumbstruck. He *was* talking about the fragging weather. With an effort, I brought my thoughts back under control. "A change is as good as a rest, that's what they say, at least." I glanced away from his face to the view behind him. "Wouldn't you agree?"

He chuckled. "There are some significant . . . *perquisites*

. . . to corporate rank," he admitted. "I do rather like Kyoto. Have you ever visited the city?"

"Never had the time."

"Unfortunate." He pursed his lips momentarily. "But you do like to travel, I trust?"

"Only if I get to keep any frequent-flier points they give me," I said dryly. "Look, Mr. Barnard, despite appearances, I'm assuming that this *isn't* a social call."

He blinked, and his expression changed. For an instant, I could have almost believed that there was disappointment in his eyes. It was gone in a microsecond, and his face became the cool mask of the seasoned negotiator. "As you wish, Mr. Montgomery." He paused, as if to order his thoughts. "As you might have guessed, there is a . . . a *matter,* one might say . . . on which you can help me. Do you have a passport? Not in your own name, of course"—he chuckled softly—"considering that Derek Montgomery officially died in twenty fifty-two. But one that will pass muster?"

I nodded.

"Good. Then I have a request for you. I have a message that I need delivered to a . . . a *colleague* of mine. I would like you to deliver it for me, Mr. Montgomery."

I snorted. "You want me to be a delivery boy?"

"I wouldn't put it quite like that," Barnard hedged.

"But it's accurate."

He shrugged. "If you wish."

"Why can't you do it electronically?" I asked. "Or virtually, over the Matrix?"

Barnard's dark eyes hardened, and I felt my internal temperature drop a couple of degrees. "I have my reasons, I assure you," he said coldly. But then his mien softened an iota. "Personal contact is required in this situation, Mr. Montgomery. Circumstances are such that nothing else would be acceptable."

He was trying to win me over by being reasonable, by actually *explaining*—to some degree, at least. But I wasn't going to get sucked in that easily. "So why not send one of your flunkies from Kyoto?" I shot back. "There's got to be hundreds of keeners just *dying* to"—*to kiss hoop,* is what I started to say, but at the last moment I reconsidered—"to do the executive veep a personal favor. *Neh?*"

Barnard frowned. "Perhaps. But that would be . . . *inappropriate* . . . in this case."

"Why?"

"Because the contact must be untraceable, Mr. Montgomery. I need a deniable asset."

"You mean an *expendable* asset, don't you?"

Barnard sighed in mild frustration. "Not in this case, Mr. Montgomery." He gave a wry half smile. "Under other circumstances"—he shrugged—"who knows? But not in this case, I assure you."

"*Why* not?" I asked sarcastically. "You'd hang someone else out to dry, but not me. Because of my winning personality, no doubt?" I snorted again. "Look, Mr. Barnard, I'm willing to go along with you because I owe you for the arm, and I'd rather pay off my marker than be hunted down by Yamatetsu hard-men. But please don't insult what I like to consider my intelligence, *so ka*?"

For a moment I thought I'd gone that one step too far. For nearly ten seconds Barnard just stared at me out of the screen, his eyes like targeting lasers. Then he leaned forward, and again the vid pickup adjusted, putting the statues out of focus. "Listen," he said, "I'll tell you this once, and only because I want you to understand. I'm not calling in a marker, Mr. Montgomery. You've already paid back for the arm, and more." He smiled faintly and gestured around him. "Do you think I'd be sitting in this office if Adrian Skyhill was still undercutting me with the Board of Directors at every turn?" The smile faded, and for a moment the executive looked even older than he had before. "And there's more to the debt, of course, but I'd rather not discuss it, even via a cold relay."

I nodded slowly. He meant the insect spirits, of course.

"The way I view the matter, Mr. Montgomery," Barnard continued smoothly, "Yamatetsu owes *you* for your services." He spread his hands in a disarming gesture. "This is part of the payback. I understand you need the work, and the credit."

I forced a laugh. "Mr. Barnard, you'd better give your information conduits a swift kick. I've got contracts out the hoop; I don't have the time to be your glorified messenger boy and—"

His voice was no louder, but the edge to it cut me off as short as a gunshot. "No, Mr. Montgomery, you *haven't* got contracts, as you say, 'out the hoop.' The one matter you have to concern you at the moment—since you so smoothly discharged the matter with The Avalon for one Jennifer Arnequist—is a minor contract with Sharon Young." He smiled—he was enjoy-

ing this, the slot. "And, as a matter of fact, the business for
which Ms. Young has contracted you is directly connected with
my request, so there's not even any conflict there."

I sighed. Corporators. I should have known better than to
try and run a bluff. I raised my hands in mock surrender.
"Okay, okay, you've got me."

Barnard paused. Then he said quietly, "You know, I *would*
rather you take this matter on voluntarily."

"*Why?*"

He paused again—longer, this time. "Do you want the
truth, Mr. Montgomery?"

"If it wouldn't strain you too much."

His expression changed. Not quite a smile, but something
very close. "Because I *respect* you, Mr. Montgomery. And
further, I *like* you."

He waited, as if he expected me to come back with some
hard-hooped rejoinder. I always like being unpredictable, so
I kept my trap zipped. Eventually, he smiled, his "business"
smile again. "You know, Mr. Montgomery, you haven't
asked the major question yet."

He *was* enjoying this. "Okay, Barnard," I said wearily.
"Where am I going?"

He chuckled. "Have you ever been to the Kingdom of Hawai'i, Mr. Montgomery?"

I must be losing my fragging mind . . .

I sat back, staring at the telecom screen. The vidphone
pane had cleared and vanished, but the data display still
burned with its plasma glow. According to the data on-
screen, I had an open ticket on the Global Airways suborbital hop from Casper to beautiful downtown Honolulu
about twelve hours from right then. A corp ticket, no name
on the manifest, and enough "don't-worry" flags that ticket
agents, customs officers, and the like wouldn't dig too deep
into my supposed identity. According to the datawork, which
I could download onto my own credstick whenever I felt
like it, I'd be traveling under the auspices of some outfit
called Nebula Enterprises. A minor subsidiary of Yamatetsu,
no doubt . . . or maybe not, come to think of it, if Barnard
was so hinky about this whole thing getting traced back to
him. Maybe Nebula was some independent that owed
Yamatetsu as a whole, or Barnard individually, a Big One, or
that chummer Jacques had under his corporate thumb.

In addition to the ticket itself, the flatscreen display showed me that my account at the Sioux I-face Bank had just more than quintupled, with an infusion of 22-Kay nuyen "contingency funds."

Finally—also for download onto my credstick—was an "electronic password," I guess that's the best way of describing it. The message I had to deliver to Barnard's "colleague" in Hawai'i wasn't something I could memorize and recite verbatim—of course not, that would mean I'd know what the message was. Instead, it would be delivered to me on optical chip—no doubt encrypted and loaded with enough ice to chill a good-sized lake of synth-scotch—when I arrived at the Casper International Airport for my boost to the islands. The electronic password would identify me to the appropriate gofer at the airport for the handover.

I stared at the data displayed on the screen, and I fretted. Not because my comfortable little life was getting turned upside down and shaken out like a garbage can—well, not *only* because of that, at least. No, what worried me the most were my own reactions. Just a few hours before, I'd been thinking I didn't have the instincts to survive in the shadows anymore (if I'd *ever* had them . . .), and now I had proof.

Proof? Yeah.

I found myself wanting to trust Jacques Barnard, wanting to believe he was telling me the chip-truth about the trip to Hawai'i. About the fact that he didn't consider me in hock to the corp. That he'd picked me for the messenger job because he respected and—maybe—liked me. Worse, I found myself wanting to like him.

Trust him? *Like* him? Get fragging real. Barnard was the Johnson to end all Johnsons—I'd had enough personal proof of that four years before, hadn't I? If I thought he would—or *could*—feel any genuine human emotion for a convenient tool like me, I was naive at best, schizophrenic at worst. And the fact that I felt an urge to reciprocate those nonexistent feelings . . . well, maybe it was time to hang up the old trenchcoat and hip flask and carve out a nice, safe career selling greeting cards or some drek.

With a snarl I shoved my credstick into the telecom's slot and punched Download. As the system transferred the data—ticket, operating funds, and password—I forced myself to think through the situation coldly and logically.

Okay, no matter how Barnard couched the "request" in

polite and friendly terms, the fact was that I didn't have
much choice but to go along with him. Debts are debts, and
megacorps are even harder on welchers than loansharks. I
was going to Hawai'i, carrying a message that I couldn't
read, to a person that I didn't know, under circumstances
that I couldn't control. Anything I'd missed? Oh yes—facing
potential opposition that I couldn't analyze or estimate.
Great, better and better. In other words, this situation was
the exact opposite of the "shadowruns" I usually chose, I
thought bleakly. Maximum exposure, minimum leverage,
and probably zero backup. Going in blind and stupid.

Well, at least I could do *some* research. I groaned as I
thought of spending the next four or five hours whipping together another smartframe like Naomi to scope out any and
all connections that Yamatetsu as a corp, and Barnard as an
individual, had with the independent Kingdom of Hawai'i.
Well, hell, I could sleep on the plane, I supposed.

Wait a tick here—there might be another option. I had one
resource that might be able to tell me something useful. This
resource seemed to have an almost encyclopedic memory for
facts, factoids, and scurrilous rumors about corps the world
over, and key players within them. Considering that he'd
been involved with Yamatetsu and Barnard himself—albeit
indirectly, through the intermediary of one Dirk Montgomery—he might be able to shed some interesting light on
the subject, on what I was getting myself into.

I leaned forward again, rattled a command string into the
telecom's keyboard, then waited while it dialed a CalFree
State LTG number. For the second time tonight—my time
for cold relays, apparently—I watched the icons blink as my
call was routed through a couple of intermediary nodes.
Then, finally, the Ringing symbol flashed on-screen.

Someone answered immediately—through a blank screen,
audio only—a thin, somewhat asthmatic voice that brought
to mind images of a weasel-faced punk. *"Do desu ka?"*

"Get me Argent," I told the screen.

The weasel paused. "And who the frag are you?" he demanded.

"The fact that I know about this relay means I don't have
to answer that, doesn't it?" I pointed out.

"Look, *priyatel*," the weasel snarled, "you want to play
fragging games, you play them somewhere else, *neh*?"

I imagined him reaching for the Disconnect key with a

dirty forefinger and shrugged. "Okay, *omae,*" I told him, "we'll play it your way." It didn't really matter anyway. "Tell Argent that Dirk Montgomery wants to talk to him, okay?"

"Montgomery?" The weasel's voice changed, the habitual hostility vanishing. "Hey, the Man talked about you, *priyatel,* told me some stories. We got something in common, you know that?" I didn't really want to think about what that might be, but the weasel went on, "We're both refugees from the Star. How about that, huh? Small fragging world, *neh?*"

"Yeah," I said, muffling a sigh. "Small fragging world. And you are . . .?"

"You can call me Wolf."

"Oh." I tried again. "I need to talk to Argent, Wolf."

"Can't do it, *priyatel,* he's over the wall and out of the sprawl. On biz."

"When's he due back?"

Wolf/Weasel chuckled thinly. "You ever known Argent to give you a straight answer to that one?" He paused, then went on more seriously, "I'll get him to call you when he gets back, that's the best I can do. Got a relay number?"

I gave Wolf the LTG number for a voice-mail service in Cheyenne. Nowhere near as secure as a true cold relay, of course, but since the voice mailbox was rented in the name of a dead man, at least it wouldn't lead interested parties *directly* to my doorstep. I exchanged a few more empty pleasantries with Wolf/Weasel and logged off as soon as I could.

I sighed again and checked the time. Close to eighteen hundred. It had been a full couple of days, all in all, and it didn't look like the pace would be slowing any time soon. I reviewed the details on my S-O ticket: departure, oh-six-hundred, check in and be in the boarding lounge no later than one hour before dust-off. No worries there . . . at first glance. Unfortunately, however, the only airport in the Sioux Nation capable of handling full-on suborbitals is in Casper, *not* in Cheyenne—and almost 300 klicks away. Which meant a short-hop "Skybus," which left from downtown Cheyenne. Which, in turn, meant a cab from my doss to the Skybus terminus, unless I wanted to pay an arm and *two* legs for parking my car. Which meant . . .

I sighed one more time. I'd better start packing.

4

Traditionally, the screamsheets and datafaxes have absolutely nothing good to say about the many short-hop carriers in the Sioux Nation. Too many companies, too little inspection, too many cases of pilot error, too few meaningful after-incident investigations, drekcetera. So when I boarded the Federated-Boeing Commuter VTOL, all shiny in its Sioux Skybus livery, and strapped myself into the window seat, I was expecting a hairy ride.

No flap, chummer, smooth as synthsilk. Okay, it's true, I *could* see past the little bitty curtain into the flight deck, and it *did* disturb me a tad to watch the pilot and copilot—jacked into the flight systems via fiberoptic cables—playing a heated game of crib while we were climbing out. But other than that, no problems.

We put down at the commuter terminal of Casper International at oh-four-forty-five, which gave me fifteen minutes to collect my baggage and hump it over to the international terminal. According to the signs, there was an automated people-mover to carry passengers the klick or so from one terminal to another. But, according to other signs—hastily hand-lettered—the people-mover was down for maintenance, and should be back up and running three days ago, thanks for your patience. There were shuttle-buses too, but the one I tried to catch was full—or so the big, burly Amerind driver told me, even though I could see a dozen empty seats—and fragging near rolled over my toes as it pulled out. Well, it was a nice morning for a brisk walk anyway.

Not only did I get my exercise, but I also got a good view of the international terminal that I would have missed if I'd ridden the underground people-mover. It's a sight I wouldn't have missed for anything ... *null!* In the darkness of pre-dawn, under the harsh glare of arc lights, it looked like an overgrown bomb shelter or missile bunker: prestressed ferrocrete with less aesthetic appeal than a brick.

The suborbitals, though—they were a different story. As I hiked my way beside the access road—cursing silently at the two shuttle-buses that blazed on by me without even slowing—I could see three of the things out on the apron beyond the terminal building. Gleaming white under the carbon arcs, they were beautiful—geometrically precise, like the crystalline purity of mathematics itself somehow made tangible. Okay, I admit it, I copped that last line from a trideo talking head. But he was right. The suborbitals were unbelievably striking, unbelievably beautiful in a kind of heart-stirring way. *They don't belong here, on the ground—* that's the thought that struck me. *Any time they spend down here in the dirt is just waiting, just marking time before they can re-enter the element for which they were born ...*

That heartwarming feeling of awe lasted until I'd entered the international terminal, and vanished precisely one microsecond after I'd laid eyes on the hard-case customs and safety inspectors waiting for me at the security gate. Sigh. You'd think the fact I was carrying an open corp ticket would give me some kind of clout with the inspectors, wouldn't you, would guarantee me some special treatment? No luck there, chummer. (Or maybe—and this was a scary thought—what I went through *was* special treatment ...) In any case, as a gaggle of technicians poked and prodded and X-rayed and assensed and MNR'ed my bag, a couple of hard-eyed and horny-handed trolls in undersized uniforms did much the same thing to me. Metal detectors to analyze the composition of my dental fillings. Chemsniffers to check if I was wearing clean underwear. Magical examinations to make sure I wasn't actually a fire elemental trying to fool them. The whole enchilada. Finally—and only after the fine uniformed gentlemen had made a detailed manifest of every speck of lint in my possession—was I gestured on.

Then came Immigration Control or Emigration Control, or whatever the frag the Sioux government's calling it now. Once again, I was looking up at a couple more uniformed Amerind trolls while their 'puter whirred and clicked and tried to decide whether it liked the passport data on my credstick. And I was trying not to sweat; it was supposed to be the best fake datawork (a lot of) money could buy, but you never really knew how good this kind of drek was until it was put to the test. My sphincter contracted as the 'puter went *brack* sharply. But the trolls handed my credstick back without a word and gestured me on. Signs directed me to the departure gate, so I followed them.

And almost had a childish accident when a heavy hand landed on my shoulder. I spun, and I *think* I stopped myself from yelping aloud. I looked up, expecting another troll . . . then quickly down when the slag who'd stopped me cleared his throat rattlingly. A dwarf, he was, even stockier and more dour than most of his metatype, still on his toes after reaching up for my shoulder. He was wearing the nondescript black suit I've come to associate with government agents, and a cold fist squeezed my stomach. Somehow, I managed to force a well-meaning smile onto my face. "Is there some problem?" I asked genially.

"You're Brian Tozer?"

I nodded; that was the name on my fake datawork. "That's me, er . . . sir. Is there a problem with my ticket?"

"Follow me, please." And he turned his back on me and walked off without looking back, fully expecting me to follow him blindly.

Which I did, of course—not that I had much choice. I followed him through an unmarked door into a small, bare room, and I braced myself for a cavity search or worse.

The dwarf didn't say anything once he'd shut the door behind me. He just scrutinized me, dark eyes narrowed beneath beetling brows. If he wasn't going to say anything, neither was I. If we were going to play the old "who speaks first" waiting game, some years from now an airport employee would open the door and find two desiccated corpses in this bare room, still glaring at each other.

Finally, he frowned, and his brows merged into something that looked like a road-killed squirrel. "You *are* Brian Tozer?" he asked.

And that's when I got it. I pulled out my credstick—the one with the digital signature on it—and extended it to him. He sneered—"*Fragging twinkie*," I could hear him thinking—and he slipped it into the oversized chipjack mounted in the base of his skull. His eyes rolled up in their sockets for a moment. Then, with a quick movement, he clicked the stick free from his slot, tossed it back, and held something out to me. An optical chip: a tiny sliver of impure

silicon the size of a pen-point, in a plastic chip-carrier the
size of my first thumb-joint.

"That's your payload for our mutual friend," he grunted,
already starting to turn away.

"Hold it," I said quickly. He turned back, and one of his
eyebrows tried to crawl up into his hairline. "Look," I told
him, "I don't have any of the details on where I'm going,
who I'm supposed to give this payload to, and when. Don't
you think it might make my job a little easier if—"

He cut me off with a sharp, "You'll be met." And again
he turned his back on me and strode off. This time I let him.
I glanced down at the chip-carrier in my hand, and for just
a moment I had the impulse to throw it to the floor, grind it
under my heel, and just *run like hell*. The pleasant fantasy
didn't last long. I sighed, opened the door, and re-emerged
into the concourse.

In the course of following the dwarf, I'd lost track of my
gate. Fortunately, some airport employee—a flackish-
looking slot with a carcinogenic tan and plastic smile—
noticed me looking lost. He was actually *polite* to me—a
first for the day—and he led me directly to the Global Airways departure lounge.

That's when things started to look up a tad. I'd expected
the usual barren, sterile-looking holding pen with its plastic
seats designed to make it categorically impossible to find a
comfortable position in them. The usual stained, institutional
gray carpet. The usual boarding and departure announce-
ments that might as well have been made in Urdu, for all the
meaning they conveyed. The usual crush of (meta)humanity,
where you try to avoid having your toes stepped on while
you play the old game of "Spot the Hijacker."

Buzzz, thanks for playing! *This* was where the open corp
ticket came into play big-time. The flackish kind of guy led
me right through the holding pen where the hoi polloi were
contained, past an armed sec-guard who actually touched his
cap to me as I passed, and through a pair of double doors
that could have been real mahogany. As we stepped through,
me and my flackish shadow, I saw arrays of tiny LED ripple
and flicker on both sides of the doorway. Yet *another*
weapon-detector of some kind. I congratulated myself once
again for deciding to travel completely unarmed except for
my rapier wit.

The Global Priority Class Stand-By Lounge—that's what

the nameplate on the door identified it as—looked like a cross between a gentleman's club in Edwardian London (or, at least, the BBC rendition thereof), and a high-tone computer dealer's showroom. Heavy wood paneling, burgundy plush carpets, wingback leather chairs, crystal decanters on mahogany sideboards ... and everywhere, suit-clad travelers tapping away on palmtop computers, babbling into cel phones, or staring off into space with fiber-optic spiderwebs trailing from their temples. Of the fifteen or so people in the lounge, the only people who weren't engaged in some form of electronic or verbal intercourse were me, the flack—who, with one final unctuous comment, made himself scarce—and a particularly shapely bartender (bartendress? bartendrix?) whose smile hinted she *really* needed my patronage to make her day complete. Out of the goodness of my heart I obliged her, and spent the next ten minutes savoring the best of all possible kinds of single-malt Scotch whiskey—free single-malt Scotch whiskey.

Finally, the boarding call came—delivered in person by a shapely, and decidedly mammalian, flight attendant—and we started to make our way through the priority boarding tube. This was a transpex cylinder—scrubbed so clean you could see the walls only by the way they diffracted lights outside—which extended from the terminal building to the first-class passenger door of the suborbital. Twenty meters away was another, similar tube—which suddenly reminded me of those "HabiTrail" things kids use to incarcerate gerbils—used by the *déclassé* from the economy-class holding pen.

I took a couple of steps into the HabiTrail, and then stopped dead, earning a bad look from the *shaikujin*—still jacked into his portacomp—who tripped on my heel and collided into my back. I couldn't help it; I'd never had a chance to look at a suborbital from this close up before, and I certainly wasn't going to pass it up so he could get to his complimentary pretakeoff gin and tonic a couple of seconds sooner.

The thing was *huge,* much larger than I'd expected. Hell, suborbitals only carry about 150 people. How much space do you need for *that*? But of course, there's a lot more to a suborbital than the passenger compartment. There's all the stuff that goes into any standard civilian transport: turbojets, fuel, landing gear, navigation drek, baggage bays, and that place up front where the crew and the flight attendants have their parties. And then there's the *extra* stuff needed when you're flying at altitudes of 23 klicks (75,000 feet, for the metrically challenged) and speeds of Mach 20+. SCRAMjets to get you to cruising altitude and speed. Fuel for those SCRAMjets . . . and lots of it (SCRAMjets aren't known for their fuel economy). Cooling systems to keep your hull from melting under the air friction. And on and on. All in all, the suborbital was longer than a football field, a big integral lifting-body with tiny stub wings bolted on apparently as an afterthought. The body lines followed some complex—and very beautiful—multiple-recurve pattern, making the thing broad and high at the nose, but narrower and thinner toward the tail: something like an asymmetrical teardrop, maybe.

Finally, the pressure of *shaikujin* behind me got too much to ignore any longer, and I had to move along. Once I was inside, I could just as well have been in any plane—row upon row of seats in a three-aisle-three arrangement—except for one detail: no windows. The entertainment suite mounted in the seatback ahead of me made up for that lack, I decided quickly once I'd found my spot. As well as the usual selection of mindless movies, and even more mindless "classic tri-V" reruns, several of the program selections offered views from various microcams mounted on the hull. While the cabin attendants handed out free drinks and flavorless snacks—to the first-class passengers only, not to the great unwashed flying cattle-class, which started one row behind my own seat—I thoroughly enjoyed watching the baggage handlers conduct torture tests on people's suitcases as they threw them aboard.

Then we got the standard safety lecture—what to do in an emergency, like if the galley runs out of Bloody Mary mix— then we were rolling, and then we were climbing out. On my seatback screen I saw the ground drop away behind us, becoming a detailed scale model, then a contour map. Speed and angle of climb seemed—in my limited experience, at least—pretty extreme. But then the SCRAMjets kicked in— the pilot actually warned us before he lit them off—and I got a taste of what "fast" and "steep" really mean. Some ridiculously short time later, a voice came over the intercom, telling us we were at cruising altitude—23,000 meters, give or take—and flying at a mind-buggering 29,000 klicks per hour.

"We're on course and on schedule," the friendly voice announced, "and we should have you on the ground at Awalani a couple of minutes shy of four-fifty A.M. local time. Have a good flight." I checked my watch, which I'd already adjusted for Hawai'i time: a couple of minutes past four in the morning. That put total flight time at something under one hour, gate-to-gate, Casper to Honolulu. Ain't progress wonderful?

With some regret, I wiped the external view—a distant horizon, showing some definite curvature—from the seatback screen, and tried to concentrate on biz. I'd never been to the Kingdom of Hawai'i before and knew next to squat about it (apart from what I'd seen on trid pabulum actioners like *Tropical Heat*). Sure, some of the runner wannabes who hang out in low-life bars copping a 'tude will tell you that the shadows are all the same, no matter where in the world you are. But I've never bought into that. Hell, from my own experience, not extensive, I *know* it's not true.

The shadows of Cheyenne are *very* different from the grungy underbelly of the Seattle sprawl. Maybe not if you take a big enough, *abstract* enough view, I suppose. If you think in terms of dynamics, there's much that's similar. The sex trade, the chip/drug industry. Organized crime and iconoclastic freelancers. Gangs of various stripes and flavors. Grifters and abusers, stalking the grifted and abused.

But when you get down to the personal scale—where it *matters* from a practical, rather than academic, point of view—there's a world of difference. In terms of dynamics, the threats are the same: the cops, the corps, the competition. In personal terms they wear different and unfamiliar faces. In the shadows sometimes the only way to win the game—whatever it happens to be at the moment—is to cheat. That's much harder when you don't know all the rules, and when to bend or break them.

Leaving Seattle for Cheyenne, I left familiar territory behind. I left behind my support network and many of my resources. I left behind my personal knowledge of the way the underbelly of the city worked—where to go to buy a piece of cold iron, what alleys not to flop in at night, what bartenders will swear up and down that they haven't seen you for weeks while you hide behind the beer fridge. Now I was doing it again, and it made me *very* uncomfortable.

I folded out the membrane keypad from the seatback entertainment unit and started checking out the system's data retrieval function. Not bad for a mobile unit. Somewhere deep in the plane's electronic guts an optical chip contained the latest editions of the *Columbia HyperMedia Encyclopedia,* plus the *World Almanac and Book of Facts,* plus some fairly funky search algorithms. All for the convenience of Global Airways' cherished passengers (and to keep them occupied so they wouldn't drink too much and hit on the stewardesses). As the suborbital hurtled on, five times as fast as a rifle bullet, I started working out some search strings.

We were well along on the glidepath by the time I'd done what I could, and the stewardess had already warned me three times to return my seat to its upright and most uncomfortable position. I had a lot to think over as I folded up the seatback system's keyboard, and tried to keep my stomach out of my mouth as the suborbital pitched over even steeper for final approach.

The on-board data retrieval system had given me *some* background, but I'd soon come to the conclusion that the *Columbia HyperMedia Encyclopedia* seemed to be targeted at elementary-school kids who were considerably less streetwise than I'd been at that age. Sure, it was a great source for data on the kingdom's population (four million and change), its capital (Honolulu, natch), its average per-capita income (20,000¥), and the other superficial drek a kid would want to plagiarize for an essay. But for the real meat, I soon realized I'd have to access sources with a slightly more mature worldview.

Fortunately, the seatback system offered a gateway to the plane's communication systems, and from there an uplink to the Amethyste system of low-Earth orbit comm satellites. Through the Amethyste grid, I could sidelink to Renraku's DataPATH system, and then downlink to the public databases with which I'd been familiar in Seattle. Hell, returning to my old electronic stomping grounds was easier from 23,000 meters over the Pacific—once I'd figured out the gateway protocol—than it was to navigate the Sioux RTG system to get to the same nodes. (Of course, it was also a hell of a lot more expensive. When I finally logged off and the system reported my connect charges, I went pale for a moment, then thanked the fine folks at Yamatetsu—*in absentia*—for picking up the tab.) The only thing I'd wanted that the system *couldn't* give me was access to a Shadow-land server. (Well, I suppose it probably *could* have, but the audit trail stored in the guts of the big suborbital would have been like garish flags reading "Shadowrunner On Board.")

So here's what I managed to dig up about the independent Kingdom of Hawai'i, summarized in the inimitable Dirk Montgomery style. (Oh yeah, one quick aside. Mainlanders probably aren't used to seeing Hawai'i spelt with the apostrophe. Back in the weird old days, when the islands were actually a state of the now-defunct U.S., the name had been spelt *Hawaii*. No longer, chummer. An easy way to slot off an islander is to spell the name of his country without the apostrophe. An *easier* way is to mispronounce it, apparently: it should be pronounced *ha-VEYE-ee,* with a noticeable glottal stop before the last syllable. At first I thought this anal retentiveness about pronunciation was stupid, but then I considered what I'd think of someone who pronounced my city of birth as *SEE-tul.* Point taken.)

Okay, so anybody who's attended elementary school in the United Canadian and American States will know that Hawai'i used to be the fiftieth state of the union. What I hadn't known was that this was originally accomplished not by negotiation, but actually through the actions of a U.S. naval officer who'd placed his gunboat at the disposal of some American robber barons who considered that the incumbent national government was actually an obstacle to doing business. (Who says history never repeats itself? A corporation effectively taking over a sovereign state? Sounds like the early twenty-first century, *neh*?) Once the incumbent monarch, King Kamehameha III, was ousted, one Sanford B. Dole—a high corp muckamuck who'd made his fortune in pineapples, or some damn thing—named himself head of state of the entire island chain.

That was in 1893. After five years, the good old U.S. of A. decided that having a corp suit as head of state wasn't a Good Thing. So *they* moved in and annexed the islands from the robber baron who'd annexed them from the native Hawaiians . . .

And immediately started peppering the islands with military bases—naval, air force, etcetera, drekcetera. In 1959 the U.S. government decided to legitimize this shotgun marriage of an annexation, and declared the islands to be the fiftieth state. Again—judging by the historical records I could access, at least—nobody bothered to consult the native Hawaiians about this change. (Hey, they were just primitive Polynesians, weren't they? And they couldn't even vote . . .)

That's how things stayed, more or less, for fifty years. Oh, sure, there were occasional resurgences of nationalism, of "Hawai'i for Hawai'ians" sentiment—led most notably by a group calling itself *Na Kama'aina* ("The Land Children")—but nothing much happened until the first decade of the twenty-first century.

Back on the mainland, trouble was brewing. The U.S. government—and mainly the U.S. military—saw the writing on the wall, and knew that the "Indian problem" would soon be coming to a nasty, violent head. Suddenly the military bases on the islands of Hawai'i became even more important than they were before. Here were bases and assets that the SAIM "terrorists" couldn't sabotage or infiltrate easily. (Much harder for some militant Sioux warriors to blow the drek out of Pearl Harbor than to terrorize Colorado Springs—so the reasoning went, at least.) More and more major military research projects were moved to the islands, "out of harm's way."

Hah, and again *hah! Na Kama'aina,* and more hard-hooped splinter factions like the whimsically named ALOHA (*A*rmy for the *L*iberation *O*f *HA*wai'i), started looking to the SAIM hotheads as role models. Hey, if the mainland aboriginals could kick the drek out of the Anglos, why couldn't they?

Between 2011 and 2013, ALOHA and its bomb-throwing brethren went on a rampage, car-bombing government buildings, army barracks, and military installations. During the two-year reign of terror, ALOHA claimed to have greased some 150 "legitimate" targets. (Its leaders didn't have much to say about the three hundred-plus innocents offed in "collateral damage.")

Predictably, this made it heat-wave time. At the request of the state government, the feds sent a battalion of troops to Kaneohe Bay Marine Corps Air Base, renamed the combat troops the "Civil Defense Force," and proceeded to break heads. According to my research, there was a surprising incidence of suspected ALOHA sympathizers "killed while resisting arrest" or "shot while trying to escape." Who would have thought it? (Yeah, right.)

The heat wave went on, and *Na Kama'aina,* ALOHA, and

their fellow-travelers dropped from public ken. For a while, at least. To (mis)quote Shakespeare, the Civil Defense Force had scotched the snake, not killed it. The ALOHA boys and girls kept working, but in the shadows now rather than out in the bright tropical sun.

Some bright spark decided that a PR coup was needed, so ALOHA and the rest started looking for a legal lineal descendent of King Kamehameha I, the *Ali'i* ("king") who'd united the islands initially, turning a bunch of squabbling islands into a single nation. Surprise, surprise, they *found* one. (Well, *sure* they did: Look for something hard enough and you're going to find it ... whether it actually exists or not.) Seems that one Danforth Ho—a twenty-four-year-old management consultant on the island of Maui, who happened to be one-quarter Polynesian by blood—was actually the direct lineal descendent of King Kam I ... and hence the True and Rightful King of the Islands. Now that ALOHA and crew were able to produce—or at least *talk* about—a "rightful king in exile," more and more of the islanders started to swing over to their cause. (The fact that the Civil Defense Force wasn't exactly discriminating in which heads it broke couldn't have hurt.)

Now, *Na Kama'aina* and ALOHA apparently thought that their "*Ali'i* in exile" was just puppet, a mouthpiece they could use to build up support from the populace. And at first, that seemed to be the truth. Danforth Ho wasn't really what you'd call king material; both Ho himself and his "handlers" agreed on that. But then, when he saw that people were really starting to follow him, to *believe* in him, Danforth had something of a change of heart. He did some studying and learned more about his true heritage, about what his umpty-ump-grandfather had actually done for the people of Hawai'i. And he realized that he could actually *do* something about the situation. Without the knowledge of his handlers, he started to *become* an "*Ali'i* in exile," not just a figurehead. On his own initiative he started negotiating for support and funds with various megacorporate interests in the islands. (Want to take a wild guess about one of the key corporations he dealt with? Three guesses, and the first two don't count. A clue for you: the corp name starts with a *Y* ...)

It was in 2016 that Ho started cutting his own private deals. It wasn't until 2017—when various megacorps started throwing their resources behind *Na Kama'aina* plans—that

Danforth's handlers realized what had happened. Apparently some hotheads came *this* close to icing Ho on the spot—probably by arranging for a "tragic accident"—so they could keep the reins in their own acquisitive hands. But wiser heads prevailed, realizing that having promoted Danforth Ho as the True and Rightful King and all that, now they were stuck with him. And by this time, the people were following *Ho,* not the leadership of *Na Kama'aina . . .*

While *Na Kama'aina*'s leaders were still trying to get Ho back under their control, they found out to their absolute horror that he'd cut a deal with the local yakuza, along the same lines as the ones he'd penned with the corps. (Now, this surprised me a little when I learned it. I guess I hadn't thought that there was much yak activity in Hawai'i. I should have known, though: Wherever there's a large proportion of Japanese, you're going to find yaks.) *Na Kama'aina* felt control *really* slipping away now.

By late summer 2017 the federal government mobilized its armed forces on the mainland and set forth to implement the Resolution Act of 2016—in other words, the "Genocide Campaign" against Native Americans. We all know what happened immediately thereafter: Multiple volcanoes blew their tops under the influence of the Ghost Dancers, and that was the end of the Genocide Campaign. When word reached the islands of just what kind of drek had gone down, Danforth Ho decided that *der Tag* had finally arrived. He issued his orders to the army of followers he'd built up throughout the islands.

Whole assault teams of *kahunas*—the local flavor of shamans, I think—engaged the Civil Defense Force, and tied them up real good. Where resistance was especially strong, Great Form spirits backed the *kahunas*. Simultaneously, the yakuza mobilized a "civilian army" which, supplemented by heavily armed megacorp security forces, closed down basically all military and government communication channels on the islands, and blockaded various key government buildings.

Meanwhile, Danforth Ho—backed by the street-fighters of *Na Kama'aina* (who'd finally realized on which side their bread was buttered) and by thousands of devoted civilians—marched on the capitol building next to the old Iolani Palace in downtown Honolulu. The mob broke down the doors, rousted out the government officials and functionaries, and basically installed Danforth Ho as *Ali'i*. On August 22, 2017, King Kamehameha IV—born Danforth Ho—officially declared Hawai'i's sovereignty.

Predictably, the U.S. government back on the mainland didn't take too kindly to a bunch of jumped-up pineapple-pickers—led by a *management consultant,* for frag's sake!—taking over their major military staging area in the Pacific basin. It seems that most of the Pacific fleet wasn't in Pearl Harbor in late August of 2017. In fact, it was in transit to the west coast of the U.S., presumably to provide support, if necessary, to the abortive Genocide Campaign. (And you can bet that Danforth Ho, aka King Kam IV, knew that, and planned on it. Otherwise things might have gone *very* differently in the streets of Honolulu.) When word reached D.C. about Hawai'i's declaration of independence, encrypted messages downlinked from military satellites to the flagship of the Pacific fleet—no doubt the military equivalent of "get your sorry asses *back* there, and clean this mess up."

While the new King Kam was consolidating his control at home, his new allies weren't idle. A delegation of megacorps—led by Yamatetsu, it seems—was already pressuring Washington to recognize Hawai'i as a sovereign state. The feds told the corps precisely what they could do with that idea, and ordered the Pacific fleet to flank speed.

I wish I'd been there for the next act of this saga—it must have been quite a show. Mere minutes after Washington's rejection of the megacorps' "polite suggestion," a barrage of "Thor shots" bracketed the *USS Enterprise,* the flattop that was the flagship of the Pacific fleet.

("Hold the phone," I hear you say. "What the flying frag is a 'Thor shot'?" Thought you'd never ask.

(Project Thor dates back—*way* back, apparently, to the middle of the last century or thereabouts—but it's an idea whose time had come. Project Thor envisioned putting a whole drekload of "semismart" projectiles in low Earth orbit, equipped with little more than a retro-rocket, some steering vanes, and a dog-brain seeker head on the tip. No warhead, because one isn't needed. Basically, they're just "smart crowbars." When you need to send a blunt message to someone, just send the appropriate commands to a couple dozen Thor projectiles. They fire their retros to kick themselves out of orbit, then plummet free toward the ground at some horrendous speed. Their seeker heads now start looking for an appropriate target, depending on their programming—a Main battle tank, maybe, or the dome of the Capitol Building ... or something that looks like an aircraft carrier. Down they come, packing Great Ghu knows how much kinetic energy, and whatever they hit just kinda goes away ... probably accompanied by much pyrotechnics. In essence, then, Thor shots are just guided meteorites. Elegant idea, *neh*?

(That was the idea, but as far as anyone knew—up to 2017, at least—nobody had actually implemented Project Thor. To this day, nobody's *precisely* sure who fired the rounds that vaporized a couple of tons of seawater off the *Enterprise*'s bows.

(But I can make a pretty good guess, based on some interesting coincidences. Coincidentally, 2017 was the year in which Ares Macrotechnology took over the old *Freedom* space station, the one they eventually modified and renamed Zurich-Orbital. Just as coincidentally, Ares was the only megacorp with orbital assets anywhere near the correct "window" for a Thor shot into the central Pacific. And—also coincidentally, of course—Ares was one of the megacorps with which our friend Danforth Ho had enjoyed the longest and most intense private discussions ... *Quelle chance* ...

(End of digression.)

So that was it. Screened by Aegis cruisers or not, there was no way a carrier battle group could intercept Thor shots, or survive them if they landed. Once more, the task force reversed course, and slunk dispiritedly into San Diego harbor. The feds recognized Hawai'i's independence, and King Kam IV became the head of a constitutional monarchy that still exists today. And they all lived happily ever after ...

Null! As I said before, megacorps don't give gifts; they make investments. Now they came to King Kam looking for some major return on their investments. Like special trade deals, extraterritoriality, and basically almost complete freedom to do biz as they saw fit in the islands.

The people of Hawai'i liked the idea of independence from the U.S., and they weren't convinced that immediately giving up that independence to the megacorps was such a swift idea. The leadership of *Na Kama'aina*—yep, it was still hanging around—decided that this was a perfect lever to pry away King Kam's popular support (and, ideally, to put their own figurehead—a *real* figurehead this time—on the throne). Campaigning on the platform of cutting back—way back—on the megacorps' freedoms, *Na Kama'aina* politicos won a significant number of seats in the legislature. King Kam suddenly found himself confronting a strong faction within his own government that was dedicated to tossing him out on his hoop. He managed to keep control of the majority, but it was a very close thing.

King Kam IV died in 2045—no, the *Na Kama'aina* didn't off him . . . I don't think—and the faction of the government that had backed him retained *just* enough influence to put the successor he'd designated on the throne: his son, Gordon Ho. At age twenty-five, our boy Gordon became King Kamehameha V, and still wears the funky yellow-feathered headdress of the *Ali'i*.

I was still chewing over all the facts I'd absorbed and trying to make overall sense of them when the suborbital touched down at Awalani—"Sky Harbor."

"Welcome to Hawai'i," the flight attendant announced.

5

Call it the Montgomery Principle of Inverse Relationships. The faster you can get somewhere, the longer the wait for customs at the other end. Honolulu's Awalani Airport added another nice, big data-point to my mental graph.

I timed it. After spending only forty-some minutes to travel six thousand klicks, it took more than *sixty minutes* to traverse the fifteen meters from the end of the customs/immigration lineup to freedom in the lobby of the airport.

The only difference between the Hawai'ian customs officials and the functionaries who'd hassled me at Casper was the tans. Other than that, it was the same trolls in undersized uniforms watching from the sidelines while humorless drones asked me questions about whether I was importing meat products in my luggage. (I've always had the perverse impulse to ask a customs drone whether a dismembered body in my suitcase qualifies as "meat products . . .")

As I waited in the "Foreign Visitors" lineup, I watched with growling bitterness the speed with which the returning *kama'ainas*—the locals, Hawai'ian citizens—were processed through. No probing questions about meat products for them, and smiles and greetings of "Aloha" instead of a cold-voiced "Travel documentation, please."

At last I was through, though, into a pleasantly spacious and airy lobby, which suddenly struck me as packed with a disproportionate number of trolls and orks—at least in comparison to Cheyenne and even Seattle. Now that I thought about it, I remembered that the juvenile *Columbia HyperMedia Encyclopedia had* stated that the combined proportion of orks and trolls was something like *thirty-three percent*. What was it in Seattle? Closer to twenty-one, I thought. Well, I'd always heard that the Hawai'ians bred them big.

* * *

Through the customs nonsense at last, I started thinking about my next problem. Namely, *where the frag was I going, and to do what*? I'd be met—that's what the dwarf with the road-kill eyebrows had told me at Casper. By who, though, that was the question?

A question that was answered almost immediately. As I stood there looking vaguely lost, a figure separated itself from a passel of camera-laden Nihonese tourists, and approached. A *large* figure—an ork with a rather astounding set of shoulders and small tusks that looked impossibly white against his tanned skin—wearing a well-tailored business suit. In his big hands he held a little laser-printed sign that read "Tozer." This time I didn't have any trouble remembering that was supposed to be me, so I beckoned him over.

He gave me a broad smile that would have looked much more friendly without those fangs. "Mr. Brian Tozer?" he asked me in a voice like midnight and velvet.

I nodded. "That's me." I reached in my pocket and pulled out my credstick, the one with my digital password stored in memory, and offered it to him.

He chuckled—a sound like big rocks rolling in a fast-flowing stream—and waved it off. "I know you're you, Mr. Tozer," he said. "You look a lot healthier in person, y'know."

He'd probably seen my driver's license holo, or something like it, I figured. (If you ever actually *look* like your license holo, you're too sick to drive . . .) I shrugged. "Have it your way . . ." I hesitated, not knowing what to call him.

"Scott," he told me. "You can call me Scott, Mr. Tozer."

"Dirk," I responded automatically, then quickly corrected, "My name's Brian, but everyone's always called me Dirk." Frag, I had to be jet-lagged or something.

Scott's big brown eyes twinkled. "Dirk's chill with me," he said. "Let's get your luggage."

First-class passengers' luggage was routed to its own carousel, and most of my flight-mates had already collected theirs and cruised before the first bag even showed up in the cattle-class area. I pointed out my single bag, which Scott scooped up like it weighed nothing, then tossed it onto a little automated baggage cart that followed him around like a loyal spaniel. We led the spaniel-cart out of the terminal onto the road.

That's when the heat first hit me. Hell, it was only a little past oh-six-hundred, but I guessed the temperature was already around twenty-seven degrees, and the humidity was something horrendous. In seconds I felt my shirt start to stick to my back. Scott must have sensed my discomfort, because he chuckled again, and announced, "Going to be a nice toasty one, today. We're looking for thirty-one, thirty-two by midafternoon." He touched the cloth of my black shirt. "Hope you brought something a little more practical to wear, brah." I glanced pointedly at his suit, and he smiled again. "Yeah, but I'm *paid* to be uncomfortable."

The sky was still dark—that's right, it was the tropics, wasn't it? Dawn would be later and more sudden than I was used to in Cheyenne—but the sodium lights were almost as bright as day. Under their yellow glare, I saw where Scott was leading me: a metallic charcoal gray limo, a Rolls-Royce Phaeton, or some close cousin. A huge, low-slung thing that looked like it was doing Mach 2 while still parked at the curb. I let out a long, low whistle to show I was impressed.

Scott shrugged those massive shoulders. "Yeah," he acknowledged. "I still feel like that sometimes." From his pocket he pulled a little remote and pushed a button. With a silky whine like a high-speed turbine, the engine lit, and a moment later one of the oversized doors into the passenger compartment swung silently open. As the ork-chauffeur retrieved my bag from the spaniel-cart and tossed it into a trunk big enough for a game of Urban Brawl, I climbed into the back of the Phaeton.

Mental note: I *must* acquire myself one of these things at some point. Not to drive. To *live* in.

The passenger compartment looked bigger than some lower-class dosses I've rented; a huge, overstuffed couch where you'd expect there to be a rear seat. No, I corrected instantly, it wasn't a couch ... unless you consider four-point harnesses to be standard equipment for your living room furniture. I settled down and felt the opulent upholstery wrap itself lovingly around my fundament. (Did the limo come with some device—a crane, perhaps—to pry passengers *out* of the deep seat again as an optional extra?) Impulsively, I pulled off my shoes and made fists with my toes in the deep-pile carpeting. (One of my favorite flat-film movies from the last century recommends it as a cure for jetlag, and who am I to disagree?)

From the outside the big wraparound windows had been opaque, charcoal mirror-finish to match the coachwork. From inside they seemed to totally disappear . . . except for the fact that some subtle polarization removed the glare from the brilliant sodium streetlights. Between me and the driver's compartment was an array that looked like a waist-height entertainment wall unit: trid set, various formats of optical players, a stereo system that would give my technophile buddy Quincy wet dreams for the rest of his life, and something that looked like a scrambled satellite uplink commo unit. And, oh yes . . . a small liquor cabinet/wet-bar arrangement. Above the entertainment suite was a transparent kevlarplex screen. Through it I saw Scott slide into the front seat, push back a hank of hair, and slip a vehicle control line into his datajack. He turned around and grinned at me through a centimeter of reinforced kevlarplex. "Ready to go, Mr. Dirk?" His voice came from a hidden speaker somewhere behind my left ear.

"Only when you get rid of *this* thing," I told him, leaning forward to rap on the bulletproof screen. "I feel like I'm in an aquarium."

His chuckle sounded clearly from the hidden speakers as the screen whined down into the top of the entertainment suite. "Better?"

"Much." Another couple of centimeters of my anatomy was engulfed by the upholstery as Scott put the Phaeton into gear and pulled out smoothly. "Scott," I said after a moment, "your call. Do I need the four-point?"

"Hey, I know some tourists *pay* to be strapped down." I saw his large head shake. "You can get by with the lap-belt if you like, but you want *something* to keep you from rattling around if I have to do any heavy evasion."

As I fastened the lap-strap, I asked the next logical question. "Is that particularly likely? Evasion, I mean?"

My chauffeur shrugged. "Likely? No. Possible? Yeah." He snorted. "We've had a couple of wild moves against corp higher-ups this year, and the shooters might not bother to find out who's in the limo before they start busting caps, y'know what I mean?"

"Who's behind the wild moves?"

"ALOHA, who else?"

I blinked. "ALOHA? They're still around?"

"They're *always* around, brah. Some people are never satisfied with what they got. Yanks out, Japs out, *haoles* out . . ."

I cut him off. "Howlies?"

"*Haoles.*" He spelled the word. "Anglos, brah. White folk. Foreigners . . . like you, okay?" The smile I could hear in his voice robbed the words of offense. Then he continued, "Like I said, *haoles* out, corps out . . ." He snorted again, letting me know what he thought about that attitude.

We pulled out of the airport compound, and onto a modern six-lane freeway. Scott opened up the throttle, and the Phaeton's turbine sang. I glanced at the wet bar, thought about it, then—what the frag anyway?—cracked it open and searched through the miniature bottles inside for some Scotch. Glenmorangie, twenty-five-year-old single-malt—well, *that* would certainly make the grade. The limo's active suspension ate up the road vibration so I had no trouble pouring a healthy shot into a heavy crystal glass and adding a splash of water. I silently toasted the back of Scott's head, and in the rearview mirror I saw his eyes crinkle in a smile. I sipped, and let the Scotch work its magic.

"Scott," I said after a couple of minutes, "you know who I am, right?"

He paused, and I knew he was thinking about how best to answer. "Of course I do, Mr. Tozer," he said at last.

I smiled. "Call me Dirk," I reminded him quietly.

He smiled again and admitted, "Okay, yeah, I know who you are."

"And Jacques Barnard told you what I was here for?"

"Don't know any Jacques Barnard," he lied firmly. "My boss is Elsie Vogel at Nebula." He paused. "But yeah, I know you're here to deliver a message, and I know who you're going to deliver it to."

"Tell me."

He shook his head. "You don't need to know that yet," he said, and for the first time I could hear the hint of steel under the friendliness. This well-dressed ork wasn't just any corp gofer, I realized, he had some juice. "I'll drive you there when the time comes," he went on, and again his voice was geniality itself. "Don't you worry about that."

"When?"

"Tomorrow, probably. The man you're to meet—he's on one of the outer islands today—won't be back till late tonight, early tomorrow morning. Emergency trip, or something like that." He turned for a moment and grinned at me over his shoulder. "Means you've got the whole of today and tonight to see the sights, brah. And me at your disposal." He hooked a large thumb at his chest. "Number one tour guide, that's me."

I sighed and contemplated that over another sip of Glenmorangie. I didn't really want to admit it, but I was enjoying myself. I kind of liked Scott—even knowing he had corporate steel under the good-ol'-boy exterior—and I *certainly* liked the idea of having a chauffeured limo at my beck and call. But . . .

But I had to keep my level of paranoia up. Despite all the trappings, this wasn't a vacation, this was biz. And, worse, I was in the dark about a lot of what the biz entailed. I didn't know who I had to meet, or why. I didn't know what would happen to me afterward. And I didn't know who or what had any interest in getting between me and the objective. I was out of my territory—I had to keep reminding myself of that—playing in someone else's yard, and out of my comfort zone. Who knows: Everything might come off as smooth as synthsilk. I deliver the message, maybe receive a reply, then Scott ferries me back to Awalani, and I'm winging my way home to Cheyenne. But if it didn't, and I suddenly found myself rather dead because I hadn't taken precautions, then I wouldn't even have the satisfaction of being able to haunt Barnard through all eternity. The fault would be my own, not his. I *was* exposed—that's what I had to remember, every moment of every day. And I had to do what I could to minimize that exposure. Which reminded me . . .

"Scott."

"Yes, Mr. Dirk?"

"I had to leave some . . . *personal* effects . . . behind me on the mainland, if you know what I mean." The back of his neck wrinkled, and I knew he was grinning like a bandit. "I want to correct that problem. Can you help me out?"

"You really don't need it, y'know." He rapped on the driver's side window with a bulging knuckle. "Do you have any idea what it takes to punch through this stuff?"

I wasn't going to be put off that easily. "Even so," I pressed. "Call it a good-luck charm . . . like a rabbit's foot. I just wouldn't feel comfortable without it."

He laughed aloud at that. "Yeah, a nine-millimeter rabbit's foot, I bet." He sobered quickly. "Okay. It's chill, brah, I'll buff you out." He glanced back again. "And I'll get you some appropriate clothes, too. Okay?"

"I've always been partial to kevlar," I told him, "if you can get it in one of my colors."

Ahead of us, against the blackness of the sky, I could see the lighted ziggurats of skyrakers. For a moment I had one of those moments of disorientation. I could as well have been cruising north on Highway 5 toward downtown Seattle as west on Hawai'i Route 1. In the dark most cities looked the same.

Again, Scott seemed to pick up my unspoken thought. "Too bad you had to catch the red-eye. This is a real nice view—a good intro to the city, y'know what I mean?"

"So what's Honolulu like?" I asked him. "You live in the city, don't you?"

"Yeah, I've got a place in the Nebula complex." He shrugged. "It's a city, y'know? It's got its good points and it's got its bad points. Places you shouldn't miss, and places you shouldn't be caught dead. It's got its corporators, it's got its *burakumin*"—he used the Japanese term for the homeless or dispossessed, an insulting word that was gaining currency among corp suits to refer to people without corporate affiliation—"and it's got its tourists." He laughed. "*Bruddah*, does it have its tourists."

"High-level corps types?"

"Most of them, yeah. Whole swarms of them coming over from Asia, and some from Europe. But there's still the mom-and-pop types who've saved for years to get away and splash money around for a while."

"That's what drives the economy, isn't it? Tourism?"

"That's what the mainland guidebooks say," he agreed. "But most of it's corp-driven, really. Hey, Hawai'i's the biggest corporate free port going. Where do you *think* the money comes from?"

I thought about that for a while as the skyrakers reared up around us, constellations of electric stars in the firmament. "So what are the bad points about the city?" I asked at last.

"The politicians," Scott responded at once with a humorless laugh. "I don't know what they're like where you come from, brah, but here they're like the trees: crooked with their palms out." He chortled as he pointed out the window to a coconut palm on the street corner.

He slowed and swung the big limo around a tight corner.

We sighed to a stop, and he killed the engine. "We're here," he announced unnecessarily.

"Which is where?" I asked him a few moments later as I watched him unload my single bag from the limo's hangar-sized trunk. I looked up at the building looming over me: white as only artificial marble can be, multiple complex curves that seemed to give the building a sense of movement in the faint pink of the predawn.

"The Diamond Head Hotel," he told me, "right next to—you guessed it—Diamond Head itself."

"Open to the public?"

"You've got to be kidding, brah," the big ork snorted. "Even *I* don't have high enough corp connections to stay here. You pack big juju, even if you don't know it."

I nodded as I followed him up the ramp toward the lobby. There were corporate hostelries in Seattle—places open only to various ranks of corporators, regardless of their actual affiliations—but the concept hadn't really caught on there yet. (In Cheyenne? Maybe that backwater burg will catch up in a decade, chummer.) Apparently, the high-tone suits like the hostelries because they contribute even more to the sep-aration between them and the *burakumin* . . . a class that in-cluded me, which gave the whole thing a nice touch of irony, didn't it?

We breezed right through the lobby. Scott didn't even glance at the smooth-faced slot behind the front desk, so I didn't either. Up the elevator we went—I noticed the ork had to wave a keycard at the control panel before the door would open and again before the elevator would start—and out onto the landing on the seventeenth floor. The hotel—corporate hostelry or not—had the same feel and ambiance as modern hotels anywhere in the world, all the individuality and character pressed out of them. I could just as well have been in the Sheraton in Seattle.

I followed Scott all the way down to the end of the hall and waited while he waved the keycard again at the door. The maglock snapped back, and he pushed the door open with his foot, stepping aside to let me enter first.

Well, okay, this *wasn't* like the Sheraton . . . at least, those rooms in the Sheraton I've had cause to visit. Come to think of it, it was conceptually the nonmobile analog of the Pha-eton's passenger compartment: similar overstuffed couches, similar entertainment suite, similar wet-bar arrangement.

Pure, packaged hedonistic luxury, in peach and aqua. Chuckling softly at my reaction—probably a pretty good gaffed-fish imitation—Scott carried my case through into the bedroom of the suite and placed it gently on a bed big enough for one hell of a party. As he came back toward me, I had the momentary urge to slip him a tip.

"You want to grab some shut-eye?" he asked.

I thought about it, glanced at that bed, and thought about it again. "Not a bad idea," I admitted.

"No problem." He checked his watch, a pricey Quasar chronograph (yet more evidence, if I'd really needed it, that he was more than a simple limo driver). "How's about I swing by in about three hours?"

"Make it four," I told him. "And—"

He cut me off with a grin. "Don't worry, Mr. Dirk, I'll bring you your rabbit's foot. *And* some real clothes."

True to form—whenever I really feel like I need sleep, it happens this way—I didn't slip into the deepest, most restful phase of sleep until fifteen minutes before I'd set the alarm to go off. So my eyes were still dry and gritty, my thoughts just a touch fogged, when I rolled out of the party-bed.

Sun was pouring through the picture window, and I was diverted for almost a full minute by the view as I stood there naked in the middle of the room. I was looking out toward Diamond Head—I assume that's what it was, at least—a huge outcropping of weathered rock. From this angle it didn't look so much like a diamond as a slightly crooked anvil, but at that moment, I couldn't have cared less. It was beautiful as all hell, wreathed around its base by lush foliage and even lusher mansions, silhouetted against a sky that was a clearer and purer blue than any I'd ever seen before. If there was any drek in the atmosphere—particulates, NO_x, and other miscellaneous nasties—there wasn't enough of it to take the edge off the view's clarity. Not like Seattle—in fragging spades—or even like Cheyenne. One of the advantages of being an island in the middle of the Pacific, I figured, watching the trade winds stir the coconut palms lining the shore: The prevailing winds blow all your pollution problems out to sea. Not a bad system, if you can arrange it.

I shook off my fascination with the view and headed for the bathroom to take care of the fur that had built up on my teeth, in addition to other matters. I'd thrown on a bathrobe and was debating doing something drastic with my hair—mousse, maybe or (better yet) some fragging varnish—when the suite's door signal chirped.

You know how you can tell a *real* luxury hotel from a wannabe? A front-door intercom in the bathroom, within easy reach of both drekker and bathtub. The Diamond Head Hotel definitely fit the first category. I leaned over and hit the intercom switch. "Yeah?"

The two-centimeter thumbnail screen lit up, and I saw Scott's grinning face. "You up and around, Mr. Dirk?"

"More or less. Come on in, make yourself at home. I'll be out in a couple of ticks." I hit the key labeled Door Unlock.

When I emerged a few moments later, the big ork was standing in the middle of the living room staring out the picture windows, transfixed by the same view that had nailed me earlier. He was in mufti. He'd looked big enough in his tailored business suit. Now, the impression of overwhelming size was emphasized by the fact that he wore a Hawai'ian shirt—yes, those things were still in fashion, apparently—that made him look like a profusion of jungle flowers that had decided to take a stroll. On the couch near him were a couple of parcels.

He turned as I emerged from the bathroom. "Sorry to keep you waiting," I told him, running my hands through my hair, which still stood out in places like stickpins.

Scott chuckled and patted one of his own unruly cowlicks. "I hear you, bruddah." He gestured to the parcels on the couch. "Brought you some things. Want to try them on?"

"Did you guess at the sizes?" I looked again at the chauffeur's two-ax-handle shoulders. How good would he be at judging the size of anyone with a normal physique?

"No need, I just checked your file. One-eighty-five height, eighty-nine mass. One-oh-five regular in the chest, eighty-four centimeters in the waist. Right?"

"Not quite." I was perversely glad that he'd got *something* wrong. Christ . . . if Barnard had my fragging *measurements* on file, what else did he have in my docket? An itemized list of sexual conquests? An estimate of my daily calorie intake? "Closer to eighty-six in the waist these days."

Scott grinned triumphantly. "I figured they might be old figures, so I took the libery of letting the waist out a touch. Check 'em out."

With a sigh I picked up the parcels and headed into the bedroom to change.

The clothes fit perfectly, and I had to admit that they *were* a hell of a lot more practical than what I'd brought. A couple of pairs of light-colored, lightweight slacks—five-pocket things, with slightly baggy legs, pulled in at the ankles. A couple of Hawai'ian-style shirts—floral prints, but a lot more muted than Scott's choice—slightly oversized, short-sleeved, cut to be worn outside the waistband of the pants. A second package contained a set of Ares Arms form-fitting body armor—short-sleeved, of course—that fit me like a re-inforced second skin. I selected bone-white slacks and a dusty blue shirt with a red hibiscus pattern. As long as I kept the shirt buttoned up high, you couldn't see I was wearing armor underneath.

Scott nodded approvingly as I re-emerged. "Much better," he told me with a grin. "You look almost like a *kama'aina*."

"What abou—?"

"Your rabbit's foot?" he finished for me. "Here." He reached up under the waist of his shirt, pulled something out, and tossed it to me.

I snagged it instinctively and examined the object. A Seco LD-120 light pistol, in a compact, cut-down waist holster. I pulled out the blocky black macroplast weapon, dropped the clip, worked the action. Perfect condition—as I'd expected, when you came down to it. The holster had two side pouches, each holding a spare clip—thirty-six rounds in to-tal, then. The little pistol didn't have anywhere near the stopping power of my trusty old Manhunter, but if the fertil-izer hit the ventilator, I'd at least be able to give an opponent *something* to think about. With a nod of thanks to Scott, I slipped the holster into the waistband of my pants over the left hip, attaching the clip to the belt. I checked in the mir-ror, and saw that the loose-fitting shirt concealed the weapon almost perfectly.

"Feeling luckier now?" Scott asked.

The first order of business was food. I hadn't bothered with the light meal served on the suborbital flight, so the last time I'd eaten was almost eighteen hours ago. My stomach was starting to suspect my throat had been cut.

Scott led me downstairs to the restaurant—opulent, as I'd expected—and out onto an open patio where white-coated staff were tending a breakfast buffet. For a moment I wondered about the tactical wisdom of an open patio, but then I saw the little warning signs positioned every three meters along the patio rail. Notice: Protective Magic in Use, they read. I nodded in understanding. A physical barrier of some kind, I figured, backed by some kind of spell barrier. It couldn't have been a mana barrier, because birds flew unhindered between the patio and the surrounding palms.

The patio was empty, apart from me and Scott, and the serving staff ... and about a dozen little beige birds that looked like some kind of dove. The big ork led me to a table by the patio rail and asked me what I wanted for breakfast.

While he went off and filled my order—I could get used to this kind of personal service, I realized—I enjoyed the view. The view of Diamond Head was blocked by some buildings from this vantage point, but I could look out to the west, toward downtown Honolulu and, beyond that, toward Awalani Airport and Pearl Harbor. The still, azure water of the bay was dotted with pleasure craft of all types and sizes. Brightly colored spinnakers gleamed in the sun, while here and there speedboats kicked curtains of spray into the air as they cut tight turns. In the distance, halfway to the horizon, I saw a high-speed craft of some kind, going like a bat out of hell but leaving almost no wake. Some kind of hydrofoil, I figured; possibly an interisland ferry.

As Scott returned with my loaded plate—he'd either erred on the side of generosity or else judged my appetite based on his own—I heard a distant ripping sound. I looked up and to the west.

Two vicious little darts were shooting through the air, climbing and accelerating out over the ocean—fighters of some kind, no doubt launched from Pearl. Even though I knew they weren't any faster than the suborbital I'd ridden a few hours earlier—hell, they might even have a lower top speed—they looked much faster. Pure, violent energy, that's the way they seemed to me at that moment: volatile, apparently ready to maneuver in an instant or lash out with weapons of grotesque power.

Now that I was looking to the sky, I noticed something else, something that I'd seen only a couple of times on the mainland. It was the contrail of a high-altitude plane, but this wasn't the geometrically perfect straight line of a high-speed civilian transport. No, this was like donuts on a rope—a central line contrail surrounded by evenly spaced torus-shaped loops. From what little I knew of aerospace technology—the kind of drek you pick up from scanning the popular press—the only kind of engine that could create that characteristic donut-on-a-rope structure was a pulse-detonation propulsion system. As far as I knew, pulse-detonation engines were used on only one kind of craft: hypersonic spy planes, Aurora class and up.

I frowned, thinking. Pulse-detonation is pretty hot fragging stuff. Even now, decades after it was introduced, it was still a touchy thing. Anybody could make a standard jet engine—turbofan, ramjet, even SCRAMjet—but only a very few engineers could design and build a pulse-detonation drive that actually worked without blowing itself into shrapnel. I wouldn't have imagined that Hawai'i had the resources—monetary and personnel—to develop something that sophisticated.

But then, I realized, maybe the kingdom didn't have to develop it from scratch. When Danforth Ho's civilian army suppressed the Civil Defense Force and basically took over the islands, he might well have "acquired" a lot of interesting tech by default, as it were.

And that thought brought up a whole drekload of other questions. Now that I considered it, I realized that the descriptions I'd read of Danforth Ho's coup and the islands' secession from the U.S. had been pretty fragging superficial on a couple of pretty major points. The Pacific fleet business—that I could understand. A task force commander doesn't argue with Thor shots. But what about the materiel at the military bases throughout the islands? And the bases themselves? Would the U.S. government have let them go so easily, without a fight? Or had there been a fight, and the official records modified to gloss it all over?

I turned to Scott. He'd gotten his own plate of food—heaped even higher than mine—and was already halfway through it. "You're native-born, aren't you?" I asked him.

He nodded. "Oahu born and bred," he acknowledged around a mouthful of Belgian waffles.

"So tell me about the Secession."

He chuckled and wiped syrup and whipped cream—real whipped cream, for frag's sake—from his lips. "How old do you think I am, brah?" he asked. "That was back in 'seventeen. I wasn't even an itch in my father's pants."

"But your parents were around in 'seventeen, right?" I pressed. "And you'll have met a drek-load of people who were around, maybe even involved. People talk."

Scott shook his head as he finished off another gargantuan mouthful. "That's the thing, bruddah—they don't talk, not about Secession. Well, okay, they do—but, like, about the stuff leading up to it, and about the days after it. What actually went down, what the *kahunas* did to the CDF, all that *kanike*—all that bulldrek—nobody talks about it much."

"Why?"

The ork shrugged. "Don't know, *hoa*, really I don't. I'm just a simple *wikanikanaka* boy here."

"Wikani-what?"

"You got to learn to sling the lingo around here, brah," the ork said with a laugh. "Everybody speaks a kind of pidgin—lots of Polynesian loanwords, okay? Like *hoa*—that means 'friend,' 'chummer.' *Kanike*—that means the sound of stuff clashing and clattering together, but it's used like 'bulldrek.' And *wikanikanaka*—that's 'ork.' You'll get used to it.

"Anyway," he went on, getting his thoughts back on track, "like I said, nobody really talks about the Secession."

"Like there's stuff they don't want other people to know?"

"Maybe," he allowed, "or maybe stuff they don't want to remember."

"Like what?"

The ork shrugged, apparently a little uncomfortable. "You hear stories, sometimes," he said vaguely. "Old people talk, sometimes . . . but then you ask for more details, and they clam up on you." He paused. "You talk to enough people, you hear really weird stuff. Dragons, for one. Big storms—unnatural storms—rolling down out of Puowaina. That's Punchbowl crater, just north of the city. Weird drek going on in Haleakala Volcano on Maui. Kukae, some old geezer even told me once he saw something big—something real big—moving under the water in Pearl Harbor, next to the old *Arizona* battleship memorial. Said whatever it was, it was bigger than the battleship and it looked at him with eyes the size of fragging basketballs." He shrugged again. "Believe as much of that *kanike* as you want. I don't know the answers."

He folded his napkin and put it on the table. "Now eat up and let's roll, *hoa*, okay?"

6

I waited in the open-air lobby while Scott pulled the Phaeton up and out of the underground parking lot. The big Rolls sighed to a stop in front of me, and the rear passenger door swung open.

I gestured no to that, crossing my hands edge to edge like karate chops meeting each other. Scott's voice sounded from an exterior speaker. "Problems, Mr. Dirk?"

"I don't want to ride in the playpen," I explained—feeling a touch foolish at talking to a car that was so obviously buttoned-up. "Any objection to company up front?"

I heard the ork chuckle, a slightly tinny sound through the speaker. "Your call, bruddah, but you're going to have me forgetting I'm a chauffeur here." The passenger compartment door shut again, and the right side front door clicked open. I walked around the big car, slid inside, and *chunked* the door shut. The driver's compartment was nothing compared to the playpen in back, predictably, but it still was more comfortable and well-appointed than some dosses I've lived in.

Scott grinned over at me. The hair-thin optic cable connecting his datajack to the control panel seemed to burn in the sun. "Okay, Mr. Dirk, anything in particular you want to see?"

I shrugged. "You're the *kama'aina*," I said. "You tell me what I *should* see?"

His grin broadened. "You got it, *hoa*." At the touch of a mental command, the limo slipped into gear and pulled away. "Any objection to a little music? Local stuff."

I shrugged. "Just as long as it's not 'Aloha Oe,'" I told him.

He laughed at that. "Not in *this* car, you can bet on that. Ever hear traditional slack-key?" I shook my head. "You're in for a treat, then." As Scott sat back comfortably and

crossed his arms, the stereo clicked on and the car filled
with music.

I've always had a taste for music—*real* music, stuff that
shows some kind of talent, some kind of musicianship, not
the drek that anyone with an attitude and a synth can churn
out. Old blues or trad jazz preferably, but I've got a relatively open mind. Hell, I've even listened to country on occasion. Slack-key was something new—acoustic guitars,
alternately strummed and intricately finger-picked. Something like bluegrass in technique, but with a sound and a feel
all its own.

"You like?"

"I like," I confirmed. "I've got to get some of this for my
collection. Who're the musicians?"

"An old group, they recorded back before the turn of the
century. Kani-alu, they're called. None of them still alive:
they all kicked from old age, or got cacked by the VITAS.

"I just picked up this disk a couple of days back. Some
guys have gone back through the old catalog and remastered
a bunch of this stuff." He paused. "If you want, you can
have my copy when you leave. I'll pick up another."

"Thanks. I'd like that." To the lush strains played by musicians long dead, we cruised off the Diamond Head Hotel
property and headed toward the city.

Scott was a good tour-guide; he had amusing and interesting stories to tell about nearly everything we passed. We
cruised roughly northeast, then turned northwest to pass
through Kapiolani Park in the shadow of Diamond Head itself. Then we cut down onto Kalakaua Avenue (what is it
with Hawai'ians and the letter *K*?), which flanked the beach.

You could tell the tourists from the locals, both on the
sand and in the water. The tourists were pale white—like
slugs under a rock—or turning a painful-looking pinky-red.
(I started thinking about sunscreen and the thinning ozone
layer. I'd brought some spray-on SPF 45 goop, but would
that be enough? I looked down at my arms: as slug-white as
the other newbies.) In contrast, the locals—there weren't
that many of them, for some reason—were all bronze or mahogany, the comfortable deep-down tan I'd seen on Sharon
Young back in Cheyenne.

There was a little surf rolling in—breakers all of a meter
high or so. A couple of pale tourists were trying to catch
those waves on surfboards garishly emblazoned with the

name of the company that had rented them out. It looked like an awful lot of work just to get wet. As we cruised slowly on, I saw one slag—an ebony-haired elf with ivory skin—actually get up onto his surfboard and ride it . . . for a whole two meters before he submarined the nose and went *sploosh*.

Then, out beyond him, somebody else caught a wave perfectly and was up in an instant. A troll, he was, on a board larger than some dining tables I've owned. His long black hair whipped in the wind as he cut his board back and forth across the margin of the small wave, dodging through the heads of swimmers like gates in a slalom. Swishing into the shallows, he dismounted smoothly, and in one motion he picked up his board—shoulders and arms bulging—swung it around, and started paddling out again. I watched the muscles working under the golden-brown skin of his massive back.

Scott had been watching the same show. "Nice moves," he said approvingly.

"Do you do that?"

"I do it," he confirmed with a chuckle, "but not around here. If you've got time, let me take you to see some *real* waves, brah. Thirty-footers, and one after another. Pretty close to heaven."

As I nodded, I realized something a little surprising. There was something disturbing about the view on the beach, and it took me a moment to make sense of it. All that bare skin—*that* was what bothered me.

Don't get me wrong, I'm no prude. Bare skin is great; I fully and wholeheartedly approve of bare skin, under the right circumstances, and particularly with the right companion. But . . .

Bare skin means *no armor*. I looked at all the frying tourists sprawled on the sand. Most of them would be *shaikujin*—corporators from one or another of the megas. Where in Seattle would you see this many corporators wandering around in public without the benefit of any armor whatsoever? *No*where, that's where. Here, a disgruntled sniper with a grudge to settle would have no trouble with one-shot-one-kill. Either the tourists were pretty fragging confident in the security provisions—pretty fragging *over*-confident, if you asked me—or the tropical sun had cooked the sense of self-preservation right out of their pointy little heads.

I pointed that out to Scott, and he nodded slowly. "A bit of both, that's what it is," he suggested. "*Na Maka'i*—that's the cops, the Hawai'i National Police Force, the HNPF—they keep things buttoned down pretty tight in Waikiki. This part of town *ain't* a good place to make trouble, *hoa,* trust me on that one. If you ain't corp, you ain't *here,* if you take my meaning."

"You're saying the whole of Waikiki's a corporate enclave?"

"More or less, brah, more or less." He nodded his big head. "It's a security thing. If you're walking the streets and you don't look the part, Na Maka'i's going to pull you over and ask you some questions—real polite, and all, but you'd better give them the right answers and have the datawork to back it up."

He shrugged. "But clamp-downs and heat-waves can do only so much, right? Security's good in Waikiki, but it's not *that* good." He gestured through the window at the scantily clad bodies on the beach. "If I *really* wanted to take down some suits, I could do it . . . *and* get away afterward."

I nodded slowly. That's basically how I had it scanned. "What about the locals, then?" I asked. I pointed to the surfing troll, who was already riding another wave. "You'd expect *him* to know better than to trust the cops. But he's not wearing any armor."

Scott chuckled. "No, he's not *wearing* armor, *hoa,* he *is* armor. You know the second most popular elective medical procedure in the whole of the islands?"

"Dermal armor," I guessed.

"You got it, brah. *Nui* dermal armor—dermal armor big-time. Along with bodysculpt to make it look good . . . or as good as you can get. See, now check out that slag over there? Classic example."

I looked where he was pointing, saw an ork strolling along the beach, wearing nothing but a pair of shorts even more garish than Scott's shirt. His arms and legs were scrawny; his shoulders weren't broad. But by Ghu did he have pecs and abs—massively cut, incredibly defined, as if they were chiseled out of some material other than flesh. Which they were, I realized. His chest and back were layered with enough dermal planting to stop a Manhunter round. The Seco on my hip would barely scratch him.

"Want to guess the *most* popular procedure?" Scott asked.

"Tell me."

"Sun-shielding, brah. Genetic treatment of the skin to block UV. They tried various chemical treatments, but you had to keep going in for a refresher because you'd eventually just exfoliate the treated skin. The genetic route, new skin is as resistant as the old. See this?" He extended his hand to me, pinched a fold of his skin. "This is SPF eighty-five, *hoa*. Permanent sunscreen.

"I got my eyes done, too—modified iris and photosensitive chemicals in the lens. I don't need shades no matter how bright it gets."

"Expensive, I guess?"

"The eyes, yes," he admitted. Then he chuckled. "Glad Nebula picked up the tab.

"But the skin treatment? No, brah, it's not bad at all. The clinics have got it down to a real assembly-line process, and you've got *nui* kinds to pick from. Full treatment costs five thousand nuyen, good for life. And lots of the clinics, they offer special family packages—you, the wife, and all the ankle-biters for seven-Kay." He poked my pale forearm. "If you decide to stay here, you might consider it yourself."

"Hey," I protested quickly, "I'm not staying. Just doing my job, then I'm gone."

The chauffeur shrugged. "That's what everyone says," he told me, "at first."

Still on Kalakaua Avenue, we rolled westward into downtown Waikiki.

I didn't really know what to expect from Waikiki, except that I thought it would be *different,* somehow. I was disappointed. It was just another city, really. Apart from the curving beach, the rich blue ocean, and the perfect weather, it could just as well have been the corporate enclave in just about any metroplex anywhere in the world. Okay, it *was* cleaner than most other cities I've seen. But apart from that, this could just as easily have been the rich corporate quarter of Tokyo or Chiba.

Why did I pick two Japanese cities as examples? The people on the sidewalks, chummer, that's why. Nine out of ten of them were Nihonese. I wondered about that for a while, but then I remembered something I'd read a long time ago.

Apparently, during the last decades of the last century, lots of Japanese—and lots of Japanese money—moved into the islands. (The smart-ass who'd written the article I read said something like, "After the Japanese couldn't conquer Hawai'i in World War II, they came in afterward and *bought* it.") Add a large resident Nihonese population to the influx of tourists from Japan-based megacorps, and that would explain it.

Scott tooled the Phaeton along the broad, spotless street of Waikiki, showing me all the major sites. The Royal Hawai'ian Hotel—"The Pink Lady," Scott called it—a flamingo pink extravaganza of pseudo-Moorish architecture that was more than a century old, but was still recognized as one of the most sumptuous hotels in the islands. The International Market Place, an open-air market comprising scores of booths and stores, under the spreading branches of a banyan tree. (Scott explained that the original International Market Place had been turned into a convention center around the turn of the century, but that after a fire destroyed the center in 2022, the City Council ordered another banyan planted, and the Market Place returned to its earlier glory.) And on and on. Eventually, the sumptuous-looking hotels started to blur into one another, and my eyes started to glaze over.

Scott noticed almost immediately, pulled the car over, and turned to me. "You getting bored, is that it?"

I shrugged. "Call it culture shock, maybe."

The ork snorted. "You call *this* culture? This is glitz, brah, pure and simple."

"That's what I mean," I told him. "I'm not used to this much money concentrated in one place."

"I got it now, Mr. Dirk." Scott laughed. "You want to see the other side of the coin, right? Okay, you'll get it." And he pulled the car back out into the traffic.

As soon as we were out of the Waikiki enclave, into the *real* Honolulu, I felt a lot more at home and comfortable. (Depressing, in a way, but there it is.) According to Scott, the official population of Honolulu is almost three million—just a hundred thousand or so less than Seattle's. That's the *official* figure, of course, in both cases. In Seattle, if you lump in the SINless—the homeless, the indigent, the transient, and the shadowy—the total rises to, depending on which estimate you believe, just short of four million to well over five and a quarter million.

The Honolulu number is probably an underestimate as well, but—cruising down its highways and byways—I couldn't believe that the difference between official population and real population was that great. Don't get me wrong, I *did* see vagrants and homeless types. (I made sure that Scott included appropriate places on the tour.) But they were nowhere near as numerous as in Seattle, or even in Cheyenne. There were some pretty drekky low-rent areas, and one or two ancient tenement complexes that prompted ideas of urban renewal using high-explosives, but there wasn't anything I'd really class as slums. And there *certainly* wasn't anything as squalid and soul-killing as Hell's Kitchen, Glow City, or the Barrens back in Seattle.

The most interesting thing about Honolulu, to my mind, was the proximity of the drekkier parts of town to the corporate heart. Around the intersection of King Street and Punchbowl Street, you've got the financial guts of the city, all pristine skyrakers and corp smoothies on the street. Less than half a klick away, there's the "vice shopping mall" that is Hotel Street, lined with sex shows, tough-looking bars, and porno chip outlets, populated by broken-down jammers of all four orientations (hetero and homo male, hetero and homo female), by chipleggers and flashmeisters, and by the fresh meat strolling by to do business with same. Even Seattle has managed to segregate the two facets of its economy a little more.

Hotel Street was the heart of Chinatown, according to Scott, but I didn't see too many ethnic Chinese on the streets. Lots of big slags and biffs who I guessed were native Polynesians and an almost equal number I tentatively labeled as Filipinos. As we cruised slowly by, I watched the action—contract negotiations of various sordid kinds—come to a stop as the participants stared at the Phaeton gliding past. There probably weren't that many Rolls-Royces to be seen in this neck of the woods, I figured. (Come to think of it, that slow cruise pointed out another difference between Honolulu and the underbelly of Seattle: nobody so much as took a potshot at the car.)

From Chinatown we headed west again, swinging past the airport, past the huge restricted area that was the Pearl Harbor military base, and into the region known as Ewa (*EH-*

vah; Scott made sure I got the pronunciation right). As recently as thirty years ago, my tour-guide told me, Ewa had been a city in its own right, close to but still distinct from Honolulu itself. No longer: The larger city had sprawled out, eventually absorbing the smaller. (Much like Everett and Fort Lewis, now that I came to think about it.) Apart from the weather and the clarity of the air, as we drove the streets of Ewa I could easily imagine I was in Renton.

I checked my watch. We'd been cruising for almost two hours, and my stomach was starting to make growling noises again, despite the big breakfast. "I need a bite to eat," I told Scott. "And it's getting on to Miller time, too."

"The bar's fully stocked in the back," the ork told me, "and if you look in the bottom of the fridge there's food—"

"No," I cut him off, "I want to stop somewhere around here. Consider it part of the tour."

He smiled at that. "What do you have in mind?"

I told him, and his smile grew even broader. "Mo' bettah, brah, that's okay. I got just the place in mind."

The place was called Cheeseburger in Paradise, and it was in the grimy heart of Ewa. Scott told me the name as if it was a joke, but I didn't get it. He had to explain about a song by some dead country-folkie called Jimmy Buffet whom I'd never heard of, and by that time it wasn't really funny anymore. In any case, he explained, Cheeseburger in Paradise was originally a chain that had started up in Maui during the nineteen eighties, and eventually spread to the other islands. The chain had gone belly-up in the 'twenties, and recently this place had picked up the name as an ironic commentary. Something like a rat-bag flophouse calling itself the Hilton.

I felt at home the moment I walked in the door. Almost subliminal waves of tension, of intensity, of danger and violence only barely held in check, washed over me. In the semidarkness of the tavern, I could easily imagine I was back in The Blue Flame in Seattle, or even The Buffalo Jump in Cheyenne.

I went in first—Scott had wanted to lead, but I'd insisted—and I *felt* the eyes on me from the darkened booths and tables. The bartender, a grizzled ork with chipped fangs, gave me a welcoming sneer. From the rough direction of the dance stage—currently vacant, although the lights gleamed on something that could be oil on the worn carpet covering—I heard a muttered comment, something highly derogatory by its tone, and a harsh laugh. Yep, this was just the kind of place I was looking for.

The door opened again behind me, and I felt the looming presence of Scott at my back. Instantly, the feel of the place—the strange dynamic that you can always feel, if you're tuned in closely enough to your instincts—changed. I couldn't believe that the locals of Cheeseburger in Paradise knew Scott personally, but they had to recognize *what* he was, if not precisely who: a bodyguard, and a very competent one. I could *feel* the shift as the patrons quickly reoriented their perceptions of me.

I jandered across to an open booth, thinking about the gun on my hip as I walked. That's all it takes, really—just *think* about the heat you're packing, and where you're packing it. It changes your walk, the way you carry your weight, very subtly. Anyone with street instincts is going to pick up on that change and interpret it correctly. In a totally nonconfrontational and nonthreatening way, I'd made it abundantly clear to those who mattered that I wasn't traveling unheeled. Scott followed me, and we slid into the curved booth, sitting side by side with our backs to the wall.

A waitress—a hard-faced woman with black roots to her bottle-blond hair—was with us in a minute. "What can I get you?"

"Nothing for me," Scott started, but I shot him a look. He hesitated, then beamed. "Gimme a dog, then," he said.

I raised an eyebrow in question.

"Black Dog beer," Scott explained. "A microbrewery out Kailua way makes it. Real good, if you like your beer dark."

"I'll have a dog too, then," I told the waitress. She walked away without acknowledgment, but a few minutes later returned to place two half-liter glasses filled to the brim with dark liquid on our table.

I tried to pay, but Scott was too fast. "I'll get this one," he said, slipping some money—real folding money, which surprised me—to the waitress. "You got breakfast."

"Did I?"

He chuckled. "It got charged to your room, anyway." He glanced down at his glass. "I shouldn't be doing this, not on duty, but"—he grinned like a bandit, and raised his glass—"*okolemaluna!*"

I toasted him in return. "Whatever you just said." The beer had a nice head to it, and a sweet, slightly nutty taste. I took a second swig and nodded approvingly. "Good. How's the food here?"

By the time we'd finished our lunch—a large soyburger with Maui chips, two of the same for Scott—the afternoon crowd had started to roll in. A succession of dancers—quite pretty, most of them, and some could even dance—disrobed and strutted their stuff for the indifferent audience. As the patrons gathered along the bar and in the shadowy booths, I felt even more at home. Apart from style of dress and the preponderance of deep tans, these slags were almost exactly like the crowd that frequented my favorite watering holes in Seattle and Cheyenne. Hard-edged customers, most of them—totally at home in the reality of the streets, if not full-on denizens of the shadows. Many were packing—I could see it in the way they moved—and those who weren't looked as though they could more than hold their own even without a weapon.

I sipped at my second beer. Scott was still nursing his first and refused my offer of a refill. "Drinking and driving ain't a good thing with a vehicle control rig," he told me firmly.

A knot of real hard cases were talking biz in the back corner. Macroplast glinted momentarily in the light as a credstick changed hands. I leaned over toward Scott and nodded toward the negotiators. "What are the shadows like around here?" I asked quietly.

He sipped beer to give himself a moment to think. "Pretty dark, brah," he said at last. "When the sun's bright, the shadows can get pretty fragging dark."

"Big shadow community?"

He shrugged. "Depends on how you define it, I guess. There's a fair bit of biz to be done, that's what I hear at least." He grinned crookedly. "Comes from having such a big megacorp presence, that's the way I read it."

"But the core group, the real players?" He shrugged again. "Not too many of them, I guess. Probably fewer than where you're from. And fewer wannabes, too."

"Why's that?"

The ork smile turned predatory for a moment. "Nature of the islands, *hoa,* that's all. It's a small community here. You frag up, and there's no space to run. The way I hear it, you're good . . . or you're dead."

I nodded slowly. That made a disturbing kind of sense. As a kind of mental exercise, I ran through a few contingency plans for getting off the islands if things went screwy in a hurry . . . and quickly realized how few options there really were. Disturbing. I always liked to have running room. "How much actual biz goes down here?" I asked after a moment.

Scott raised his eyebrows. "Hey, you're asking the wrong *wikanikanaka*, brah," he protested mildly, "I'm just a chauffeur, here."

My expression communicated just what I thought of that disclaimer. "Get actual, chummer," I told him. "You're connected. Somebody like you has *got* to be. Right?"

I watched his eyes as he debated standing pat with his bluff, and eventually decided against it. He smiled a little self-consciously. "Yeah, okay, I got my ear to the ground. I hear things." He paused. "*Some* biz goes down here, and in other places like this. But the shadows are different here than they are elsewhere—that's the way I hear it, at least. On the mainland, if you got a good brag-sheet, you get biz. Fixers deal with you on the basis of your street rep, doesn't matter whether they know you or not. Right?"

"Sometimes," I allowed.

"That's not the way it happens here, *hoa*," he said firmly. "Not the way I hear it, at least . . . and keep in mind this is all secondhand; I'm a driver, not a runner, okay?" He paused, ordering his thoughts. "The way I hear it, in the islands it's personal relationships that matter more than a brag-sheet, even more than a street rep. People deal with people they know personally, people they've come to trust. Some *malihini* newcomer to the islands rolls up with a brag-sheet as long as your fragging leg—'I shaved Fuchi ice, I blew away a division of Azzie hard-men, I took Dunkelzahn in a con game'—and nobody's going to touch him, 'cause he's an unknown quantity, see? The *kalepa*—the fixers—they're going to go with the runners they know, the ones they've dealt with personally before . . . even if it means going with some *hawawa* who's not as good as the newcomer. At least the *kalepa* knows exactly what to expect."

I nodded slowly. That made a certain amount of sense in a tight community with limited running room. You're less likely to bet on an unknown quantity, because if the drek drops into the pot *you* might find you don't have anyplace to run.

A tight knot of people—lots of black synthleather and studs—jandered in and cruised over to the bar. I could almost *feel* the attitude from where I sat. Beside me, Scott looked up and grinned. "Somebody you might want to meet, *hoa,*" he told me. Then he raised his voice. "Te Purewa. *Hele mai.*"

One of the black-clad arrivals turned and looked our way. I felt his eyes on me like lasers, burning out of a face that could well have been chiseled from black lava rock. Hawk nose, thick brows, short black hair. And tattoos all over his fragging face: swirls and geometricals and curlicues around his eyes until he looked like a paisley necktie. He smiled— the kind of expression I associated with thoughts of ripping out someone's liver—and he strode over toward our table. He was one big son of a slitch, I saw as he loomed up over us. Big and broad; the bulges of his muscles had bulges on them. "Howzit, Scotty?" he rumbled.

Scott shrugged. "Li' dat." He gestured my way. "Want you to meet somebody, Te Purewa. Bruddah from the mainland, Dirk Tozer."

Te Purewa—was that his name, or some Hawai'ian phrase I hadn't caught yet?—turned those burning dark eyes on me. "*Kia ora!*" he barked at me. And then he bugged out his eyes and stuck out his tongue.

My natural response was to laugh; and when I saw the anger flare in those eyes I knew I'd made a mistake. The big guy scowled, and his tattoos seemed to writhe. Then, without another word, he turned his back on us and strode away.

I turned to Scott. "Oops," I said quietly.

"You got *that,* bruddah." The ork shook his head. "Shoulda warned you, I guess. Te Purewa—"

"That's his name?"

"Yeah, it's Maori, from Aotearoa—used to be called New Zealand." Scott sighed. "Every time I see him, he's more Maori. Good guy, at heart, but sometimes he takes things too far, y'know? All this heritage *kanike* . . . Last year it was the tats"—he traced imaginary lines on his face—"then a coupla months back he got himself a linguasoft so he could speak Maori. And now he's doing the traditional greeting crap as well. That whole tongue stuff? He says Maoris look fierce at you as a sign of respect." He shrugged. "Sounds like *kanike* to me."

"So now he hates me forever?"

Scott chuckled. "Honestly? Te Purewa doesn't have the attention span for holding long grudges, *hoa*. Next time you see him, snarl at him and say '*Kia ora!*', and he'll treat you like a long lost bruddah." He paused, and his smile faded. "Thought you might like to meet him 'cause he's the closest thing I know to a real shadowrunner. Te Purewa's SINless, he hangs with some of the fringe *kalepa*, the fixers on the edge of the action. Don't know what kind of biz he does for them—don't really *want* to know, is it—but he's the closest thing to real street action I know around here."

He glanced at his watch. "Another beer?"

I thought about it, then shook my head. "What's the next stop on the tour?"

The cultural/historical part of the tour was next, it turned out. Scott tooled the big Phaeton back through the financial heart of downtown Honolulu, then continued east into the government sector of the city. First stop was a relatively undistinguished two-story building that looked as though it was made of dressed lava rock. Despite the fact that the place was nothing special, it looked vaguely familiar, as if I'd seen it before. It took me a few seconds to tag the memory. That was it—an old two-D TV show I'd seen at some retrospective festival up in Seattle, something about cops in Hawai'i; that's where I'd seen the place before.

I mentioned this to Scott, but he just shrugged. "Don't know about that, brah, but it's possible, I guess. That's the Iolani Palace. Old place, century and a half old."

"But what *is* it?" I asked.

The ork looked at me like I'd just misplaced a couple of dozen points of IQ. "It's the palace, *hoa*. The capitol, where the *Ali'i* lives and holds court with his *kahuna*."

"His shaman?"

Scott shook his head. "No. Well, maybe, but ... You'll find words in Hawai'ian can have a drek-load of meanings. Take *aloha*—'hello,' right? Also means 'love,' 'mercy,' 'compassion', 'pity,' maybe half a dozen others.

"And *kahuna*? Shaman, sure. Priest. But it also means 'advisor,' particularly when you're talking about the *Ali'i* and his *kahuna*." Scott chuckled. "Also means someone who's *nui* good at something, okay? Remember that guy we saw on the surfboard? He's one big *kahuna* when it comes to surfing."

He paused and shrugged. "Where was I? Oh yeah. The Iolani Palace, it's the 'working' capitol. On some big, *nui* important ritual days, the *Ali'i* and his court fly over to the old capitol on the Big Island. But most of the time, this is where King Kam does his stuff."

"This is King Kamehameha V, right?"

"That's it, brah." The ork pointed across the street. "You want to see King Kam I, Kamehameha the Great? There he is."

I looked where he was pointing and saw the large statue he meant. It showed a perfectly proportioned man with mahogany skin and noble features, holding a spear. He wore a yellow cape and a weird kind of curving headdress, both apparently made of feathers. "Quite the outfit," I noted.

"The traditional dress of the *Ali'i*," Scott agreed. "King Kam wears the same stuff for official business." He paused. "From what I've heard, that statue's life-size, by the way. Kam the Great was one big boy."

I glanced back at the statue. At a guess, I'd have said it was at least 2.2 meters tall—7'3" for the metrically challenged—and that didn't include the headdress. "Big boy, all right," I agreed. "Any troll blood in the king's lineage?"

Scott chuckled at that as he pulled ahead.

Our last stop was maybe a block from the palace, the other side of the government business. Scott pointed to a big ferrocrete building whose vertical lines evoked images of both classical columns and waterfalls. Over a set of large double doors hung a massive disk of metal—bronze, probably, judging by its color—bearing a crest. "That's the *Haleaka'aupuni*," Scott announced. "I guess you could translate that as 'Government House.' The legislature sits here, and this is where the administrators and the datapushers do their thing."

I remembered some of the material I'd scanned on the flight in. "Is the king still scrapping it out with the legislature?" I asked.

The ork shot me a speculative look. "You're not as out-of-touch as I thought, brah," he said with a hint of respect. "Yeah, King Kam's still butting heads with the *Na Kama'aina* hotheads in the legislature." We turned a corner, cruising down another side of Government House, and Scott pointed ahead. "There's some of the hotheads' constituents now."

I looked.

It wasn't large as demonstrations go—I've seen larger mobs protesting a hike in monorail fares in Seattle—but there was something about it, something I couldn't quite put my finger on, that made me think it was well-organized. There were maybe a hundred people massed before the steps of Government House. Not many, in the grand scheme of things, but every time the news photographer who was standing at the top of the steps panned his vidcam over them, they all packed in tighter in the area he was scanning. To make the crowd look denser, and hence much bigger, when the footage aired on the news tonight, I realized. That was too much media awareness for a "spontaneous gathering." I could well be looking at the Hawai'ian version of something an old Lone Star colleague had once called "rent-a-mob"—professional agitators, or at least a group *led* by professional agitators.

All the protesters seemed to be Polynesian, I noticed. Lots of orks and trolls, with only a few humans and dwarfs tossed in for spice. (No elves, though, I noted, or none that I spotted. Interesting, that . . .) Lots of bronze or mahogany skin, lots of black hair. Most wore more or less the same as Scott—the same as me, for that matter—but some were dressed in traditional aboriginal costumes of one kind or another. Lots of straw, and grass, and feathers. Most of the placards were too small for me to read from this distance, but I could make out one. *"E make loa, haole?"* I sounded out to Scott.

He frowned, then snorted in disgust, but didn't translate.

"What's it mean?" I pressed.

"It means, 'Die, Anglo,'" he admitted after a moment. "Like I said, hotheads."

I gestured toward the crowd. "Are these people ALOHA?"

Scott laughed. "Are you *lolo,* bruddah? You stupid? You think I'd get this close to a pack of ALOHA goons with a fragging *haole* in the car?" He paused, and when he spoke again his voice was more serious. "ALOHA doesn't go for this kind of *kanike,* Mr. Dirk. Peaceful demonstrations? Not their style. They blow drek up, *that's* how they get their ideas across."

"*Na Kama'aina,* then?"

He shrugged. "The leaders, sure—one or two of them, the slags who arranged for the newsvid boys to be here. The rest? They're just twinkies come along 'cause they've got nothing better to do with their time."

A couple of the demonstrators at the back of the pack had turned to watch the limo as we rolled by. One of them had the same kind of facial tattoos as the Maori in the bar. Instead of black leather, though, she wore only a loincloth and a kind of skirt made from dried reeds or some drek. "I can't complain about the costume choice," I remarked, and Scott chortled appreciatively.

"Some people get an idea in their heads, and they just run with it," he said. "The costumes. Trying to speak the old languages ... or what they *think* are the old languages—some died out, but that doesn't stop the hotheads from pretending." He snorted again. "Look at them. Refugees from the *luau* shows put on for the tourists ... except these *ule* don't know the show's over."

I blinked in mild surprise at the vehemence in his voice. "Is that what you think of what's-his-name?" I asked quietly after a moment.

"Te Purewa?" He paused. Then, "More or less," he admitted. "I don't think he's taken to waving placards at the government yet, but ..." He shrugged.

"Te Purewa's not his real name, is it?" I guessed.

Scott gave a bark of laughter. "You got *that*," he agreed. "Mark Harrop, that's his real name, can you beat that? Mark fragging Harrop. Couple years back he decided he had Maori blood in his veins—like, a couple drops, maybe—and picked the name out of some book."

I was silent for almost a minute as Scott swung the limo around a corner and headed back toward Waikiki and Diamond Head. At last I asked gently, "What about you, Scott? You don't have any sympathy for *Na Kama'aina*? You're Polynesian by descent, aren't you?"

He didn't answer right away, and I wondered if I'd offended him. Then he smiled, a little shamefacedly. "I'm a *kama'aina,*" he agreed. "I'm a 'land child'—quarter-blood, but I get it from both sides of my family. My mother, she was a Nene *kahuna.*"

"Nay-nay?" I asked.

"Nene, Hawai'ian goose," he explained. "Looks kind of like a Canada goose—except it's not extinct, it's got claws on its feet, and it likes volcanic rock. One of the local Totems.

"Anyway," he went on, "you can be a *kama'aina*, a local, without being part of *Na Kama'aina*, if you get my drift."

"And you've got no desire to take a Hawai'ian name and run around in grass skirts?"

"Grass makes me itch." He paused. "I've already got the Hawai'ian name," he added quietly after a moment, "I don't have to take one. My mother, she gave me one."

I waited, but he didn't go on. "Well?" I pressed at last.

He sighed. "My given name is *Ka-wena-'ula-a-Hi'iaka-i-ka-poli-o-Pele-ka-wahine-'ai-ho-nua*." The polysyllables rolled off his tongue like a smooth-flowing river.

"Holy frag," I announced when I was sure he was done.

"Yeah, quite the mouthful."

"And it means?"

" 'The red glow of the sky made by Hi'iaka in the bosom of Pele the earth-eating woman,' if you can believe that."

"You must get writer's cramp signing your name."

He laughed. "That's why my father called me Scott," he explained.

7

My body clock seemed to have finally adjusted to the time difference and everything. I slept when I went to bed, and I woke up when I wanted to, a couple of minutes before my alarm went off. I rolled out of bed feeling like a new man—or at least a creditable retread—drew open the drapes, and stared for a couple of minutes out the bedroom window. The sun glinted off the azure sea, and the few clouds only served to emphasize the depth and clarity of the sky. Another drekky day in paradise.

As I dressed, I noticed for the first time the two holos on opposite walls of the bedroom. One showed Waikiki as I'd seen it the day before from a vantage point somewhere near the west end of the bay—a view of Diamond Head in the distance, people on the beach, a big auto-rigged trimaran anchored offshore. The other hologram had a sepia tone, like a holo taken of an old black-and-white flatphoto. A dark-skinned native was pushing a dug-out outrigger canoe up onto the beach out of the surf. Something looked familiar about the shot somehow. I compared the two mentally and realized that both holos were from exactly the same camera angle! The sepia one had to date from the nineteenth century. There was Diamond Head ... with nothing but jungle all the way down to the beach and only a couple of tiny buildings around the curve of the bay. I turned back to the contemporary shot—yes, the holographer had matched the camera angle and the composition exactly. Fascinating.

It was oh-eight-thirty by the time I finished dressing, and my stomach reminded me not to skip breakfast. So down the elevator I went and breakfasted in the company of those little ring-necked doves on the outdoor patio.

I was savoring my third cup of coffee and debating whether I had room for another waffle when I felt a presence beside me. Glancing up, I saw one of the self-effacing hotel functionaries holding a small cellular phone out to me. "Mr. Tozer?"

I nodded to him, and he vanished from sight as I flipped the phone off standby. "Hello?"

"Good morning, Mr. Dirk." It was Scott, of course. "I hope you're feeling up to a little business today."

I almost asked him the details, but my natural caution—better yet, my paranoia—kicked in at the last moment. "When?" is all I said.

I was waiting outside the hotel when the Rolls pulled up thirty minutes later. Dressed in a finely tailored business suit today, Scott climbed out and held the rear passenger compartment door for me. (No slotting around with sitting up front today . . .) As I settled myself in the couch, he slid back into the driver's seat, buttoned the car up, and pulled away.

"Okay, Scott," I said once we were out in traffic, "*give*. Who, what, where, when, and why."

He glanced back at me. (At least he'd left the kevlarplex divider down.) "You've got an appointment with Mr. Ekei Tokudaiji," he told me flatly.

"Who is?"

The ork shrugged his broad shoulders. "An important man around these parts, that's all I can tell you."

Well, frag, I could have maybe guessed that much. "Where are we going?"

"Kaneohe Bay. Mr. Tokudaiji has a . . . a *place* there."

I frowned. The friendliness, the volubility, had vanished from Scott's manner. This was more than being businesslike, it was as if the big ork were under some kind of major stress. Was visiting this Tokudaiji so daunting, even for a fragging chauffeur? Just how important *was* this slag? "Why couldn't we have gotten this over with yesterday?" I asked.

"Like I said, Mr. Tokudaiji had biz on the outer islands yesterday," Scott explained patiently. "He's under no obligation to see you at all, see? He could just dust you off, and nobody could say drek about it."

I digested that as Scott turned the limo onto a northbound highway that soon plunged into a tunnel through a range of hills. Either Scott didn't know on whose behest I was working—this Tokudaiji wouldn't be dusting *me* off, he'd be dusting off Jacques Barnard, executive vice president of

Yamatetsu North America—or Tokudaiji was a *very* important man indeed.

"Are you packing?" Scott asked suddenly.

The Seco suddenly felt heavy on my hip. "Yes," I said slowly.

Scott made a *tsk* sound. "Should have warned you about that. You'll have to leave it in the car when you go in to see Mr. Tokudaiji."

Like frag I will . . . That's what I *wanted* to say, but I held my tongue with a sigh. "I'm not sure I like the way this is working out." For a moment the old Scott reappeared in his smile. "Hey, brah, at least *you* won't have to go through a cavity search."

The highway emerged from the tunnel, and the whole landscape had changed. The north side of the island was much lusher than the south, which implied more rain. (Hadn't I read somewhere that changing wind patterns had really fragged with the weather in the islands over the last half century? Well, whatever.) The highway curved northwest, judging by the position of the sun, then switchbacked to the northeast, descending a hillside. Directly north was a rocky promontory, with something that looked like a military installation at its base. On the west side of the promontory, the coastline opened out into a sweeping bay so beautiful it almost couldn't be real. "Mr. Tokudaiji's got himself a pretty fair view, you ask me," Scott said, again seeming to read my mind.

We pulled off the highway and followed a harshly weathered secondary road that flanked the bay. After a klick or two, Scott took an unmarked turn, and the quality of the road improved drastically. Private road, I guessed . . . and a glimpse of a surveillance camera tracking the car from a hibiscus bush confirmed it a moment later. I patted my pockets to be sure I hadn't misplaced Barnard's message chip after all this, and, a little grudgingly, unclipped the Seco's holster from my waistband. "You can just leave your piece in the back there," Scott suggested. "It'll be safe."

The limo sighed to a stop at a security gate, but not any kind of security gate I was used to. No electrified chain-link fences here, no strands of cutwire, no powered metal gate running on reinforced tracks. Instead, we faced a large palisade—that's about the best word I can find for it—made of finely finished dark wood. A Japanese-style arch topped the gate. I saw the motif worked into that arch and into the double gate itself and felt a faint chill in my gut. A chrysanthemum, that was the key image, replicated everywhere. Just fragging peachy.

As we sat, waiting, I examined the gate and the palisade. Though the whole setup looked like a set from an old Kurosawa flatfilm—*Ran*, maybe—it didn't take much brains to guess that things were a lot more secure than they seemed. Maybe the facade of the gates and the fence *were* real wood—if I hadn't noticed the chrysanthemum pattern, I'd have wagered they were cheaper macroplast—but they certainly covered material a lot more resilient. Reinforced ballistic composite at the very least, possibly armored ferrocrete. Though it looked as though those carved gateposts would fall like bowling pins if Scott gunned the Rolls into the gates, I'd have laid a very big bet that even a light panzer would have difficulty taking down Ekei Tokudaiji's first line of defense.

After a minute or so—enough time for security personnel to scan the car with every available frequency of the electromagnetic spectrum, presumably—a small postern gate opened and two figures emerged. They wore expensively tailored suits, not the ancient Nihonese armor I'd half expected, but their faces, their manner, and the general way they carried themselves wouldn't have seemed out of place in a samurai epic.

Neither had any visible weapons, but one of them took up a perfect position for covering fire anyway. The second approached the driver's side. Scott powered down the window and gave the guard a formal nod. *"Konichi-wa,"* the driver said, then went on in Japanese faster than my limited comprehension could match. I heard *Tokudaiji-sama* once, and my own name—I think—a couple of times, but beyond that I couldn't make any sense of it.

When Scott had run down, the guard nodded again. "Go ahead," he said in unaccented English and stepped aside to join his comrade. The double gates swung silently back, and the Rolls sighed forward.

Outside the compound, the forest had been allowed to run more or less riot. Inside, everything—the position of every tree and shrub, even the proportions of the winding driveway—seemed to be laid out with mathematical precision. I felt like I was cruising through a tropical version of a Japanese formal garden ... which is exactly what I was doing, of course.

I gave a heartfelt sigh and shot Scott a sour look. "You could have told me Tokudaiji was a fragging yakuza *oyabun*," I pointed out.

"Hey, don't give me that stink-eye," he protested. "Not my idea, brah. Just following orders."

"What an original excuse," I muttered.

The *oyabun*'s mansion nestled up against the steep slope of a greenery-clad hill. He'd obviously got himself a good architect, had the yak boss—every line of the house and its outbuildings harmonized perfectly with the contours of the terrain around it. How many million nuyen would a place like this set you back? I wondered. More than I'd ever see.

As we pulled up, I found myself looking around for more of the suit-clad samurai who'd greeted us at the gate. I couldn't see any, but I could *feel* their presence. Nothing happened for almost a minute. Scott killed the Rolls's engine, but he didn't open the door, didn't even move. I figured he knew what he was doing, so I concentrated on doing the same kind of nothing. Again, I imagined invisible fingers of electromagnetic energy scanning the car and our bodies, counting rivets and fillings and the like.

Finally, a figure emerged from the front door of the mansion—another suit-clad samurai—and stopped a couple of meters from the front quarter of the car. As if that had been his signal—which it probably was, of course—Scott climbed out, came around, and held my door open for me. As I emerged from the air-conditioned comfort of the car, the heat and humidity—and the unmistakable smell of jungle—was like walking into a door.

"Just take this all chill, okay?" Scott whispered, without moving his lips. I snorted. What the frag did he expect me to do? Go ballistic for no good reason, and try to cack the samurai with my bare hands? Yeah, right. For an instant my left hip felt awfully lonely without the weight of the Seco. Scott took up station to my left and one step back as I walked toward the Armanté-clad samurai.

When I was a couple of strides away, the man turned wordlessly and strode off toward the front of the house, obviously expecting me to follow. With a shrug, I did. Through a set of large double doors we went—the chrysanthemum motif was carved into those doors as well, just in case a visitor hadn't gotten the message already—and into the atrium of the house.

And "atrium" is exactly the right word. The place was laid out like a Roman villa with a central open area. I guess I expected something more in the neighborhood of a Japanese rock garden complete with fishpond and *koi*. Wrong, chummer. No rocks growing in the sand, no mutant immortal carp. The atrium was paved with marble and sported a couple of benches plus a handful of classical-style statues. (Suddenly I flashed on the formal garden in the background of Barnard's vidcall. Did he and Tokudaiji share the same fragging decorator or what?) In the bright Hawai'ian sunlight, the white marble *glared*.

Our samurai guide turned left down a . . . well, if this was a church, I'd call it a cloister—a corridor open on one side, looking out over the atrium. (Weird mixture of styles and symbols in this house. But somehow they seemed to mesh and the amalgam worked.) Two more side-boys materialized out of nowhere flanking me and Scott a couple of paces back. Again, no weapons were visible; but, again, the way they carried themselves convinced me they wouldn't *need* weapons to take down anything less than a fragging dzoo-noo-qua.

We played follow-the-leader halfway down the cloister, then hung a left through another heavy wooden door. (No chrysanthemum on this one, as if it mattered.) Two more suit-clad sammies were waiting for us in the room—a small antechamber decorated in muted tones, very serious and elegant. The two new sammies pulled out scanners and went over every centimeter of my body. Very polite about it, they were—as polite as you can be when you're doing something like that—constantly murmuring "*Sumimasen, chotto,* excuse me." Never once did they touch me—no pat-down, no search of my pockets or whatever. The process took a couple of minutes and evidently they were satisfied with the results, confident that I didn't have a heavy pistol concealed in my left ear or a hand grenade in my cheek. Both sammies bowed formally to me with one last "*Sumimasen,*" and focused their attention on a resigned-looking Scott.

His anxiety about a cavity search was misplaced—they never so much as touched him either. Granted, they were a little more intrusive in terms of how close they brought the scanners, and they didn't give him even one "*Sumimasen,*" but there was nothing invasive or proctological about the procedure. One of the sammies, an older slag, with strategically silvering hair and hollow cheeks, showed specific interest in a stickpin Scott wore in his lapel. To me it looked like some kind of Hawai'ian idol, a pot-bellied little guy with big wide eyes, made out of sterling silver. The old slag didn't scan it with his detectors, but just stared at it for a while, a slightly puzzled frown on his face. Then he shrugged and moved on. I shot Scott a questioning look. The big ork just shrugged.

Finally, the scanning and examining was done, and the door on the other side of the antechamber swung open. One of the Armanté-garbed sammies gestured us through. As I stepped forward, Scott again took up his position a step back and to my left. I strode through the door . . .

And stopped. I've always been a sucker for books. *Real* books, the paper-and-ink kind, the kind you can hold in your hands, the kind with real covers and bindings. (Sure, I know, it's the content that really counts—you can't judge a book, drekcetera—but if you don't already understand the pure, sensory pleasure of opening a book and flipping the pages, you probably never will . . . and your loss.) As a bibliophile, it's always been my dream to have a library—one room devoted entirely to books. If I had to envision that room, it would have a couple of large windows for natural light, but every other square meter of wall space would be taken up with bookshelves. There'd be one chair specifically for reading—a big old wing chair, preferably (although I'd probably retrofit a massage unit)—a couple of small tables to hold decanters of single-malt Scotch, and maybe two or three other (lesser) chairs in case I ever invited friends into my *sanctum sanctorum.*

Rescan that description. That's exactly the room we were ushered into, all the way down to the cut-glass decanter of smoky amber liquid on the side table. My first reaction was, "Yeah, all *right.*" My second, "There ain't no fragging justice." And then I suppressed both those reactions and focused all my attention on the slag watching us from the wing chair.

He looked old and frail with bones as thin and fragile as a bird's, his skin pale and parchment-thin. He was nearly bald, and his hands—steepled thoughtfully before his lips—were scrawny and fleshless. It was his eyes that caught and held my attention, though; dark, intense eyes, the eyes of a hawk. Intelligence and awareness glinted deep in those eyes, like windows into the soul of a young and vibrant man who only happened to be wearing the body of an octogenarian. Strength of personality radiated from him in waves. Here was a man to respect, I realized—a man to fear, perhaps, but also a man to like.

I felt Scott's presence at my elbow. Behind us, I heard the library door click shut. I blinked, and for the first time I noticed the aide—another twenty-first-century samurai—standing silently behind the *oyabun*'s chair.

Mr. Ekei Tokudaiji was silent for a few moments as his eyes scanned my face and—that's what it felt like, at least—probed the depths of my soul. Eventually, his thin lips drew up in a gentle smile. "Mr. Montgomery," he said. His voice was smooth as velvet, not loud—but then it didn't have to be—and totally accentless. "Welcome. Please." He gestured to a chair—another leather wing chair, but smaller than his—that faced him.

"Thank you," I told him.

The yakuza boss watched me as I seated myself. The *oyabun* never so much as glanced at Scott, I noted, as if the big chauffeur didn't even exist. (No, I corrected, as if Scott were as irrelevant to our discussion as a piece of furniture ... or as his own aide.)

I pointedly scanned the room with my gaze, nodded approvingly. "Nice decor."

He smiled as if my opinion pleased him, as if it really mattered one way or the other. "Thank you." He gestured at the books. "A man needs a refuge where the great thoughts of the past shield him from the chaos of the world." He paused. "I apologize for ..." He inclined his head toward the door to the anteroom. "Necessity. No dishonor was intended."

"None taken." I forced myself to relax, to wait him out. I never felt really comfortable with the initial meaningless protocol of high-level meetings. Why not just cut to the fragging chase and get on with things? But it was the *oyabun*'s game, his rules.

"How is Mr. Barnard?" Tokudaiji asked after a moment.

"Tired," I responded, remembering the way the corporator had looked on the telecom screen. "But he's got a nice setup in Kyoto."

"A beautiful city," the *oyabun* said, inclining his head,

"with much history and culture. Have you visited, Mr. Montgomery?"

Yet another high-powered suit wanting to know about my travel itinerary. What was this, a trend? I shook my head. "Never made it."

Again, the *oyabun* was silent for a few moments, regarding me steadily. Then something changed subtly in those sharp eyes, and I knew we were getting down to biz. "I understand that Mr. Barnard has a message for me," Tokudaiji said quietly, "something he was unwilling to commit to the Matrix."

"That's correct, sir."

The yak smiled gently. "What would it concern, do you suppose?"

I shook my head. "Do you really think Mr. Barnard would confide in a mere messenger?" Drek, I thought—hang around with people like this long enough and you start *talking* like them . . .

"Of course not, of course not." Tokudaiji extended his hand.

In response I reached into my pocket for the optical chip in its plastic holder.

And that's when the drek dropped into the pot. I *felt* something happen behind me. It wasn't hearing, it wasn't seeing, it wasn't the sense of touch or smell—it was *something else,* but it was also totally undeniable. I felt it right down in the core of my being, sort of like the shivery feeling of an overpressure wave, but internal rather than external.

Magic. I knew that's what it was; somehow I knew.

I turned my head to the left. In my peripheral vision, I saw Scott move forward, reaching into his coat. The little pot-bellied guy on his lapel was glowing with a strange inner light, and I could feel that shivery feeling emanating from it.

At that instant time seemed to change. Everything seemed to shift into slow motion, like in an old Sam Peckinpah flatfilm.

Tokudaiji's eyes widened in surprise and alarm. Behind him his aide was going for his heat. Even in slow-mo, the sammy's move was blindingly fast.

Not fast enough, though. The sammy's heavy pistol was barely clear of its shoulder holster when his face vanished in a wet red cloud and he went over backward. The concussion of a gunshot hammered my left ear, and I flinched away from the muzzle-plume of Scott's Roomsweeper. (Scott's *Roomsweeper*? How the frag had he smuggled a drek-eating *Roomsweeper* past the security check?)

Still in slow-mo, I felt my own body responding instinctively. I came out of the chair like I was on springs, right hand slapping ineffectually at my vacant left hip.

Tokudaiji was moving, too, one of his skeleton-thin hands plunging inside his thousand-nuyen jacket. His eyes met mine, and in a flash of instantaneous communication we both knew he was too late.

From the corner of my eye I saw Scott's Roomsweeper come to bear, saw it gout flame again. The blast—shot, not a single slug—took the yakuza boss full in the face, slamming what was left of his skull back into the leather chair, spattering blood and tissue across the room. My nose was filled with the smells of a shooting: cordite, blood, drek . . .

I was on my feet, turning, still reaching for the gun that wasn't there. Time clicked back into full-speed mode as Scott swung the smoking muzzle of the Roomsweeper to point directly between my eyes.

8

... And he said, "Get out of here, brah, I'll cover you as long as I can."

Through the door to the anteroom I heard the first sounds of alarm—muffled, but still audible. If I could hear that, then the sammies on the other side of the door would *certainly* have heard the two throaty booms from the Roomsweeper. Obviously the door was locked, and the normal release was somewhere in here—probably close to Ekei Tokudaiji's blood-spattered hand—otherwise Scott and I would already be absorbing high-velocity rounds.

"Get the frag *out* of here, *ule*," the ork barked again.

I didn't know whether to drek, go blind, or wind my watch. (Actually, I was down to two choices because I think I'd already done one of those three things when the first shot went off next to my head.) My mouth moved, and I think I said something cogent and pithy like, "Gaah?" My right hand was still pawing around somewhere down at my left hip—apparently searching for the Seco that was in the backseat of the Rolls—so I stopped it by clenching it into a fist.

"*Kukae!*" Scott swore in frustration. He pivoted and fired two ringing blasts into the nearest window. The first starred the reinforced glass; the second blew it out into the foliage beyond. (Mental note: Some kinds of reinforced glass don't work worth squat if the shot's coming from the *inside*.) "Get fragging *going!*" Scott roared. He crouched, scooped up the pistol that the dead aide had been trying to draw and tossed it to me. Instinctively, I plucked it out of the air.

Finally my reflexes kicked into gear, and I got fragging going. Three running steps across the room, then a dive out the window, tucking into a smooth landing roll. Would have worked like a hot damn, too, if it hadn't been for the fragging hibiscus bush just outside the window. A silent tuck-and-roll became a loud rustle-and-crash, but at least the flowering bush absorbed my momentum and gave me a (relatively) soft landing.

I came up in a crouch and looked around wildly. Nobody coming for me, not yet. I worked the action on the pistol—a brutal-looking Browning automatic of an unfamiliar model—and checked the load. A full clip of fourteen rounds, according to the indicator, and one in the pipe. Feeling like I had a nasty big crosshairs painted on the back of my skull, I moved away from the blown-out window.

Just in time. Behind me I heard a smash, the sharp ripping of light autofire, then a godawful *whump* that felt like a troll had just boxed my ears for me. I hit the ground—not entirely my idea, as the pressure wave slammed into me—and out the corner of my eye I saw a dirty-red fireball lick momentarily out the window. On my belly I did the high-low crawl through the foliage as shrapnel, bits of wood, and assorted shreds of tissue spattered down around me. When I was what felt like a reasonable distance from the house, I bellied up and tried to calm myself.

Okay, just what the frag had happened? Scott had taken down my contact, that's what had happened. And now he was dead.

He *had* to be dead, didn't he? When Tokudaiji's samurai tossed a grenade into the library ...

No, that made no fragging sense at all. For all they knew, their boss-man, the *oyabun*, might still have been breathing. They wouldn't have fragged the room just in case.

Which meant bruddah Scott had done it himself, didn't it? Probably a belly-bomb of some kind. A suicide mission. He'd hung back to draw some more of Tokudaiji's troops in, then he'd suicided violently, taking at least some of them with him.

So why the frag was I still alive?

Later, I told myself firmly, *think about that later.* Lord knows, I had enough to worry about at the moment, like getting out of the *oyabun*'s enclave with all my anatomy intact. By now, all of Tokudaiji's samurai would know of the hit. They'd know that two people had gone in, a chauffeur and some pale-skinned reprobate name of Montgomery. They'd be cranked up, and they *sure* wouldn't be in any mood to accept the excuse, "Hey, chummer, I had nothing to do with it ..." Thanks, Scott. And thanks to you, too, Jacques Barnard, you fragging *slot.*

I had to move, and I had to move fast. It was still less than a minute since the gunshots, and only seconds since the explosion had gutted the library. Tokudaiji's sammies would be operating on instinct and training—both probably well-developed—but things would only get worse when they had a chance to *think* as well as react. By the time they got their collective drek together, ideally I'd like to be several counties away. Looking around to get my bearings, I took off in the old high-low crawl again, heading directly away from the house through the heart of a large flower bed.

It wasn't long before I ran out of bushes and had to cover some open ground. About ten meters of open ground, as it turned out, which separated me from some pretty thick-looking jungle. Ideal. A quick look around me, and I burst from cover.

Which startled the frag out of the Armanté-clad guard who was just coming around the corner of my flower bed. He was fast as greased lightning, swinging his submachine gun around to cut me in two. But fear had me so hopped up that I was even faster. Also, the fact that he saw a wild man with rolling eyes and hibiscus twigs in his hair probably set him back for a millisecond or two. I dug in and cut to the right, planning to put my shoulder into his gut. He danced back just in time, so I slammed him in the throat with my forearm.

My *left* forearm. The forearm of the boosted-strength cyberlimb that Jacques Barnard had paid to have installed. Trachea and hyoid bone and vertebrae *gruntched* under the brutal impact of synthskin-clad titanium. The samurai went one way, his SMG went another, and I went a third, hesitating only long enough to put a round from the Browning into his chest just for good measure. At a full run I plunged into the jungle. Behind me I heard the fluttering *whop-whop* noise of a small helicopter spooling up.

Don't ask me how the frag I got out of there in one piece, chummer, I couldn't tell you. I made it, but I don't think I'll ever fully recall the details. Whole whacks of time, minutes upon minutes, were total blanks for me. I know I crawled through tropical jungle. I know I dodged homicidal guards. I know I eventually climbed a fragging *palm* tree to jump over a fragging ferrocrete wall. I know I ran through more jungle—how far I ran, I don't know—tearing the crap out of the clothes Scott had supplied me, and coming *this* close to blowing out an ankle. I know I eventually came to a narrow public road in a residential area where I boosted a car and basically got the frag *out* of there. But the images—the memories—are disjointed, like scenes in a badly edited simsense—disorienting and confusing.

I was driving my stolen car, a tiny Chrysler-Nissan Buddy three-wheeler that had seen better days, roughly west when the emotional reaction hit me. I pulled over to the side of the road, killed the electric motor, and got the bubble top open just in time to yarf up my breakfast all over the curb. My right hand was shaking as if I had some kind of palsy; my left would only move in ragged jerks, which was the cyber analog of the same thing. I felt cold and tight all over, as though I'd put on skin that was half a size too small and that had just recently been pulled out of a refrigerator.

Emotional shell shock, that's what it was, coupled with the very real symptoms of "adrenaline overdose." While it ran its course, I was incapable of feeling anything, fragging near incapable of *thinking*. If Ekei Tokudaiji with his head split like a melon, had walked up to me, I'd have shaken his fragging hand.

The shakes and the nausea and the chills went away eventually the way they always do. After ten or fifteen minutes, I was almost back to normal except for the dull, thudding headache and queasy stomach of adrenaline hangover. *I'm getting too old for this drek,* I told myself. I wasn't a young lion anymore. Frag, I was thirty-five going on thirty-six . . . and feeling half a century older than that, at the moment. I was losing the edge. *Losing?* Frag me, I'd *lost* it. How long had it taken me, back there in Tokudaiji's library, to register the fact that Scott wasn't going to geek me, too?

It wasn't entirely age and diminishing capabilities, though, was it? There was more to it than that. I looked down at my left hand and clenched it into a fist again and again.

It was still with me, wasn't it? The emotional baggage of that cluster-frag beneath Fort Lewis, the op that had cost me my arm and Hawk, Rodney, and the others so much more. I was still fragged up by it. My timing was gone, my instincts were . . . well, *were* they fragged, or was it just that I didn't trust them? I didn't know. When that first gunshot had gone off next to my ear, the emotions that had paralyzed me hadn't been the emotions of the moment—if that makes any sense at all. They'd been loaded with resonances of the emotions of those *distant* moments when friends had been dying around me and when my left arm had been fried to charcoal. Somehow I'd never really recovered. It was as if I'd lost much more than my arm in Fort Lewis. Part of my self-image, part of my worldview, perhaps . . . part of my soul? It was *that* loss which hadn't allowed me to put it all behind me and move on.

I could have done things different, I recognized suddenly. What do people always say when you fall off a motorbike? Get back on the fragging thing *right now,* get back in the fragging saddle. Had *I* gotten back in the saddle after my "fall?" Not a frigging chance, *omae.* I'd slipped the Seattle border and fled on down to the slower pace of Cheyenne. And I'd built myself a rep as the master of minimal exposure. Had I climbed back on that bike? No, chummer, it's as if I'd run from it and never again gone near anything that moved faster than a slow stroll. My choice, and at the time it had seemed the reasonable one. But now I was out of my safe little no-exposure comfort zone, and I'd be *paying* for that choice.

I buttoned the C-N Buddy back up again and pulled back onto the road. I was still too close to the scene of the crime; I had to extend, had to put distance between me and Tokudaiji's samurai. I also had to think things through and decide on my best course of action, but I could think just as well driving as I could staring blindly into space.

Ten minutes later and I was heading northwest on Route 83, the coastal road that circumnavigates the island. At any other time, I'd have relished the view. Now I hardly even saw it, I had so much on my mind.

What the frag had gone down back there at the *oyabun's* compound? What the frag had I gotten myself into?

Obviously, a conspiracy to geek the *oyabun*—no prizes for guessing that much. Barnard had used me as a kind of Trojan horse, hadn't he? Used me to penetrate Tokudaiji's security, to draw the yak boss out, to let Scott get close enough to cap him.

And more than that. Obviously, Barnard—with Yamatetsu's resources behind him—had set up the magical provisions that Scott the hit-ork had needed to do the job. The physical illusion spell or whatever the frag it was, that had let him sneak a fragging *Remington Roomsweeper* through a tight search. The shattershield spell that he must have used to slam down the magical barrier that an important target like an *oyabun* would have as a matter of course. A lot of that drek, you could pour the mana into a spell focus or a fetish of some kind, something, say, like the pot-bellied little guy on Scotty's lapel. Scott himself would have to be a mage or a shaman—probably the latter, I figured, following in his mother's footsteps—to trigger it (that's the way I understood it, at least), but he wouldn't have to have much juice of his own.

So I was the cover, the camouflage under which the assassin got close enough to grease his target. Okay, I could scan that.

But why didn't Scotty take me down as well?

That was the sixty-four nuyen question, wasn't it? Frag, if he'd played it right, Scott could—maybe—have walked out of there alive. Grease Tokudaiji and his aide with the Roomsweeper, then cap me with another weapon. Claim that *I* was the assassin and that he'd been too slow to pulp me before I got my shots off. Sure, it might not have worked. Sure, Tokudaiji's sammies would probably have shot first and questioned the corpses. But it would have given him a chance, even a slim one. As it was, he suicided with a belly-bomb. Why not toss the dice and maybe—just maybe—live another day?

So why was I still sucking air past my teeth? Good question, chummer, with two possible answers. One, cacking me was part of the job that Scott just didn't feel up to doing. In other words, my winning personality had been enough to convince a corporate hit-ork to default on part of his contract. Yeah, right. Two ...

Two, leaving me alive was part of the plan. A live Dirk Montgomery would serve Jacques Barnard's purposes better than a dead Dirk Montgomery.

Why? Who the frag knew. Maybe Barnard expected me to draw off the yakuza's resources, to lead the yak soldiers on a merry chase while ... While *what*? I didn't like the logic behind this train of thought. The way Barnard figured things, leaving me alive would only *benefit* him. Leaving me on the street with a grudge to settle didn't represent a significant threat to him or to his plans. (Not the most complimentary estimate of my capabilities, *neh*?) No, the way he figured things, I'd *help* him ... without realizing it, of course. And—here was the *most* disturbing part—for the life of me (literally) I couldn't figure out *how* ...

Frag! Just fragging wonderful, better and better, oh boy.

Now wait, hold it just a tick here, there was something I was missing. Something that just didn't ring true. I slowed down and let the biker who'd been tailgating me on his gyro-stabilized crotch-rocket scream by, flipping me the finger as he passed.

It was the belly-bomb, wasn't it? *That's* what was hanging me up. Call me hopelessly naive (I've been called much worse, trust me), but I'd always associated belly-bombs and suicide missions with ideologically driven fanatics—in other words, with slogan-chanting wackos. *Not* with corporate hard-men. I'd always classed corporate assassins as the cold and logical types, the slots who plan everything down to the minutest detail and won't take a job unless there's a 99.99% chance that they'll walk away from it. Hell, corporators—whether they're managers or killers—are driven by the personal profit motive, aren't they? I've never really thought loyalty unto death was part of the corporate world. You do your job because you're paid for it—paid very well, in many cases—not because you *truly believe* in what the corp's doing. Who in their right mind would die for the Just and Righteous Cause of Yamatetsu Corporation?

Yet apparently that's just what Scott did. Where was the profit motive in his actions? It's pretty hard to enjoy the fruits of your labors when a kilo of C12 in your abdominal cavity has splattered your body hither and yon. Was I missing something here? Was there more to Scott's actions than the obvious?

Or—now *here* was a nasty little thought—had bruddah Scott even *known* he was packing a belly-bomb or that it would be detonated when it was? Maybe he hadn't *known* he was on a suicide mission. Maybe he'd really expected that he'd be fighting his way out ... possibly with me in tow.

Yes, now *that* made a nasty kind of sense. I could easily imagine some Yamatetsu covert op monitoring events—maybe through some kind of bug on Scott's person—waiting for the right moment to press the little red button on the transmitter beside him. Bang goes Scott, taking with him all evidence that could be used to trace the responsible party. (Part of that evidence, of course, was one Dirk Montgomery . . .) *That* could be why Scotty let me go: because he expected that we'd both be getting out of there in one piece. The only reason I was alive to think this through now was that the covert op was asleep at the switch, a few seconds slow on the button.

Oh joy. Now that made things *really* tight, didn't it? If my line of reasoning was anywhere near correct, I was a walking, breathing piece of evidence that could connect the *oyabun*'s assassination directly with Jacques Barnard. So now, not only did I have yakuza payback teams to worry about, I also had my theoretical Yamatetsu covert ops looking to tie up the loose ends in their operation. Oh, and just for good measure, toss in the Hawai'i National Police Force as well. Presumably murder is against the law in the Kingdom, and they might have some interest in the matter. Suddenly, I was very popular, wasn't I?

So what the frag was I supposed to do now? I pulled the C-N Buddy over to the side of the road, and I stared out over the Pacific as despair rolled over me like a dark and cold wave. Where the frag was I supposed to go?

I was hooped—well and truly hooped.

Options—let's work through them one at a time. I could go back to the Diamond Head Hotel—*null!* Suicide, basically. Yamatetsu would be waiting for me there, as would the yaks if they had any brains at all. My only hope of surviving the experience would be if the yaks and the corps were too busy geeking each other to geek me. Not an attractive bet.

I could hightail it for Awalani Airport and grab a suborbital the frag *out* of here. Hell, I still had my open corp ticket, didn't I? Sure, I could jump aboard a plane and leave all my grief behind me—*null!* I knew from experience just how much security surrounded those birds. There was no fragging way in hell that Barnard, or the yaks either, for that matter, wouldn't know I was hopping a plane out. At Awalani, in the middle of the flight, or at whichever airport I chose as my destination, there'd be that gentle tap on the shoulder that's more shocking than a punch in the teeth. I'd be dragged away, and then there'd be the bullet in the back of the head. Or who knows, maybe I'd be turned to stone and get to join the statues I saw in the background during Barnard's telecom call.

The more I thought about it, the more hooped I was. I

hadn't really paid attention when Scotty had told me why there were so few wannabes in the Hawai'i shadows—no running room if things go for drek. Now I was learning from personal experience that he was right, and I didn't like the feeling at all.

What options did I have? Was there any other way off the islands? Not that I knew about, on the spur of the moment. Was there anywhere I could hole up until this all blew over? Not that I knew about, on the spur of the moment. Was there anyone who had contacts and resources that could help me out? Not that I knew about, on the spur . . .

Wait a tick. Maybe there *was* one. It was a long shot, but when things get desperate "risk amelioration" isn't much of an option.

"*Kia ora!*" I practiced as I pulled the Buddy back onto the road, trying to get just the right tone of bellicosity into my voice. "*Kia ora!*"

9

But before I paid my respects to bruddah Te Purewa—né Mark Harrop—at Cheeseburger in Paradise, there were a couple of other things I needed to take care of. Like, hooking up with any and all resources that might prove useful even if they weren't in the islands.

That morning, when I'd gotten ready to cruise out to the meet in Scott's limo, I'd debated whether or not to bother bringing my pocket 'puter. Hell, I'd reasoned if I needed communications or data retrieval or whatever, the rig in the back of the Rolls would put my personal 'puter to shame. Out of habit, though—and a sense of cussedness, perhaps—I'd brought the scratched little unit along in my pocket.

Thank the Spirits for habit and cussedness. At a little village called Kaaawa, I pulled over and used a public phone booth outside a ramshackle grocery/ice-cream/tourist-foo-foo store. First order of biz—after polarizing the transpex so no one could see in—was to disable the vid pickup, which I did in the most efficient way by smacking it a good one with the butt of the Browning I'd inherited. Second was to haul out my trusty 'puter, jack it into the phone's data port, and trigger the sophisticated—and hideously illegal—smoke and mirrors program that my old chummer Quincy (how long since I'd seen that slag?) had once blown into the little unit's EPROM chips. Phone and 'puter clicked and hummed for a few seconds while Quincy's code seduced the LTG system. Finally, with a beep that was the electronic equivalent of, "Take me, stud, but be gentle," the phone succumbed to the 'puter's entreaties and I had the run of a very small corner of the PA/HI RTG.

First things first. Convincing the innocent, trusting phone system that I was an authorized Hawai'i Telecommunications Corporation senior manager, I set myself up a private and secured mailbox in HTC's automated datamail system. (This was only a temporary setup, unfortunately; I didn't have the time or the resources to make it permanent. At some time, a month or two down the road, some watchdog program would start barking when it noticed that nobody was paying for the datamail box even though it was still active. HTC would immediately close it down, but by that point it shouldn't matter to me. In a month or two, I'd either be dead or off the islands.) This datamail box was the electronic equivalent of a "blind maildrop" in espionage fieldcraft. People could leave messages for me there, and I could retrieve them at my leisure, but there was no way, theoretically, that any interested party, like Jacques Barnard, could track down my actual location even if he compromised the mailbox.

Step two: Get in touch with the people that I wanted to leave me messages. The first of those was simple. One of the ever-wiz little utilities on my Quincy-modified 'puter let me send off a text-only message through a series of cold relays to a certain telecom in deepest, darkest Renton. The message contained no names, nothing that could compromise either sender or recipient. The header addressed the message to the president of Demolition Man Building Services Inc. The body text of the message was the digital address of my new datamail box cyclically encoded (again thanks be to Quincy, forever and ever amen). The way I figured it, only one man still alive would recognize the reference and know who was trying to reach him. When he got back into the sprawl, Argent would pick up the message and hopefully contact me through my blind drop.

The second person was harder, but again Quincy's codebashing helped me out. Within minutes I'd whipped up a simplistic little gofer of a smartframe and fired it off through the Matrix to the Cheyenne LTG. Once there, the gofer would search for any references to one Sharon Young and deliver her a message.

The content of that message was more problematic than the one to Argent. Young and I didn't have much in the way of background; we certainly didn't have any codes in common as I did with Argent. My message had to meet two criteria. First, it had to identify me without using names. Second, it had to communicate my blind-drop address in code. And third, it had to contain the key to that code in such a way that only Sharon Young would recognize it as such and be able to decrypt the address.

It had taken a fair bit of skull-sweat, but I'd finally come up with something that *should* serve. "Exposure has become direct," the message began, echoing the conversation between Young and me at The Buffalo Jump. "Discussion necessary on extraordinary disbursements. Confirming terms of payment: deadline forty-eight hours, twenty percent on twelve, ten on eighteen." And beneath that was the encrypted bit-string that was my blind-drop address.

Subtle. *Too* subtle? The terms of payment I'd quoted in the note were totally out to fragging lunch with regard to what we'd actually agreed, and I hoped Young would notice that and recognize the significance. Take the numbers I'd quoted: 48, 20, 12, 10, 18. That was the key to decrypt the address, of course: 48201–21018. Smart, *neh*? We'd see soon enough. I checked that everything was kosher, then used the 'puter to tell the phone system to forget everything that had happened over the last ten minutes. I unjacked my 'puter, climbed back into the cramped cockpit of the bubble-topped Buddy, and turned the little three-wheeler back toward Honolulu.

It was getting on to evening by the time I made it back to the Ewa area of Honolulu. Blame it on my being too distracted to read highway signs accurately. When you've got a megacorp *and* the yakuza gunning for you, it's easy to mistake Kapaa for Kapua and get totally fragging lost. The sun was sinking down toward the ocean, one of those spectacular views tourists pay the big cred to see, and all I could think was "Hurry the frag *up!*" I'd feel much better with the cloak of night around me, I figured.

I ditched the three-wheeler a couple of blocks from the Cheeseburger in Paradise, using every shred of tradecraft I could muster to spot anyone who was affording me an abnormal degree of interest. I didn't seem to have any shadows, but it's a tenet of the street that you'll never spot anyone who's *successfully* shadowing you, right? As I approached the door of the tavern, I saw a reflection of myself in a store window. My flowered shirt was torn down one side, my pants were stained in places with something I hoped was mud (and not residue from Tokudaiji's blasted skull), and I still had hibiscus twigs in my fragging hair. I had looked better, I had to admit. I did what damage control I could under the circumstances—damn near squat, to be honest—and then I jandered into Cheeseburger in Paradise.

The crowd looked pretty much the same as when Scott had bought me a couple of beers—the same hard-bitten locals, the same street-rats not quite watching the strip show. The same ork with the same chipped tusks was behind the bar, and he gave me a solid dose of what Scott had called "stink-eye" as I walked in. Yet again, I was the only *haole* there, and you can bet your *okole* that I felt it. I was out of my element and out of my depth, and the patrons at Cheeseburger in Paradise weren't going to let me forget it.

What I most wanted to do at that moment was to turn round and slink back out into the predusk where nobody was ·ying to glare holes in me. I couldn't do that, of course, so I jandered on in like I fragging owned the place. I kept thinking about the heavy Browning crammed down my waistband—not that it was an easy piece of hardware to forget—for the benefit of those patrons who liked to play "spot the heat." The booth Scott and I had taken the day before was vacant, so I slid into it, settling my back firmly and reassuringly against the wall. Now that I felt about as safe as I could under the circumstances, I looked around for friend Te Purewa.

No, he wasn't there. (Frag, of course not. The old Montgomery luck was continuing to run true to form, I thought disgustedly.) I thought I recognized one or two of the slags he'd come in with yesterday, but I could well have been mistaken. One leather-clad Hawai'ian ork with a lousy attitude looks very much like another to the untrained eye.

A waitress came up to me—not the same one as yesterday, but they could well have been sisters—with a "Well, *what*?" expression on her face.

I sighed. "Give me a dog," I told her. And I settled down to wait.

Thank the Spirits I didn't have to wait that long, not much more than an hour and a half. I swallowed about a liter and a half of Black Dog beer and sweated out what felt like twice that much of cold, rank fear-sweat. A couple of tables full of hard-hooped locals were giving me the speculative eye. I knew they'd picked up on my heat when I'd come in, but they were getting to the point where it was even odds they'd try the *haole* just to see if he knew how to use the hardware he was packing.

When Te Purewa swaggered in at about nineteen hundred hours, I was glad enough to see him that I'd have gladly stuck out my tongue at him—or any other portion of my anatomy, for that matter—if it would make him look on me more kindly. He saw me the moment he came in the door, and his scowl raised the stink-eye quotient by a significant factor. I glanced over to the hard-eyed waitress—I'd already explained to her what I wanted her to do and slipped her a big enough tip that she might actually remember—and gave her the nod.

I couldn't hear exactly how she phrased things—probably something like, "See that wild-assed *haole* in the corner? Says he wants to buy you a drink. If you happen to drop your credstick, kick it home before you bend over to pick it up, huh?"—but it didn't really matter. Te Purewa—Mark Harrop—shot me a fulminating glance from under his night black brows, but I saw there was a new element in his glare—curiosity.

He didn't come over immediately—that wouldn't have been chill, of course, and chill is all. He stretched it out for a good fifteen minutes before he jandered on over to glare at me from closer range. I glanced meaningfully at the chair across from me, but he didn't take it. The silence stretched, then he grunted, "Maletina say you wanna talk."

"*Kia ora,* Te Purewa," I responded. "What are you drinking?"

He hesitated, then he shrugged his burly shoulders. "Vodka."

I nodded at the waitress, Maletina, who'd been hanging close, probably to catch the fun if the big pseudo-Maori decided to beat the drek out of the *haole.* She gave me anther dose of stink-eye, but she did cruise off in the general direction of the bar.

"We got off on the wrong foot yesterday," I said levelly as we waited for the drink to arrive. "I had no intention of insulting you." I gave him my best disarming smile. "Us dumb-hooped tourists don't know any better, *neh*?"

"Dumb-hooped tourists get heads broke in," he rumbled. But despite his hard-assed act I saw he actually wanted to smile. For the first time in a long while, I allowed myself to feel a little hope.

Maletina showed up about then with the quasi-Maori's drink. It looked like a triple, easy ice. Maletina was obviously playing "soak the *haole*," but I wasn't about to complain. I raised my glass of dog and struggled to remember Scott's toast. "*Okolemaluna*," I said at last.

Te Purewa hoisted his own glass. "Li' dat." He polished off about half the vodka in one pull, then puffed out his cheeks with a satisfied *pah* sound. His hard glare had softened a little.

"You've known Scott for a while, have you?" I asked after a reasonable interval.

The Maori wannabe shrugged. "Some time, yah," he agreed. He smiled. "Get drunk, raise *pilikia*—raise trouble—and li' dat. *Aikane*—friend." His eyes suddenly narrowed suspiciously. "Where Scott at, *ule*, huh? Where?"

There wasn't any really smooth way of breaking the news—not that would get me the overall result I wanted, at least. "Dead," I told him flatly. "Some guy called Tokudaiji had him killed."

He was half out of his chair, his hand reaching for a bulge under his leather coat. I rapped the barrel of my Browning on the underside of the table—I'd pulled the piece from my waistband while he was busy with his vodka—and when I knew I'd got his attention I thumbed the safety off. The way his eyes widened at the metallic *snick,* I knew he recognized the sound. Slowly, he moved his hand away from his heat, and he settled back into his chair. His eyes didn't leave my face though, and I could *feel* the rage he was fighting back.

"*Haole,* you dead," he whispered. "You *pau,* all over, no moh, yah? Not now, maybe. Sometime, you *pau.*"

It was hard to pretend that much hatred didn't faze me, but I managed to shrug unconcernedly. "You're right about that, Te Purewa," I said evenly. "I was with Scott when he was geeked. You think Tokudaiji's not going to have me aced too, to finish the job? Of *course* I'm fragging dead, brah. But you think I'm scared of *you* when I've got yakuza samurai on my hoop?"

That got through to him as I'd hoped it would. "Yak?" He blinked. "*That* Tokudaiji? He *da kine* . . . he *oyabun. Nui* big yak."

"You've got *that* right," I confirmed.

"Yak kill Scott? Tokudaiji kill my *aikane*?"

"That's what happened," I paused. "I don't know any of

the background, Te Purewa. I came to Hawai'i to deliver a message—Scott knew who I was supposed to deliver it to, I didn't. I never heard of Ekei Tokudaiji before today. I need to know more. What can you tell me about him?"

It had worked, I saw. The multiple shocks—Scott's death, the identity of his "killer" (the way I was telling the story, at least), then the straightforward admission that I needed his help—had done their job. Te Purewa didn't know quite how to take me. Eventually, he might decide the *haole* had to die. But for the moment, I'd broken down his resistance.

The almost-Maori blinked again. Then, "Lots of Japanese in the islands," he began. I noticed that the intensity of his accent and his pidgin dialect were a lot less, as though in the effort of remembering he'd forgotten to be *quite* so Polynesian. "You know about the yakuza, yah? Traditionally, they always been the 'defenders of the people.' When some lord causes too much *pilikia,* the people can go to the yaks, say 'help us out with this *ule,*' and the yaks do it. Even today. No lords no moh, but corps and cops and politicians and li' dat, yah?

"So yaks, they got *nui* respect from the Japanese, the common folk, like, yah?" he went on. "Tell 'em no worry, no *huhu* when they get riled up. Settle 'em down, like.

"Happen wi' *Na Kama'aina,* happen wid ALOHA ..."

I raised a hand, asking for a time-out. "Hold the phone. *What* happened with *Na Kama'aina* and ALOHA?"

Te Purewa snorted. "Corps out, *haoles* out, yah? All that *kanike,* li' dat." He hesitated and frowned again. "Scott didn't tell you 'bout that? Scotty, he got big hard-on for ALOHA *kanike.*"

My turn to blink. *He did, did he?* But now wasn't the time. "Yeah, he told me some of it," I said reassuringly, "but he didn't give me much in the way of details. Dumb-hooped *haole,* remember?"

He chuckled, and I knew I'd set his suspicions to rest again ... for the moment. "ALOHA, they try to stir up big *pilikia,*" Te Purewa continued, "big trouble, everybody *huhu,* yah? Some yaks say, 'So what? Not *my* problem, Jack.' "

I thought I was starting to understand—some of it, at least. "But not Tokudaiji?"

"You got *dat, hoa,*" he agreed vehemently. "Tokudaiji say ALOHA stuff all *kanike,* make no sense, yah? Hawai'i *need*

corps. Hawai'i need *haoles*—some, maybe." He snorted
again. "Hawai'i need money, bruddah, I know *dat* for true.
No corps, where we get money, huh? Where we get food?
Can't eat scenery."

I nodded slowly. "So ALOHA and *Na Kama'aina* tried to
get the people up in arms against the corps, is that right?
And Tokudaiji calmed them down again?"

"Calmed *Japs* down," Te Purewa corrected. "Japs only
people really listened to him." The Maori wannabe paused,
and his face set. I thought I knew what he was going to ask
next.

I was right. "What Scotty do to get whacked, huh?" he
asked me quietly. "Step on *oyabun*'s toes? Spout ALOHA
crap? Get *oyabun* all *pupule*—all pissed off, yah?"

What the frag, I'd have to tell him sometime. "You could
say that," I agreed.

"What Scotty do to *oyabun*, huh?"

"He killed him," I said.

I'd been here before, and I hated it.

Well, not *here* precisely, but enough places just like it that
the surroundings were depressingly familiar. After a while,
one single-room rundown squat is just like another—they all
kind of blend together in the memory. Granted, there were
differences—cockroaches replaced rats in this one, and it
was air-conditioning I craved instead of central heating.
Other than that, though, little enough difference.

I lay on the mistreated mattress, shifting around to find a
position where as few springs as possible dug into my flesh.
I stared at the ceiling.

What the frag had I gotten myself into here? (That question was depressingly familiar, too.) I thought I'd gotten a
handle on it; I thought I'd gotten at least part of the story
chipped. Suddenly, it didn't look like I knew *squat* about
what was really going down. I sighed.

At least I had a resource now; I had a sometime ally. Te
Purewa, of course. I couldn't depend on him too far. At
some point he might notice some of the inconsistencies in
the story I'd told him and come on by with some of his overgrown friends to ask me hard questions. Better not to push
my luck.

For the moment, though, he'd come through in spades. I
needed a doss—he'd gotten me a doss, a squat in a trashed-

out rooming house on the fringe of downtown Ewa. I needed wheels—he'd gotten me wheels, a fifteen-year-old 250cc Suzuki Custom motorbike. I needed cold iron—he'd gotten me cold iron, a Colt Manhunter that he swore up and down wasn't registered and wasn't in anyone's ballistic database. And I needed sleep. I was on my own for that one.

But I *couldn't* sleep, of course. I was still stoked up from the hit and its aftermath, and my mind was racing like a high-speed flywheel. I kept going over things again and again, trying to slide the puzzle pieces around into their proper places, so everything would make sense. Fat fragging chance.

It had all looked so simple, for a couple of hours there. Corporate hit against Tokudaiji—orchestrated by Barnard—using me as camouflage and Scott as the hitter—both expendable, of course, and to *be* expended via belly-bomb. About as straightforward as anything ever is, these days, *neh*?

But there had to be more to it than that. For one thing, Tokudaiji the *oyabun* seemed to be a major corp supporter ... if I could trust Te Purewa on that point. When ALOHA and the other hotheads tried to stir up the population against the megacorps, it was Tokudaiji who worked to calm them down again. Surely then, it would be in Barnard's best interest—in Yamatetsu's best interest, and in the best interest of *all* megacorps making big cred out of Hawai'i—to keep Tokudaiji breathing. With him gone ...

Well, Te Purewa's reading on the situation—and I had to agree with him—was that there'd be some major backlash. The hit would be seen as a megacorp operation. Rumors to that effect had already been buzzing down the streets while I was still sipping dog with the quasi-Maori. How would the general populace—particularly, the numerous (and quite influential) *Japanese* populace—read that? The evil, wicked, mean, and nasty megacorps had just whacked an important "defender of the people." Suddenly, ALOHA and *Na Kama'aina* would find it a frag of a lot easier to stir up the populace against the corps, right? I could easily imagine retaliation against corporate facilities and personnel.

So why—why, and again *why*—would Barnard arrange to off the *oyabun*? Unless he was *trying* to stir up the locals against the corps.

How did *that* hang together? Pretty well, actually.

Cack the *oyabun*. Provoke the locals. Lose some megacorp resources. Then—more in sorrow than in anger, of course—move in corporate security personnel, private armies to "pacify" the islands. While they're at it, remove the government that had proven itself incapable of protecting megacorporate interests within its jurisdiction. Frag, drek like this had gone down before successfully. Ask any historian.

Was *that* it, then? Was I involved in a plot—*another* plot, for frag's sake—to oust the sovereign government of the fragging Hawai'ian islands and put a plutocrat on the throne? Sanford B. Dole in the nineteenth century, Jacques Barnard in the twenty-first . . . ?

All the facts fit—or I could *make* them fit—but I had to admit it was all circumstantial evidence at best. Frag it, like I do all too often, I was getting my exercise by jumping to conclusions. The "corp coup" theory answered some questions, but it left a couple of puzzling queries unanswered. Those queries continued to nag at me as the rusty bedsprings creaked under my back. Specifically, I couldn't stop thinking about the wide discrepancy between how Te Purewa had described his friend's political outlook and the way Scott had presented himself to me. When we'd seen the protesters outside Government House, he'd expressed no sympathy, no solidarity with them. *Why,* when according to Te Purewa he was a staunch *Na Kama'aina*/ALOHA supporter?

Could Barnard and Yamatetsu be in bed with ALOHA in some way?

I rolled over on the bed, and something prodded me in the hip. Not another bedspring, something else . . .

And with a bellow of "You're a fragging *idiot!*" I jolted bolt upright in bed and dug in my pocket. There it was, where I'd stuffed it unconsciously when the first Roomsweeper shot had pummeled my ear.

The message chip that Barnard had given me to pass to Tokudaiji.

10

My fingers were trembling slightly as I slipped the optical chip into the reader slot of the doss's ancient telecom. Trying not to let myself hope too hard, I ran a directory of the chip's contents. A single file—BARNARD.TXT. Pretty fragging self-descriptive, *neh*? I rattled in the command to copy the file under another name—in case there was some kind of protective virus that would delete the original if someone jacked with it—then tried to open the copy, not the original.

The screen filled with a flurry of graphical symbols—happy-faces, Greek characters, and such drek—and the speaker fired off a fusillade of beeps. Well, *that* wasn't so hard to predict, was it? The file was encrypted, encoded so a curious third party—like me—couldn't read it.

Okay. Now the question was, how "robust" was the encryption? There are thousands of ways of encrypting a file; maybe a dozen are in widespread use. Of this dozen, they range from theoretically unbreakable (practically speaking, there's no such thing as totally unbreakable encryption) all the way down to as insecure as a safe door sealed with nothing but masking tape. My next step would depend entirely on the kind of encryption Barnard had selected for his message.

(Now hold the phone a tick. Didn't the fact that there *was* a message at all tell me something? If the whole "message delivery" scam was just camouflage, why bother . . . But no, that didn't hang together. Barnard had no guarantee that I wouldn't scan the chip before delivering it. There had to be *something* there to set the mind of the Trojan horse at ease.)

I scrolled back up to the beginning of the encrypted file and examined the header—that string of bytes that basically tells decryption/display software, "This is a message encrypted *so,* and here's where it begins," I connected my personal 'puter to the telecom's dataport, and let another one of Quincy's busy-beaver programs loose on the header.

The results showed up on the portable 'puter's small screen, and I cursed. Public-key encryption, with a 70-bit key code. It could have been worse . . . but not much.

I don't know how much you savvy public-key encryption, but it's a slick little system that's been around for nigh on eighty years now. Everyone who uses the system has two key codes (both 70 bits long, in this implementation, equivalent to a 22-digit number): a private key that he tells no one and a public key that he can tell all and sundry, or even publicize. The way the system is most commonly used today in 2056, if Adolf wants to send a secret message to Barney, Adolf encrypts the message using two keys: his own private key and Barney's public key. To decrypt the message, Barney uses two keys: his private key and Adolf's public key. Theoretically, only Barney can read the message, since only Barney knows his private key. (Well, duh.) As an added bonus, he *knows* it had to come from Adolf—or, at least, that it had to have been encrypted using Adolf's private key—otherwise it wouldn't have decrypted properly. Clear as mud? Good, then we'll continue.

The point is that, according to the cryptographic theories in fashion when the public-key system was developed and for thirty-odd years thereafter, it was theoretically impossible to crack a public-key system within the projected life span of the universe. Theories have changed, though—they tend to do that. Today, some bright sparks claim that using Eiji recursion and other bits of black art, it's possible to crack a 70-bit code in a couple of days of churning on a fast enough computer. Which is why few people bother with anything less than an 85-bit code as of 2056. (Should the fact that Barnard plumped for a less secure system tell me something? Or was I still reaching . . . ?)

The upshot? It *should* be possible for a nova-hot cryptographer to bash through Barnard's security in somewhere between twenty-four and seventy-two hours. The problem?

I was fresh out of nova-hot cryptographers at the moment. With a sigh, I remembered some of the resources I had access to back in Seattle. Rosebud the dwarf, a quasi-legal technomancer with computing power equivalent to a MultiVAX installed right in her braincase. And, for bigger challenges, the ex-decker called Agarwal ... no, he was dead now, wasn't he? Deeper sigh.

Here, out in the middle of the fragging Pacific? Nobody, chummer. *Still* deeper sigh. (Okay, okay, don't say it, I know: I could do it all virtually, spew it all through the matrix to whatever decrypt artist struck my fancy, all without leaving my doss, yattata yattata yattata. In principle, true. But when your life's on the line, chummer, sometimes you *really* want the hands-on control that only a face-to-face can give you. You scan? So get off my back.)

Moral of the story? I had to *find* the nova-hot cryptographer I needed, using the limited resources I had. Which meant, sad to say, Te Purewa, and that was about it. *Deepest* sigh.

The pseudo-Maori was better than nothing, but he definitely wasn't the drek-hot resource I'd hoped for. From the way Scott had introduced him, I'd figured him for a part-time fixer. What did they call them around here?—*kalepa*, that was it—with a stable of contacts. No banana on that one, chummerino. He was SINless, true, surviving by doing odd jobs and getting paid under the table ... so by some people's measure, that made him a shadowrunner. He *did* know a few fixers, but only socially—or so I gathered. Translation? He was *in* the shadows, but not *of* them, if you see the distinction. He might have met some people with the skill-sets I was looking for, but he might not have known it.

Still, he was the only entrée into the Honolulu shadow community I had at the moment. If I could figure a way of getting him to put the word out—while keeping it from the various and assorted hard-men who wanted to see me dead—I'd have to do so. That was going to take some thought ... which, in turn, was going to require some sleep. My brain was soya-paste. I reached out to power down the telecom ...

Then stopped. What the hell, I might as well check my blind maildrop while I was at the keyboard. It didn't seem particularly likely that Argent or Sharon Young had gotten back to me already, but it was worth a look. Using the nicely hidden back door that Quincy's gofer had installed in HTC's system, I accessed my datamail box and requested a directory listing.

Wonder of wonders, there was a message there: voice, not just text. No name—predictably, and the originator address was one of the many anonymous remailer services that thrive in the Carib League. Curious, I keyed playback.

"Mr. Montgomery, we need to talk."

My left hand flashed out and hit the Pause key almost hard enough to crack the macroplast enclosure. Ah, drek . . . how the frag had he tracked me down already?

The voice was Jacques Barnard's, of course, the slag who'd gotten me into this nasty mess and who no doubt now wanted me out of it . . . permanently and terminally. For a moment I stared at the telecom with real fear.

Then I fought back that emotion and snorted with absolute disgust at my reaction. What the frag did I think? that Barnard was going to crawl out of the fragging telecom if I played back the rest of the message? Get a fragging *grip*, Montgomery. (More evidence that my reactions were fragging *shot*, part of my mind nagged. Shut the frag up, another part of my mind told the carping mental voice.) I reached out again and keyed Rewind, then Play.

"Mr. Montgomery, we need to talk." The recording was as crystal clear as if Barnard were in the same room—no static, no sound degradation. One of the advantages of being able to afford the best corp-class datalines, no doubt. "I'm very concerned with events, and with your response to them, Mr. Montgomery," he went on coldly. "I need you to make contact *now*. I need you to tell me the exact details regarding the demise of . . . of our mutual friend. I'm disappointed that you have not seen fit to get in touch with me and wonder whether I should interpret your actions as evidence of complicity in the . . . the *events*. You may contact me at your earliest convenience using the provisions already established. We have things to discuss and further actions to schedule."

Barnard's voice paused, then continued icily. "I do expect to hear from you soon, Mr. Montgomery. Do I make myself clear?" With a click the recording ended.

I glanced at the telecom's blank screen. What the fragging hell was I supposed to make of *that*? If I were to take Barnard's message at face value, he didn't know the whys and the wherefores of the hit on Tokudaiji any more than I did. If I were to believe him, his impulse—and a very natural one it was, too—was to wonder if I hadn't pulped Tokudaiji myself, for my own reasons. If I were to believe him, he was asking me to come back into the light so he could debrief me on Tokudaiji's death and so we could plot out our logical next move.

If. That was the operative word, wasn't it? If I believed him, he wanted me to come into the light so he could do damage control. If I *didn't* believe him, he *still* wanted me to come into the light so he could do damage control . . . by blowing my brains out. Why were these things never easy and clear-cut?

Well, at least I didn't have to make a decision at the moment. Mr. Jacques Barnard, Yamatetsu veep, wouldn't be going anywhere, would he? I could take some time and think through the consequences. I could also try and get his message to Tokudaiji decrypted and see if that led me anywhere. For the moment, though . . .

I slumped back on the bed and tried to sleep.

There was more to this Barnard message than I'd considered, wasn't there?

The air in my face was refreshing as hell as I rode "my" Suzuki Custom toward Cheeseburger in Paradise, and it helped blow away the mental cobwebs and lingering remnants of nightmares. Cruising at sixty klicks, the air temperature was almost bearable. When I stopped for lights or traffic, though, the streets of Ewa felt like radiators, or maybe sophisticated cooking surfaces dedicated to the preparation of grilled *haole*. The bike's little petrochem engine sang and hauled hoop when I cracked the throttle. (Somebody told me that as little as sixty years ago, there was no way you could crank 100 horsepower out of a 250cc engine. Maybe *some* things have improved with time after all.)

As I weaved through the slow midafternoon traffic, I frowned. Barnard had gotten a message to me . . . and the fact that it was in my secured datamail box was a message in itself, wasn't it? I'd only given that address to two people: Argent and Sharon Young. Argent would rather chew his own leg off than help Yamatetsu Corporation with *anything,* I knew that. That left Young . . .

. . . Who, now that I thought about it, had been on Barnard's fragging payroll back in Cheyenne. *Frag!* I'd *known* that; Barnard had told me so himself, indirectly: The contract Young offered me was related to this whole Hawai'ian cluster-frag. And I had given my secure datamail box address to Young . . . and thus, indirectly, to Barnard. If I made it out of this thing in one piece, without fragging something up so badly I got myself geeked, I'd dance a fragging jig, I swear it.

I parked the little Suzuki in the alley behind Cheeseburger in Paradise and jandered into the tavern. I guess my two visits qualified me as a regular, because the chip-tusked bartender started to draw me a half-liter of dog the moment he saw me. As I took what had become my regular table, Maletina brought the frosty glass over and put it down in front of me. For a wonder, she didn't look as though she wanted to kick me in the pills today. Hell, she even talked to me: "Te Purewa say he be by later. Got some people you wanna meet, maybe."

I thanked her and smiled sweetly . . . even though I really wanted to swear a blue streak. So Te Purewa was coming in later with some people I wanted to meet, huh? I'd asked him over the phone if he could put out some feelers—*very* subtly—to see if he could track down a decrypt artist who could handle a 70-bit public-key job. Apparently he'd gotten busy on it right away . . .

. . . And then he'd *told the fragging waitress about it.* Slot! Who *else* had he told? His girlfriend? The slag who cut his hair? The yak soldier who lives down the street . . . ?

My first instinct was to cut and run, to bail out of Cheeseburger in Paradise and never come back. Short-term survival-wise, it probably was the smartest thing I could do . . . but I had to take the long view as well. I needed the decrypt artist. And, more important, I needed who the decrypt artist *knew.* Any code-slicer capable of handling a 70-bit would *have* to have better contacts with the real shadow community than Te fragging Purewa. Thus I needed to hang chill at the tavern. So my logic went at the moment, at least.

That didn't mean I had to make myself a big, glowing *haole* target, of course. I gave the place the once-over, a closer visual scan than I had to this point. Keeping in mind that this was a watering hole in one of the badder parts of town, and that it had a rep as a borderline shadow hang-out.

Yes, there it was, I was sure of it. The security camera whose fish-eye lens could cover the entire floorspace, mounted in the (apparently nonfunctional) smoke/dust precipitator over the bar itself. Like the cameras in most places like this, it was out of obvious view, to remove a very real temptation. When gutterpunks get into their cups, obvious security cameras often seem to be interpreted as an invitation to small-arms target practice.

A surveillance camera, of course, implied someplace to view the surveillance data. Taking my half-liter of dog with me, I made my way over toward the bartender.

Have you ever spent two hours watching a tavern through a distorting fish-eye lens while drinking Black Dog beer in a windowless room with no ventilation or air-conditioning on a hot tropical day? Let me save you the trouble. You can get exactly the same effect by driving twenty-centimeter nails into your temples, and you won't even have to pay for the beer.

I rubbed at my eyes and massaged my throbbing temples. The bartender had been incredibly understanding when I'd asked to use his office—after I'd shown him the balance on my credstick, of course—and I *did* feel a frag of a lot safer watching for Te Purewa via electronic intermediaries. But at the moment, if a yak had come in and prepared to blow my head off, I'd have thanked him, since I was out of aspirins.

Okay, looking on the bright side, I *did* have a much better feel for the tavern's clientele. Take *those* two, for instance. Over in a darkened corner was an overweight, middle-aged man wearing a thick toupee . . . oops, sorry, I guess the socially acceptable term is "alternative hair," isn't it? He was making a long, drawn-out—and probably pointless—attempt to hit on a bored-looking biff who I reckoned sported a pair of "alternative breasts." And over there were two kids, obviously underage but trying to look mature, while they *almost* avoided staring at the dancer giving herself a gynecological exam on the stage. And there, nearer the door, was an older native woman—bird-thin, fragile-looking in the same way as Tokudaiji—ignoring the drink on the table in front of her as she stared off into space. (Well, from this angle, it looked as if she were staring right into the camera lens, as a matter of fact. Coincidence, of course, but still creepy.)

The front door of the tavern swung open. The light level wasn't enough for any details to show on the security system, but I could make out three relatively large silhouettes. Te Purewa and his chummers? The three figures moved forward into the light, and I was *seriously* glad I'd invested in this vantage point.

Japanese, they were. Humans, all of them, but any one of

them could have applied for promotion to troll at any point. They wore conservative business suits. Their augmented eyes glinted unnaturally on the screen as they looked around the barroom.

Frag, couldn't these guys have tried for at least *some* local color? The closest thing to conservative business fashion around the Cheeseburger in Paradise was a tailored black leather armored jacket. Still, I shouldn't really be complaining, should I? If the yak soldiers—what the frag *else* could they be?—had bothered with camouflage, I might not have seen them coming. I congratulated myself for my foresight in setting myself up back here. If the yaks even thought to check the back room, I'd have plenty of warning. I'd be able to bail out the back door, hop on my Suzuki and lay rubber before they'd even talked their way past the bartender. Perfect, right?

If it was so goddamn perfect, how come the door behind me burst open, and somebody yelled, "Ice, *hoa!*" at me?

I spun in my chair, trying to haul out the Manhunter Te Purewa had provided. But I was staring into the muzzles of two large-caliber weapons, and instantly gave up on that pursuit. I showed empty hands and tried a tentative, "Okay, let's chill here, huh?"

It took me a long second or two to notice the slags behind the big guns. They weren't yak hitters as I'd expected . . . or if they were, then the Hawai'i yakuza has gotten a lot more behind affirmative action with regard to women and *kawaruhito* then their mainland cousins. The figure on the left was an ork with even bigger shoulders than Scott. He wore jeans and a sleeveless black leather vest a few sizes too small for his armored-and-bodysculpted torso. To his right was a woman—ork too, but whip-slender, with steel cord muscles. She wore dark pants and an aloha shirt, but the shirt's pattern was a pretty fragging good approximation of urban camo, I noticed. Both had their pistols—nasty big fraggers—Savalettes with a gleaming chrome-steel finish— leveled at my head.

"Clear your weapon," the woman snapped. "Two fingers. *Do* it!"

I did it—what the frag else was I supposed to do?— pulling out the Manhunter between the thumb and forefinger of my left hand. I dropped it to the floor and kicked it toward the two gillettes.

To my amazement, they relaxed visibly the moment I did, safing their own weapons and holstering them. I felt my mouth gape open, and the man chuckled as he scooped up my pistol. "Hey, *shaka*, brah, we just didn't want you doing nothing hasty, you scan?"

"We're chummers of Marky," the woman added. It took me a moment to twig to who "Marky" was—Mark Harrop, aka Te Purewa.

With a sharp inclination of her head she indicated the security screen—and, by implication, the yak soldiers. "You want to come with us, or wait for *them*?"

"Lead on, *hoa*," said I in heartfelt tones. As I rose to my feet, I glanced back at the screen. The older woman in the barroom was still staring into the camera, and for a disturbing moment I felt as though she was staring right into my skull.

As soon as we were out of the office, into the narrow hallway that led to the alley, the woman indicted her companion and said, "He's Moko. I'm Kat."

"I'm—" I began.

But she cut me off sharply. "Ice that, *hoa*. Know all I need to know. You're a chummer of Marky, that's good enough, huh?" She glanced at Moko and got a nod of acknowledgment. Suitably chastened—one of these days I've really got to get myself a street handle—I nodded, too.

As if an afterthought, Moko tossed me back my Manhunter, I felt the way a kid must when getting his security blanket back from the laundry. I shoved it back into my waistband.

Out into the alley we went. There were two new bikes there, parked next to mine. A Yamaha Twin-Turbine Rapier II—one of the newest rice-rockets. Driven by two contra-rotating gas turbines, it looked as lean and sharp and downright lethal as ... well, as a rapier, I suppose. Next to it was a big, brutal Honda Viking mega-hog painted a nasty matte black with blood-red trim. Instinctively, I played "match the bike," pairing Moko with the Viking, Kat with the Rapier.

And got it totally back-assward. Moko swung aboard the lean-lined Rapier and fired up the engine with a high-pitched whine. Kat, meanwhile, was pulling on a full-face helmet and a riding jacket angular with body armor. (Moko's sole concession to riding safety was to button his sleeveless vest shut across his bulging pecs.) A moment later, Kat was astride the Viking—not so much "astride," actually, as "nestled in the guts of"—and she hit the starter. The big 1800cc engine roared, then settled down to a contented purr as if the bike had just eaten a Suzuki Custom.

"Mount up and follow us," Kat told me.

Obediently I mounted up, and when they took off down the alley, I followed along. Considerately, they kept the speed at something my little Suzuki could handle without blowing a gasket. We kept to the alleys for a few blocks, then swung out onto a main road.

We rode for ten, maybe fifteen minutes . . . after the first five of which I was hopelessly lost. We were still in the heart of Ewa, I figured, but *where* precisely? Well, I suppose it didn't really matter. Eventually, Moko, who was riding directly ahead of me, flicked on his right-turn signal—the first time in the ride that he'd bothered with such niceties—and I slowed for the turn. The two lead bikes leaned way over, the Viking's pipes almost scraping the asphalt and headed directly for the closed up-and-over door of a warehouse . . .

Which opened just in time for them to cruise through. I'd hung back too far, and the door had already started to close again as I scooted under. The metal roof echoed back the thudding of the Viking's engine until it sounded like a .50-cal machine gun on full-auto. Slowly, the lead bikes rolled across the open warehouse floor and into what looked like a low alcove in the far wall. I followed and cut my engine as Kat gave me a slash-across-the-throat kill signal. For a few seconds my ears still rang with the concussion of the Honda's big engine.

The floor jolted under me, and I almost lost the Suzuki, whose kick-stand wasn't down yet, as the "alcove" started to rise. A freight elevator. As the elevator continued up, the two orks dismounted, and Kat stripped off her riding gear. The floor eventually stopped moving, and the two shadowrunners—what *else* could they be, *neh*?—led me out into the low-ceilinged second floor of the warehouse.

It was set up as a large ops room, I saw at once. Over against one wall was a weapons area—a fragging arsenal with various and assorted implements of mayhem mounted on hooks. In one corner was a sophisticated-looking commo suite; in another, a collection of computers and miscellaneous other tech-toys connected by a medusa's-head of wiring harnesses. Moko led me over toward a briefing table—the high-tech kind with a complex array of flatscreen display panels built into the tabletop—and slumped down in a swivel chair.

For the first time in a long time I felt my muscles start to relax. I was among professionals. I could feel the "vibes," and I recognized them. I knew Argent, the sole surviving street op from the late, lamented Wrecking Crew, would feel very much at home here.

And as I relaxed, my brain finally acknowledged various physical signals that parts of my body had been sending for some time. I glanced over at Kat, suddenly a touch embarrassed. "Where's the . . . um, the . . ." She chuckled and pointed.

That part of the ops facility was sophisticated, too. I took care of immediate needs and did a little damage-control on my appearance before I re-emerged.

Another member of the team—so I assumed, at least—was waiting to use the facilities. Yet another ork, yet again with a Polynesian cast to his features. His large eyes narrowed when he saw me—suddenly encountering a stranger in a place like this was probably as disconcerting as catching an unidentified tourist using your drekker at home—but then I saw understanding dawn. I stepped aside to let him into the facilities . . .

But he didn't go, not immediately. "You were with Scott, huh?" he asked me without preamble. His voice sounded like a bunch of rocks in the hubcap of a moving car.

I hesitated, then, "Yeah," I admitted slowly.

"How'd he go out?"

I glanced over toward the briefing table, where Moko and Kat were, for guidance. But they were deep in conversation with each other. I shrugged and said, "Belly-bomb, I think."

"Yeah, but he got the *oyabun* first, huh?"

"He did that," I confirmed.

The ork smiled. "Good. He did it up right, then, the way he wanted to go out." And he strode past me into the drekker.

I blinked in surprise at the closed door. That certainly hadn't been the reaction I was expecting. I didn't get any time to think about it right then, though, as Kat called, "Hoi!" and beckoned me over.

A third figure had joined them at the table by the time I'd crossed the open floor. Hawai'ian or Polynesian or whatever in coloration, but this one was an elf, complete with the pointed ears and almond eyes. (For the first time, I realized just how few elves I'd seen here in Hawai'i.) Apart from the coloration, he wouldn't have looked out of place in Seattle . . . or in Cheyenne, for that matter. Instead of what I'd mentally labeled as "tropical adventure gear," he was wearing close-fitting black leathers bedecked with a fashionable assortment of chains, studs, and plates. His quasi-Mohawk coiffure left his forehead and temples bare, and three datajacks and a chipslot glinted in the overhead lights.

Kat indicated the elf. "Poki," she told me. I nodded a greeting. The elf just looked right *through* me, too chill to even acknowledge my existence. *Like all too many elves,* I added mentally.

"I hear from Marky you got a chip you need decrypted, huh?" Kat said.

I hesitated for a moment. Then—this was what I'd been looking for, wasn't it?—I reached into my pocket and pulled the chip carrier out. I slid it across the tabletop to Poki.

He picked it up, again not acknowledging my presence. It was Kat he asked, "What's the scan?"

"Seventy-bit public-key," I told him.

That got him to actually look *at* me rather than *through* me. "Yeah?" He grinned, a real predatory expression on his thin face. "Meat for the beast, *hoa*. By when?"

"Soonest." Kat and I spoke the word almost simultaneously.

The elf picked up the chip carrier. "When are you going to get me something *tough?*" he asked Kat with a decidedly evil chuckle. And with that he strode over toward the computer corner.

11

For the next six hours I sat in a corner well out of the way and watched the shadow team—if they had a name, they (predictably) hadn't told me—go about their biz. Poki, the elf decker, spent all that time hunched over his computers, singing tunelessly along to some three-year-old shag rock fed directly into one of his secondary datajacks. The others . . . well, they did "shadowrunner stuff." The ork I'd met outside the drekker—his name was Zack, I'd learned—was the team's equivalent of a gunnery sergeant, and seemed to thoroughly enjoy his job of stripping down and cleaning some of the lethal-looking weapons in the team's arsenal. A Chinese dwarf—I never caught her name—helped him from time to time, occasionally going over to Poki and giving him a deep shoulder massage as he worked. Moko slept most of the time away, sprawled in a net hammock hung between too support pillars. Kat and another female ork—Beta, Kat called her—had networked a couple of pocket 'puters together and seemed to be doing administrative datawork. (I'd never really thought about it, but I guess even shadow teams can't avoid that joyless task.)

Of the seven people in the sprawling ops room, only I had nothing to do, assuming that Moko's current assignment was catching up on his zees. I've never handled down-time all that well, particularly when I've basically put my life in the hands of people I don't really know. The wait should have given me time to think things through, to come to some significant conclusions, but my brain just wasn't up to incisive analytical thinking at the moment. I couldn't stop my mind from churning; I couldn't stop my thoughts from running around and around in the same, well-worn track. I wished I could sleep, but I knew that wasn't in the cards.

About four hours in a receiver in the team's commo suite chirruped. Beta hurried over and slipped a hushphone headset on. I could see her lips move as she subvocalized, but I couldn't hear squat of either incoming or outgoing communication. After a minute or two she set the headset down and came over to Kat. Beta glanced in my direction before she spoke, but I'd already made sure I was staring blankly into space, quite obviously paying no attention to the proceedings. I quieted my breathing, trying to hear everything I could and momentarily wished for cyberears and enhanced peripheral vision.

"It's him," I head Beta say.

"Neheka?"

Beta shook her head. "The big worm," she corrected. (Or that's what I *thought* she said, at least. It could just as well have been "the bookworm" or "the big word," or even "the bakeware," really . . .) Whatever it was Beta had said, it was enough to break Kat away from her datawork and send her hurrying over to the hushphone. That piece of hardware did its usual fine job of work, and I couldn't make out a single syllable of the conversation, which lasted more than five minutes.

When Kat was done and had terminated the circuit, I watched her expression and body language out the corner of my eye as she walked back to the briefing table and the networked 'puters. Nothing meaningful; maybe Hawai'ians have their own *body* language as well.

It was something like two hours after the conversation with "the bakeware" that Poki let out a creditable rebel yell. I was on my feet in an instant and hurrying over to him. Kat got there before me, though—chipped? I wondered—and it was to her that the elf decker announced, "Got it."

"Yeah?"

Poki smiled nastily at my skepticism and told me, "Hey, slot, seventy-bit's old news. Where you been anyway?"

I shook my head, isn't there *anything* that doesn't change so fragging fast you can't keep up? The elf had sliced a corporate code in less than a fragging *quarter* of the time I'd expected. Whatever is the world coming to, etcetera etcetera drekcetera. I held out my hand for the chip, but the decker just pointed to a high-res data display.

I shot a meaningful look at Kat, and she picked up on it right away. "Got a couple of ticks to check my 'puter's memory, Poki?" she asked. "Think I might have picked up a virus."

The decker looked absolutely scandalized for a moment, and he opened his mouth to bag about it. But then he saw the hard edge in Kat's eyes, swallowed his kvetching, and nodded. (I'd already scanned that Kat had the juice in this outfit, but it was nice to get a little confirmation.)

"Yah, okay," he said, though his voice told me and everyone else that it definitely was *not* okay. He stood up, unjacked, and followed Kat to the briefing table . . . but not before giving me a solid dose of stink-eye. I shot him my best "Hey, I'm just a harmless idiot who *probably* won't reformat all your storage" smile, and sat down in the chair he'd just vacated.

It took me a few moments to make sense of the 'puter's user interface. (Sure, modern systems are supposed to follow the same paradigm, but just because you can drive a Volkswagen Elektro doesn't mean you're immediately competent behind the wheel of a 480-kilometer-an-hour Formula Unlimited racing machine, right?) When I thought I had everything under control, the first thing I did was scope out how many copies of the chip's contents Poki had in memory or in long-term storage. As far as I could tell, there was only the one: a single copy of the file in volatile memory displaying on the screen. Unfortunately, the key phrase was "as far as I could tell." If a nova-hot decker wanted to hide a backup copy from an amateur code-jockey like me, he'd sure as frag be able to do it. Once I'd done what I could in the way of security, I actually read through the message on the display.

Apparently, Barnard had never learned how to write concise letters. (But then, of course, by-the-bit charges for message traffic don't mean much to a corporate suit.) The message from Jacques Barnard to the late Ekei Tokudaiji filled three screens. I read it over twice, word for word, then scanned again for overall content.

For all the meaningful content I pulled out of the text, Barnard could as well have kept it down to two or three lines. If I'd been asked to give a high-school-style précis of the letter, it would have come out something like, "Keep on doing whatever it is you've been doing with regard to the subject under discussion, and be aware that some other, unidentified people might take steps to stop you from doing so. Have a nice day."

Sigh. I should have expected it, I suppose. There are more

ways to conceal meaning than by using 70-bit public-key encryption. Veiled language, cryptic references that mean something to no one but the two principals, "closed" allusions to things like "our communication of 12/18/55" and "the matter that so concerns our mutual friend" . . .

In addition to my simple précis, I *could* conclude one thing from the message with a fair bit of certainty. Namely: Tokudaiji and Barnard weren't strangers, and their interests had definitely aligned several times in the past. That's all I knew for sure after reading the message.

I could make a couple of guesses, of course. First, considering what Te Purewa—"Marky" to these folks—had told me, it seemed reasonably logical that "whatever it is you've been doing" was calming the populace down when *Na Kama'aina* and ALOHA tried to stir them up. And second . . .

Second . . . I couldn't be at all sure about this, but I couldn't shake the feeling, gut-deep and so very disturbing, that this *wasn't* a fake message whipped up just to set the mind of a soon-to-be-dead courier/Trojan horse at ease. If someone had asked me to bet on the instigator of Tokudaiji's death, not so long ago I'd have put a whack of cred on one Jacques Barnard. Now? No bet, chummer. Sure, I've been known to be wrong, but deep down where instinct sends you messages, I just didn't buy it anymore.

So, what the flying frag was going on?

I checked that the chip I'd given Poki was still in the 'puter's chipslot, then downloaded a copy of the plaintext message to it. Once I was sure it was safely ensconced on the optical chip, I deleted the copy from memory. Then I removed the chip using the same carrier and slipped it into my pocket.

Kat and Poki were watching me as I walked back to the briefing table. "Thanks," I said with a nod at the decker. Then I focused my attention on Kat. "I need to go back to my doss in Chinatown." I'd misstated the location of my flop, of course, and I watched her eyes closely for any reaction.

There was none—none beyond a frown of disapproval, that is. "Your safe-house is insecure," she pointed out. "The yaks might have compromised it." She gestured around at the ops room. "Just hang here, *hoa,* you're covered here. You scan? If you need to catch some sleep . . ."

I shook my head. "There's gear there I need," I lied sincerely. "If I don't get it, I'm dead. Not now, but pretty fragging soon."

She glanced over at Moko, still sprawled in his hammock. "I can send—"

"No good," I cut in. "It's secured. Unless I cut off my thumb and give it to Moko . . ." I shrugged and let the thought hang.

Kat considered it. The fact that my implication I was using a thumbprint security system of some kind didn't even faze her told me something more about this group's resources. "Moko can come with you," she suggested after a moment.

I shook my head. "That's just asking for trouble, isn't it?" I pointed out. "It's not as if Moko isn't a memorable type, after all." She half smiled at that and I knew I'd won. "I'll be back in touch the minute I've got my gear," I told her, to soften the victory. "Give me a cold relay so I can contact you."

After a moment she nodded once, and recited a string of digits. I committed them to memory. "Get his bike ready," she told Zack. Then she turned back to me. "Hope you know what you're doing, bruddah."

"So do I," I told her fervently, and that was the only truthful thing I'd said in the past few minutes.

I had to ride around in circles through the depths of Ewa for almost ten minutes before I spotted a landmark I recognized. From there it only took me another five to make it back to my doss.

I was cautious going in, of course. I didn't think it particularly likely that the yak soldiers had a line on my flop, but you don't bet your life blindly on vaporous things like "likelihoods." There were no unusual-looking people in the stairwells or the hallways, and when I reached the door to my room all the telltales I'd left were still securely in place. Confident for the first time that I *was* doing the right thing, I went in and locked the door behind me.

Then the confidence vaporized. I knew what I had to do—what I *thought* I had to do, rather—but that didn't make it any easier. I'd lived this long trusting my gut, but one of these days that well-tuned organ was going to let me down, violently and terminally. I sat down in front of the telecom, slipped my Manhunter from my waistband, and set it on the table beside the keyboard. Then I just stared at the screen for a couple of minutes.

Did I have the jam to do it? Did I have the jam *not* to do it? Frag, I *hate* these questions. Finally, I accepted that, a) I really didn't have that much choice; and b) if I played it right, it wasn't going to increase the danger I was in—already maximal—by any meaningful degree. I sighed, and then I keyed in the LTG number I'd taken off my voice-mail back in Cheyenne, what seemed so long ago.

I fidgeted and fretted as the telecom clicked its way through the intermediary nodes of the cold relay. Finally, the Ringing symbol blinked on the screen. Belatedly, I ran through the math to figure out the time in Kyoto, Japan. Nigh on midnight unless I'd slipped a time-zone somewhere. Would Mr. Jacques Barnard still be in the office? I doubted it. If not, would he have the call redirected, or would I get that most hateful of voices, the one that says, "Please leave your message after the beep?"

The Ringing symbol cleared, but the screen stayed blank. Then I heard the electronic click of yet another relay. After a few more seconds the screen cleared, and I was staring into the face of Jacques Barnard.

He was at home, I figured. Behind him, slightly out of focus, was a nighttime cityscape, viewed from a decent height—like from the penthouse of a downtown skyraker, for example. He was awake and alert, but he looked mentally cooked. When I'd first called him from Cheyenne, he looked to have aged a good decade in four years. Now he'd added another five years to that figure. He leaned back, brushing an invisible speck of dust from the sleeve of his maroon velvet smoking jacket—a fragging *smoking jacket*—and he gave me a smile that reminded me of sharks and barracudas.

"Mr. Montgomery," he said. "I'm so glad you saw fit to contact me. Can you please do me a large favor and tell me just what the *frag is going on*?"

I mentally flinched at the ferocity of his words. I'd never seen Barnard lose his temper, and I'd never expected to see it. I wished I'd been able to forgo the pleasure. "Tokudaiji's dead," I told him.

"I do understand that," he said coldly. "I would like to assume that you were not responsible—"

"You got *that* right," I said fervently. Then I went on to

give him a capsule description of what had gone down. He didn't interrupt or ask any questions, but I could see his brain spinning at 1,000 rpm behind his eyes. "I thought Scott was one of yours," I finished at last.

"A reasonable assumption," he acknowledged slowly, "since it was the same one I had made." He paused. "What is the . . . the tenor of the islands, concerning this matter?"

"I don't know directly," I told him, "but I can guess how things are going to shake out. You were using Tokudaiji to counter ALOHA's 'corps out' rhetoric, weren't you? When word gets around that a corp hitter whacked him"—I raised my hand to forestall the inevitable objection—"I know you're saying Scott didn't do the dirty deed on Yamatetsu's behalf, but who's going to believe that?"

"Even *you* have some difficulty believing it," he put in incisively.

I didn't have to acknowledge it; he could see it in my eyes, no doubt. "Anyway," I went on doggedly, "ALOHA's going to be able to play this one for all it's worth. 'Corps cack defender of the common people,' and all that bulldrek. They'll have the people behind them, and they'll be able to give you some serious grief."

"They would be *exceptionally* foolish to try," Barnard said flatly. "There are individuals in the corporate sphere with less . . . restraint . . . than I. And many of them have close connections with Zurich-Orbital and the Corporate Court." He paused. "Still, I have to agree with your analysis."

"Well, that makes me feel just so warm and fuzzy inside," I said sarcastically. "Get me the frag out of here, Barnard, *Now.* Hawai'i's getting a little too hot for me, if you'll pardon the wordplay."

Barnard smiled, but there was no real amusement in the expression. "Impossible at the moment, I'm afraid," he said flatly. "Perhaps in a week or two . . ."

"I'll be dead in a *day* or two."

"Not if you use those skills that so impressed me during our first acquaintance," he pointed out. Normally I like an ego-stroke as much as the next slag, but this one grated on me. I kept my reactions under control, though. "There is a further small matter on which I would value your assistance," he went on.

"A *further* . . . ?" I laughed out loud. "Frag you, Barnard, and the hog you rode in on. Your last 'small matter' is *already* going to get me geeked."

"I understand your animosity," the corporator said reasonably. "I would assure you that I had no intention for things to turn out this way . . . but of course you wouldn't believe me." He paused.

"Mr. Montgomery," he went on, leaning forward intently, "it is exceptionally important that we be clear about this. There are larger matters at work here than the death of an *oyabun* . . . and *certainly* larger than the fate of an erstwhile shadowrunner from the Sioux Nation." His mouth quirked into an ironic smile. "Larger than the senior vice president of a megacorporation, if it comes down to that.

"I need you to make one more contact, Mr. Montgomery."

"No fragging deal," I told him. "Not after the last one. Frag, you want me to 'contact' the CEO of Renraku, maybe, watch him get splattered, and then spend the rest of my short life running from the Red Samurai as well? No dice."

"That is unfortunate," he said sadly. "Truly unfortunate. If that's your final position . . ."

"It is."

" . . . Then your death is assured. Followed by the deaths of others—perhaps *many* others. However . . ."

He let the thought hang, like a baited hook dangled in front of the nose of a fish. I hated myself for it, but I wanted to hear that "however."

"*However,*" Barnard continued slowly, "if you were to help me in this, you would be in a position to still the turmoil that all this has caused. You would save the lives of countless others. And, incidentally, you would find yourself under the protection of those who even the yakuza's soldiers would think twice before challenging. Once the situation has settled down, there would be no problem—no problem whatsoever—in . . . *extracting* . . . you from the islands, and returning you to wherever on the mainland you may wish to go. *With,* I should point out, the gratitude of Yamatetsu Corporation, expressed both in monetary and other terms."

Frag, I knew I was hooked, and I knew Barnard knew. It wasn't much of a choice really, was it? "Die now, or maybe get out of this with skin intact." Kind of a no-brainer, all in all, *neh*?

I sighed resignedly. "Whom do you want me to contact?"

"A gentleman by the name of Gordon Ho."

I choked at that one. "Gordon *Ho*? King fragging Kamehameha the fragging Fifth? The fragging *Ali'i*? What the frag have you been slotting? *Jesus!*"

Barnard just watched me calmly as I ran down. "That *is* who I mean."

"Why don't you just ask me to go deliver a fragging pizza to Dunkelzahn, or something?"

"I understand your reaction," the corporator said calmly, "but you, in turn, must understand the importance of this. It is necessary—*vitally* necessary—to reassure the *Ali'i* that there was no corporate involvement in the assassination of Ekei Tokudaiji. Which there was not."

"Call him yourself, for frag's sake."

"Impossible," Barnard shot back. His voice was totally calm and controlled, and at that moment I hated him for it.

"*Why* impossible? Frag, Barnard, you're *Yamatetsu*, for frag's sake. How many commo satellites does Yamatetsu own? Send him a screened and encrypted message—"

He cut me off again. "Impossible," he repeated. "For various reasons, actually. The first is that a face-to-face meeting will almost certainly be required to set his doubts at rest."

"Then *you* go see him!"

Barnard chuckled. "I wish I could, actually. I had the chance to meet Gordon Ho on several occasions—he and my son went to university together, as a matter of fact—and I would enjoy the chance to talk to him again." I digested that one; I didn't even know Barnard *had* a son, couldn't picture him doing anything so normally human as popping kids. "Still, the political situation is such that a senior corporate executive can*not* be seen visiting the *Ali'i* of the Kingdom of Hawai'i. How much do you understand about the political situation in the islands?"

"I've had other things on my mind, if you hadn't noticed," I pointed out dryly.

The suit chuckled again. "Quite." He paused. "You do know how Gordon Ho's father—Danforth Ho, King Kamehameha IV—ascended the throne, though?"

I thought I knew where he was leading. "Deals with the megacorps, among other things."

"Correct. There were many of Danforth Ho's advisors who counseled against making deals with the . . . the corporate *devil*. They were outraged when Ho made the deals initially. They were even more outraged when he stood by those deals, after Secession.

"Have you heard of *Na Kama'aina*?"

"Of course. I'm not totally brain-dead."

"I never thought you were," Barnard said, stroking for all he was worth. "Then you will understand that there is still a large and powerful *Na Kama'aina* faction within the government?"

I nodded. That jibed with what I'd scanned from the suborbital's data system during the flight in.

"The *Ali'i* must balance economic realities with popular perceptions," Barnard continued smoothly. "He must not be *perceived* to be too close to the corporate interests, while still maintaining the status quo. Can you imagine what the *Na Kama'aina* opposition would make of a private meeting—and it would *have* to be private—between King Kamehameha V and a senior representative of a megacorporation with extensive financial interest in the islands?"

Okay, I could see that. I didn't like it—I ground my teeth, I disliked it so intensely—but I could see it. I tried one last counterbattery shot. "But he's the fragging *king*, isn't he? He can do what the frag he wants."

"He *is* the king," Barnard agreed, "but of a constitutional monarchy, with an elected legislature."

I had to cede him the point. Anyone who's been to school knows what happens to a constitutional monarchy when the electorate gets fed up with it. Just ask the Windsors, erstwhile Royal Family of the United Kingdom. Barnard had won one battle, but I wasn't about to pack it in on the whole war. "So send him a message," I tried again.

He laughed. "Do you really think that anyone's electronic communications, even a king's, are immune from interception? There is a possibility—no, a certainty—that the *Na Kama'aina* faction of the government monitors and records all of the *Ali'i*'s communications. How would a supposedly secret message from a megacorporate executive be any different from a private visit?

"No, Mr. Montgomery, once again, I need the message to be delivered, face-to-face, via a deniable asset."

What the frag was it about me? Did I have a slogan blazoned across my forehead—"Hi! I'm a deniable asset. Frag me over"—that only corporate suits could read? "If I did this—I'm not saying I will, but *if*—how the frag would I go about it?" I demanded. "Just stroll on up to the palace and say, 'Got a secret message for King Kam. Oh, and don't *tell anyone*.' Yeah, right. I need some kind of 'in'."

"I can't give you one," Barnard replied at once. "For the reasons I already mentioned, plus others." He smiled, knowing he'd won. "Someone with your talents should have little difficulty arranging a private audience."

Yeah, right. "You're telling me you can't do anything to help me."

"Nothing you should depend on to the exclusion of other options," he corrected smoothly. "Through various other assets, I *am* sending word to the *Ali'i* that he might expect a visit from one Dirk Montgomery, and that he would find value in what you have to say." He shrugged—a little apologetically, I thought. "For obvious reasons, I can't make those messages too ... *noticeable*, if you understand. They may pave your way, however."

"So that's it? You want me to go see the fragging king, and tell him, 'Hey, Brah, Yamatetsu *didn't* cack the yak, cross my heart and hope to croak?'"

"Stripped of the sarcasm ... yes."

I shook my head. Better and better, oh boy. "I'll think about it."

"Don't think too long," he warned me quietly. "There are various factions who wish to see you dead. The yakuza, of course, and the *real* killers of Tokudaiji-*san*."

"Who are ... ?"

Barnard blinked. "ALOHA. I would have thought that was obvious. They would like to see you unable to testify that it was *not* a corporate-sanctioned assassination."

I hadn't thought that one through all the way, but frag it, it made an ugly kind of sense.

"Think fast," the corporator stressed again, "and *act*. There is no need to contact me again on this matter. Either I will hear of your success through other channels, or word will reach me of your unfortunate death."

"You've got a nice way with words, anyone ever tell you that?" I ground my teeth again, so hard I expected enamel to flake off.

"Do you have any questions, Mr. Montgomery?"

I considered a smart-ass answer, but decided against it. "Just one," I said after a moment. "Off point, I suppose, but I'm curious. You said Sharon Young was doing some work for you in Cheyenne, and it was connected to this cluster-frag. *How*?"

He smiled faintly. "I wondered if you would get around to asking that. The individual I asked Ms. Young to trace—Jonathan Bridge, if you recall—has connections with the islands. In fact, under the name 'Kane' "—he pronounced it *CAH-nay*—"he is one of the major human and metahuman leaders of ALOHA."

My turn to blink in surprise. "Hold the phone," I said. " 'One of the major human and metahuman leaders'? What the frag does that mean?"

"The true leader of ALOHA is actually a feathered serpent," he told me. "A vassal of the Great Dragon Ryumyo, if my intelligence is correct."

"So the group that wants to give you grief is run by a fragging *dragon*?" I shook my head. "Remind me not to hang out in your backyard anymore, Barnard. I don't like your playmates."

The suit chuckled once more. Then his face grew deadly serious, and something cold and nasty twisted in my gut. "There's one more thing I should tell you, Mr. Montgomery," he said quietly. "There is even more to this matter than you understand . . . or to be honest, than *I* understand. It would seem that some . . . *previous acquaintances* of yours have some involvement."

"What the frag does that mean?"

"I take it this is not a secure line." He didn't phrase it as a question. "Then all I can tell you is that Adrian Skyhill would appear to have some interest in the outcome.

"Good day, Mr. Montgomery." And the screen went blank.

12

Barnard *couldn't* have meant that.

Could he? I sat on my doss's Torquemada bed and I stared at the wall.

He *couldn't* have meant it . . .

Why the frag did he *say* it, then? There was only one way I could possibly interpret his words, and, by frag, Barnard must have known that. Adrian Skyhill . . .

Memories bubbled back up—the terror and pain and death and chaos under Fort Lewis four years ago. Fragments of *The Dream*. Oh, fragging Jesus.

Insect spirits. What the frag *else* could he have meant? Dr. Adrian Skyhill—erstwhile managing director of Yamatetsu's Integrated Systems Products facility in Fort Lewis—had been a shaman. An *Insect* shaman. He, or someone like him, had summoned the Queen of the Wasp spirits. The same Queen that had killed Toshi and Hawk and Rodney and many others. The same Queen that had burned off my left arm. The same Queen that had run the . . . the *hive,* I suppose is the right word . . . that had tried to *assimilate* my sister, Theresa. Oh fragging Christ on a crutch. How the frag were *insect spirits* involved in this?

Fragging hell, didn't the bugs have other things to worry about at the moment? The pogroms. The "cleansing" of the Universal Brotherhood across North America. And—for Christ's sake—the fragging bugs taking over Chicago . . .

My sole encounter with insect spirits had left me maimed; I'd only survived because others had given their lives to destroy the Queen. With a supreme effort I bit back on the fear, forced it down. Barnard's words were something to remember, his warning something to take to heart . . .

But in the future. For the moment there weren't any insect spirits or Insect shamans around (*were* there?). I was still up to my nostrils in drek, but—at this precise moment—the putative involvement of insect spirits didn't make the drek any deeper. I fell back on the bed, shifted my sightless stare from wall to ceiling.

So fragging Barnard wanted me to get in touch with the fragging *Ali'i,* did he? How in frag was I going to do that? For all the ego-stroking Barnard had given me, I had the nasty, twisty feeling that he had more confidence in my abilities than I did at the moment. I could hope that his estimate was more accurate than mine, but that didn't help my lousy self-esteem one iota.

How was I going to contact King Kamehameha V ... without getting geeked in the process? I needed resources. Maybe Kat and those other shadowrunners ...

That thought fired off all kinds of subtle warning bells in my gut. I paused and mentally worked it through. Just what was it that was bothering me so much? Something Barnard had said, partially, but there were other elements to it as well. I replayed the telecom conversation in my mind.

It was Barnard's comments on ALOHA that were bothering me, I figured that one out at once. Why? He'd said one of the sub-bosses of ALOHA was Kane, aka Jonathan Bridge. The real head honcho was a feathered serpent, who might or might not be a vassal of the Great Dragon Ryumyo.

"The bakeware." "The big worm." A pretty decent description of Ryumyo, *neh*? Which implied, if I took it at face value, that Kat and her little friends ...

... Were ALOHA. And suddenly a bunch of other puzzling little elements fell into place. Zack the ork's reaction at hearing about Scott's death—his interpretation of death by belly-bomb as "doing it up right." That certainly fit in with the idea of ideologically driven terrorists, didn't it? Add to that the fact—which I'd almost forgotten—that Kat and the rest, who claimed they were helping me merely because I was a friend of Te Purewa, didn't seem to *know* much about Te Purewa at all. They called him "Marky," not the new Polynesian name he'd taken for himself. If they were really his close chummers, as they'd implied, wouldn't they respect his rather earnest wishes and call him Te Purewa (and maybe stick their tongues out at him from time to time)?

You're reaching, Montgomery, I told myself firmly, *really reaching.* There wasn't one thing I could point to and say "proof." Intriguing hints, maybe. Totally circumstantial evidence—well, not even that. Who the frag knew—maybe

Te Purewa only did his more-Maori-then-the-Maoris trip with new acquaintances, and didn't mind close chummers calling him the familiar Marky. And even if the phrase Beta had used *was* "the big worm"—and not "the bakeware"— was I justified in making the logical leap and implicating Ryumyo? Got me, chummer.

Still, it *was* a possibility, and I had to take it into consideration. No more contact with Kat and crew, then. And, a sudden chilling thought, I had to get the frag out of this doss and find somewhere else to flop. Kat had told Zack to "get my bike ready." What if that preparation had included the addition of a homing beacon of some kind? So frag it, I had to ditch this doss, and I had to ditch the Suzuki while I was at it. With a general curse at corporations, yaks, terrorists, kings, and the whole fragging Kingdom of Hawai'i, I forced myself to my feet and headed for the door.

Thanks be to chummer Quincy, *again*. Another one of the wizzer little features with which he'd juiced my pocket 'puter was the software that allowed me to make the next best thing to certified credsticks at a moment's notice. Slip a real credstick—the kind that has personal identification datawork and all that drek, on it—into one slot; slide a credstick "blank" into the other. The software smoothly transfers cred from the ident stick to the blank. (Okay, hold the phone, I know *any* 'puter can do that. The feature that sets Quincy's code apart from the usual 'puter facility is that it erases all "audit trails" in the process. Normally, when you transfer cred from stick to stick, both "donor" and "recipient" sticks archive details of the transaction. Anyone with the right toys—cops, mainly—can backtrack this kind of transfer without breaking any skull-sweat. With Quincy's toys, both sticks *think* they're archiving the appropriate data . . . but neither is. Try to trace the audit trail later, and you'll come up empty. And *no*, the software *isn't* good enough to slam a credit balance onto a blank stick *without* taking that sum from a legitimate stick. Quincy's a technomancer, not a miracle worker.)

So that's what I did, sheltering like a squatter in the entry alcove of a boarded-up building. I transferred a couple of hundred nuyen from "Brian Tozer's" credstick to a virgin blank. Reassured that I wouldn't be leaving a great, glowing electronic trail that yaks and ALOHAs and other assorted reprobates could follow, I got to work on finding a new squat.

First order of biz was to get out of Ewa. I'd have loved to have taken the little Suzuki Custom—I'd actually come to like it—but I couldn't be totally certain I'd cleared it of any homing beacons. So I hopped The Bus—that's what it had emblazoned on the side in bright yellow, The Bus, in case anyone mistook it for, say, The Art Gallery, or something— and cruised north into Waipahu. Apparently, this used to be another distinct city, like Ewa, recently absorbed into the sprawling mass that was Honolulu.

If I hadn't been paying attention to the street signs and pestered The Bus driver with idiotic questions, it would have felt like I'd never left Ewa. Waipahu felt much the same, kind of like Renton on a good-air day, and that made me feel at home.

I checked into a hotel called the Ilima Joy. The sign out front advertised rates by the day, week, or month, but judging by the scantily clad individuals who amorously accosted me on the way in, the place could probably have done good trade charging by the hour. I got myself a "convenience suite"—in other words, with its own drekker, telecom, and hot plate—and slotted my "blind" stick to pay a week in advance (a bargain at 350 nuyen). In most parts of the world, it's a legal requirement that hotel guests provide some kind of ident. I was all ready with one of my secondary aliases— not good enough to get a credstick or to travel, but *certainly* good enough to register at the Ilima Joy. I needn't have bothered. The bored-looking clerk just handed me a stylus and told me to sign in on the touchscreen of the battered registration computer. I overcame the urge to sign in as "I.M.N. Alias" or something similar, but made sure my signature was absolutely illegible, even after computer enhancement. Taking the grimy key-card the clerk handed me, I walked up the two flights of stairs and found room 301.

If this was a convenience suite, I wondered at once, whose convenience was it supposed to enhance? Not mine, chummer, that's for damn sure. The drekker was private— probably because nobody else would want one that didn't work—and the door to its alcove was distinctly missing. The hot plate apparently *did* work, judging by the scorch marks on the wall and the countertop; I couldn't imagine myself trying it out. And the telecom was also functional, if limited to outgoing calls only (no doubt monitored, and charged for, at the front desk). Still, it was all I really needed at the moment.

The first order of business was to check out the legitimate approaches to the *Ali'i* . . .

No, the *first* order of business was to get some sleep. Being hunted takes it out of you, chummer, trust me on that one. It wasn't so much my body that was tired as my mind, my emotions. Sleep is a weapon—somebody (Argent, maybe?) had told me that once—and I figured it was time to bring that weapon to bear.

The sun was just rising over the skyrakers of downtown Honolulu—or I guessed it was, at least; the view from my convenience suite at the Ilima Joy didn't give me much of a view, apart from a noisome alley and the back of another decrepit rooming house.

Now it was time to check out the legitimate approaches to the *Ali'i* . . . if nothing else, to eliminate them. I had it in the back of my mind that some monarchies—I don't know where I'd picked this up—have always allowed the populace to contact their ruler directly—to "cry Harold," or whatever the frag the term was. Who knew, maybe King Kamehameha V had something similar in place. I fired up the telecom and started browsing through the online directory.

It didn't take me long to track down the number of the information desk at the Iolani Palace. I placed the call, and then had to sit through a recorded message telling me about the availability of tours and other such useless drek. Only when that chip had played out did I have the option of speaking to a flesh-and-blood receptionist.

Well, what do you know—there *was* a simple procedure through which citizens of the Kingdom of Hawai'i could arrange for an audience with the *Ali'i*. So the plastic-faced receptionist told me, at least, through his fashion-model smile. All that was necessary was for me to give my name and SIN and make an appointment. There even happened to be a slot open in the king's schedule . . . in early spring of '57. If I wanted to take it, all I'd have to do was to arrange for the requisite security and background check . . . I hung up, of course.

What next? For almost an hour I wracked my brain. Frag, if this had been Seattle, I was pretty sure I'd be able to arrange a meeting with good old Governor Schultz. But that would have required a whole bunch of shadowy contacts and resources I just didn't have here in the islands. Back to the directory again, and this time I dredged up a number for the Executive Offices at the Iolani Palace. Again, I placed a call.

With much the same result. A polite functionary informing me that of *course* I could arrange for a message to be passed to the *Ali'i*. All I had to do was give my name, SIN, arrange for the requisite background check ... I hung up, of course.

I was starting to come up dry at the old mental well. On a wild-assed hunch, I even checked the directory for listings under the name "Ho." When the first of seven screens filled with names and LTG numbers, I fragging near despaired. I hung up, of course.

I needed a break, I needed something to jump-start my synapses. If I were really hard-hooped about security, I'd never leave the damn room, but that just wasn't going to work. I needed food, and—more important—I needed coffee. (That was *one* major thing I'd decided I liked about the islands, incidentally. Nobody seemed to have heard of soykaf; even coffee shops served the *real* thing. Bliss beyond measure.) So I strolled downstairs and into the ratty coffee shop next door to the Ilima Joy.

And almost had a coronary arrest on the spot as I saw a face I recognized. Over in the back corner, sitting at a table, idly watching the comings and goings of the patrons, lingering over a mug of coffee. It was the same little bird-boned woman I'd spotted at the Cheeseburger in Paradise. Her eyes lit on mine as I walked in, and I almost had a childish accident. It took me a moment to calm myself down. *Coincidence, for frag's sake,* I told myself firmly. It *had* to be coincidence. This was a free fragging country, wasn't it? Little bird-boned women could take coffee wherever the frag they liked. Sure, she seemed to be paying an inordinate amount of attention to my face, but that was just my paranoia playing up. "The guilty flee where none pursueth," and all that drek. Frag it, she'd never so much as seen my face before, had she? She hadn't been there when I'd walked into the Cheeseburger in Paradise yesterday, and the only time I'd laid eyes on her was via the security camera system. Even so, it took me a lot more effort than it probably should have to turn my back on her and jander over to the counter.

I didn't stay there long—not just because of the bird-boned woman, though her presence certainly didn't help any. I drank several cups of fine coffee, scarfed down a sandwich billed as *ono*—some kind of fish, apparently, even though it could well have been Styrofoam packing material, judging by the dry texture—then I left. On the way out through the lobby and up the stairs, I used what tradecraft I could to pick out anyone tailing me. Nobody, specifically not Mrs. Bird-Bone. Thank the spirits for small favors. I returned to my room and locked the door.

If I'd been hoping my sojourn in the coffee shop would jar something loose from my brain, I was sorely disappointed. I sat back down at the telecom—trying to convince my body and brain that it was time to get back to work—but then I just stared at it for a good five minutes. To meet a king . . . how do you go about it? And, more to the point, how do you do it *fast*?

The telecom beeped, and I jumped so hard I almost sent the chair over backward. I glared at the screen. Yes, the icon told me it was an incoming call . . . despite the placard on the wall over the unit saying NO INCOMING CALLS. I blinked at it.

And then I brought the telecom online to receive the call. What else could I do?

It wasn't Barnard, as I'd half expected. It wasn't Kat or Moko or an urbane-looking Japanese assassin, as I'd half feared. No, it was a handsome Polynesian man about my own age. Strong-featured, he was, with the kind of nose you could classify as "noble," and eyes as dark and hard as flint. His black hair was worn long, shoulder-length in the back, a little shorter on the sides, and was perfectly groomed. The framing of the image was such that I couldn't see his clothing, but beneath his chin there was something that could maybe be a corp-style split collar. He smiled at me, showing perfect teeth. "Mr. Montgomery," he said with a slight accent that sounded faintly British, "please don't hang up. I understand you need to talk to me."

"And who the hell are you?" I demanded, though I had a nasty, nagging feeling I already knew.

"My name is Gordon Ho," the man said calmly. "You may also know me as King Kamehameha V."

13

King Kamehameha. Frag me blind.

"Your Majesty," I said slowly—was that the correct form of address?—while I tried to get my racing, panicky thoughts in order. Then I blurted out the question that was in the forefront of my mind—probably not the most politic thing to say to a fragging king, but there you go. "How the frag did you get this number?"

King Kamehameha V smiled. "Think about it for a moment, Mr. Montgomery," he suggested quietly. "The Kingdom of Hawai'i is a sovereign nation, and I'm head of its government. While our capabilities don't match those of UCAS, for example, they're still fairly formidable." His smile grew a touch broader. "Certainly formidable enough to track down the number of someone who's called the switchboard at the palace several times in the past few hours." The smile twisted, became an ironic grimace. "I still have the loyalty of *some* members of the nation's military intelligence service, at least."

I thought about that for a moment. You got it, chummer, I was playing *way* out of my league. I thought I'd covered myself pretty well—well enough to keep prying corps and yaks and terrorists off my back. *Not* well enough to block the military intelligence service of a fragging nation-state. Oh, my aching head . . .

I nodded acceptance, or maybe it was surrender "Okay. So . . . ?"

"So why am I contacting you?" The king shrugged slightly. "I'd rather thought you'd be the one telling *me,* Mr. Montgomery. I've heard through . . . various sources . . . that you wished to speak to me on a matter of some grave concern."

That set me back for a moment. Sure, Barnard had said he'd be spreading the word "through various other assets"—

his phrase—that one Dirk Montgomery would be trying to arrange a meeting. But I hadn't expected an instant response—well, I hadn't expected *any* response, to tell the truth. And I *sure* hadn't expected that the fragging *Ali'i* would take the time and trouble to track *me* down to talk.

"That's true, Your Majesty," I said slowly. "Er . . . is that the correct form of address?"

That brought another smile to Gordon Ho's face. "Not precisely," he told me. "The correct phrase is *e ku'u lani*—'O my royal one'—but I'm only a stickler for the old forms when the *kahunas* are around." His smile faded, and his expression became that of a professional poker player or, I suddenly thought, a corporate exec. "I've invested considerable time and effort in arranging to speak to you, Mr. Montgomery," he went on, his voice even and calm. (*Yeah, right,* I thought, *the time and effort of lackeys, maybe.*) "I'd like you to tell me a reason why I should invest any more in you."

I paused. "This isn't a secure line," I pointed out at last, "not at this end at least."

"I'm well aware of that," Ho said drily. "But I'm certain you can find ways around the problem, am I correct?"

Again I paused, thinking through exactly what I could get away with saying on a potentially compromised line and still pique his interest. "According to the news, some heavy happenings have been going down recently," I began.

"True."

Jumping into what sounded like a real non sequitur, I made my voice as casual as I could. "Oh, by the way, the father of a college pal says hoi."

He blinked in momentary confusion. Then I saw his eyes narrow as he made the mental connection . . . or, at least, I *hoped* he did. "Yes," he said musingly, "yes, he might well be sending greetings.

"Do you still wish to speak with me face-to-face?"

I swallowed hard. "Yes, *e ku'u lani*," I said, butchering the pronunciation. "Or maybe it'd be better all around if I did it over a secure line." That wasn't according to Barnard's instructions, but it wasn't his hoop hanging out in the wind.

"Unacceptable," the *Ali'i* responded immediately. "There's no such thing as a totally secure line, as you should know. If the matters you wish to discuss are truly weighty, then a personal meeting is the only thing that'll serve."

"I'm not sure I'd feel too comfortable just jandering up to the front door of the palace," I pointed out.

"But that's exactly what you *must* do," Ho told me coldly. "If this is really important, that's exactly how you'll handle it."

"I'd prefer neutral ground," I tried again.

"Of course you would, but that, too, is unacceptable. 'Neutral' for you is potentially hostile territory for me." I digested that one quickly. Were things getting *that* dicey in the political in-fighting game? "You will visit the palace," he repeated, "and present yourself at the reception desk at"—he glanced off-screen—"one o'clock this afternoon. That gives you two hours to decide whether to accept my invitation, Mr. Montgomery." He smiled frostily. "Would that suit you?"

No, it *wouldn't* fragging suit me at all, I wanted to say. "There are other concerns—".

"There always are," he broke in. "But I leave it to you to deal with them in whatever manner you see fit."

Great. Thanks, Kam. I had to try once more. "If you've figured out what the matter is I want to talk to you about—"

And again he cut me off, "Are you insinuating that the *Ali'i* of the Kingdom of Hawai'i might want to take personal retribution against you?" he asked icily.

"Well . . . *yes*, in a word."

"Then you have my word that isn't the case."

"No insult intended, *e ku'u lani,* but—"

"You need something a little more tangible than my given word—than the given word of the descendent of King Kamehameha the Great, is that it?" His smile was back, but now it had a real nasty edge to it. "Then perhaps *this* would suffice."

His eyes stayed locked on mine, and his lips moved. I couldn't hear a sound, maybe because he was using a kind of hushphone or something. His barracuda smile grew broader.

And, just like that, something *snicked* through the window of my doss, and slammed into the wall beside me. Instinctively, I threw myself to the ground, scrambling across the small room to flatten myself against the wall under the window. For a couple of seconds I just crouched there, hyperventilating.

I could still see King Kam's face on the telecom screen,

though I knew I was out of range of the unit's vidcam. "Is that sufficient support to my word, Mr. Montgomery?" he asked my empty chair.

Message received loud and clear, O my royal one: *If I'd wanted you dead, you'd be dead.* "Quite sufficient," I told the telecom, trying vainly to keep my voice steady.

"One o'clock, then. I expect an interesting conversation." And with that, King Kamehameha V signed off.

I took off my shoe, threw it at the telecom keyboard, and the unit disconnected. It was another three minutes before I felt comfortable standing up.

Frag, I was boned. No, I was so far *past* boned that it would take light twenty years to get from here to there. I was playing with the government of a sovereign state. A fragging *government*. What kind of resources could a fragging *government* bring to bear at the whim of its ruler? Heavy-duty electronic interception and tracking, for one. A fragging sniper for another. What the hell else? I didn't know, and I didn't *want* to know.

Idly, I stuck my little finger through the bullet hole in the window—nicking myself, incidentally, on the sharp material. Clean-edged, perfectly circular—a little larger than nine millimeter, I judged. The round had been so fast that it had basically drilled through the window composite, too quickly for the brittle material to even crack, let alone shatter. The bullet hole in the opposite wall was a touch bigger, and so deep that I couldn't reach the bottom with my finger. It was a weight-bearing wall—good fragging thing, otherwise the round would have cored its way through my room and several others, before coming to rest in a wall or a hot plate or someone's headbone. (But of course the sniper had probably *known* it was a reinforced weight-bearing wall.)

Okay, I got the point. I wasn't dead, which meant I probably wouldn't *become* so on my appearance at the Iolani Palace. After my meeting with Gordon Ho, of course, all bets would be off. If he figured I wasn't telling him all I knew or wasn't giving him the answers he wanted to his questions, there wasn't much stopping him from sending me downstairs into a small, dark room—palaces had dungeons or something, didn't they?—where large men would ask the questions again under less agreeable conditions. Fragging swell.

Maybe I should just pull the quick fade. Maybe Kat and

the rest—ALOHA or not—would help me disappear into the shadows. Maybe—and this was a *big* maybe—I'd be able to stay one jump ahead of the factions already out looking for me. Oh yes, and add to the playlist the Yamatetsu payback team that Barnard would send after me when he learned I hadn't delivered his message to the *Ali'i*. I was pretty good at keeping a low profile, I knew that . . . but over the long haul, "pretty good" wouldn't cut no ice. I figured my odds at surviving a week at about fifty-fifty. A month—call it seventy-five–twenty-five. A year? Maybe a one-in-ten chance. Long enough to look back on all this and laugh? I'd rather bet on the survival of a snowball in a plasma furnace, chummer.

Looked like I'd be visiting the Iolani Palace in about an hour, didn't it?

The telecom—the one supposedly locked out to incoming calls—chirruped again. I glared at it. When it stubbornly refused to disassociate into its component atoms, I sighed. Gordon Ho calling back with some additional instructions? Whatever. I sat down at the keyboard, pressed the keys to accept the call.

It wasn't Gordon Ho's face that appeared on the screen. No, if I had to describe a face that was diametrically opposite from King Kam's in all facets, it wouldn't be too far from the man I saw before me. Smooth skin so pale it looked almost translucent. Silver hair, long and flowing. Eyes the color of arctic ice in Global Geographic trideo shows—maybe blue, maybe green, maybe gray, depending on the light and your mood. Hollow cheeks, small nose, small mouth. Ageless, too. If you'd asked me to peg his age, I'd have put it anywhere between twenty and a hundred. Instinctively, I looked at his ears—no points, he wasn't an elf.

There was something . . . well, *disturbing* is the closest I can come to it . . . about his appearance. Austere, he was, aloof, distant . . . almost inhumanly so. I didn't really want to think about what those eyes might have seen.

"Mr. Montgomery," he said. His voice was . . . *strange* . . . too, thin, reedy, almost piping, but also strong, in the way that a stiletto is both delicate and lethal.

"Sorry," I said, trying to keep my bravado up, "someone's already won the prize for guessing that one. Who the hell are *you*?"

"A friend." No smile, no expression at all, accompanied the declaration.

"Could have fooled me. Are you sure you don't have the wrong number? Wrong Montgomery, for that matter."

"I don't think so." Again no smile, although there was a tinge of something in his voice that could be detached amusement. "I have a message for you, Mr. Montgomery. A warning, in fact."

"I don't *want* any—"

His voice didn't rise in volume, but it cut me off as effectively as a gag. "A friendly warning, Mr. Montgomery. I'd advise you listen."

My bravado was wearing kind of thin at the moment, so I just shrugged.

"Through no fault of your own, you've become involved in matters much too weighty for you," the austere face told me. (*No drek, Sherlock,* I managed not to say.) "A long-standing conflict is coming to a head in Hawai'i. Forces are marshaling."

"ALOHA and the corps. No drek."

"Yes, those too," Mr. Parchment-Face paused. "Even when one fully understands the dynamics of a conflict, it's often difficult to keep from getting overwhelmed by it ... overwhelmed and crushed. When one is unaware of what the conflict is truly about, it's usually impossible."

"So *tell* me."

This time the amusement—cold, distant, but unmistakable—was clear in his voice. "I think not, not at this time. I merely suggest you take my words to heart. Terminate your involvement in matters beyond your control and comprehension. In more familiar terms ... stay out of it, Mr. Montgomery. *Right* out."

"I would if I had the opportunity," I told him honestly.

"Then *make* the opportunity."

"Who the frag are you anyway?"

"As I said, a friend," the man repeated softly.

"And you're telling me you know what's going down?" He nodded. "Yeah, right," I snorted. "*Prove* it if you want me to pay any attention to you." It was only after the words were out of my mouth that I remembered the last "proof" anyone had provided me. Out of reflex, I glanced at the bullet hole in the window.

And so I missed the first instants of the change. By the

time my eyes were back on the screen, the man's outlines were flowing, shifting—*morphing*. Nothing I saw on that screen was beyond the capabilities of a hot-shot kid with a Cray-Amiga submicro running FX Oven . . . but, deep down, I *knew* what I was watching wasn't any kind of special effect. The man's skull expanded, elongated. Those icy eyes swelled, shifting apart, migrating toward the sides of the skull. His mouth opened, showing dagger teeth. Beyond the serried rows of teeth, something moved—a black tongue, forked like a snake's.

"Is this sufficient proof?" asked the dragon.

14

The big worm. The fragging bakeware.

That's who it had to be, didn't it? Ryumyo the fragging Great Dragon. Great fragging Christ on a crutch. Whatever happened to a low fragging profile?

My hands were shaking, making it harder to hot-wire the car I was boosting—a nice, nondescript Volkswagen Elektro, rusted out here and there. I wiped the sweat from my eyes with the back of my hand and tried not to drek myself.

A nice, relaxing sojourn in the islands. Just deliver a message, soak up a few rays, get wasted on mai-tais, then it's all over. That's how Barnard had pitched it to me.

Yeah, *right*. Ryumyo, the fragging dragon, had it chipped, didn't he? "You've become involved in matters much too weighty for you," that's what he'd told me. No drek. Corps and yaks and terrorists, oh my. And now kings and fragging *dragons* ... Oh yes, and we can't forget the insect spirits, can we? My dance card was already full, and more guests kept showing up at the cotillion. Frag it to hell and back. I must have been something *real* nasty in a past life— nun-rapist, maybe, mass murderer, or perhaps tax collector—to warrant this kind of drekky karma.

I finally managed to get the Elektro to admit that I *did* have the right keycode, and the little flywheel deep in the car's guts spun up to speed. I tried to burn rubber, but the mobile coffin just whined at me accusingly and pulled away from the curb at a slow walk. (According to some Volkswagen propaganda I'd scanned a while back, the Electro is supposed to have a top end of 75 klicks. *Sure*, chummer. The Volkswagen engineers must have dropped the fragging thing off a bridge to get that figure.) I pointed the Elektro east, and cruised through the noontime traffic.

Spirits ... I would purely *loooove* to take the nice dragon's friendly advice and just butt the hell out of all this. It hadn't been my choice to stick my nose into anyone's biz. Now, if I made one wrong step, my nose was probably the largest fragment of my anatomy anyone would find left in one piece. Maybe after I'd talked to King Kamehameha V. Yeah, right.

I was ten minutes early for my appointment—audience?—when I pulled into the public parking facility a block from the Iolani Palace. I bid a less-than-fond farewell to the Elektro—Volkswagen's ergonomic gurus must have left it up to a band of munchkins to spec out the headroom—and took the elevator up to street level.

And that's where I stopped and listened for a minute or two to my pulse beating a wild tattoo in my ears. Logic fought with instinct. It was instinct that told me to use all the tradecraft I knew, to look for shadows and tails, to watch my hoop, to approach my target without being spotted. Logic told me that was a load of bollocks. I was going to be jandering into a fragging *palace*. Lot of good tradecraft was going to do me there. And anyway, I recalled, looking down at the nicks the window composite had left in my finger, Gordon Ho's sniper had given me convincing evidence that the *Ali'i* didn't want me dead yet. Still, it took a good two minutes for logic to suppress the whimperings of reflex. Finally, I strode across the road—almost getting greased by a courier on a pedal-bike, despite the fact that I had the light—and toward the Iolani Palace.

The building itself sat in the middle of more than half a hectare of grassy turf, almost indecently green and vibrant. It didn't look big enough to be the capitol of a sovereign nation. Frag, you couldn't fit more than a hundred bureaucrats and datapushers into the place. But then I glanced across the road at the *Haleaka*-something, the big, ferrocrete Government House. I supposed it made sense; separate the day-to-day biz of the government from the symbolic, ritualistic drek. The wrought iron gate leading onto the grounds was open, flanked by four guards—all big boys, trolls or orks dressed in white uniforms that were almost blinding in the brilliant sun. (*Stupid,* I thought at first, but then I realized these guys were just symbolic. If you're going to stand at attention out in the beating tropical sun, white gear makes a lot more sense than dark camo. The *real* hard-men would be out of sight, somewhere in the shade, but able to respond to trouble in an instant.) I jandered on through. One of the trolls gave me my daily dose of stink-eye, and I saw his big, horny knuckles whiten on the forestock of his H&K assault rifle. Chummer, I just *smiled.* At the moment trolls with assault rifles were low on my priority list of things to drek myself over.

Up the driveway I jandered, up the low steps, in the front door. And into the blissful cool of a lobby/reception area. Scott had told me the Iolani Palace was about a hundred and fifty years old, and now I could really *feel* it. Not that the place looked rundown. Far from it, it was perfectly maintained. But the very feel of the air hinted at the history that had passed through its doors, up its stairways, across its dark wood floors.

There were four more white-clad ceremonial guards—trolls, again—one in each corner of the room. More stink-eye. In front of me was a huge reception desk made from the same dark wood as the floor. Behind it sat a young Polynesian woman, her attractiveness undiminished by the fact that she was an ork. No stink-eye here. She was watching me with a welcoming smile that, under other circumstances, might have had me running around in circles, dragging a wing and whimpering. I walked up to the desk. "My name's Dirk Montgomery," I told her.

"Yes?" Then she blinked and looked down at a 'puter flatscreen set into the desktop. "Oh, yes," she said brightly, "I'm sorry, Mr. Montgomery, you *are* expected, of course. If you'll just wait a moment . . ." Her eyes rolled up in her head, and for the first time I noticed that a fiber-optic line connected her to the desktop system. In a couple of heartbeats her dark eyes were smiling up into mine again. "Mr. Ortega will be with you momentarily," she told me.

When she said, "momentarily," she meant it. I'd barely finished thanking her when a door in the wall behind her opened and a suit emerged.

Not "suit" as in "corp." No, "suit" as in Zoé or one of the other upper-tier designers. When Mr. Ortega came through the door, it was the suit I noticed first, and only as an afterthought the man who was wearing it. A pasty-faced little guy, pale skin, salt-and-pepper hair. He looked kind of dusty, like a librarian who hadn't been let out of the stacks for a couple of years. But the suit and the eyes—flinty-hard, rather like the *Ali'i*'s, I thought suddenly—were enough to tell me this was a honcho with real juice.

Those eyes gave me the top-to-toe scan, sizing me up . . . and narrowing as though he didn't particularly like the conclusions he'd reached. "Mr. Montgomery," he said politely, but with no human warmth. He extended a thin hand. "Your weapon, please."

Out the corner of my eye, I saw the white-suits stiffen as I reached—*very* slowly, with my left hand—under my shirt-tails and pulled out my Manhunter. I safed the weapon, going so far as to pop out the clip before I handed it over to Ortega. Distastefully, as though I'd offered him a dead fish, he took it and passed it in turn to the receptionist, who made it disappear into a drawer. "You will, of course, receive it back once your business is concluded," Ortega told me. Then he turned his back and strode toward the door, the lines of his narrow shoulders indicating he fully expected me to follow.

Follow I did, through the door—through a sophisticated suite of metal detectors and chemsniffers, I had no doubt—and into a kind of anteroom with three doors. Ortega turned around again, and again he gave me the top-to-bottom scan. "Yes, well," he said at last, "you must, of course, wear a jacket and tie for an audience with the *Ali'i.*" I almost chuckled aloud—the last time I'd heard words to that effect I'd been trying to sleaze my way into a restaurant called La Maison d'Indochine back in Seattle—but suppressed my amusement. Aide de camp, maître d'—I guess there *wasn't* that much difference, when you thought about it. I watched the laser-eyed little man, surprised that he didn't look even slightly Polynesian, as he opened a closet set into the richly paneled walls and pulled out some clothes. "A one-oh-five regular should fit." (This seemed to be my week for meeting people with a haberdasher's eye.) He handed over a double-breasted jacket—deep blue with a conservative emerald pinstripe—and a white-and-navy paisley tie. And then he waited.

The collar of my tropical shirt wasn't made for a tie, and if the jacket actually was a one-oh-five regular, I'd put on some weight. But I made do the best I could, and did a model's turn for Ortega. "Yes," he said dryly—I suppose a sense of humor wasn't *de rigueur* this season—and turned his back on me once more.

I followed him through another door and down a short hallway. We stopped at yet another door—some dark, dynamically grained wood this time—and paused. He turned back to me, gave me one last once-over—his frown telling me he didn't like what he saw any better this time—and started in on a protocol lecture. "The *Ali'i* will acknowledge you," he said. "Until that point you will stand with your eyes averted. You will not speak unless addressed, and then you will limit yourself to answers to the *Ali'i's* questions. You will not—"

Mr. Manners was cut off by a click as the door opened behind him. He shot me a scowl—didn't appreciate *pedantus interruptus,* apparently—but turned to whisper something to the white-suit who'd opened the door. After a quiet exchange Ortega stepped aside and gestured for me to go ahead. I did, but not before wishing I had a small-denomination coin handy to tip him (and *really* slot him off). I walked through the door . . .

. . . And into a throne room. I mean a *real* throne room, complete with throne, up on a low dais at the far end. Like a magnet the figure on the throne drew my gaze. A bronze-skinned warrior god—that was my first impression. Tall, muscular, in the prime of his vibrant, vigorous life. He wore pretty much the same getup as the statue of Kamehameha the Great that Scott had shown me: loincloth, a cape of brilliant yellow feathers hung over his shoulders, and a big forward-curving headdress also covered with feathers. His chest was bare, well-muscled, and decorated here and there with tattoos of a geometrical design. If he'd held a spear or a war club in his big hands, it would have looked totally appropriate. In fact, however, what he held was a sophisticated pocket 'puter on which he was taking notes. He looked up as the door clicked shut behind me, and those flinty eyes seemed to pierce me to the core.

It was Gordon Ho—it had taken me this long, a couple of seconds, to recognize him in his glory. Gordon Ho, King Kamehameha V, *Ali'i* of the Kingdom of Hawai'i. When I'd seen him on the telecom screen, my mental impression had been of a young, up-and-coming corporate exec. The telecom hadn't conveyed the size of him—just shy of two meters tall, I guessed; not up to Kamehameha the Great's standard, but still one big boy—and it certainly hadn't done justice to his . . . his *aura.* (I hate the word, but it's the only one that fits.) I could *feel* his personality, his strength of will, like radiant heat penetrating to my core. I'd never met a king before, and for the first time I realized there might be something more to this monarchy drek than a title and—maybe—congenital defects from inbreeding.

He glanced back to his computer, and the removal of his gaze seemed to free me from a spell. For the first time since I'd stepped through the door, I was able to look around at the rest of the room.

It wasn't big, this throne room, about the size of a major corporate boardroom. The floor was hardwood, the walls paneled in the same rich-grained wood as the door I'd passed through. On the wall behind the *Ali'i* was a large coat of arms or seal or something—circular, with words around its circumference. *Ua mau ke ea a ka aina i ka pono,* I managed to pick out . . . whatever the frag that was supposed to mean. In the center of the seal was some kind of emblem incorporating a hibiscuslike flower, a tree that looked like a banyan, and—I drek you not—a fragging *goose.* Framing it were drapes of rich maroon velvet.

Beside and to the left of King Kamehameha another man was on the dais—standing; the only seat in the room was filled with *Ali'i.* An older man, he was, scrawny and weathered, looking like he'd been carved from nut brown wood. He too wore a cape—no feathers, just red fabric—and a loincloth. Around his brow was a headband, and a single feather of some kind protruded from the back, to sag forward—forlornly, I thought—over his forehead. An advisor of some kind, I figured at once. What had Scott called these guys? *Kahunas,* that was it. The *kahuna* looked only a couple of years younger than God himself, but he had the same steely edge in his eyes as Gordon Ho. Not a slag to trifle with.

Two white-suits flanked the dais, and another loomed over me and Ortega, who'd joined me in the room. These boys *were* holding spears, but I noted they also had big-time handguns holstered on their belts.

And then there were the three . . . visitors? supplicants? what would you call them? They stood before the dais, eyes averted as I'd forgotten to do. All humans, all Polynesians . . . and all suits (in the corp sense, this time). One of them turned and shot me a bad look—I was getting pretty goddamned tired of stink-eye by this time—before getting back to his averting.

The *Ali'i* looked up from his notes, and fixed one of the

suits with a sharp look. "Is there any more I should hear on this matter?"

The suit looked up and said formally, "No more, *e ku'u lani.*"

"Good," the king said with a nod. "Then you'll hear my decision within twenty-four hours."

Another of the suits—he looked younger than the rest—opened his mouth to bitch, but the look the *Ali'i* shot him shut him up before he could start. The young suit shifted uncomfortably, then he got back to the averting, too.

The *Ali'i* glanced over in my direction, and I thought I saw a faint smile. "Mr. Montgomery," he said. That wasn't a question, so I didn't speak. Ho shifted his gaze to Ortega by my side. "Please escort Mr. Montgomery to my private office."

Ortega stiffened. "*E ku'u lani,* is that proper?"

Oops, mistake. Regal stink-eye is very different from the run-of-the-mill kind, and I was glad this dose was directed at someone else. Surprisingly, it was the scrawny *kahuna* who said, "It is for the *Ali'i* to decide what is proper and what is not." The reprimand was delivered in a quiet voice, little more than a whisper, but Ortega flinched as though he'd been whipped.

The aide/maître d' nodded and seemed to be trying to swallow his prominent Adam's apple. He tapped me on the arm, and I followed him back out the door.

Leading me through the bowels of the palace, he didn't utter a word for the next few minutes, which suited me just fine. Finally, he stopped before another rich-grained wood door, nodded to the requisite white-suit on guard outside, and turned the knob. Wordlessly, he gestured me in, and this time he didn't follow. I let the door shut behind me before giving the place the once-over.

State-of-the-art, cutting-edge corporate office—that was my first impression. Tech everywhere—not obtrusive or overbearing, but always to hand. Anything and everything to make the life of a busy executive just that one little bit easier or more comfortable. Huge holo unit against one wall; one of those high-tech whiteboard displays, the kind that automatically networks to multiple pocket 'puters via infrared links and lets a dozen people make and annotate drawings and notes; a telecom/commo suite that you'd need an electrical engineering doctorate just to turn on; an electrostatic

printer only marginally bigger than the pieces of paper it
printed on; and—thank God for *something* I fully
understood—a slick little coffee/espresso maker on the credenza.

I suppose I'd expected the decor of the *Ali'i*'s private
office to be something like that of the throne room: dark,
polished woods, somber drapes, that kind of drek. Good try,
but no cigar. The place was light and airy, painted in pale
pastels that made it feel larger than it actually was. The desk
and credenza were macroplast finished in a contrasting pastel. The chairs—there were four of them, one behind the
desk and three in front—weren't the antiques I expected either; instead, they were this-year's-model self-adjusting
units.

Behind the desk was a huge window looking out toward
the mountains north of the city. It looked like a storm was
blowing in, black clouds boiling up over the ragged peaks.
I shook my head, tempted to go over and touch the window
material. There wasn't any of the color-shift I'd always associated with reinforced ballistic composite. If that window
was standard transpex, any yahoo with a rifle could cap the
fragging *Ali'i*, put a pill in the back of his noble skull. Hey,
just wait one tick ... What was wrong with this picture?

A couple of things. First of all ... this shouldn't be an
outside office. Unless I'd gotten myself totally turned
around—possible, but not likely—this place was right in the
fragging middle of the Iolani Palace's second floor.

Second, the view of the mountains I was enjoying was
simply impossible from the site of the palace. Sure, you
could spot the mountains ... but only between corporate
skyrakers, none of which appeared in the view through the
"window." A sophisticated holo display, that's what it had to
be—like the "window" in Adrian Skyhill's office at Fort
Lewis, now that I came to think of it. The sense of *déjà vu*
gave me the shivers. I sat down in one of the visitor's chairs,
and tried to relax while I waited.

I didn't have long to wait—convenient, since I couldn't
relax anyway. The door behind me clicked open, and I reflexively jumped to my feet.

Gordon Ho, King Kamehameha V, had changed again.
Not just his garb, although he had doffed his regalia for a set
of hideously expensive casual clothes. No, his whole
manner—his aura, to use that stupid word—had changed,

too, as if in setting aside his royal trappings he'd set aside the strength of personality I'd sensed in the throne room. Was that strength of personality some kind of magical effect, then, incorporated into the headpiece, perhaps?

Uh-uh, I revised after a moment. The strength was still there; it glinted in his eyes. It was just that Gordon Ho made a strong distinction between ceremony and business, like any good executive.

"*E ku'u lani,*" I began.

Ho gestured casually for me to be seated. "I told you on the phone, it's the *kahunas* who are so set on the old forms, not me." He sat down in the chair behind the desk and leaned back luxuriously. Then, for almost a minute, he just watched me from under his dark brows. His scrutiny wasn't hostile—more curious than anything, I thought—but that didn't make it any more comfortable. I shifted edgily in my chair, and I felt a bead of sweat start to trace its way down my ribs. I tried to match his stare with my own, but it wasn't long before I had to drop my gaze—look at the "picture-window" behind him, at the desk, at the whiteboard, at anything but those flint eyes.

Finally the *Ali'i* stirred, and I felt the intensity of his gaze ease. "Mr. Montgomery," he said slowly, almost speculatively. "Derek Montgomery." He smiled. "I know a little about you, Mr. Montgomery. Born on July 22, 2019 in Seattle, Washington—it *was* still Washington state at that time, wasn't it? One sibling, a younger sister. Both parents killed." His tone of voice was like he was reading, though his gaze was still fixed on my face. It was only when I noticed a faint artificial glint from his corneas that I realized some kind of unit in the desk was projecting my personal data directly into his eyes. "Attended the University of Washington," he continued, "but didn't graduate. Served a tour of duty with Lone Star Security Services Corporation." He shot me a wry grin. "An *abbreviated* tour," he amended ironically, "after which you left the corporation on less than amicable terms.

"Since then"—he shrugged—"very little, really. Occasional hints that you might have been contracting out your services to various individuals, and even to a couple of corporations. But not much concrete data.

"Until your death, confirmed via gene typing and dental records, in 2052." A thick eyebrow quirked. "Interesting,

Mr. Montgomery; I've never chatted with a dead man before."

I shrugged . . . and tried not to show how chilled I was by the ease with which he'd dug up background information on me. Date and place of birth, family details, employment history . . . all of which should have dropped out of public ken when I tubed my SIN number after my break with Lone Star. I'd always thought "zeroed" meant just that—you don't exist anymore, no connection between who you are and who you were, and no easy way of tracking down that drek after the fact. Live and learn, I suppose.

The *Ali'i* leaned forward. "So tell me, Mr. Montgomery, what is a dead man doing in Hawai'i?"

I hesitated. Frag it, I realized Barnard hadn't briefed me enough. Yes, I was supposed to deliver a specific message to King Kam, but what else should I or shouldn't I tell him? "Trying to do something about that graveyard pallor," I temporized, giving myself time to think.

He chuckled softly at that. "Well, perhaps we'll come back to that later." He paused, then his voice changed—time for biz. "You implied you had a message for me. From whom, Mr. Montgomery?"

"Jacques Barnard," I told him. "Senior veep or something at Yamatetsu."

"I know Jacques Barnard," he acknowledged, "a fine gentleman. I assume you've spoken to him recently. Is he enjoying Chiba?"

"Kyoto," I corrected.

"Of course, Kyoto. I wonder . . . did you ever have the chance to see his estate in Beaux Arts?"

"I *did* see his exercise room . . . but it was in Madison Park."

"Quite. And how's his lovely wife—Marie, isn't that it?"

I sighed. "Never met his wife, don't know her name," I told him wearily. "Two questions out of three right. Does that mean I don't win the grand prize?"

The *Ali'i* paused again, and his gaze seemed to pin me to the chair. "Do you always joke so much, Mr. Montgomery?" he asked quietly.

I blinked, and—to my surprise—I told him the truth. "Only when I'm drek-scared."

He smiled at that. "I think I understand." Another pause.

"All right, Mr. Montgomery, I think I can accept your *bona fides*."

Considerate of you, *slot*, is what I *didn't* say. I just nodded.

"So what was Jacques's message?"

I couldn't think of a graceful way of dancing around the issue, so I just said it flat. "He wants me to reassure you that he wasn't behind the assassination of Ekei Tokudaiji."

Gordon Ho's eyebrows shot up at that. "Indeed?"

"Honto," I confirmed. "Indeed."

"Then who was behind it, does Mr. Barnard think?"

"ALOHA," I stated. "Who else?"

The *Ali'i* smiled again. "Quite a number of people, I'd think. Tokudaiji-*san* was an *oyabun* of the yakuza, after all. But I rather think you're right about ALOHA." His hard gaze softened. "Thank you, Mr. Montgomery," he said. "You may consider your message delivered. I didn't really think that Yamatetsu *was* behind the matter, but it's good to receive one more reassurance.

"I'd be very interested in hearing any insight Jacques has on developments," he went on, more conversationally. "Some of my sources are already starting to report increasing popular support for ALOHA on the streets. And in the legislature the opposition party is starting to apply pressure. I'd like to be able to speak with Jacques personally, but . . ." He shrugged. Then his smile changed, and his gaze drilled into me again. "Perhaps *you* can help me with this, Mr. Montgomery," he said deceptively lightly.

Oh frag, not *again* . . .

My thoughts must have shown in my face, because Gordon Ho chuckled. "You look as though it's continuing to be one of those days."

"One of those lifetimes," I corrected.

"Not your first choice on how to spend your stay in the islands, running messages back and forth, is it?" He hesitated, and real curiosity showed in his eyes. "Just how did you get involved in this, Mr. Montgomery?"

"Just lucky, I guess." I sighed. What the frag, if anything about my involvement was a secret, it wasn't *my* secret, and I figured I didn't owe Barnard anything further.

So I told him the story—the short version, the one starting in Cheyenne, not the complete saga including how I'd fallen in with Barnard in the first place. Probably I shouldn't be doing this, I thought while babbling, but frag, there are times when you've just got to talk to *someone*. I couldn't see what practical harm it would do. King Kam had my life in his hands anyway, and I couldn't think of any ways—well, not many ways, at least—that he could glitch things up for me worse than they already were. Besides, now that he wasn't wearing his feathered drek, Gordon Ho didn't seem that much different from me, and I felt myself drawn to like him.

(Which, truth to tell, scared the drek out of me. I'd been drawn to like Barnard, too, hadn't I? And look where that had gotten me . . .)

When I was finished, the young *Ali'i* nodded slowly. "The direct involvement of Ryumyo is somewhat disturbing," he said slowly. (*Somewhat* disturbing? Understatement of the century, *e ku'u lani* . . .) "If that *was* Ryumyo you spoke with, of course."

"One dragon kind of looks like another," I acquiesced dryly.

"Quite." Ho paused. "But it might not have been a dragon at all. Oh, I know it certainly looked like one, but many *kahunas* and hermetic mages could produce an illusion that only another magic-wielder could penetrate."

I blinked at that one. That line of thought hadn't even occurred to me.

"Whether or not Ryumyo *is* personally involved, however, I think the ALOHA connection is fairly certain," the *Ali'i* concluded. He studied me speculatively for a few moments. Then he opened one of the desk drawers, extracted a small item and extended it to me. "Take this, Mr. Montgomery."

I reached out for the object and studied it in my palm. It was a lapel pin or badge—almost a brooch, judging by its size. Intricately worked into the likeness of the crest I'd seen behind the *Ali'i*'s throne, it massed heavy in my hand. "Gold?"

Ho's dark eyes twinkled. "Electroplated. Sorry." He indicated the badge. "This identifies you as officially under the protection of the *Ali'i*, Mr. Montgomery. As far as members of the government service are concerned, it marks you as carrying my authority—some of it, at least."

I snorted. "You mean I've been deputized?"

"You might think of it that way," the *Ali'i* confirmed with a smile. "When you display the badge, you can expect at least some degree of cooperation from servants of the

Crown—government agencies, even *Na Maka'i,* the police. Not the military, however." He shrugged. "You might even find that Tokudaiji-*san*'s security personnel will think twice before gunning you down if they see that," he added thoughtfully. "After all, Tokudaiji-*san* was a servant of the Crown, in his own way, and his help did not go unreciprocated."

I looked skeptically down at the badge in my hand. Maybe the *Ali'i* was right, maybe Tokudaiji's samurai would feel some kind of ... I don't know, patriotic loyalty to the Crown or some drek ... and decide not to pulp me if they saw this. Maybe not. I certainly wasn't going to depend on it. I'd made the mistake of thinking a badge could protect me during an earlier phase of my career, and it hadn't taken me long to realize how fragging wrong I was. Still, it couldn't hurt. I nodded thanks to the *Ali'i* and pinned it onto the collar of my shirt.

Ho's eyes never left my face. "I wouldn't force you into a situation that you find uncomfortable ..."

I finished the thought for him "... But you *do* want me to get word to Barnard that you're trolling for ideas." I sighed again. "Yeah, okay, I'll see what I can do ... *if* it doesn't mean too much exposure." Frag, intermediary *again.* Why oh why don't people *ever* learn that killing the messenger just isn't a good idea?

"I appreciate that, Mr. Montgomery. Now—" Ho stopped as a knock sounded on the door. *"Hele mai."*

The door opened, and a functionary—not Ortega, though he could have been the gray-faced man's Polynesian half brother—stepped into the room. *"Kala mai ia'u, e ku'u lani,"* he began, then noticed me for the first time and clammed up on the spot. He looked at the *Ali'i* with a "what the frag do I do?" expression on his face.

Gordon Ho chuckled. "This man is in my confidence," he told the functionary quietly. "You have a report for me?"

" 'Ae, e ku'u lani," the older man said with a bobbing nod. *"I luna o ka Puowaina."*

"In English, please," the *Ali'i* said sharply.

The functionary looked almost as scandalized as Ortega had in the throne room. Just to make sure he got the idea, I pulled back the lapel of the jacket Ortega had loaned me, so he could spot my deputy's badge nice and clearly.

He spotted it, all right, and I could see in his eyes just

how little he thought of the whole thing. But at least he managed to control himself. *"Ae, e ku'u lani.* Yes, O my royal one, of course.

"The"—he shot me a sidelong look, and I could *see* him mentally editing what he'd been about to say—"the *incidents* on Puowaina seem to have escalated, *e ku'u lani.* The most recent one is quite disturbing—that's how the chief of *Na Maka'i* describes it, 'quite disturbing.' The . . . *level of activity* is more intense."

"But nothing could come of it, correct?" Ho asked.

The functionary looked really uncomfortable . . . and not just because of my presence, suddenly. "The *kahunas* think not, *e ku'u lani.*"

"Think not?" Ho sounded surprised.

"That's what they told me, *e ku'u lani.*"

"Interesting. *Na Maka'i* are continuing their investigation, of course?"

"Yes, *e ku'u lani,* they have the area sealed off."

"Good." The *Ali'i* nodded approval. "Do you have anything more to report?"

"Not at this time, *e ku'u lani.*"

"Thank you, then." Ho dismissed him with a nod.

Once the functionary had shut the door behind him, the *Ali'i* leaned back in his seat and shook his head.

"What was that about?" I asked.

Ho sighed. "Puowaina," he said, then waited.

"Punchbowl," I said after a moment.

"That's right," he confirmed. He turned in his chair and pointed to an area of the holo "mountains" behind him. "There. Puowaina, just north of the city. Its name means 'Hill of Sacrifices,' referring to the old religions. It seems as though someone is taking that name a little more seriously than they might."

"Sacrifices?" I asked.

The *Ali'i* nodded. "It's not unheard of, unfortunately," he admitted. "Hawai'i has its fringe cults, just as the UCAS does. In the first eight years after I assumed the throne, there were half a dozen . . . *incidents* of that kind. Animal sacrifices—dogs and pigs, mainly, the sacrificial animals most commonly used in the old faiths. Usually, the sacrifices would be just that and nothing more: some unfortunate animal with its throat slit, then burned. Once or twice, there were hints that someone was trying to link magical activity with the sacrifices—incomplete hermetic circles and things of that sort." He shrugged. "My *kahunas* assured me that the people conducting the rituals were totally deluded. The magical trappings would never have worked.

"Things change, though," he went on quietly. "Have you ever given any thought to the fact that fringe religions—crank religions, you could say—become more pervasive when a people is troubled? It's true," he confirmed with a nod, "check it out yourself. UFO fever a century ago, during the height of the cold war. The proliferation of psychics and spoon-benders in Russia after the collapse of the USSR. The 'Church of Christ, Geneticist', during the throes of the VITAS epidemic. The fascination with reincarnation during the 'teens . . ."

I nodded at that one. I remembered reading once that two—count 'em, *two*—scam artists had built careers on their claims that they were the reincarnation of proto-angst rocker, Kurt Cobain.

"The Brotherhood of the Eternal Now," the *Ali'i* was going on, "in the years before the Treaty of Denver. The Universal Brotherhood—*that* perversion—when 'future shock' really hit the UCAS. And here? Here, we've got the people sacrificing dogs and pigs and goats up on Punchbowl." He smiled wryly. "I suppose I might take it as a criticism of my rule."

"It's becoming more common, then?" I suggested.

"Precisely. Six or seven times in the first eight years of my rule. Then, in the past two years . . . would you care to guess?" I shook my head. "Seventeen incidents. No," he corrected himself quickly, "eighteen now." He sighed. "Crackpots."

For some reason I suddenly didn't feel so sure about that. "Your chief of police seems to be taking it more seriously," I pointed out.

"It's his job to take it seriously . . . if only because the people behind the sacrifices might decide to . . . to *graduate* . . . from dogs and pigs."

I waited, but the *Ali'i* didn't continue. Well, if a king chooses not to share all his thoughts with you, what the frag can you do? After a few moments Ho smiled. "Thank you for your cooperation, Mr. Montgomery," he said warmly. "I've enjoyed our discussion. Please, make what efforts you can to communicate with Mr. Barnard. And please stay in touch, to inform me of anything you should learn. Agreed?"

"What about contact procedures?"

"Here." He handed me a mylar business card—no name or address, just an LTG number. "This node will transfer you to my private line, wherever I happen to be. If for some reason I'm unavailable, no one else will answer." He hesitated. "Be aware that I can't vouch for the complete security of the relay." He grinned wryly. "My military intelligence traffic-analysis teams have been a little zealous of late."

"Agreed," I told him.

King Kamehameha V pressed a concealed button on his desk, and seconds later a functionary arrived to escort me out. I traded in my jacket and tie to Ortega for my Manhunter, and then I jandered out of the Iolani Palace. The *Ali'i*'s deputy badge was a comforting weight in my shirt pocket. I figured that wearing it openly might attract too much attention, but I certainly wanted it close to hand.

What the frag was I supposed to do now? Contact Barnard—that's what Ho wanted ... but for the moment, at least, I felt like keeping a nice, safe distance from Yamatetsu and all the other megacorporations.

As if by magic, my eyes were drawn to the hills overlooking the Honolulu sprawl. There was Punchbowl—Puowaina. What the frag, I didn't have anything I really needed to do at the moment, did I?

I turned my back on the palace and went looking for a bus stop.

15

I remembered a little bit about Punchbowl—Puowaina—from my data search on the suborbital. Apparently, as the *Ali'i* had implied—it used to hold one mega-important place in the ancient Hawai'ian religion. It was up on Puowaina—Hill of Sacrifices—that the old Hawai'ians used to cack their human sacrifices to placate their gods. Who *were* those sacrifices? Volunteers? Criminals? Virgins bred specially for the task (what a fragging waste)? "Prisoners of war" from other islands? Search me, chummer. All I knew was that it came to an end with the *haoles*—the priests and missionaries and pineapple plutocrats—who moved in and "civilized" the place, of course.

I guess Pele, goddess of the earth and of volcanoes, got a mite ticked that nobody was placating her with blood anymore, but it took her a while to do something about it. (You know how it is with goddesses: never a free moment . . .) In 2018, Haleakala, a huge volcano on the island of Maui, blew its top. Well, not its top, really, more like its side. A ridge on the volcano's west side collapsed, and a massive lava flow obliterated the luxury hotels and tourist traps of Wailea and Keokea. (Tourist fluff still refers to the area—a lava rock wasteland—as "Pompeii of the Pacific.")

In any case, in the twentieth century Puowaina had become a military cemetery for the United States—the National Memorial Cemetery of the Pacific, a kind of "Arlington West." Predictably, it didn't stay that way after Secession. The government, under Gordon Ho's dad, exhumed all the bodies—more than 26,000 of them—and shipped them all back to the mainland, with appropriate honors. (That slotted off more than a few Americans, of course, but after the Thor shots at the Pearl Harbor task force, nobody really dared push the point too hard.)

And that's where The Bus dropped me off in the middle

of a baking-hot Hawai'i afternoon, Puowaina, now a public park. A pretty place, an ancient, eroded volcanic crater shaped something like a big bowl. Grassy and green—did that mean artificial irrigation? not necessarily, I supposed—with trees and flowers—forty or so hectares of peace just twenty minutes from the pressure of downtown. From the rim of the crater I imagined you'd get a spectacular view of Honolulu, in all its finery, but I didn't bother looking. More immediate things were attracting my attention.

The Hawai'i National Police Force copmobiles—two of them—were crisp tropical white with rainbow logos on the doors, not the blue and gold of Lone Star Seattle. But it takes more than a flashy paint job to make a Chrysler-Nissan Patrol One look anything other than brutal and threatening. Only half the strobes on the two vehicles' light-bars were operating, but I still had to shield my eyes from the glare. A couple of cops—what had Scott called them? *Na Maka'i,* that's right—were squatting down, doing something vaguely forensic, near a little copse of flowering trees. Another uniformed officer was sitting on the ground, back up against a tree. He looked drugged or chipped out of his pointy little skull, but I knew better. I recognized that vacant expression; I'd seen it all too often on the faces of Department of Paranormal Investigations officers—"Dips," to street grunts like myself—who'd butted into some of my cases while I was with the Star. Okay, I thought, so at least one cop-*kahuna* was doing the old "ghost-walk" around the area, looking for astral evidence. There was only one more cop there, bringing the total up to four. He was one big boy—a human, but with a gut worthy of a sumo wrestler—and he was talking to a couple of shorts-clad local kids. Witnesses, maybe?

Na Maka'i had cordoned off the crime scene much the same way we were taught in the Star. Where trees, picnic benches, and the like were conveniently placed, the cops had strung up that universal yellow police line tape between them. To cover open ground, they'd used the collapsible lineposts that every cop car on the planet has somewhere in its trunk. I ambled over, and when I reached the police line, I held up the yellow tape and ducked under it. I took another step toward the two cops crouching on the ground . . .

And rapped my nose and forehead against an invisible barrier that was as unyielding as a concrete wall. "Frag," I grunted. Instinctively, I tried to step back.

No go. There was an invisible wall behind me now, too. And one to the right and to the left when I checked. It was like I was in an invisible and slightly undersized phone booth. For a couple of seconds I did the old street-mime shtick, palms pressing flat against unseen walls. Then I cringed and covered my ears as a high-pitched siren shrieked from somewhere behind my left shoulder. Frag, why not? Invisible walls—why not an invisible burglar alarm, too?

I watched helplessly as the sumo-gutted cop left the kids and strode menacingly across the grass toward me. *"Mai ne'e,"* he barked. "Don't move, *haole*." I snorted at that. Like I could. "What you doing here, huh?"

"Coming to talk to you," I told him calmly. And I pointedly pinned my deputy's badge to the collar of my tropical shirt.

The cop was good, I had to give him that. His look of absolute and total disgust lasted only a fraction of a second before he slapped an expression of polite eagerness on his face. *"Aloha, e ku'u haku,"* he rumbled to me. Then he snapped something else, apparently to the empty air. I almost keeled over, off balance, as the invisible walls surrounding me were suddenly gone.

"Thank you, Officer . . .?"

"Constable Saito, sir. What can I do for you?"

"Show me around," I suggested. "What's been happening here?"

The sumo-stomached cop nodded and led me across the grass to where the two forensics boys were still poking around. One of them looked up at me and drew breath to kvetch, but Constable Saito shut him up with a foul glare. "Sacrifices again, sir," Saito said unnecessarily. He pointed at what looked like a makeshift altar, jury-rigged from flat rocks that had recently formed the border of a flower bed. Something had been burned on that altar—something that had left behind a pile of blackened, crumbling bones.

"What was it?" I asked.

"Pua'a," one of the forensics types answered, then translated, "Pig, sir. Young pig."

"Something more, too." The voice sounded from empty space, a meter to my right. I jumped, then tried to pretend I hadn't. Mages—they're always finding new ways to give me the fragging willies.

"What do you mean?" I queried.

"Something else was killed here," the mage's disembodied voice elaborated. "Not a pig."

"A metahuman?"

"Not sure," the voice said. I glanced over at the *kahuna*'s meat-body, saw it frown. "Shielded."

"What do you mean, 'shielded'?"

This time the voice came from the *kahuna*'s meat-body as he climbed to his feet. "There was a death here," he explained, "I can feel that much. I can't tell what it was that died . . . and I *should* be able to."

I nodded as if I actually understood. "Only the pig was burned, though?"

"Only the *pua'a*," the shaman confirmed impatiently.

The forensics people had finished collecting their samples of ash and bone and now were scanning the rocks of the altar with a low-intensity UV laser to bring out latent prints. Good luck, boys—the heat of the fire would almost certainly have obliterated anything usable.

I turned my back on the altar and looked at the surrounding ground. Some kind of intricate pattern had been cut into the grass—no, not cut, I realized—*burned* in. The lines were sharply defined and surprisingly narrow. You couldn't do a job like that by pouring lines of gasoline and igniting them, the way I'd figured at first. You needed something that burned much hotter and faster. *Hmmm,* I thought—someone had gone to some effort here.

I stepped back for a better overall picture of the pattern. Two concentric circles, centered on the altar, one maybe ten meters in diameter, the other maybe eleven. The half-meter-wide annulus between the two circles was divided into quadrants by radial lines. I checked the sun and guesstimated—yes, the radial lines seemed roughly aligned with the cardinal points of the compass. Around the annulus there were an even dozen strange, angular symbols. Not burned, these, but formed from scores of small, white pebbles carefully aligned. I looked around—no, as I'd suspected, there wasn't an obvious source for those pebbles anywhere in the Puowaina park.

Finished with his ghost-walk, the cop-*kahuna* was now carefully photographing each of the arcane-looking symbols around the circle. I jandered over to him and waited for him to acknowledge me. His frown told me he didn't want to, but I saw his eyes flick down to my deputy's badge. "Yes, sir?"

he asked at last. (The "sir" seemed to cause him physical pain.)

I indicated the concentric circles with my toe. "What *is* this? A hermetic circle? A medicine lodge of some kind?"

He wanted to roll his eyes, I could tell, but he managed to control the impulse. He shrugged. "Neither," he said. Then, less certainly, "Not really."

"What, then?" Another shrug. "Is it hermetic or shamanic?"

For a moment he looked really uncomfortable. He shrugged once more.

Which was interesting. Neither hermetic nor shamanic ... or maybe *both* hermetic *and* shamanic, if that made any sense. Hell, at one time or another, everyone's overheard those airy-fairy philosophical discussions about the structure of magic—the hypothesis that magic is magic and that's it. That the distinction between hermetic and shamanic is entirely artificial, one made by (meta)human minds, but not innate to the mana itself. Was that what these symbols represented? Or were they just meaningless—some fraghead mage-wannabe copying something he saw on the trid?

"What would you use something like this for?" I asked the *kahuna*.

"*I* wouldn't use it for anything," he snapped.

I sighed. "What would someone else use it for then? What *might* they use it for?" I corrected quickly, to forestall another case of literal-mindedness.

"Don't know."

I shot the *kahuna* a penetrating look. He was really uncomfortable now, and it was making him sullen. (Magicians of all stripes *hate* admitting they don't know everything—I learned that long ago.) "You've got to have some idea," I pressed. "It's got to remind you of something. What *might* it be?"

For a moment he just glared stink-eye at me. Then I saw his eyes change as he surrendered. "Could be some kind of conjuring circle," he mumbled. "Could be."

"For summoning spirits? You mean the mage or shaman or whatever stands in the circle—"

"*No,*" he cut in with a look that clearly completed the thought—*you fragging twinkie.* "Conjurer stands *out*side the circle, thing that gets conjured *inside* the circle ... till *kahuna* lets it out. Okay?"

"So what would you conjure using something like this? Elementals? Spirits? What?"

Some unreadable expression flickered across his face. *"Nothing,"* he said firmly. "Couldn't conjure *nothing* with this. Not elementals, not spirits, okay?" And—deputy's badge or not—he turned his back on me and strode away. I watched him climb into one of the Patrol Ones, shut the door, and just sit there in a sulk.

Interesting. What was it the functionary had told the *Ali'i?* Up until now, the magical mumbo-jumbo surrounding the sacrifices in Puowaina had been meaningless. This time, though, the *kahunas* hadn't been sure of that. That represented a pretty significant change in things, didn't it? The cop-*kahuna's* reaction had certainly fit with that analysis.

So this ritual-circle drek was *similar* to the stuff the mystics use for summoning—similar, but not exactly right. If I'd known more about magic, maybe that would mean something to me. It's unfortunate, in a way. Unlike a lot of people I know, I'm not a magophobe—how the frag *can* you be magophobic in the Sixth World, tell me that?—but I'm certainly no spellworm. I guess the most time I've ever spent with a real-and-for-true practicing spellworm was when I worked alongside Rodney Greybriar back in Seattle . . . before he was geeked, of course.

Well, magic or no magic, the laws of logic had to stay more or less the same, *neh?* Maybe all I needed was a little common sense.

What must you do to summon a spirit, or whatever? No, take the question one step further back. Where do spirits and their ilk hang when they're not being summoned? *Somewhere else,* obviously. On the astral plane, maybe, or on one of the "metaplanes" (whatever the frag *they* are . . .). Bringing them across takes effort. It takes magical jam, and—from what I've heard—to drag the big boys, kicking and screaming, into the material world, it can really harsh a spellworm out.

Why? Obviously—well, it's obvious to me, at least—there's some kind of barrier between the material world and the other planes. No, let's call it something pseudo-mystical—say there's a curtain between this world and the others, or maybe a veil. Okay, some kind of curtain. Sure, that made sense, otherwise people might just stumble from this world into some freaky metaplane without intending to do so, or even knowing it happened.

So, to summon something, logically you'd have to break down that barrier—pull back the curtain—or it just wouldn't work, *neh*? Could *that* be what the weirdo circle was for? To open—or maybe weaken—the curtain between what we laughingly call the real world and those other places? An interesting hypothesis . . . and, now that I thought about it, not a particularly comforting one.

Oh, *drek* . . . combine that nasty thought with another one that had just struck me. When the cop-*kahuna* said he wouldn't conjure anything using that circle, could he have meant that (meta)humans couldn't use something like that? Who could?

How about the friends of Adrian Skyhill? The fragging insect spirits. They were involved somehow—if I was to believe Barnard, and I had no reason to *dis*believe him at the moment.

Great. Hadn't I read somewhere that certain sites on the earth—typically ancient "places of power"—had high mana "background counts" that made magical activity easier? Mount Shasta, apparently. Crater Lake possibly. Why not Puowaina?

Could the insect spirits be trying to use the power of the Hill of Sacrifices to do to Hawai'i what they'd done to Chicago? To bring forth hordes of their kind from whatever hell had spawned them?

Or was I a paranoid slot getting his exercise by jumping to *really* out-there conclusions? (Go back, go *waaay* back . . .)

I shook my head. It was a dead fragging certainty I wasn't going to figure it out just by standing here and pummeling my brain. Who knew, maybe the kids—the ones that sumo-Saito had been questioning—had seen something relevant.

But the kids were gone when I looked around. The forensic boys had finished their work, and were piling into the car with the still-sulking *kahuna*. Saito was standing by the open driver's door of his car, watching me—and *almost* concealing his impatience—in case the "deputy" might want to waste his time with more dumb-hooped questions. I waved to him and gestured that he could take off if he wanted. He wanted, and I was left to breathe in the dust of his departure. With a sigh I started walking toward The Bus stop.

I felt eyes on me, that creepy feeling that the academics

say doesn't exist but that every nonacademic has felt many times. I stopped and looked around.

He was standing, totally motionless, leaning casually against the trunk of some kind of flowering tree, watching me. Rapier-thin, he seemed to radiate a sense of pent-up energy, explosive movement. He was an elf, I was almost certain. From this distance I couldn't see his ears, but the morphology looked right. His eyes were hidden behind those radically styled shades that advertise they can stop a 12-gauge shotgun blast—reassuring only as long as the slag busting caps on you confines his aim to your sunglasses—but I could *feel* his gaze on me. I raised an eyebrow questioningly.

He stepped away from the tree and jandered over toward me—slowly, casually—yet purposefully. (A contradiction, true enough. But that's exactly how he moved—with the lethal casualness of a predator.) I gave him the top-to-toe scan as he approached.

Thin face, high cheekbones, a nose that an eagle would kill to possess. He wore his hair—red, streaked with silver gray—long, pulled back in a ponytail that reached the middle of his back. He was dressed in dark clothes—a slate gray synthsilk shirt, black pants wide at the thighs and tapering to the ankle. Expensive, high-quality clothing, but anachronistic in style. When was the last time *you* saw a shirt buttoned to the neck with no tie, and bloused cuffs? It was almost as if the elf had stepped right off the virtual pages of *Gentlemen's Monthly Online,* but from an issue twenty years old. Instinctively, I played "spot the heat." No luck—if he was packing anything larger than the smallest of hold-outs, he'd found a damn fine way of concealing it.

He stopped a short distance away, and it was his turn to give me the once-over. It took no more than a second, and then he smiled.

Suddenly, I realized I feared this elf.

It was a disturbing realization. Hell, there was nothing overtly threatening about him. His smile seemed to be genuinely amused, not a power smile intended to impress or intimidate. His body language was, well, I didn't know quite what to make of it, but *it* wasn't threatening either.

Yet the fear was real, chummer. For some reason, it chilled my guts like an ice-water enema. Some people you automatically like at first glance; others you automatically despise. Never before had I met someone to automatically *fear.* I think I managed to keep my thoughts from showing on my face, however.

The elf nodded a greeting—a gesture with an Old-World formal air to it. "Mr. Montgomery," he said. His voice was a musical instrument, almost inhumanly perfect in timbre, tone, and resonance; any trideo personality would gut his mother for a voice like that. "I rather thought I might find you here."

"Then you know more about it than I do," I told him truthfully.

He found that amusing, and his smile broadened. "Well, there is always that possibility, isn't there, Mr. Montgomery? Or may I call you Derek?"

"Why don't you call me Brian Tozer?" I said. Then—what the frag anyway—"But Dirk will do. Your turn."

The elf nodded again, almost a bow, this time. "Quentin Harlech, at your service. But you can call me Quinn."

I ignored the obvious opening.

Harlech removed his bullet-proof shades—blue eyes, sharper than a monoblade—and looked pointedly around the area. "Quite fascinating, isn't it?" he remarked lightly.

I shrugged. "If you understand it, I suppose."

He laughed then, Harlech did. Not the sinister cackle that part of my mind had expected, but a full-throated, *free* rush of genuine mirth. "Oh, of course, Dirk, of course. Will you be returning with interesting reports?"

"Huh?" Not overly witty, of course, but it was all that occurred to me at the moment.

Quinn chuckled again. "Reports, Derek, *you* know. To those who sent you. Give them my greetings while you're at it, will you? But then, of course you'd do that even without my urging, wouldn't you?"

Slowly, I shook my head. "Pardon the dumb question, but are we both reading from the same script here? Or maybe you're confusing me with another Dirk Montgomery?"

The elf sighed and made a disapproving *tsk-tsk-tsk* sound with his tongue. "Basely spoken, Mr. Montgomery," he said. His tone of voice sounded more disappointed than anything else. "Dissembling so clumsily? It suits you ill, sir."

I showed him my empty palms. "Chummer," I said quietly, "I haven't got a fragging clue what you're talking about."

"Of course you don't, of course you don't," Quinn said patronizingly, and he laughed again. "And of course you don't know that the game is up," he went on sarcastically. "You don't know that your cover's blown, and that you're wasting your time. I've seen to that, you know. You really *should* tell your master that." I saw his gaze flick down to my deputy badge, saw his expression change subtly. "*Both* your masters," he amended.

Before I could speak, he turned away with a final, "Well, good day to you, *makkaherinit.*"

"Hey, just a fragging moment," I called after him.

Or that's what I tried to call after him, at least. I tried to draw breath . . . and couldn't. I tried to move . . . and couldn't. I tried to blink my fragging eyes . . . and couldn't.

Magic, obviously—a powerful paralysis spell. Harlech must have cast it on me to give himself walking-away time. That's what I guessed later, at least. At the moment there was only one thought running through my mind.

I was fragging *paralyzed,* and I was fragging *terrified.* Spirits, have *you* ever been paralyzed? Let me tell you it's not the way you think it'd be . . . or not the way *I* thought it'd be, at least. Maybe there are some kinds of paralysis spells that control only voluntary muscles, that leave the involuntary functions alone. Not this one. I couldn't breathe, in or out, and I couldn't even hear my pulse. Every muscle fiber in my body seemed frozen in the position it held when Harlech cast his spell or whatever it was.

I watched him stroll away; then he was out of my field of vision, and I couldn't move my eyes to follow him. I was stuck there, staring at some turf and a flowering tree—the tree was slightly out of focus, and I couldn't even focus my eyes—and I started wondering if that was the last sight I was ever going to see. The elf had implied that he didn't want me dead, which meant he'd eventually drop the spell . . . but soon enough? How good was his estimate of the anoxia-tolerance of a thirty-something erstwhile shadowrunner who's not in the best of fragging shape? By the time he dropped the spell and my cardiovascular system got back on the job, how much of my brain would have suffocated? Not a pleasant thought . . .

My vision was starting to tunnel down, and little floaty stars were drifting around the dark periphery of my visual field. In growing desperation, I tried once more to draw a breath . . .

And fragged if it didn't work this time. I filled my lungs, a great whooping inhalation. (Who says orgasm is the best experience in the world? I'm here to tell you, chummer, it's *breathing* . . .) My heart kicked in, a triphammer beat in my ears. I fell to my hands and knees and just relished the sensations as my chest and diaphragm did what they were supposed to do. The little floaty stars and the black tunnel receded, and eventually the aftertaste of terror followed them. By the time I could think of anything beyond personal survival, the elf was gone without a trace.

16

I sat in the back of The Bus, morosely watching the assortment of (meta)humanity sharing the vehicle with me. Mostly working-class Hawai'ians, I figured, but there was a significant minority of younger people I tentatively labeled as the kids of corp vacationers. (Did mummy and daddy suit know their little darlings were riding a fragging *bus* instead of cruising in a limo? Not that it mattered ...) The "recently dead" look seemed to be back in fashion, with bleached skin, black-dyed hair, and makeup to give the eyes a sunken look. Anything that could be pierced was pierced. The only thing that set these pre-suits apart from sprawl guttertrash was the quality—and obvious expense—of their clothes. Oh, sure, they wore the *de rigueur* biker jackets and weathered jeans. But their jackets were *real leather,* not synth, and they'd obviously bought their jeans prefaded and preslashed.

And then there were the T-shirts and sweatshirts they wore under their jackets—emblazoned with logos from fashionable corps. I don't know jack about fashion, really, but I do know how much a trendy label adds to the price of something. I sighed. In the grand scheme of things the only difference between cows and some people is that cows don't pay mega-cred to get branded. Maybe it's time to cack us all and give the cockroaches their shot ...

It was continuing to be one of those days, all in all. Through no fault of my own, I'd gotten myself mixed up in the affairs of kings, corps, and dracoforms. I'd witnessed an assassination, I'd been shot at repeatedly, and I'd almost asphyxiated under a paralysis spell. And the day wasn't even over.

It was Miller time with a vengeance. Of all the things I could think of, what I most wanted right at that moment was to head back to my doss, flop down on the bed, and watch eyelid movies for twenty-four hours. Maybe by the time I woke up again, things would have started looking a little better.

Problem: I didn't *have* a doss at the moment. Or, more correctly—I had two dosses, but they were about as compromised as it's possible to get. Maybe I should just head on back to the Iolani Palace, ask for political asylum, and throw myself on the mercy of the *Ali'i*. Maybe King Kamehameha V needed a *haole* courtier or a eunuch or some damn thing.

Sitting there in the back of The Bus, I scanned through the memory of my pocket 'puter. I still had a couple of aliases stashed away in the little box's optical chips. They were all on a par with the one I hadn't needed to check into the Ilima Joy: good enough for low-level, routine drek, but certain suicide if I tried to travel on them.

I tried to think back to when I'd snagged the Ilima Joy room. *Had* I used one of those aliases? I knew that the desk clerk hadn't asked me for ID, but . . .

But didn't the credstick with which I'd paid have an ident stored on it, just in case? I thought so. Okay, so assume that ident—"Emory Archambault"—was compromised. Quickly, I set myself up another "blind" credstick, this time under the name "Mike Bloemhard." When that was done—a matter of minutes—I started watching The Bus stops and figuring out exactly where I was.

Two transfers and twenty minutes later, I was in a Bus rolling northwest on Highway 99. When I hit Pearl City—older than Ewa, apparently, but better maintained—I swung down off The Bus and started trolling the backstreets for a place to flop. In the west another perfect sunset was burning its way down behind the skyline. Tropical twilight is always short, and maybe ten minutes later the streetlights were coming on to hold back the night.

Maybe Pearl City hadn't been such a good bet, I started thinking after another half hour or so. All the hotels I'd found, even the ones well off the beaten track, were surprisingly high-tone. Sure, they were old, but they'd been seriously gentrified, like the New Ritz Hotel in Seattle, using their age as a selling point instead of a drawback. Typically, places that invested that much cred into the physical facilities wouldn't have scrimped on the electronic side, either. It wouldn't take much in the way of data back-checking to figure out that "Mike Bloemhard" was as much a fiction as

"Neil the Ork Barbarian." For a moment I debated hopping The Bus back to Ewa—at least I knew I could find some sleazy flops there—but quickly discarded the idea. If Kat and her little friends had bugged my bike, it just wasn't a reasonable risk to go anywhere near where I'd dumped the Suzuki. So I walked on.

I must have been tired—that's the only excuse I can come up with—tired and emotionally battered. Otherwise, I like to think I'd have noticed the Renault-Fiat Eurovan creeping up on me a little sooner.

The puke green van was no more than ten meters away when my cerebral cortex finally got with the program and tagged it as something to be concerned about. Just in time, too. In my peripheral vision I saw the passenger-side window roll down and spotted the movement inside the cab. Reflexes kicked in, and I flung myself to the sidewalk.

The weapon the van's passenger was aiming went off—a dull *pum* noise instead of the usual sharp crash—and I felt something split the air above my falling body. A myopolymer net appeared—magically, it seemed—immobilizing and incapacitating a datafax kiosk a meter or two behind me.

I hit the sidewalk hard, rolling to try and absorb the impact. My sartorial splendor downgraded itself yet again, but at least the light armor underneath saved me from losing much skin. I did another tuck-and-roll into the shelter of a parked car. My Manhunter was in my hand, safety off and finger on the trigger, but I kept it down, out of sight. The slag in the Eurovan had taken his first shot with a netgun, meaning he wanted me alive—for the moment, at least. It didn't make sense for me to return fire and escalate matters to a more lethal level. Cautiously, I raised my head above the hood of the car behind which I was crouching.

And all nonlethal bets were immediately off. The side door of the Eurovan slid back, and three laser sights winked on in the darkness beyond. I dropped flat to the ground, as autofire stitched the car and blew out the windows, showering me with transpex. Over the rattle of gunfire I heard another door open on the Eurovan. The passenger's side door? Probably—the guy with the netgun was taking advantage of the "suppression fire" to come and finish me off.

Mentally, I reviewed my tactical options. It didn't take more than a fraction of a second—there were only two, and only one of them involved staying alive. Before I could think about it too much and immobilize myself with fear, I forced myself to my feet, put my head down, and *ran*. Directly away from the car, jinking and weaving, but concentrating more on pouring on the speed and opening the distance. Ideally, I wanted to keep as low as possible, to minimize my exposure, but speed was more important than anything else. Without looking, I squeezed off four shots from the Manhunter back over my left shoulder.

Bullets whipcracked by my head. Ricochets whined off into the darkness. I felt something pluck at the collar of my shirt—now *that* was too fragging close.

On this part of the street the buildings, largely light-industrial facilities, were separated by narrow walkways ... or, more accurately, breezeways. I faked right, then cut hard left, and hurled myself headlong down one of these darkened passages. I yelled with pain as something slammed into my left shoulder blade—a love-tap with a baseball bat. The impact was enough to throw me off balance for a second, and I caught my right elbow a nasty crack on the corner of a building. I howled, my right hand and forearm feeling like they'd been dipped into molten lead, but I kept on running.

The firing continued behind me—no more *pum*s, all the cracking of real-and-for-true guns—but nothing came close. I tore down the walkway/breezeway like a boosted sprinter and hung a skidding right when I reached the end.

An alley—a fragging, noisome, garbage-strewn alley. Even though I knew I couldn't really spare the breath, I cursed out loud. Was it just me, or did *everyone's* life seem to gravitate to drek-choked alleys and dumpsters? I pounded on. The gunfire had stopped behind me, but I could hear the echoes of pursuing footfalls. I risked a glance over my shoulder and was rewarded with a momentary glimpse of two figures bursting from the breezeway. One was big and hulking, with klick-wide shoulders; the other was small and wiry. Moko and Kat, two of the runners connected with "the big worm?" A pretty safe bet, I figured. Both of them popped some caps in my direction, but the visibility was drek, and the range was extending. I sprinted on, until the air was like knives in my lungs when I breathed in.

Questions churned through my mind as I ran. First off ... how the fragging hell did they track me? They might have put a tracer on my bike, but I'd dumped the bike ...

Hold the phone. A tracer on the bike was an obvious play, but I'd also given Kat and the others plenty of chances to put a tracer on *me,* hadn't I? Frag, it doesn't take much these days, not with the microminiaturized drek on the market. A casual pat on the shoulder and you've transferred a self-adhesive tracker the size of a pinhead.

If that was the case, the "why" could only have to do with Ryumyo—assuming it *was* Ryumyo who'd done the morphing trip on my telecom screen—and his warning to stay out of matters. So what had I done almost immediately thereafter? I'd run to the fragging *Ali'i,* hadn't I? Not a particularly good way of keeping my nose out of trouble. When the big worm realized I hadn't taken his friendly advice, he'd decided to send Kat and her little friends out to settle things once and for all. (What was with the netgun if they were simply going to open up with lethal ordnance the moment the nonlethal takedown failed? Obviously, the ALOHA runners were planning to cack me anyway, but their primary plan was to bag me and then put a pill in my ear in private. When I inconsiderately refused to be bagged, they went to Plan B: Hose the place down.)

Kat and Moko were still on my hoop, maybe fifty meters back but closing the gap. (Fear and adrenaline can do wonderful things, but they *can't* make up for too many months as a couch-tuber.) They weren't firing indiscriminately anymore. Hell, they didn't have to; they knew they'd catch me eventually. Panicking seemed to be the only logical plan at the moment, so that's what I did. Wildly, I started looking around for somewhere to make my last stand.

And that's when guns opened up behind me again. Not Moko's and Kat's—someone else's. The two ALOHA runners were packing SMGs of some kind; the reports and cyclical rates were unmistakable. The guns that suddenly cut loose were something very different, with a much higher cyclical rate of fire. Not miniguns—the reports were from small-arms rounds—but with a similar rate of fire, sounding like giant zippers. Standard SMGs stuttered in response, but the zippers spoke again, and the SMGs fell silent.

Part of me wanted to know what the frag was going down behind me, back down the alley. Who the hell was hashing it out with Kat and Moko? The more logical part of my mind wrote the question off as meaningless. Anything that eliminated pursuit was all to the good, wasn't it? "The enemy of my enemy is my friend," and all that jazz ...

The alley ended, and I was out onto a backstreet. Another skidding turn—left, this time—and I started to slow down. There was silence behind me—no gunfire, no running footsteps. Were Kat and Moko down, or had they just broken off pursuit? If the latter, they—or their friends, come to think of it—could still be tracking in on me, using the hypothetical locator that had led them to me in the first place. Frag, I had to ditch that thing *fast* ... but doing a striptease in the middle of the street probably wasn't tactically sound, for various obvious reasons.

My heart was pounding in my ears, and my calves felt like somebody had worked them over with a nightstick. Had I eaten dinner, I'd probably have been busy losing it. I jogged on, trying to decide what to do next ...

... And slammed on the brakes just in time to avoid plowing into the figure that emerged from the shadows ahead of me. Instinctively, I brought up the Manhunter.

No, I *tried* to bring up the Manhunter, but my right arm was damn near paralyzed from the crack on the elbow. My left hand snatched the big pistol from my numb right. I triggered the sighting laser and set the red dot center-head.

Dark, liquid eyes widened in panic. A tastefully made-up mouth dropped open.

She was beautiful, was the elf facing me. Just shy of two meters, I guessed, willow-slender, with the kind of face that might best be described as "why men fight."

Hooker, joygirl, sex-worker—that's how I labeled her initially, but then I saw her clothing. Top-tier corp garb, that's what she was wearing. A skirtsuit that probably cost as much as a small car. Polished titanium jewelry: earrings, necklace, matching bracers on her wrists. Those bracers flashed in the streetlights as she showed me empty hands. "Don't shoot. Please!"

Instinctively, I lowered the Manhunter. The more rational part of my brain knew it was a bad idea, but the knight-in-shining-armor lobe seemed to have suddenly taken over. The instant my gun was off-line, she extended one of her slender palms toward my chest.

And then fragging *shot* me. Flame flashed from the bracer, and pain drove deep into my chest, a long, lancing needle of agony that went through the light body armor as if it wasn't there. I tried to bring the Manhunter back up, to return the favor on my way out, but the thing suddenly weighed a couple of hundred kilos.

I was still trying to think of a witty exit line when blackness crested over me like an ocean wave and carried me down, deep deep down.

17

Light. Morning.

I lay there—wherever there happened to be—for an unmeasurable time, just staring up into a mellow, sourceless light. If this was death, I kind of liked it. No pain, no worries, no fears. No real thoughts either, and certainly no analytical awareness of the future. I was just the eternal, living *now*, with as much concern for the past or the future as a fragging bunny rabbit. It was pleasant, and for I don't know how long I just grooved on it.

It didn't last, of course—the good drek never does. Way too soon, I started to become aware of my body. The lazy *lub-dub* of my heart. The slow, deep bellows action of my lungs. The touch of soft sheets and a firm mattress against my back.

And the throbbing pain of a puncture wound in the center of my chest.

That realization brought an end to the timeless grooving, let me tell you, chummer. As if the realization of pain had opened some kind of stopcock, memories of the past and fears of the future come flooding back into my brain. I think I whimpered then. Somebody had bagged me, and bagged me good. The elf-biff had distracted me with her looks and body language, then driven a narcodart into my chest. Good tactics, with forethought and planning. That still left a couple of important questions, though.

Who? And, more important, why? Work on the "who" first, I decided.

Moko and Kat? Doubt it, chummer. A drive-by was more their style. (Frag, if I'd been a millisecond slower, it would have worked and I'd be dead right about now.) Ryumyo? Doubt it; Kat and her friends were almost certainly after me on the worm's orders. King Kamehameha? Doubt it; he'd had me in his clutches in Iolani Palace and let me walk. Harlech the elf? Doubt it, for much the same reason. Which left . . .

Which left the fragging yakuza, didn't it? The yaks could be as brutal and direct as anyone else when circumstances warranted, but they could also pull something pretty elegant if they wanted. Like the elf-biff and her bracer.

And that answered the "why" all too well. I'd cacked their *oyabun* . . . or, at least, I'd been closely involved in his cackage. The yaks had always been deep into payback, teaching lessons, and sending messages. That meant the fact that I was still alive wasn't necessarily a reassuring thing. It simply meant they were planning to take their time over making me dead.

Wonderful, oh joy.

My body wasn't yet under perfect control of my mind, but at least I managed to sit up and look around. I was in what looked like a hospital or clinic room, judging by the powered bed and antiseptic white walls, at least. There was no furniture beside the bed—no chairs, no bed tables, nothing else that could serve as a weapon of opportunity. No window, either.

The door was to my right, flush with the wall. No knob, just a push-plate, which meant the door opened outward. Which, in turn, meant I was denied that old trick of hiding behind the door and cold-cocking the first person to come a-visiting. Locked, of course.

And that was it for the room. No closet, no door to an adjoining room. Not even a light fixture in the ceiling, just standard-issue flatpanel lights set right into the acoustical tile.

I threw back the single sheet covering me. I was naked, of course. That didn't surprise me; it was just one more move in the familiar security game. My captors knew how much harder it is to be heroic and innovative when you're bare-ass naked. With a silent curse I pulled the top sheet off the bed and wrapped it around me. Better to look like a refugee from a toga party than display my shortcomings in public, I figured. Then I began prowling around the room, looking for . . . well, looking for anything that might help me get out of there. I didn't know exactly what that anything might be, but I figured I'd know it when I saw it.

My captors didn't give me much time. The click of a maglock disengaging froze me in midprowl. I was all the way on the other side of the room, much too far for me to reach the door in time for anything heroic. (And, of course, my captors would have known that, timing their entry by watching me on a surveillance monitor.) I gathered what shreds of dignity I still had to hand, drew myself up to my full height, and prepared to give the first yak soldier through the door a serious dose of imperious stink-eye.

It wasn't a yak soldier who came through the door, though. Not what *I* imagined to be a typical yak soldier, at least. She was elf and Polynesian—three strikes, as far as the yaks I'm familiar with are concerned; male, human, and Nihonese is more their style. She gave me a coldly polite smile and said, "Good morning, Mr. Montgomery."

(I sighed. What was the deal here? Everyone and his fragging hamster knew my name . . .)

She looked competent and confident, did this elf-woman. She didn't have any obvious weapons—sensible, since it was conceivable I could have taken any heat away from her and used it myself—but she *did* look poised and ready, like a martial-arts expert. She was dressed in conservative corp-type fashions—nothing extravagant or flashy, but still definitely well-heeled.

In my peripheral vision I caught movement in the hallway outside the door. There were two more figures out there. I couldn't see details, but it was a sure bet *they* were packing serious heat, and were ready to take me down if I made the first wrong move against the elf-slitch. I sighed again and just stood there in the middle of the room, wrapped in my sheet.

"Here," she said, tossing a small, soft-sided suitcase onto the bed. "Get dressed please, Mr. Montgomery," she went on emotionlessly. "Someone will come to fetch you." And with that she turned on her heel and walked out. The door shut behind her, and the maglock snapped back into place.

I crossed to the bed and sat down heavily on it. For a couple of minutes I stared at the suitcase as though I was expecting it to sprout fangs and go for my throat. Just what the frag was going on here anyway? Maybe it wasn't the yaks who'd bagged me after all. Unless there was something big that I was missing—not an unreasonable possibility, I had to admit—the only interest the yaks would have in me was to make me dead, in as protracted and messy a way as possible. That kind of game wouldn't involve giving me clothes beforehand, would it?

I shook my head. Then I reached over and undid the latch of the suitcase.

If this had been an old-style action-espionage flatfilm, the clothes in the suitcase would have been a finely tailored dinner jacket with black tie and patent leather shoes. No luck there, chummer. The case contained simple tropical-weight casual wear: shirt, slacks, shoes, and undergarments. All in my size—or close enough to it—incidentally. No armor, predictably, and definitely nothing I could use as a weapon. Even the shoes had apparently been chosen to minimize their effectiveness as weapons, in case I'd happened to be an expert at savat. The uppers were rough fabric almost like burlap, and the soles were rope. (No drek—hemp rope.) They were comfortable enough, though, and that was all that mattered at the moment. The bag also contained my wallet, my 'puter, and all my credsticks.

So I dressed. Shrugging into the shirt introduced me to a complex spectrum of pain radiating from the region of my left shoulder blade. I breathed in deeply and worked the shoulder . . . immediately regretting it. The pain was almost enough to knock me flat on my hoop. I tried the deep-breath thing again, a lot more cautiously this time.

Okay, the pain was bad, but more the dull, throbbing kind you get from a major contusion. The light armor I'd been wearing had spread the kinetic energy of the impact over a wide enough area that it hadn't punctured my precious skin. Also, the fact that the pain wasn't knife-sharp stabs told me that my ribs weren't broken. Be thankful for small favors, I told myself.

I'd just finished dressing when the maglock snapped back again. (Yes, I *was* definitely under observation.) The same elf-slitch appeared in the doorway, backed by the same two barely glimpsed figures in the hallway behind her. "Come with me, please, Mr. Montgomery," she said.

I came. What the hell else was I supposed to do? I followed the corp-biff out from my room into the hallway, hanging a good pace back. The two shadows—elves too, but surprisingly beefy for that metatype—fell in behind me and to the sides. Both had tasers on their belts and held oversized stun batons ready to swing. Chill, brah, I wanted to tell them, I'm not planning anything militant unless you force me into it. But I held my tongue.

Along the corridor we went, the elf-biff walking point, me walking slack, and my two armed side-men picking up the rear. Decor-wise, the place still looked like a hospital, but it didn't take me long to start second-guessing that conclusion. Hospitals—the ones I've visited, at least—have antiseptic-looking people always hurrying to and fro, carrying pocket 'puters and portable scanners. The air's always filled with that hospital smell—equal parts rubbing alcohol, urine, fear, and despair—and PA systems are always telling Dr. So-and-So to do such-and-such *stat.* Not here. We were alone in the hallway, me and my escorts. The air smelled of nothing whatsoever, and the loudest sound was the tap-tap of the elf biff's stiletto heels on the acrylamide tile floor.

We reached a T-intersection and turned left. An ideal place for a nurses' station if this were a hospital. Here, though, there was just a bank of three elevators. One opened its doors as we approached, and the elf gestured for me to stop.

If I'd wanted to make a break for it, this would have been the time. Something I'd learned early in my training in the Star is that getting into an elevator with a captive is—like getting into a car—an activity that requires good technique if you don't want your captive to take advantage. The three elves had good technique. One of my burly side-men went in first, holding his stun baton ready. Then the biff gestured me in. The second muscleboy followed, his baton lightly touching my kidney. Only once I was inside and secured—one stun baton at your kidney, another touching your groin is a *frag* of a disincentive against trying something stupid—did the corp-biff step inside.

Hey, they could have saved themselves the trouble if they'd only asked me. Making a break for it when I didn't know where I was or which way to run just didn't seem to be a reasonable option at the moment.

Take, for example, the fact that the "hospital" was apparently two levels underground—judging by the elevator control panel, at least. Frag, if I'd made a break before this, I'd probably have bolted *down* a fire-escape stairway, and found myself running out of options in a real hurry.

The door sighed shut, the corp biff touched the UP button, and off we went. Moments later, the macroplast doors hissed open again, and our entire entourage stepped out.

Into the reception area of what was obviously a high-tone corporate building. Lots of chrome, lots of polarized mirrorfinish, lots of technoflash. All the trappings you'd normally expect: holos on the wall of suits schmoozing with politicos and other reprobates; waiting-room furniture that costs more than an apartment in downtown Seattle; reception desk, complete with glamour-faced receptionist jacked into the system; big corp logo on the wall behind said reception desk. For a moment I focused on that logo.

TIC, it said in a curlicued, stylized font. And below that, in smaller letters—almost as an afterthought—the expansion: Telestrian Industries Corporation.

Telestrian. Where had I heard that name before?

Memory flashed back. It was a Tir Tairngire corp, wasn't it, with an arcology somewhere in Portland? Not much activity outside the Tir itself—or so I'd *thought*. This facility seemed to indicate otherwise. I wouldn't have so much as recognized the name if there hadn't been all that hash-up some time back during a highly publicized reorganization of the elven corp.

The receptionist behind the desk—elf, natch—flashed me a fifteen-gigawatt smile as I passed by. It didn't seem to matter one iota that I was being escorted by two muscleboys, each prodding me in the back with a stun baton. It occurred to me that, even if I'd run through the lobby buck-naked and on fire, she'd still have fired off that same practiced smile.

On we went, my friends and I, past the reception desk into the atrium of the TIC building.

That stopped me in my tracks—earning me two painful pokes in the kidneys, but I hardly noticed. I've never been much for typical corp architecture. Too many corps seem to get into the old macho "I've got the biggest architect" kind of drek, forgetting that people actually have to live and work in their monuments to too much cred and too little taste. Not TIC—at least, not here.

The place was bright and airy, the atrium open to the azure blue sky above. Open-sided corridors looked down onto the atrium from all three stories of the building. People were doing about their corp business along those corridors. As I watched, one slag on the second floor reached over the railing and plucked a blossom from one of the flowering trees—that's right, *trees*—that grew in the open area. He sniffed the flower appreciatively, then stuck it into his buttonhole before moving on. Birds twittered and cheeped from the boughs above me, and the air was full of perfume.

Under one of the trees was a small conference table. Half a dozen intense-looking corp types were discussing something—discussing it quite heatedly, judging by their body language. I couldn't hear the first word of what they were saying, however; the "conference room" was obviously equipped with white-noise generators.

"All right, already," I said peevishly as my two sideboys poked me in the back, and off we went again. Over to the far corner of the atrium, and up a movator to the second floor, then up another to the third and top.

Top floor—executive suite. I could tell immediately. The pearl gray carpet on the floors was deeper-piled. The art on the walls was more understated, elegant, and obviously expensive. The people passing by in the halls were better-dressed. (Don't get me wrong: Even on the ground floor, people wore suits that would cost as much as a car. The only difference on the third floor was the *model* of car—Jackrabbit or Westwind.) I could almost *smell* the cred in the air.

Along one of those open-sided hallways we walked, then turned away from the atrium and into serious suit-land. We approached a big set of double doors that had to be real mahogany and not wood-grained duraplast. The doors silently swung open before we reached them. The corp-biff jandered on through with me at her heels. The two muscleboys peeled off, though, and stayed outside the doors, which immediately swung shut behind me. Which implied serious security on this side of the doors, of course. Surveillance cameras at the very least, and probably spirits or elementals on a very short leash. Just as well I wasn't planning anything untoward at the moment.

On jandered my escort, past various office doors—all mahogany, all notably missing nameplates; presumably, if you didn't know where to find the office you wanted, you just plain didn't belong here. Another couple of turns, and another double door; this time floor-to-ceiling transpex with some kind of chromatic coating that made the doors look like huge opalescent soap bubbles. Again the doors swung back as we approached and again closed silently after us.

End of the line, apparently. The elf stopped in the middle of an antechamber or waiting room and gestured silently to one of the coral-hued leather couches. And then, still without saying a word, she turned on her heel and strode back out through the soap-bubble doors.

On a whim, I tried to follow. Predictably, those doors didn't open for me the way they did for her.

Okay, so I'd been bagged by pros and taken to see some

high corp suit who had something he/she/it wanted me to know . . . presumably. (Unless TIC was a yak cover, and this was the waiting room for the torture chamber.) I remember reading once that, "Life is just one damn thing after another." Wrongo. It's the same damn thing over and over again.

I wandered back into the middle of the waiting room and took a good, hard look around. The soap-bubble doors took up much of one wall. In the center of the opposite wall was a single wooden door. (Not mahogany; something even richer-looking, with an even stronger grain pattern. A native Hawai'ian species, maybe?) Again, there was no nameplate on the door. But it didn't need one. I can recognize the office door of the head muckamuck without any outside cues.

Along the other two walls were couches, a delicate coral in color, perfectly coordinated with the pastel carpets and wall-coverings. On the walls were three large paintings.

Yes, I mean *paintings*. Flat things with no 3-D to them. Paint manually applied to some kind of backing material. Rare, these days, and generally *very* expensive because of it. Out of curiosity—and because I didn't have much else to do at the moment—I strolled up to the nearest one and gave it the scan.

Strange drek, chummer. It was an undersea scene, complete with coral and brilliantly colored reef fish and happy, smiling dolphins. (*Dolphins*? I guess that was some indication of the painting's age. Dolphins went out quite a while back when they couldn't adapt to the concentration of toxics we were tossing into their oceans. And you can bet they weren't smiling for quite some time before the end.) So far so good, I guess. Then it started getting weird. There were Grecian-style columns, temples, and other crap—even *pyramids*, honest to Ghu!—on the bottom of the ocean, and the happy, smiling dolphins were swimming in and out among them. Hmm.

I moved on to the next painting. Much the same thing: same reefs, same ruins, same happy, smiling dolphins. Except this time there was some kind of glow emanating from inside the ruined buildings. And maybe the dolphins looked just a tad happier, I don't know.

Third painting, exactly the same, but more so. And this time, over the glowing door of one of the pyramids, there was some strange symbol carved into the rock. The Eye of Horus crossed with the biohazard trefoil, that's what it looked like, but I know squat about art, so I might have been wrong. Weird drek. Atlantis?

I bent closer for a look at the signature: an incomprehensible scrawl that might have been "*Andrew Annen-*something", or maybe not. The date was 1996.

"What do you think, Mr. Montgomery?"

The husky contralto voice sounded from close behind me. I tried to keep tight rein on my sphincters, and struggled to keep my movements smooth and urbane as I turned around.

The dark-grained wood door had opened silently, and, just as silently, an elf had emerged. Tall and slender she was, with fine blond hair curled into a coif that seemed to defy gravity. Her eyes were pale—faint blue, maybe, or gray. She was dressed in a broad-shouldered, tab-collared corp skirtsuit that could have been made of liquid gold. On one epaulet was the designer's marque—the stylized Z of Zoé. On the other was the Telestrian Industries Corporation logotype.

The elf smiled at me, and extended her hand. On reflex I took it. Her grip was firm, her skin cool and silk-smooth. "Again I feel like I'm at a disadvantage," I told her as calmly as I could manage. "You know my name . . ."

She smiled. "I meant no disrespect, Mr. Montgomery." Under the right circumstances that voice could curl my toes. At the moment, though, I wasn't in the mood. "My name is Chantal Monot." She gave the name a strong French inflection.

I racked my brain for any details I could recall about TIC. "James Telestrian's . . . daughter-in-law?" I guessed, naming the CEO of the overall TIC empire.

The elf's smile broadened. "Nepotism isn't *that* bad in the company," she chided me lightly. "Not *every* executive is related to James. Many, but not all."

I yielded the point with a nod. "And your position is, Ms. Monot . . .?"

"President and chief executive officer of Telestrian Industries Corporation, South Pacific Operations."

I blinked. *Ookaay* . . . It always pays to know what level you're working at. (In this case, the highest.)

Monot inclined her head toward the painting and repeated, "What do you think, Mr. Montgomery?" She chuckled. "And *please* don't tell me you 'know nothing about art but know what you like.' "

Since that was exactly what I *had* been about to tell her,

I thought about it for a moment. "Strong colors and pretty good technique," I said finally. "But it's going to overwhelm the wrong decor."

She quirked an eyebrow in what seemed to me genuine amusement. "And the subject matter?"

Fragging squirrely didn't seem to be a politic thing to say, so I settled for, "Interesting."

"Yes," she agreed with an arch smile. "Isn't it?"

Frag, that's one of the reasons I *hate* dealing with elves. No, correct that—with *some* elves. It's that pervasive "I know something *you* don't, nyah nyah" attitude so many of them have. Irritating, big-time.

Chantal Monot gestured to the open door. "Please," she said. "There are some things I'd like to discuss with you."

Of course there were. I shrugged, and I preceded her through the door into her office.

I was familiar with the way Diamond Head looked from the west—from the Honolulu side. Now I got to see it from the other side, and I had to admit it was just as striking. The TIC building was only three stories tall, but it seemed to be built on some kind of ridge or bluff, so there was nothing to block the president's view of the old, eroded crater.

While I was still staring, Monot took a seat behind the large desk. She gestured to one of the comfortable-looking guest chairs, and I sat down. "Tea?" she asked. Before I could either refuse or accept, she'd turned to a silver samovar on the credenza beside her and prepared two cups. Glasses, actually, in the Russian style. She handed one over to me. I sniffed, then sipped appreciatively. Never tried *real* Oolong tea? Your loss.

"I was serious about the subject of the paintings outside," Monot said at length. "Have you ever realized quite how pervasive the legend of a sunken continent, a lost world, actually is?"

I shrugged. "It's never really kept me up nights," I had to admit.

"It is interesting, though. What do you know about Lemuria?"

Again I shrugged. "It's where lemurs come from?"

I'd meant it as a smart-hooped comeback line, but she nodded approvingly. "In a way, yes. Did you know that, before geologists understood about continental drift, scientists were puzzled by the fact that fossilized lemur bones were found on two distinct continents, separated by thousands of kilometers of ocean? How had the lemurs crossed from one continent to another ... if there hadn't once been a land bridge, a midoceanic continent, connecting the two? Since there was no land bridge in existence, the only logical conclusion was that it had sunk centuries or millennia before."

I decided to stick with my response to the paintings. "Interesting." (Actually, I could hardly have cared less, but I figured it's best to be polite about the crank beliefs of the president and chief executive officer of Telestrian Industries Corporation, South Pacific Operations.)

"Isn't it?" she agreed. "What I find even more interesting is that the legends of Lemuria indirectly involve the islands of Hawai'i. Do you know who originally colonized the islands, Mr. Montgomery?" I shook my head, and she answered her own question. "Polynesians from Tahiti. According to some beliefs, they crossed the ocean, looking for their own sunken continent. There are even some who claim that this sunken continent will one day re-emerge from the water, with the volcano of Haleakala as its highest mountain peak."

She smiled enigmatically. "It's interesting how different, seemingly unrelated factors are actually connected, if you look below the surface." She paused, and I knew she was getting down to biz; all this drek about lemurs and sinking continents was just preamble.

"Like you, Mr. Montgomery," Monot continued after a moment. "*You* seem to be one of those unrelated factors. Yet you're *not* unrelated, are you? You're actually connected, directly or indirectly, with many different ... well, let's call them *threads*."

I snorted. A tight feeling had been building in my chest throughout her lemur prattle. Now I realized what that feeling was—anger. "Look," I said sharply, "I've had enough of all this vague, oblique and veiled-reference crap, you scan? Everybody's talking at me like I know a lot more about what's going down than I do, and it's torquing me off. Barnard did it, Ho did it, fragging *Ryumyo* did it, Harlech did it, and now *you're* doing it ..."

I stopped in midpurge as Monot raised a slender hand. Her brows knotted in a frown. "Who?" she asked.

It took me a moment to get my derailed train of thought

back on track. I ticked them off on my fingers. "Barnard, Ho, Ryumyo, Harlech—"

"Harlech," she repeated, interrupting again. "Who was that?"

I hesitated. There was something strange in Monot's expression—something that made me suspect she knew all too well, and didn't like it one bit. "Quentin Harlech," I told her. "He said to call him Quinn."

She went slightly pale, and she whispered something then, under her breath. It could have been a repetition of the name I'd given her, but in the order you'd find it in a 'puter database, last name first. Or it could have been something else. ("Big worm"/"bakeware" time again . . .)

"That's the slag," I confirmed. Even though I didn't know jack about what was going down, I kept a good dose of bluster in my voice. If something had knocked Monot off-stride, maybe I could use it to my advantage. "But what's the big deal?" I asked. "He's an elf, too."

Chantal Monot's pale eyes flashed with momentary anger. Then her professional control took over, and I watched as she forced herself to calmness. "He may be an elf," she said at last, "but elves don't speak with one voice. Particularly on an issue as important as this." (Important, *neh*? I filed that gem away for future reference.)

I shrugged. "From what I've read, TIC is *in like this*"—I held up crossed fingers—"with the Tir government. Sometimes, your corp's an instrument of policy for the Tir nation. And if that isn't speaking with one voice—"

She broke in again. "We may be an instrument of policy for the Tir's *leadership*," she corrected coldly, "not for the *nation*." (And I filed *that* one away, too. It didn't make any sense at the moment, but maybe later . . .)

Monot gazed out the window at Diamond Head. The rock face was washed with the ruddy light of early morning. After almost a minute she turned back to me. "You spoke with . . . *Quinn Harlech*, didn't you, Mr. Montgomery? What did he tell you?"

"It didn't make much sense," I told her truthfully. "He said he was going to blow the lid off something. Let him do it, for all I care—it's no skin off my hoop."

Monot nodded slowly. "Did he say how?"

"Not as far as I could tell." Then I hesitated. "Now I think about it, he implied he'd already done it."

"And I assume he knew of your association with Gordon Ho."

I nodded at that one. "He knew, all right." He'd seen my deputy's badge—gone, now—and certainly seemed to know what it meant.

Apparently that wasn't good news. Chantal Monot looked like one troubled elf. After a few more moments of thought she sighed. "Thank you for coming in, Mr. Montgomery. I appreciate your candor."

I snorted. "If it's candor you wanted, you could have gotten it without the narcodart," I pointed out.

Monot at least had the grace to look a little embarrassed. "I apologize for that, Mr. Montgomery, but our operative"—she must have meant the biff with the bracers—"evaluated your mental condition as being dangerous, to her and to yourself." (Translation: scared to the point of drekking myself. Granted.) "She made the field decision to incapacitate you rather than risking something a lot more unpleasant for all concerned."

Okay, I could understand that. If *my* job was to arrange a meeting with some wild-eyed spacecase who'd just burst out of an alley brandishing a gun, I'd probably have narked him in his tracks, too. That didn't mean I had to like it, though.

Monot pressed a key on the sophisticated telecom built into the desk. "A driver will take you anywhere you wish to go," she told me.

"Hold the phone," I said. "Is that it? You track me and dart me and bag me . . . and that's it? No more questions?"

Monot looked at me bleakly. "The questions I had are no longer relevant."

I think I blinked in surprise . . . and then again in understanding. "Aren't you even going to warn me to keep my nose out of things that are too big for me?"

The elf looked genuinely sad as she said, "I think it's far too late for that, Mr. Montgomery."

18

And so, yet again, I got to ride in a fragging Rolls Phaeton. It was almost too much *déjà* fragging *vu* for me to handle. If the driver had run down the bullet-proof partition, turned round to me, and grinned with Scott's face, I'd have taken it in stride and offered him a fragging drink.

Once we were off the TIC facility grounds—the corp building looked just as wiz from outside as it did from in—the driver wanted to know where to take me. That took some deep thought. All the places I'd already flopped were blown, one way or another, and my invitation to a meet with Chantal Monot had interrupted my search for another. I chewed on it for a few minutes while the driver "orbited" Kapiolani Park. Finally, I gave up, and did what I probably should have done from the outset. I asked the driver.

Frag, it's not *that* illogical, is it? Cab drivers know all the best bars, the best restaurants, the best flops, and the best places to get into deep trouble. And when you get right down to it, a corp chauffeur's not that much different from a hack driver, is he?

I laid out my requirements to the chauffeur—low profile, no questions asked—and let him think on it. Not so much as a minute later he nodded his head, and we took off in the direction of Waikiki.

(Hold the phone: Wasn't getting the chauffeur involved a major breach of security? Well, yeah, talking solely in terms of fieldcraft, it was a drek-headed move. Speaking practically, though? If Monot and her colleagues at TIC wanted me dead, I'd be dead. If they wanted to know where I went, they'd had several hours to plant a tracer—inside some body cavity, if they wanted to make it secure—that I'd never be able to find. The way I had it figured, getting the chauffeur to help me out didn't increase my exposure any. In fact, it *de*creased it, by saving me from blundering into something unwelcome as I'd done the night before.)

The Phaeton rolled west on Monsarrat, then turned right onto Kalakaua Avenue. Into the gleaming heart of Waikiki we drove, then the chauffeur cut right and cruised down a ramp into an underground parking lot. The security guard in his little booth flipped my driver a quick salute and raised the blast-proof barrier. Without slowing, the limo rolled on into the parking concourse.

We pulled up right in front of a bank of elevators. A big crest identified the place as New Foster Tower.

I rapped on the transpex partition and gave the driver a "what the frag *now*?" look.

"Ms. Monot always has a number of rooms reserved here in TIC's name," the chauffeur replied via the intercom, "to handle unexpected visitors." (I reckoned I certainly fit that categorization . . .) "Room nineteen-oh-five is yours for as long as you need it."

I raised an eyebrow at that. Once he'd figured out where he was going, it wouldn't have taken the driver much effort to link the car's computer system with the hotel's and check me in, but . . . "What about the key?" I asked.

"It's already programmed for your thumbprint," the driver answered.

Oh, really? That meant Monot had scanned my thumbprint into the TIC computer system while I was sleeping off the narcodart, and my records were accessible from a mobile computer system, i.e., the limo. The driver had obviously contacted the TIC central system, and had it download my print data to the security system at New Foster Tower. Efficient as all hell.

But I didn't like it, not one bit. Throughout my career, I've gone to great lengths to keep personal data flags like prints out of corporate records. I can think of too many ways to frag with someone's life once you've got access to flags like that. Of course, there wasn't squat I could do about it at the moment. When I had some time—and some cred—to spare, I'd have to make arrangements for new fingerprints.

I pushed the limo door open and climbed out, heading for the elevator. I turned at the soft whine of a power window behind me.

"Here, I was told to give you these back." The driver tossed me two objects, which I caught a little clumsily. My deputy's badge from King Kamehameha V. And, more important, my Manhunter. I drew breath to thank him, but he'd already powered the window back up and was pulling away. Just as well—I didn't have any cash to tip him anyway.

Room 1905 at New Foster Tower wasn't anywhere near as luxurious as my room at the Diamond Head corporate hostelry. That still left it one giant step above anywhere else I'd stayed in my life, though. The entire convenience suite at the Ilima Joy would have fit into the bathroom—fragging near, at least—and while the bed wasn't *quite* big enough for a Roman-style orgy, I couldn't imagine that I'd have any opportunity to be disappointed by the fact.

The view was nice, too—a southwestern exposure, looking out over Mamala Bay. The hotels on the other side of Kalakaua Avenue—the ones that actually lined the waterfront—were too tall to give me a view of Waikiki Beach itself. They were "terraced," though; the buildings between me and the ocean were lower than New Foster Tower . . . as, presumably, the ones behind the Tower were taller. (Good civic planning there, now that I thought about it.) That meant that, even if I couldn't see the beach, I could still see the ocean, in its impossible blue. As I watched, a huge ocean-going trimaran—forty-five meters along the waterline, if it was a millimeter—was outbound under full sail, its garishly colored spinnaker seeming to burn with its own internal light. For the first time in a *long* time, I actually saw Hawai'i through the eyes of a tourist rather than as a shadow-slag running for his life.

It didn't last, though. Biz was pressing. Doss at New Foster Tower or no, my nuts were still in a very tight vise. It was time to do something about that.

Room 1905's telecom didn't measure up to the one at the Diamond Head hostelry either, but that didn't matter. I didn't need any more than the most rudimentary of features at the moment. Jacking in my Quincy-modified 'puter, I quickly established my own equivalent of a blind relay—a simple little subversion of the telecom's programming so it wouldn't append an accurate "originator address" to any messages I sent. Once I was happy with my attempts at security, I placed a call.

Jacques Barnard picked up almost at once. (Didn't the slag ever do *anything* but hang by a phone?) His face clouded up the moment he recognized me, and he opened his mouth to bitch, but I overrode him. "I want out, Barnard," I almost yelled. "*Now*, chummer, okay? You got me into this, now you get me *out*."

The corporator blinked wordlessly for a moment; I guess senior veeps or whatever don't get screamed at very often. Then his brows drew together in a nasty-looking scowl, and he snarled, "You've got a lot of gall—"

"That's not all I've got, you slot," I broke in again. "You *owe* me, okay? You said so, and I'm holding you to it. I've found out a few things over here about Yamatetsu's operations that might attract a little unwanted attention, *karimasu-ka?*" That was pure bluff, of course. I didn't have any dirt on Yamatetsu—nothing I could use, at least. But Barnard didn't have to know that.

Not that the gambit worked anyway. His nasty scowl became an equally nasty smile. "I doubt it, Mr. Montgomery. I seriously doubt it. And as to debts? Well, I consider any beholding I might have felt toward you to have been voided when you broke security."

That set me back a little. "Play that one back," I told him. " 'Broke security'?"

Barnard looked almost pityingly at me. "I expected better of you, Mr. Montgomery." And with that, he reached out to cancel the connection.

"Wait," I barked. "Just wait a tick, okay?" Barnard's face shifted into an expression of much-put-upon patience, but at least he didn't hang up. "I'm not running a scam here," I told him as sincerely as I could. "I don't know what the frag you're talking about."

"I seriously doubt that."

"It's *true*, frag it all," I shouted back. "Tell me what the frag you're talking about. Then, if I *did* 'break security,' I'll snivel and crawl and kiss your hoop at midday in downtown Kyoto, or whatever the hell you want. But at the moment I honestly don't know what the frag you're accusing me of."

Barnard gave a long-suffering sigh. "The *Ali'i*, Mr. Montgomery," he said wearily. "Your meeting with the *Ali'i*. It was supposed to be confidential." He hesitated. "Or, at least, the fact that you were serving as my agent was supposed to be confidential.

"Yet what did you do? Virtually the moment you left the Iolani Palace, you started spreading the word that you were a corporate emissary, conveying personal messages from the Corporate Court to King Kamehameha V. Do you have any understanding of how damaging that has been?"

I shook my head. "Bull*drek*, I did that!" I shot back. "Pure, unadulterated *kanike*, okay? I didn't tell anyone. Look somewhere else for your security leak, goddamn it."

Barnard's voice was deceptively quiet, and his expression had settled into a cold, emotionless mask. "But I did look elsewhere, Mr. Montgomery. With no success whatsoever. *You* are the only possible leak."

"Bull*drek* I am!" I shouted again.

"If not you, then who?"

"What about Ho himself?"

"Ho?" Barnard laughed aloud at that. "That's the last thing Ho would leak. If the rival faction in the legislature plays their cards right—and there's no reason to expect that they won't—he stands to lose his throne ... and possibly more. Try again, Mr. Montgomery, hmm?"

"Christ, *I* don't ..." I pulled up in midbluster. Maybe I did know. "Do you know someone named Quentin Harlech?" I asked.

"The name doesn't mean anything to me."

"Then maybe you should run it through your 'puters and your databases and your legions of fragging *informants,* Barnard. I'd lay long odds that Harlech's the one who blew your op." Yes ... as I spoke, I grew steadily more convinced that it *had* been the strange elf. After all, hadn't he as good as admitted that he'd blown my cover? I hadn't known what he was yapping about at the time, but now I thought I had it chipped.

Barnard's expression made it clear that he wasn't even a little convinced that I was telling the truth. But at least he didn't seem to be quite so convinced I'd ratted him out. "I'll run the name," he said slowly.

"While you're at it," I suggested, "why don't you tell me what the frag's going on here? Okay, so the word's out King Kam's talking to the megacorps. So what?"

Barnard sighed again, and shook his head. "Haven't you been paying any attention whatsoever to the political situation in the islands?"

"Like I told you before, I've had other things on my mind recently," I said dryly.

He didn't dignify that with a response. "Gordon Ho's position depends on a kind of balancing act, you might call it," he went on as if I hadn't even spoken. "The megacorporations on one hand, certain factions within his own government on the other."

"*Na Kama'aina,*" I put in, just to show I wasn't totally brain-fried.

"*Na Kama'aina,* yes. If the *Na Kama'aina* faction can prove to the populace that their king is toadying to the megacorporations, the people will remove him from power. If, on the other hand, the corporations are dissatisfied with Ho's efforts to maintain a stable business climate, *they* will remove him from power."

I nodded: pineapple plutocrats all over again, *neh*? "So what's going on?"

"The former, of course," Barnard said flatly. "Events have obviously been manipulated to stir up anticorporate sentiments—among the people as a whole, but more important among various militant groups . . ."

"ALOHA."

"Of course," he acknowledged. "You know, of course, that the assassination of Tokudaiji-*san* has been positioned as a corporate maneuver.

"And there have been other . . . *provocative actions* . . . as well."

I blinked at that. I hadn't heard of anything else, but then, as I'd told Barnard, I'd had other things on my mind of late, like dragons and high-velocity ordnance.

Barnard continued, "And now, your revelation that . . ."

"It wasn't me, frag it all!"

"It hardly matters," he pointed out coldly. "The revelation that the *Ali'i* has been enjoying private meetings with representatives of the megacorporations is damaging enough, regardless of its source."

"But hell, he's *got* to meet with megacorp reps sometimes," I pointed out.

"Of course. But it's the secrecy surrounding your actions that makes them appear so damaging. If Gordon Ho were truly acting in the best interest of his people—and not feathering his own nest through private concessions to the megacorporations—why would such secrecy be necessary?

"Consider the situation," Barnard went on. "How would *you* interpret a clandestine meeting between the head of *your* government and the personal representative of a senior megacorporate executive, hmm?"

Okay, frag it, I got the point. Sure enough, my paranoia would kick in, and I'd conclude the government muckamuck was cutting a private deal, and had his tongue firmly up the corp-rep's hoop. "So what kind of drek's coming down?"

"Just what you'd expect," Barnard said grimly. "*Na Kama'aina* spokespeople in the legislature are putting pressure on the *Ali'i*. Others are stirring up the populace against him."

"Any violence?"

"Not yet." There was a nasty tone of inevitability in his voice.

"What about ALOHA?"

"Policlub members are involved in the agitprop, as one would expect," Barnard explained. "So far, though, they seem to be keeping a low profile."

"But you don't expect that to last."

"No."

"And then what?"

Barnard shrugged, suddenly looking even older than he had the last time I'd seen him. He might as well have been withering away from some ugly wasting disease. (*Frag*, I found myself wondering, *why do people go to the trouble of climbing the corporate ladder if it's going to harsh them out like this*?) "It depends, I suppose," he said quietly.

"On what?"

"On ALOHA's actions. On Gordon Ho's replacement, if his throne is actually usurped. The megacorporations don't take kindly to threats against their operations."

"They'll take over Hawai'i?"

Barnard nodded. "If forced to do so, yes, they will."

"So it all might come apart?" I leaned toward the screen. "Then get me the frag *out* of here, Barnard. This isn't my country. It's not my fight, and it's none of my fragging business, okay?"

"Unacceptable," he snapped instantly. "I need someone on-site to keep me informed on developments."

I pounded the table; the telecom jumped. "*Frag you*, Barnard!" I yelled. "You don't need me. You've got Christ-knows-how-many spooks and stoolies and squeals and yaps and informants!"

He nodded. "And every one will lie to me if it's in his best interest to do so."

"And I *won't* lie to you, if it's in *my* best interest? Get actual!"

"Of course you'll lie if forced to it, Mr. Montgomery," Barnard agreed with a smile. "But your needs are different from my normal contacts, and your ... er, *bias* ... will be different from theirs. The truth will, presumably, lie somewhere between your description and theirs."

"Oh, just peachy fragging keen. 'Let's hang Dirk Montgomery's hoop out in the wind so we can contrast *his* lies with the lies from some other yaps.' Thanks tons, Mr. fragging Barnard."

My anger left him totally untouched. Well, hell, why not? All my bitching was about as meaningful in his worldview as the mewling of a fragging kitten. "Perhaps it will never come to that extreme," he pointed out quietly. "Who knows, Mr. Montgomery? Perhaps cooler heads will prevail in all of this." He was trying to convince me, but was a long fragging way from sounding terribly convinced himself.

The explosion woke me from troubled dreams at about oh-four-hundred.

I didn't know it was an explosion at first. In fact, I didn't know what it was that had roused me. For a few seconds I just lay in bed, staring at the ceiling. But then a second concussion hit the transpex picture window, sounding a dull thud. I was on my feet in an instant, dashing over to the window.

The second fireball was still roiling into the sky, a dirty red fire-flower blooming from the dark ground. It was far to the right as I looked out the window—that made it to the west. What was in that direction? The airport, for one thing, but I didn't think the explosion was that far away. (Hell, if it was, it must have been one fragger of a blast ...) I wracked my brains.

Yeah, that's right ... I remembered part of Scott's quickie tour of Greater Honolulu. There was an island off the shoreline of Honolulu—Sand Island, or something equally uninspired—that was a kind of Special Enterprise Zone for corporate activities. From what I remembered of the geography, Sand Island was about the right distance away. ALOHA had been busy.

Think about it—what else would the story be? Two explosions? Despite what you see on the trideo or in the sims, drek doesn't just blow up on its own—not very often, at least. Almost invariably, when something goes boom, it's because some slag arranged for it to go boom.

The distant fire-flower faded, and I turned my back on it, crossing the room to slump back onto the bed. I'd hit the sack at about nineteen-hundred the night before, after spending the whole day just keeping a low profile around the hotel room. That meant I'd already gotten nine hours of sleep—more than I normally enjoy. So how come I still felt like a wet bag of drek? Aftereffects of the narcodart, obviously, or so it pleased me to tell myself. The other alternatives—"getting old," "slowing down," "burning out," "too drek-kicked to cut it any more"—were a lot less conducive to good self-esteem.

I snagged the remote from the bed table and keyed on the trideo. Quickly, I flipped through the channels: late-late-late show, early movie, *Zelda Does Zurich-Orbital,* a twenty-four-hour sports channel (What do they run at oh-four-hundred? It looked like Albanian-rules badminton or some drek.), two talking heads arguing economics, a brain-dead charcom, two more talking heads arguing but in Japanese this time, and on and on. I settled on one channel—*Zelda* got the nod, surprise surprise—and waited it out.

Maybe I *am* getting old. I nodded off before Zelda had boffed her way through half of the (remarkably well-equipped) "corporate executives" in the low-budget pornovid. Brassy music jolted me out of a doze, and I struggled to focus eyes and mind on an animated News Bulletin banner dancing across the trid screen.

Well, I'll condense what I saw. Like so many on-the-spot news reports, this one comprised a frag of a lot of "Well, Marcia, we don't really know squat about what's going on here, but at least we're the first network to tell you that live ..." By flipping between channels, I managed to piece together most of the story, however.

I'd been right about the location: The two blasts *had* taken place in the corp zone on Sand Island. Apparently—this was the official story, at least, confirmed by a *Na Maka'i* spokescop—terrorists had penetrated the corp zone's security and planted three jury-rigged "devices" in various locations. Intrepid security guards had found one of the bombs on Mitsuhama turf and managed to disarm it before it went bang. Unfortunately, two other "devices" had detonated, doing minimal damage to the property of Renraku and Monobe. There were no casualties, damage was extremely limited, and the *Na Maka'i* spokescop was confident that the guilty parties would be apprehended within hours.

Yeah, right. I was playing "spot the lie," and I caught three of them. First, there was nothing "jury-rigged" about the devices—not judging by the fireball I saw, at least. Unless the bombers had wheeled it into place inside a fragging moving truck, that was an efficient, high-yield bomb.

Second—again judging by the fireball—there's no fragging way the damage done was "minimal." A blast powerful enough to rattle double-glazed transpex at three klicks? Cut me loose, here.

Third—no casualties? Give me a break, boys and girls of the media. In one of those herky-jerky on-the-spot tridcasts, I saw at least two body bags getting loaded into a meat-wagon. If you're going to lie, at least make sure your own trideo footage doesn't contradict you too blatantly.

As it turned out, I was treated to a little more than the official story. While scanning the channels, I came across something that had to be a local pirate tridcaster. The production values chewed, and the announcer seemed to be halfway out of his head on some choice mind-bender, but at least he had an innovative take on the whole thing.

According to the pirate, the whole fragging thing was the corps' faults. Peaceful demonstrators had been protesting outside the corp zone on Sand Island, and at about oh-four-hundred, the zone's corp sec-guards had—without provocation—opened fire. It was only then, with scores of their comrades injured or dying, that some of the protesters did *something*—the pirate announcer wasn't precisely clear on what—that caused the explosions as "fair and just retribution" for the corp-instigated carnage.

Yeah, right. "Peaceful demonstrators" packing satchel-charges of C12 "just in case?" Pull the other one.

Still, I thought as I lay back on the bed, Barnard had raised an interesting point earlier, one that could also apply here. When you've got two contradictory reports, coming from two sources with vested interests, assume that both are tissues of lies. The truth probably lies somewhere in the middle. Maybe some relative innocents *were* cacked ... either before or after the blasts. (Frag, if I were a corp sec-guard and the site I was supposed to protect just went kaboom, I'd probably be a little less stringent than normal about identifying targets before shooting . . .)

So, predictably, the Powers That Be were trying to down-play the story, while the hotheads were trying to blow it out of all proportion. I could see already how it was going to po-larize. Gordon Ho and his supporters would champion the official line—no casualties, minimal damage. *Na Kama'aina* and ALOHA would be hard-selling the pirate's take on the whole thing.

I climbed back into bed with a sigh. It didn't much look as though cooler heads were going to prevail after all.

19

The situation had gotten even worse, I discovered as I watched the trid over my room-service breakfast. Monobe security forces had tracked the bombers—or some convenient "suspects," at any rate—and gotten into a high-speed pursuit through the streets of Aiea. All the suspects had been shot while trying to resist arrest (tell me another one). What was worse, all in all, was the total casualty count: four suspects killed, two innocent bystanders geeked when a Monobe MPUV "Hummer" T-boned their car, another noncombatant winged by stray gunfire and not expected to make it, plus four more civilians messed up to one degree or another. Frag it all, if the corps had decided to go out of their way to stir up popular sentiment against themselves, I couldn't think of many more efficient ways of going about it.

The news crews also showed several pretty nasty demonstrations against the *Ali'i*—one right outside the Iolani Palace. The protesters must have had a shaman or mage among their number because the statue of King Kamehameha the Great had been magically altered to include bugged-out eyes, a bleeding tongue, and a noose around its neck. Nice.

I know a little about demonstrations from my time with Lone Star. No matter how nasty they may look, their real significance depends on who's involved. Average slobs-on-the-street, who really believe in what's going down? Troubling, chummer. Professional *agents provocateur*—"rent-a-mob?" Much less troubling ... although it's still something you don't want to turn your back on. Which was it in this case? I had no way of knowing.

The tridcam focused again on the magically altered face of Kamehameha the Great, prompting a new thought. Did Gordon Ho know what was going down? I don't mean the bombings and the protests and that drek—of course he'd know about that. But maybe he *didn't* know that someone—probably Harlech—had blown my connection with the *Ali'i.* I'd promised to tell him anything that Barnard passed on to me about the situation, hadn't I?

And besides, I had the gross and chilling conviction that things were starting to come apart around me, which was giving me the strong urge to talk with somebody—*anybody*—about it. Ho just happened to be the closest and most convenient. I pulled out the mylar card the *Ali'i* had given to me, crossed to the telecom, and punched in the number.

I waited out the usual delays and ghost-clicks; by now I was getting used to cold relays. Finally, the Ringing symbol flashed on the screen. A few seconds later, one last click indicated the circuit was complete.

"Ia wai?" The screen stayed blank.

I hesitated. The voice didn't sound like Gordon Ho's . . . or was I just being paranoid? "I want to speak to the *Ali'i,*" I said.

"Ka?" the voice asked. Now I was sure—it *wasn't* King Kamehameha V. "Who is this?"

I struggled to keep my face expressionless, silently cursing myself for placing this call with my own video pickup online. "The fact that I know this number means I don't have to tell you that," I said coldly, playing my corp hardman act to the hilt. "Put the *Ali'i* on. Now."

"I'm afraid that's impossible," the voice said, matching my tone chill for chill. "The *Ali'i* is indisposed at the moment. Leave your name and contact information, and I'll pass it on."

I was already reaching out to slap the Disconnect key. With a sigh I leaned back in the chair.

Frag it to hell. Something was seriously wrong here. Ho had stressed to me that the number on the mylar card would reach his personal line, no matter where he was. If he couldn't answer for whatever reason—if he was "indisposed," for example—*no one else* would pick up the line. Obviously, the ground rules had changed. Maybe "indisposed" was just a polite circumlocution for "*deposed.*" Was Gordon Ho still *Ali'i* of the Kingdom of Hawai'i?

I turned and stared out the window. Almost since this thing had started, I'd felt like a rat in a trap. Now the trap seemed to be shrinking. Options and alternatives were slowly being stripped away. For a while, I'd fooled myself into thinking I had a powerful patron in the *Ali'i*. No more, chummer. For all I knew, maybe Gordon Ho was swinging at the end of a rope, eyes bugged and tongue bleeding like the magically altered statue. Even if he wasn't, it was a pretty good bet he had more important things on his mind than the travails of one Dirk Montgomery.

And Barnard? Frag, I'd already given him my best pitch, and he'd decided to leave me "in-country" to reality-check his other informants. How could I convince him to pull me out? Snivel and whimper.

Maybe ALOHA was hiring. I wondered what the going rate for burned-out *haole* street ops was these days . . .

The telecom buzzed, and I almost went over backward in the chair. I glared balefully at the incoming Call symbol on the bottom of the screen.

Who had this LTG number? Monot, obviously, and anybody else she'd happened to tell at Telestrian Industries Corporation. And that was about it . . . wasn't it?

A little apprehensively, I tapped the key to accept the call, but only *after* turning off the telecom's video pickup. "Yeah?"

The screen filled with an image of Gordon Ho's strong features. "Mr. Montgomery?"

I hurriedly keyed my vid pickup back on. "It's me," I told him unnecessarily. "Where the frag *are* you?" And then an ugly thought hit. "And how the frag did you get this number?"

The *Ali'i* of Hawai'i gave me a tired smile. For the first time I noticed the bags under his eyes, the lines of strain in his face. "As to your second question, Mr. Montgomery, I think I told you once before that some members of my military intelligence community were still loyal to me personally. Fortunately, that still seems to be the case. As to your first question, I'd rather not discuss that, for reasons that should be obvious."

"What the frag's going down, *e ku'u lani*?" I asked.

His tired smile grew sad. "That form of address isn't appropriate anymore, Mr. Montgomery."

I nodded. "A palace coup?"

"More or less. The throne has been taken—I prefer the term 'usurped,' of course," he added with a wry grin—"by a distant cousin of mine who apparently has been groomed for the position by certain factions within the legislature."

"A mouthpiece for *Na Kama'aina,*" I translated.

"Of course."

"And you?" I asked him.

"Accused of high treason, what else? How else could *Na Kama'aina* have played it?" He shrugged his muscular shoulders. "I left the palace one step ahead of a warrant for my arrest."

I shook my head. Things fall apart; the center cannot hold, and all that drek. "You've got some people with you?"

"Some," he acknowledged. "Trusted friends."

"And a safe place to hang?"

"For the moment, yes."

I rubbed at my eyes, which suddenly felt very tired. "So what happens now?"

The erstwhile *Ali'i* smiled. "I think I'd rather not discuss that at the moment, Mr. Montgomery," he said quietly. "After all, *my* people have compromised this line . . ." He didn't have to finish the thought.

I sighed. "Yeah." What the frag else was there to say? Things had gone way too far beyond my ability to affect them—that's the way it felt, at least. I was adrift on some dark, empty ocean, with no compass or rudder. "Well," I told the ex-*Ali'i,* "if there's anything I can do to—"

He interrupted gently. "That's not why I called you, Mr. Montgomery."

I blinked. "Oh?"

"I've been asked to pass on a message to you."

"From whom?" Suddenly, bleak fatalism morphed into paranoid imaginings.

"Someone who claims to know you." Ho's voice and body language were giving nothing away, no matter how hard I scrutinized him. "Someone who wishes to meet with you. It's your choice whether you accept the meeting or not, of course."

Well, thanks for *that,* at least, I thought. "Who?" I asked again.

"Two people, actually," Ho replied slowly. "That was made quite clear to me. Apparently, one of them you'll particularly want to speak with."

"Why? And who the frag are they?"

Ho seemed not to have heard my question. "If you wish,

I can help you arrange the meet, Mr. Montgomery," he went on. "Some of my people can escort the . . . the *parties* . . . to any meeting site you wish and guarantee that nothing untoward happens."

"Yeah, thanks, sure," I said distractedly. "But who the frag *are* they, huh?"

Ho looked a little uncomfortable. "I'm assuming this means something to you. It certainly means nothing to me. I was asked to convey to you that there is a message from 'friends of Adrian Skyhill'."

Oh, just fragging great. The fragging *bugs*. Wonderful, excellent, oh joy.

I accepted the meeting, of course. Frag, what else would I do? Sheer, drek-headed curiosity was enough of a motivation. After the pogroms and all that drek, after the infestation of Chicago by the bugs, after the revelation of insect spirits and their shamans as the next worst thing to the Antichrist himself . . . wouldn't a bug shaman have to have one fragging good reason to risk his precious, creepy little skin, arranging a meeting with me? (Curiosity—it's a wonderful thing, *neh*? Think of all the marvelous boons curiosity has brought humanity—thermonukes, germ warfare, trideo sitcoms . . .)

Once that decision was made, it was a no-brainer to accept Gordon Ho's offer of resources. Although I couldn't imagine that a bug shaman would go to all this trouble just to geek a null like me, I figured a couple of hard-men would be good to have around. (If for no other reason than to stop me from geeking *him*. I figured I still owed the "friends of Adrian Skyhill" for what happened to my sister, Theresa.) And come to think of it, physical protection wouldn't be enough, would it? I'd need someone who could do the astral thing as well—preferably a shaman rather than a hermetic, on the assumption that "like understands like." A shaman on my side might be able to predict any assorted weirdness the bug-guy might be considering.

So that's what I asked Ho for: a shaman plus three hoop-kicking bodyguards. I wanted two of the razorboys with me before the meet; the shaman and the other gillette could pick up the bug-boy(s) and escort him/them to the spot. Ho agreed at once; I think he was almost as curious as I was about the whole scam, and expected his people to give him a complete debrief afterward.

As to the site, well, why not right here, room 1905 at New Foster Tower? I ran a quick mental cost-benefit analysis of security concerns, and on balance the risks seemed lower if I stayed put, avoiding any undue exposure on the streets before, during, or after the meet. If necessary, I'd bail out of the Tower afterward, and find myself another flop. A fragging alley, if nothing else presented itself.

So that's the way it shook out. The meet was set for eighteen hundred; a gillette and a shaman provided by Ho would escort my visitors to room 1905 at that time. Two hours before the appointed time, the other two assets were knocking on my door.

My paranoia was in full flood, so I checked the door viewer before snapping back the maglocks. Through the distorting lens I could easily imagine I'd seen the two slags before. Even though facial features and other superficial details vary, I've always felt there's an underlying sameness about the really good bodyguards. Maybe it's the level of confidence, of belief in and understanding of their own capabilities. Or maybe it's the recognition that their job could require them to kill, or die, at any moment. Whatever the truth of it, I always get a vaguely hinky feeling around people like that. Of course, this wasn't a social occasion, and I was glad this pair looked competent.

The taller of the two figures held something up to the door viewer—a duplicate of the deputy's badge I still had in my pocket. I unlocked the door and swung it back.

The two muscleboys didn't so much as acknowledge my presence. Silent as wraiths in their dark suits, they seemed to teleport by me. The shorter of the two—I noticed with a slight shock that she was female—shut and relocked the door, while her taller companion just stood in the middle of the room scanning it with a gaze as piercing as a surgical laser.

After half a minute he nodded minusculely and finally turned toward me. "Mr. Montgomery," he acknowledged, his voice as empty of emotion as a vocoder. "I'm Louis Pohaku. My associate is Alana Kono." Neither of the hard-types offered to shake hands, so I just nodded to them. "Have you done a security survey?"

"You're the experts," I said with a shrug.

Pohaku shot a look at his partner, then they split up, and basically started taking the hotel room apart.

I watched them as they worked. Pohaku was the boss-man, quite obviously, and he'd been in the game for some time. I guessed him to be in his late thirties, maybe a few years older than me, and that the world hadn't been kind to him. His face was drawn, his eyes slightly sunken, his skin sallow. Hell, he looked like a walking corpse dressed up for the prom. He moved well, though—even just walking across the hotel room, I could see he was toned and cranked up. He didn't have any obvious cybermods, but I'd have bet big cred that his reactions were juiced to some degree.

Where Pohaku was tall and spare, Kono was small and pleasantly rounded. (I wouldn't let myself so much as *think* the word "chubby," because she'd probably tear my liver out.) Broad face, dark hair in bubbly curls, and curves in all the right girl-places. Her eyes were dark and alive, and even the slightest trace of a smile would have made her fragging near beautiful. Of course, smiling wasn't part of her job de-scription. Woman-trappings or not, she could just as well have been Pohaku's soulless clone-brother.

The two hard-types in their matching dark suits gave the place the security version of a white-glove inspection. They tried the sealed windows, they checked out sightlines, they scanned every millimeter of the walls with electronic detec-tors of some kind, they hooked little black boxes up to the telecom, they even—I drek you not—looked under the bed, and test-flushed the drekker. A couple of times I considered telling them to lighten up. Hell, I'd spent one night in this room already; I'd used the drekker, even, and my anatomy was still intact. But I kept my yap zipped. They were the pros, after all, and I might as well let them have their fun.

Finally, they were done, and Pohaku came toward me. Part of my mind expected a brisk, "Crapper secured, *sah!*", but of course all I got was a cool nod. My security assets were sat-isfied with the situation, so I should be as well. Taking my cue from Pohaku, I just nodded in return and waved them wordlessly toward the couch.

I've never been particularly comfortable waiting for something to go down. I was even less comfortable sharing the room with the emotionless Bobbsey Twins. If Pohaku and Kono had done something even slightly human— belched, maybe, pulled out a book, or used the (secured) drekker—it would have made things a lot easier. No luck, chummer. They just sat on the couch, one at each end, spines ramrod straight, staring off into space.

No, that wasn't quite right. They didn't zone out. They didn't look at me or at each other, but they didn't slip into the thousand-meter stare that I always associate with boredom, or with no coffee for breakfast. Instead, their gazes kept flicking around the room, never settling anywhere for long, like the eyes of a pilot monitoring his plane's instruments. I considered trying to strike up a conversation, but that idea withered away pretty damn quick. Instead, I snagged myself a fruit juice from the fridge, but didn't offer any to the Bobbsey Twins. If they wanted something, they could crack their adamantine shells long enough to fragging ask. Then, juice in hand, I slumped down into a chair and worked on my patience.

According to my internal, subjective clock, we sat there like that for, oh, nigh on a year or so. (My watch said it was little more than an hour and a half, but what the frag did *it* know anyway?) A few minutes before the official time of the meet, a knock sounded on the door.

Pohaku and Kono were on their feet so fast I didn't even see them move. (Yep, boosted reflexes, both of them.) Kono flickered across the living room, taking up cover position in a small alcove. Pohaku fragging near teleported again across to the door. Weapons, nasty little chopped-down SMGs, were in their hands as if by magic.

Pohaku said something I couldn't make out—probably a code word of some kind—and rapped a rhythmic sequence on the door. (Why not just look through the viewer lens? Think about it, chummer. Bad guy on the outside waits for that little viewer to go dark—telling him the good guy's eye is up against said viewer—and sends a round or two right through it. Ouch.) I didn't hear the countersign, but I could hear the answering rap code; it sounded like a musical quote from *Take Five*.

Either it was the right code, or Pohaku liked jazz. The two gillettes' SMGs vanished again, and Pohaku unlocked the door. He stepped aside as one figure entered, then shut and relocked it. I looked at the newcomer, and my stomach did a one-and-a-half gainer.

It was the fragging bird-boned woman, the little old scag I'd seen through the security camera of Cheeseburger in Paradise and then later in the coffee shop next to the Ilima Joy. She was dressed the same as when I'd seen her the other two times, in a shapeless sack of a dress that had once been black but had now faded to a kind of careworn gray. Her bright eyes flickered over to me and pierced me like a butterfly pinned onto a display board. Then she returned her attention to Pohaku, and they talked in quiet tones.

"Hey, wait just one fragging tick here," I said loudly and crossed the room toward them. Two sets of dark eyes—one sunken, one sharp and almost beady—settled on me. "Who the frag's this?"

The bird-boned woman flashed me a quick and knowing smile, but it was Pohaku who answered. "You asked for shamanic support," he said flatly.

"Her?"

I hadn't thought it was possible, but his expression grew even colder. "Akaku'akanene has the full confidence of the *Ali'i*," he said sternly, leaving the rest of the thought—*"and that should be good enough for the likes of you"*—unspoken.

I raised a hand, palm out. *"Aka*-what?"

"Akaku'akanene." This from the bird-boned woman. Her voice was brisk, sharp, abrupt. "My name. Means 'Vision of the Goose'."

"Uh-huh." I paused. "Look, I don't want to sound like a paranoid buttbrain, but . . ."

Akaku'akanene flashed me another of those quick smiles of hers. (For a moment my memory superimposed an image of my old chummer Buddy over the shaman's face. The mannerisms were painfully similar. With an effort I swallowed my sadness.) "Did I follow you?" she finished for me. "Yes."

I shook my head. That wasn't the answer I was expecting. Frag, I'd been looking for a nice, reassuring, *"Don't be a dickhead."*

"How?" I asked. "Why?" Then I went back to, "How?" again. The two times I'd seen the old shaman had been before my first conversation with Gordon Ho, the *Ali'i*. How the hell did she even know I existed?

"Why?" she echoed. "Nene sang of you."

I waited for her to go on—for her to say something that actually made sense. When she didn't, I responded, "Huh?"

"Nene sang of you," she repeated patiently. "She sees your *'uhane.* Your spirit. You are the axle. Important things

turn around you." She said all this as if it were totally obvious, as if I were a pluperfect dolt for not knowing it already.

Okay, so I guess I *was* a pluperfect dolt. I didn't know
what the frag she was talking about. Nene ... that was a
goose, wasn't it? Yes, that was right, the *nene* was that Hawai'ian goose—the one with the claws, that likes volcanoes
or some drek—that Scott had rattled on about. So a *goose*
had talked to this woman ... ?

Or maybe Nene was some local totemic creature. Sure,
that made at least some sense. In the Pacific Northwest, Bear
is a popular totem, as is Wolf. On the Great Plains, Snake
and Coyote get the nod. Down in Florida, Gator's a fave. So
why not Nene in Hawai'i? Of course, that didn't settle my
doubts much. I've never been too comfortable with the idea
of totems as real, discrete entities. I guess I've always mentally labeled them as psychological constructs that shamans
use to make sense of magic, with no real distinct existence
of their own. So whether Akaku'akanene was following me
because a goose told her to, or because a voice in her head
told her to, I still felt a little hinky about the whole thing.

Well, anyway, none of this was on point at the moment.
Let the old woman listen to birds if she wanted to. "What
about the visitors?" I asked her.

"Outside," she said. "Two of them."

"Clean?" Pohaku asked.

"No," Akaku'akanene answered firmly. "No weapons,
though." Pohaku blinked at that; it made me feel a touch
better to realize that he found the shamanic worldview a little disconcerting from time to time, too.

"Lupo's with them?" the bodyguard pressed.

Akaku'akanene nodded.

Pohaku turned to me. "Ready?"

I shrugged. "No," I admitted honestly. "But let's do it
anyway."

The bodyguard nodded and made a quick gesture to
Akaku'akanene. The old woman opened the door and
stepped back outside. Behind me I heard Kono shift into a
better covering position. Pohaku's own weapon was out
again, pointed at the ceiling, but off safety. I stepped back
into the middle of the room and I did what I could to prepare
myself. "Friends of Adrian Skyhill." Just fragging peachy.

The door swung open, and another bodyguard in the same

mold as Pohaku—this had to be Lupo, I guessed—stepped inside. A small figure followed him.

A human male, he was, midheight and of midbuild. His hair was midbrown, his features were nondescript. Frag, he was the closest thing to a nonentity I think I'd ever seen. If I'd passed him on the street, I don't think I'd have noticed him. I certainly wouldn't have remembered him. The only thing that set him apart was his eyes.

Gray, they were, pale and watery gray. They glistened, as if he was on the verge of crying, or as if he'd rubbed glycerin into them. And they never seemed to blink. Those eyes, set in an expressionless face, settled on me, and I felt the urge to hide behind a couch.

Then Akaku'akanene escorted his companion in, and I forgot about the gray-faced man.

"Oh, Jesus fragging Christ, *no . . .*" My voice was a pitiful whimper. It was all I could do not to sit down in the middle of the floor, cover my face with my hands, and cry like a fragging baby.

The second member of the contingent had the same glazed eyes as the nondescript man, except that they were brown instead of gray. I knew those eyes; I'd seen them laugh and cry.

"Hello, bro," said my sister Theresa.

20

"Ah, *Christ,* Theresa ..." I felt as though all the blood had been drained from my body and replaced with ice water. I felt as though the underpinnings of my world had been kicked out from underneath me. I felt like a child who's been forced to look at the disemboweled body of his pet puppy. I felt like ... How could I describe it, even to myself?

My sister. In all my life, the one thing I'd done that I could point to with pride—the one stupid knight-in-shining-armor knee-jerk reaction that had worked out for the best—was hauling Theresa out of that little suburb of Hell beneath Fort Lewis. Helping her through the nightmares and post-traumatic stress syndrome and all the drek that followed. Seeing that she was clean, sober and *sane,* and then letting her go about her own life.

For what? What had been the use, tell me that? All the pain, all the heartache ... for what? Frag it, I might as well have just left her attached to that pus-yellow umbilicus in the Fort Lewis hive. Might as well have left the astral parasites—the Wasp spirits—in her aura. It had all been for nothing, I could see that in my sister's glassy eyes. The one thing I thought I'd done right in my life ... now *that* had turned into drek, too. Ah, what the hell anyway? Might as well stay consistent, *neh?* At least I can be proud of *that.*

My sister's body was standing before me, a smile on its face. Something looked out from those familiar eyes, those eyes that had always seemed able to see wonder and beauty where I'd only seen pain and threat. Something ... Was Theresa in there anymore? Was there any of my sister left in that shell of a body? Or was she gone forever?

It was almost as if Theresa—or the thing that now wore her body—could read my thoughts. "I'm here, Derek," she said softly. *"I'm* here. I *am* Theresa, but I'm more as well."

"Why?" My voice was a husky whisper, the sound of a torture victim.

She smiled. It was my sister's smile, Theresa's smile. It hurt so much I wished I could die right then and there. "Why?" she echoed. She glanced away, her brow wrinkling in the way it always did when she was thinking hard. "It would take me a million words to explain," she said slowly, "or just one."

"One?"

"Love," my sister said firmly. "That's the only answer, the core answer. The heart of everything."

I shook my head. I wanted to scream, I wanted to run. I wanted to grab her and shake her. But all I did was say softly, "I don't understand, Theresa."

"It's simple, Derek, really," she said, her voice kindly and gentle. The tone of voice made me think she really wanted me to understand, but could I trust something like tone and body language?

"Do you know what it's like to be loved?" she went on.

"Of course."

She raised a brow ironically. *"Do* you? Really? Loved unreservedly and unconditionally? For *yourself*—for what you *are,* not for what you do? Knowing that nothing—*nothing!*—can ever change that, can ever lose you that love?"

I couldn't bring myself to answer.

"I didn't think so," she went on sadly. "Mom loved us . . . but only if we behaved. Dad loved us . . . but only if we excelled. Isn't that the way it was, Derek?" She took my hand. I wanted to shake free of her touch, but I couldn't bring myself to move. "If we were 'good' children—if we lived our lives the way they thought we should live them—we were loved. If we weren't, they withheld their love."

"They always loved us, Theresa." I *had* to say it even though I wasn't totally convinced it was true.

"Maybe," she said with a slight inclination of her head. "Maybe they did. But they withheld the *expression* of that love, didn't they? And for a child, that's all that matters. Maybe for an adult, too."

"*I* always loved you, Theresa . . ."

My sister squeezed my hand. "I know you did, Derek. In your own way—to the extent of your abilities—you loved me. And I'll always thank you for that, and love *you* in turn.

"But . . . it's not enough, not when you've experienced something more."

She fixed me with her unblinking gaze. "I know you love me, Derek," she went on urgently, "but I could never *feel* your love. Not directly. You *can't* feel love. No matter what all the romance stories and trideos and songs say—you can't feel it. When people say they 'feel' love, what they're talking about is something inside themselves, isn't it? They *infer* the love of another, or of others. They take in what people say to them, how they act and what they do, and from that they *infer* that those other people love them. And from that *inference* comes the feeling that people call 'being loved.'

"Do you understand what I'm saying, Derek? It's important that you understand. The feeling we label 'being loved' is totally independent of whether you *are* loved or not. Don't you see? If someone actually does love you but you don't know it—you don't make the correct inference—then you don't *feel* that love. If someone doesn't love you, but you infer incorrectly that they do, then you *do* feel it. See? You're not feeling love at all, you're only responding to some state internal to yourself, to some conclusion you're making about the outside world.

"That's all I ever felt," she went on softly, "that's all anyone ever feels. I never knew anything else could exist."

"Until . . ." I whispered.

My sister nodded. "Until I felt the love of the Hive Queen," she said simply.

I couldn't hold her gaze. Frag, I couldn't stand any of this—to face someone who looked and sounded and felt . . . and Christ, even *smelled* like my sister, and listen to her spouting *this* . . . I wanted to pull my hand away, but I didn't have the fragging guts.

She squeezed my hand again, almost hard enough to hurt. "Listen to me, Derek," she said, *"please."*

"Why?" I demanded. "Why the frag should I? So you can convince me, too? So your . . . your *Hive Queen* can suck out my soul, too?"

She didn't flinch at the venom in my voice, didn't look angry. Instead she looked sad. "That's not what we do," she said.

I cringed at that terrible word. *We.*

She saw it, but pressed on. "We don't convert by force—by fire or by the sword. That's the way human religions are traditionally spread, but this isn't a religion, Derek. People come to this way of life because it's what they choose, it's what they *want*, deep down in their core."

"Bulldrek," I snarled, suddenly angry. "I found you in a fragging coma, with a fragging *umbilical* cord stuck into you, Theresa. That doesn't sound like a fragging choice to me."

My anger left her untouched, and when I saw that, the rage just seemed to bleed away, leaving me cold and empty. She shrugged slightly. "I really don't remember much about what led up to it, Derek," she admitted. "But I *do* remember what I felt when I belonged."

"Remember *how*? You were in a coma."

She shrugged again. "I don't know how I remember, I only know I do."

"You never talked about it. With me, with the doctors, with the therapists . . ."

"I know. Maybe part of me didn't want to talk about it—to remember it, or maybe to admit it. But the memories were there, Derek, they still are. I couldn't access them all the time. Mainly they came out in dreams—dreams where I'd wake up crying my eyes out because I was so lonely and empty.

"I'd travel," she went on gently. "I'd go to a new place, a new city. I'd look at the people, and they'd all be lonely and empty, too. Some of them knew it; most of them couldn't let themselves think about it. They were all alone, all of them *alone*. And the memories came back more often, and they kept getting stronger. And the sadness wouldn't go away."

"So you went back to them." In my own ears, my voice sounded like a cold wind blowing through a graveyard.

"Not at first," she corrected.

"Why not, if living your own life was so terrible?"

"Because of you, Derek," she told me. "Because I was afraid you wouldn't understand, you wouldn't approve."

I don't *understand or approve*, is what I didn't say to her. I just nodded wordlessly.

"And then I remembered something you told me," she went on, "and I made my decision."

That shocked me. "Something *I* told you?"

"Of course. You told me once that I should live my life with the end always in mind. Remember, Derek? You suggested it as a kind of decision-making tool. That I should imagine I was at the end of my life and looking back. Would there be regrets? Would I lie on my deathbed, praying for one chance to go back and do something—experience something, *have* something—I'd decided against at the time? Do you remember that, Dirk?"

Well, of course I remembered that, now she parroted it back to me. Another one of those facile oversimplifications that I seem able to dredge up on the spur of the moment. Okay, maybe it wasn't *totally* facile oversimplification. Maybe I believed it sometimes. When I was sitting at my 'puter, trying to bash out a few more lines of code and I knew there was a gorgeous sunset outside over the skyline of Cheyenne, for example. Which would I remember when I was on my deathbed, I'd ask myself: a soul-touching sunset or another dozen lines of code? If nothing else, it was a convenient excuse to slack off, couched in the trappings of "wisdom."

"I thought about what you said," Theresa was continuing. "I thought about dying. And I thought about dying without feeling that love, that belonging, ever again. I couldn't face that."

"So you went back to them," I repeated.

"They came to me, actually," she corrected. "In Denver. It was as if they knew I was there, and they knew that I needed them. They came to me, and they offered to love me, and need me."

"And *possess* you," I almost spat, "and steal your goddamn fragging *soul!*"

My sister looked at me sadly. It was a . . . a *complex* sadness, that's the only way I could describe it: regret, alloyed with understanding, and something that could almost be compassion. I hated the expression in her eyes. I *feared* it.

"That's not how it is, Derek." Her voice was as gentle as a breeze stirring the leaves of an elm tree. "I am *me.* I'll always be me. But I'm more as well. I *am* the Hive Queen. I *am* the other members of the Hive. And they are me.

"In a sense I'll never die. As long as one member of the hive remains, *I* remain. Some of my memory—some of who I am—will continue to live. Forever, maybe. There's no loss, Derek, none. It's a *gain.* I'm Theresa, just as I always was . . . but *more* so."

Now I did pull my hand back, and I did cover my face. "No," I said. That's all, just, "No." I couldn't bring myself to say what I was thinking—that she *had* lost something. Her humanity, if nothing else. And with it, she'd lost the ability to *know* that something was lost.

Someone touched my arm, gently. Not Theresa; I knew her touch. I took my hands from my eyes.

It was the gray-faced man, the insect shaman. I flinched back from him as though his hand had been a white-hot iron bar, searing my flesh. I stared at him, at his glassy eyes, at the face that had once belonged to a human. I thought I'd hated before in my life. I was wrong. I think I smiled as I reached for the Manhunter stuffed down the waistband of my trousers.

The pistol was clear. My thumb flicked off the safety as I brought the big gun up. On came the laser, and I tracked it onto the shaman's right eye. The ruby light gleamed from the watery-looking cornea. I took up the slack on the trigger, then squeezed it.

And stopped, just short of the break-point. The shaman hadn't reacted in any way. He just watched me. Frag, his pupil didn't even seem to have contracted under the laser's light.

Suddenly, I became aware of the tableau around me. The three bodyguards all had their nasty little SMGs out. Kono and the one they called Lupo held dead aim on the shaman. Pohaku's weapon panned back and forth between me and the shaman, as if he didn't know what the frag to do. The woman, Akaku'akanene, was staring at me with those bright, birdlike eyes of hers. I think she understood what I was feeling—I *think* it was understanding in those eyes. But there was determination there as well. Deep down, in the base of my brain, I had the unshakable conviction that if I'd actually tried to fire my pistol into the Insect shaman's head, I wouldn't have been able to do it. The final member of the tableau was Theresa. In her eyes was something that, in another, I'd have had to call genuine sadness.

"Chill, people," I said quietly. I put up my gun and safed it. Just to spare myself from temptation, I turned and scaled the big hunk of metal onto the bed. Then I turned back to the gray-faced insect shaman. "Well?" I said quietly. "Speak your piece."

The small man nodded. "You find yourself in an interesting situation, Mr. Montgomery," he began. His voice was as gray, as nondescript—as empty—as his face. "Through no choice of your own, you've been drawn into important events.

"These events have been developing for some time," he continued quietly. "The beginning of the pattern was woven"—his lips twisted into a smile that didn't reach his eyes, and that contained no human amusement—"well, the weaving began long before you were born, as a matter of fact. Now, circumstance has conveyed you into the middle of affairs, and the weaving of the pattern has changed because of it."

I looked at him, and I shook my head. "I haven't got a fragging clue what you're talking about, chummer," I said flatly.

"It's self-evident, isn't it?" the shaman asked rhetorically. "You have been woven into the pattern, Mr. Montgomery. You are now *part* of the tapestry of events, not just an observer. There are those who can sense this about you." And now he shot a sidelong glance at Akaku'akanene. "The weaving of the pattern is almost complete."

I snorted. "Look, I'm not in the mood for sophomoric philosophy, okay?" I snapped. "Cut to the fragging chase."

The Insect shaman paused, then nodded. "The Hawai'ian Islands have several sites of power," he said quietly. "Puowaina, Haleakala, Honaunau Bay ... among others. There are ways to draw mana from those sites, for those with the knowledge, and the willingness to pay the price.

"There are those who wish to use those sites for their own purposes," he went on. "They consider those sites to be like motherlodes of mana, from which they can draw magical energy."

"I didn't think that was possible," I put in.

"For most mages or shamans, it isn't," he confirmed. "But there are ancient techniques that allow it. They're complex, though, and they're time-consuming. And they all carry with them a significant risk."

"What risk?"

"Power of any kind has to come from *somewhere*," the shaman said. "Within the Gaiasphere, it's generated by living material—by the 'biomass' itself. Certain sites of power, though, are like conduits to other"—he paused in thought—"other *places*," he continued carefully. "Mana can be drawn through those conduits."

I nodded. This suddenly seemed to be making at least some sense. To some degree it was tying in with the thoughts I'd had when I'd visited the sacrifice site in Punchbowl. "I scan it," I said. "You don't want these slags to get their mitts on all this power, is that it?"

The shaman shook his head firmly. "That wouldn't be a concern. On a local level the amount of power available is considerable. On a more global scale, however, it's insignificant."

"Tacnukes as compared to city-buster ICBMs?" I suggested sarcastically, thinking of Chicago.

He surprised me by nodding. "A reasonable analogy. But that's not the concern." Oh, *really*? I thought. "The issue is that the . . . the *places* from which the mana comes . . ." He trailed off, as if seeking just the right word.

"They're occupied, aren't they?" The words were out of my mouth before I was even fully aware of the thought process behind them. Chilling—and even more so when the Insect shaman nodded agreement.

"There are certain *entities* in these other places," he agreed judiciously. "The same barrier that prevents the free flow of mana also denies them access to the Gaiasphere."

"And if you weaken that barrier enough to suck through the mana . . . ?" It was my turn to trail off.

His silence was enough of an answer.

"What are these 'entities'?" I wanted to know.

The shaman shrugged. "Their exact nature varies unpredictably. It's enough to say that nobody would be well-served should they be able to penetrate the barrier."

Something just didn't hang together here. "This is bulldrek," I said slowly. "What about the slags who are trying to siphon the power? Don't they know about these entities?"

"They know."

"And they're still doing it?"

"Perhaps they think they can control the entities," the gray-faced man said, "or possibly block them once the barrier is weakened. They're wrong, in both cases. The entities will overwhelm them or suborn them . . . if that hasn't occurred already."

I held up my palms to stop him. "Okay, time out, let's see if I get this. Somewhere, in some volcano somewhere, there's going to be a shaman slotting around with this barrier thing—"

"More than one shaman is necessary," the gray-faced guy put in. "There are forces of stability that naturally counter any premature weakening of the barrier. Those forces must be overcome."

Premature? Interesting word. I'd think about that later.

"Okay, amendment noted. So a whole drekload of shamans are slotting around with the barrier, trying to siphon in some mana. And instead of power, what they'll get is this cosmic nasty that'll . . . what? What'll happen?"

"Suffering," the shaman said, his voice sounding cold and distant. "Death. Devastation. Initially limited to the islands, but believe me, it will spread."

I nodded as if I understood. "And this cosmic nasty's going to make life drekky for you guys too, I assume?"

His eyebrows rose. "Members of the Hive? No," he said firmly. "The entities that come through won't waste any efforts on us. Not until more convenient prey is no longer available."

I didn't like the sound of that at all . . . if I believed this miserable slag, of course. And did I? The jury was still out. "Uh-huh," I said neutrally. Then I leaned in close and poked him in the chest with my finger. "Then why the frag are you telling me this, huh? The way you're talking, it sounds like this is going to be no skin—or chitin or whatever—off your hoop. So why bother? Why not just sit back and watch the fragging fun?" My rage was back, a cold fire burning in my chest. I could feel my pulse pounding in my temples. "Hey, it'll probably be a pretty good fragging show, won't it? Maybe you'll pick up some pointers on how to spread suffering, death, and devastation, right?" I paused theatrically. "Or maybe that's the fragging point, huh? You don't want someone else pissing in your pool, is that it? Anyone the cosmic nasty scrags is one less for you to possess or kill or turn into a fragging monstrosity, right? Frag, you just don't want the *competition!*"

The shaman was totally unmoved. Flecks of my spittle glistened on his cheeks and forehead—I'd leaned in *real* close—but he didn't seem to notice or care. "Our intention isn't to spread death and suffering," he said quietly.

"Tell that to the people in Chicago!"

"It wasn't we who detonated the nuclear device," he responded calmly—and all the more infuriatingly because he was right, of course. "All our actions were in self-defense."

"Yeah, *right,* they were!"

"You don't know us, Mr. Montgomery . . ."

"And I don't *want* to!" I spat back.

". . . But believe this if you can. We are not your enemy.

We bear no ill-will toward metahumanity. Quite the opposite, in fact, as your sister can vouch."

"Don't you *mention* my sister, drekwipe!"

"Our goals and our agenda are our own," he went on, undismayed. "Sometimes they may conflict with yours; most of the time they're totally unconnected with yours. And sometimes—as in this case—our best interest and yours coincide."

"And I'm supposed to take that on faith, is that it?" I wanted to know.

"That's up to you," the shaman said simply.

I paused. My mind was in chaos, churning thoughts conflicting wildly with each other. I wished there was some god I could believe in, some Great Referee to whom I could yell "Time out!" No luck. The Insect shaman was still watching me with his glassy eyes and expressionless face. I couldn't remain angry at him, I found, not without some kind of response from him. It was like trying to hold a grudge against a footstool or a fragging doorstop. I sighed again. "Okay, *hoa,*" I said quietly. "Just for the sake of argument, let's say I swallow the line you're feeding me. What then? What do you want from me?"

He answered at once. "Use your influence to stop this before it goes too far."

I laughed in his face. "*Influence*? Chummer, you've got the wrong slag here, let me tell you. I've got about as much influence as a fragging pawn in a chess game, as much as . . ." My imagination failed me, so I just waved my hands about eloquently. "Zilch, in other words. Zero. Zip. Null. Get me?"

"You have influence," he stressed. "You don't wish to acknowledge it for your own reasons, but you have it."

"Yeah, *right,*" I snorted. "I'm as significant in this as tits on a bull."

"Oh?" The shaman's eyebrow rose again. "That's not how it seems to others, Mr. Montgomery." He glanced pointedly around the suite, his gaze settling in turn on each of the security personnel. "This isn't the residence of someone lacking in influence."

"Them? They're not following my orders. They're the *Ali'i*'s people."

The shaman nodded. "And the *Ali'i* listens to what you have to say. You're significant in his interpretation of events. Otherwise, he wouldn't have arranged this meeting.

"The same with Yamatetsu Corporation," he pressed on

firmly. "If someone listens to your words or follows your actions, then you have influence. And there are others, aren't there, Mr. Montgomery?" he asked. "There are others who consider you significant."

"To the extent of threatening to kill me, yeah," I said sarcastically.

"And that's to a significant extent indeed," the shaman shot back, "as you'll recognize if you'll only think about it. You don't warn off or threaten to kill someone without importance or without influence. You kill them, or you simply ignore them.

"You *have* influence," he concluded. "Use it."

"I don't know how."

"You will."

I narrowed my eyes. "You really expect me to help you on this?"

The shaman shrugged again. "You want this stopped," he stated, "*we* want it stopped. Is it really that difficult to understand?"

"So why don't you just"—I gestured vaguely, searching for the right word—"just *possess* me like you did Theresa? Then you wouldn't have to convince me, would you? I'd just follow orders like a good little drone."

Again, my scorn and anger just rolled off him. "That's not our way," he said quietly. "It must be voluntary . . . on both sides. You must accept us, but we must also accept you."

"And I don't 'make the grade'?" The shaman didn't react in any way. So the bugs considered me 4F, did they? Thank God for small favors—if I could believe this slot, at least.

I stared out the window for a few moments. My eyes saw the scenery, but my brain didn't register it. More thoughts—fears, doubts, hopes, dreams—bubbled up from the swamp of my subconscious. I tried to sort through them, separate reason from irrationality. Finally, I turned back to the shaman. "What's in it for me if I do it?" I asked.

He blinked. "The entities will be unable to penetrate the barrier," he said slowly. "They will be unable to prey on—"

I cut him off with a sharp gesture. "*No.* What's in it for *me*? Me personally?"

Again the shaman paused. "Payment, you mean?" His tone was confused, as if I'd asked him something he'd never had to consider before.

"More like *quid pro quo,*" I amended. "I do something

that benefits you, you do something that benefits me. *Me.* Not metahumanity in general. *Me.* Get it?"

I watched his eyes as he tried to bend his brain around the thought. (Frag if I'd ever needed hard evidence that the Insect spirits were inhuman and alien in their outlook, this was it. The idea of bribery, a surprise? Cut me loose . . .) Finally, he nodded slowly. "Perhaps something can be arranged."

Roughly, I grabbed him by the shoulder, and I dragged him into a corner of the room. Away from the sec-guards, away from Akaku'akanene. Away from Theresa. "I want *her* back," I whispered harshly. "My sister."

He blinked again. "What?"

"Look, it's simple. I do this for you, you give me my sister back. *Normal,* understand? The way she was, with her own thoughts and her own mind and her own soul. You reverse whatever the frag it is you did to her." I crossed my arms. "That's my price."

The shaman's unblinking eyes were fixed on mine, as if he were trying to see into my mind. "Can we discuss this?" he asked at length.

"No negotiation," I whispered firmly. "That's it. You want me to do this? Then that's my price. You don't play ball, then I'll use whatever influence I've got to fuck you up, chummer. Anything you do to block these cosmic nasties, I'll throw a fucking wrench into it."

"But the entities—"

"*Let 'em come!* Doesn't matter squat to me if I don't get my sister back." I leaned in close again. "Scan me, bug-boy?"

He thought about it for a long time—two minutes maybe. It felt more like two hours. I could feel beads of sweat trickling down my spine, soaking the waistband of my trousers. It was all I could do to keep my knees from trembling.

Finally, he nodded once. "Your sister for your cooperation? Yes."

"We have a deal?" I pressed.

"We have a deal."

I thanked whatever gods were listening that he didn't insist we shake hands.

21

Okay, I'd cut myself a deal. Now the question was, how the frag was I going to see my side of it through? (And how the hell could I be sure bug-boy was going to live up to his side? Save that worry for later, I told myself.) The Insect shaman could argue until he was blue in the tits that I had influence. Who knows, maybe he was right, speaking from his own twisted, nonhuman standpoint, but I didn't know how the frag I was going to use it.

Let's say he was right, that some shamans were going to jack around with this barrier—whatever the frag it was—in one of the sites of power in the islands. Fine, take that as a given.

Which site of power? Puowaina? Haleakala? Hona-whatever Bay? Or one of Christ-knew-how-many others?

And when were these shamans going to do the dirty deed? Tonight? Tomorrow? Next month? Or had they already started?

So what the frag was I supposed to do, huh? Use my "influence" to arrange for all the sites of power to be staked out, round the clock, forever and ever amen? Yeah, right.

I sat on the couch in room 1905, New Foster Tower, staring out the window. The sun had gown down maybe an hour before. A couple of the brightest stars—or maybe they were comsats—were visible against the black velveteen sky; the rest couldn't compete with the artificial fire of the city.

Kono and Lupo had taken Theresa and the Insect shaman away a couple of hours before. They didn't say where they were going, and I didn't ask. Theresa promised she'd be in touch, and that was good enough for the moment. On his way out the door, bug-boy had given me a strip of paper from a pocket 'puter's thermal printer—a local LTG number where I could contact him.

That left Louis Pohaku and Akaku'akanene to keep me

company. Since I didn't particularly feel like company at the moment, I was relieved when they settled down to do their own thing. The bodyguard quietly field-stripped and reassembled his weapon, then seemed to tune out and go to sleep. The shaman just settled down into full lotus in a corner and stared blankly into space—maybe talking to geese or some damn thing.

It was maybe ninety minutes after sunset that Pohaku surged to his feet—no warning—fragging near scaring me to death. Silently he crossed to the window, staring out and down. City lights reflected in his eyes as he frowned out into the night.

"What?" I asked him.

"Trouble," he said quietly.

I was on my feet and beside him in an instant, straining my eyes to see what was worrying him. Nothing. No fireflowers blooming from Sand Island . . . or anywhere else, for that matter. If I pressed my forehead right up against the transpex, I could look down to the right onto Kalakaua Avenue and watch the cars—mainly corp limos, probably—cruising along it, forming streams of lights. White on one side, red on the other. I blinked. Way down Kalakaua, to the west, there seemed to be a major knot of red taillights.

No, I realized suddenly, the knot of red *wasn't* the taillights of cars. The color was subtly wrong, as was the way it waxed and waned.

Fire. Maybe a burning barricade, maybe the aftermath of a car bomb, I didn't know. Only now that I knew what to concentrate on, I could hear the distant, almost subliminal ululation of sirens. And something else—maybe the crackle of gunfire, I couldn't be certain. One thing I knew—there was trouble in paradise tonight.

Beside me Pohaku was shaking his head. *"Lolo,"* he muttered to himself . . . then noticed my attention, and translated. "Stupid."

If I'd thought the bodyguard had reacted fast before to some cue I'd missed, I hadn't seen anything yet. A knock sounded, and before my brain had even fully registered the sound, Pohaku was flattened against the wall beside the door, SMG out and off safety.

Akaku'akanene was alert, too, back from her avian conversations. Pohaku shot her a quick nod, and the woman closed her beady eyes. After a moment she opened them and announced, *"Hiki no."*

Apparently that meant "okay" or "copacetic" or something similar, because I could see Pohaku relax. His gun was still at the ready, but his finger was on the trigger guard now, not on the trigger itself. He reached out to unlock the door, then stepped back well out of the way.

I was about to grouse "Who's fragging room is this anyway?" or some such drek—until I saw who my visitor was.

Visitor*s*, to be precise, but only one of them counted. He flashed me a wry smile as his personal bodyguards shut and locked the door behind him.

"E ku'u lani," I began . . .

Gordon Ho waved that off. "I told you, that's not appropriate for the moment." His smile took on a new edge. "Since we're both outcasts, why don't you call me Gordon?"

I could see from the way his bodyguards stiffened that they didn't like it, but frag them if they couldn't take a joke. "I'm Dirk, then," I told him. I paused, "So, not to put too fine a point on it—"

"What the frag am I doing here?" he finished for me. He took off his jacket—an armored leather number, quite a change from his feathered regalia—tossed it to a sideboy, and slumped down on the couch. For the first time I noticed how drek-kicked he looked. "I've got to be *somewhere*," he pointed out, "and since I'd already assigned a significant percentage of the people I really trust to this room, I thought, 'why not?'" He sighed, rolling his head as though to relieve tension in his neck. "You wouldn't happen to have some Scotch, would you?"

I realized I hadn't checked for a minibar—which indicated just how distracted I was at the moment. Pohaku had scoped the place out, however, and opened a wooden cabinet next to the trideo to reveal a well-stocked bar. "Make that two," I told him. "Triples, while you're at it." Then I planted myself in an armchair across from Ho.

Pohaku assembled the drinks almost as quickly as he'd responded to trouble and handed them over to us—Ho first, of course. I sipped and let the peaty liquor work its magic on my tangled synapses. The erstwhile King Kamehameha V was doing the same thing, and I could almost see some of the tension melt away from his face. What the frag had he been up to before coming here? Where does a king in exile—by definition, one of the most recognizable of all people—go to avoid notice?

And what would happen to him if he *was* noticed? I suddenly wondered. "Protective custody?" Or a necktie party on the streetcorner? I guessed it depended on who noticed him first. No wonder he was looking a little ragged around the edges.

We held our peace, the two of us, for maybe five minutes and a hundred milliliters of single-malt scotch. Then Ho sighed and remarked, "Well, it's starting to get . . . *interesting* . . . out there."

I'd decided I wasn't going to be the first to talk biz, but now that he'd broached the subject, I leaned forward. "What the frag's happening out there?" Quickly, I filled him in on the fire—or whatever—we'd spotted from the window.

Ho nodded wearily. "Anticorp violence," he said quietly. "It's breaking out all over the city . . . all over the island, if what I heard is true."

"How bad?"

"Disturbingly bad," he admitted. "It's not well organized—not yet—but in some ways that makes it even more difficult to counter."

I nodded agreement. If civil disobedience, which was what we were talking about here, was organized, you could often quell it by snagging the leaders. (Or at least so they taught us at the Lone Star Academy.) But if it was spontaneous mob action? Mobs are creatures with a few hundred legs and no brain (again, a quote from my Academy days), so there's no clean and easy way of shutting them down.

"So what's happening?" I pressed.

Ho shrugged. "What *isn't* happening?" he said dispiritedly. "Cars turned over and torched—that's probably what you saw, by the way. Rocks through windows. Molotov cocktails, sometimes. A couple of sniping incidents."

That shocked me. "Sniping? Already?"

The ex-king smiled, but there was no amusement in it. "Matters *are* degenerating faster than I'd expected," he allowed.

"What about casualties?"

He shrugged again. "I'm not privy to detailed police reports anymore," he pointed out dryly, "but I'd assume they're probably still light."

"That'll change."

"Yes," he agreed. He was silent for a moment, then went on quietly, "I *did* hear about one incident. A Mitsuhama executive's limousine was blocked by a mob. No overt violence, just threats ... but her bodyguards overreacted and opened fire." I cringed as he continued. "More than thirty of the rioters dead ... plus the bodyguards and the executive herself, of course, when the mob rampaged. I understand they turned the car over, built a bonfire around it, and roasted her alive."

It's getting out of control. The thought chilled me like an arctic wind on the nape of my neck. "Somebody's behind it," I pointed out. "Somebody's stirring up the mob."

"Of course," Ho said. (He didn't voice the accompanying, *"you idiot,"* but his expression conveyed it adequately.)

"*Na Kama'aina,* right?"

"Initially, yes," Ho corrected. "But they've lost control of the situation, too." He smiled grimly. "It seems that their dogs aren't on quite as short a leash as they'd believed."

Realization dawned. "ALOHA," I breathed.

"Of course. *Na Kama'aina* never really believed in all of that fiery 'corporations out' rhetoric. They were too realistic for that. They only wanted to use it—and ALOHA itself—as a lever, to oust me from the throne." He smiled again, with bitter humor. "Well, they've achieved *that* part of their plan.

"But now ALOHA has scented blood. *Na Kama'aina* can't leash them in anymore." He shook his head and frowned. "I wonder what Ryumyo's agenda is in all of this? Does *he* know what ALOHA's doing, or has he lost control, too?"

I raised my hands, palms out. "Hey, don't ask me," I protested.

We both fell silent again, sinking back into our private thoughts. The ex-*Ali'i*'s scan of the situation seemed all too plausible, I realized. Except ...

"You said *Na Kama'aina* never bought the 'corps out' drek?" I asked suddenly.

"Of course not," Ho said, surprised. "They're realists, after all. Politicians, and ambitious, but still realists."

"But ..." I felt like I was wandering into the mental equivalent of a mangrove swamp.

"Think about it, Dirk," the ex-*Ali'i* urged. "What happens if the corporations are forced out?"

"They'll fight back. Sanford Dole all over again."

"Precisely. But, just for the sake of argument, what would happen if the corporations *could* be ousted?"

I hesitated. "Polynesia for Polynesians, I suppose," I said slowly.

"It won't happen," Ho countered firmly. "Hawaii'i was self-sufficient once . . . back when the population of the entire island chain was less than half a million. There's six times that in Greater Honolulu alone. There's no way the nation can be self-sufficient now. If the corporations are pushed out, the islands starve."

I nodded. That's what Scott had told me, what seemed so long ago now. "*Na Kama'aina* knows this?" I suggested.

"Of course they do. As I say, they're realists."

Another idea was niggling away in the back of my brain. I closed my eyes and let another healthy mouthful of Scotch encourage it to come out where I could examine it.

"If the corps *were* booted out," I went on tentatively, voicing the thoughts as they came to me, "there'd be a power vacuum, wouldn't there? The islands are strategically valuable—the U. S. thought so, for frag's sake. So somebody's going to move in. Japan, maybe?"

Ho was smiling. "It took my staff considerably more time to figure that out than it did you," he said quietly. "Yes, of course. Corporations out, Nihonese in. That's why I said 'Polynesia for Polynesians' will never happen. Neither the megacorporations nor the Japanese would allow it."

"Maybe *that's* Ryumyo's angle, then. Maybe he wants Hawai'i for Japan."

"That occurred to me, too," Ho said. "Ryumyo seems to *live* in Japan, however he and the Nihonese government have never been on particularly amicable terms."

"There *is* that," I admitted. And with that we both sank back into our private contemplations. It was funny in a way, I had to admit. Even with the drek dropping into the pot around me, it was reassuring, in a way—to calming—to have someone with me who was getting ragged over by it all as royally (no pun intended) as I was. What was the old saying: "Misery loves company"? We sipped our Scotch and we stared at the carpet and we thought our bleak thoughts.

The telecom bleeped, jolting me out of my reverie. Pohaku was standing nearby, and he shot me a questioning look. At the moment I simply didn't feel like talking to anyone new . . . or, what I particularly feared, hearing any more bad news. For a second or two I debated just letting it ring. Bad idea, probably. Not that many people had this number (I *hoped*), so it was probably important. I sighed. "I'll get it," I told Pohaku, levering myself out of the upholstery and going over to the telecom.

I disabled the video pickup and accepted the call. "Yeah?"

The screen stayed blank—the caller had selected voice-only, too—but I recognized the voice immediately. "Mr. Montgomery?"

Deeper sigh. I keyed on my pickup. "It's me," I told Barnard.

The corporator's face filled the screen. Beside me, I felt Pohaku stiffen. Apparently, the bodyguard recognized Barnard as a corporate presence, and hence a potential threat . . . or maybe he was just professionally paranoid. "Do you have any news for me?" the suit asked. "Any developments I should know about?"

"Got an hour or two?" I asked dryly. "First thing, the throne's been usurped. Ho's out on his hoop."

"Indeed? I *had* heard that. Do you have confirmation?"

I smirked at that. "All the confirmation I need," I told him.

"The *Ali'i* . . . is he safe?"

"As safe as can be expected, I guess."

"And you have confirmation of *that*?" Barnard pressed.

"All the confirmation I need," I repeated. "He's sitting right here, swilling Scotch."

Up went the corporator's eyebrows. "*Honto?* Let me speak to him."

You two should have been talking to each other all along is what I *didn't* say. I just beckoned Ho over and gave him my chair. I stepped aside, out of the telecom's axis of view, but made sure I stayed close enough to hear what was going down.

"*Aloha,* Gordon," I heard Barnard say. "*Pe-hia 'oe?*"

"*Aloha. Pona'ana'a,*" the ex-*Ali'i* responded quietly. "*Et Gilles? Comment ça va?*"

"*Très bien, à tout prendre,*" the corporator replied. "He's Commercial Services manager at Yamatetsu-U. K., making his own way up the ladder." Barnard paused. "He still speaks of his time at university with you."

Gordon Ho smiled—a little sadly, I thought. "There's something very appealing about a time when the biggest thing you have to worry about is a term paper or whether you can smuggle your girlfriend into your residence."

While those two droned on with more of that "old-home week" drek, I went back to the couch and sat down again to concentrate on my Scotch. I could still hear snippets of the conversation, but couldn't make much sense of it with Ho and Barnard apparently flipping between English, French, Hawai'ian, and Japanese as the mood took them. After a while I stopped even trying.

After maybe five minutes of multilingual chitchat, Ho turned away from the screen. "Dirk," he said, beckoning me over. I clambered to my feet and joined the ex-*Ali'i* before the telecom, this time bringing my drink with me in case I needed instant fortification.

"Uh-huh?" I said to Barnard.

"When we spoke before," the corporator said, "you implied that someone by the name of Harlech might have revealed your corporate connection and your involvement with Gordon."

"Quentin Harlech," I said.

Barnard frowned. "I have yet to find any information on an individual by that name. Do you know anything about him that might help?"

I thought for a moment, then shook my head. "Nothing," I replied. "I just saw him the once."

Barnard nodded. "Another possible angle," he mused after a moment's thought. "Are you aware of anyone who *might* have background on him?"

Well, now that he put it that way . . . "Maybe you can get some scan from Chantal Monot," I suggested. Barnard shook his head, so I elaborated. "Telestrian Industries Corporation? Prez of South Pacific Operations?"

I saw the recognition dawn in his eyes. "Monot, yes." Then his frown deepened. "And how do you happen to know Mademoiselle Monot, Mr. Montgomery?" he asked, his voice deceptively casual.

Okay, well, I guess maybe I *should* have told him before now. Quickly, I recapped my experience with TIC, starting with the narcodart in the chest and finishing with my "transfer" to New Foster Tower. "Monot recognized Harlech's name," I concluded. "At least, I think she did."

Barnard sighed. "Telestrian Industries Corporation," he said quietly, a complex expression on his face.

"Why don't you ask Monot about this Harlech slot if you think it's so important?" I suggested.

The corporator chuckled softly at that. "I rather doubt she'd tell me."

"Why?" I wanted to know. "You corps are thick as thieves, aren't you?"

Barnard looked at me as he would a child too stupid to get with the toilet-training program. "Megacorporations rarely speak with one voice, Mr. Montgomery," he said coldly, unconsciously echoing Chantal Monot's comment on another topic. "We cooperate in some areas, it's true. But don't forget that, primarily, we're in competition. Do you really think that one megacorporation would fail to keep confidential something that could prove to be a competitive advantage?"

I nodded, a little chastened. Point taken.

"It is interesting, though," Barnard continued thoughtfully after a moment. "Telestrian's representatives to the Corporate Court was initially in accord with one of the major factions that have formed around the Hawai'i issue. Now Telestrian Industries Corporation has withdrawn all involvement . . . on either side of the issue. I wonder if there's some connection?"

"Hold the phone," I began.

But Gordon Ho got there before me. " 'Factions'?" he asked sharply. "What 'issue'?"

Barnard smiled mirthlessly. "What issue do you think, Gordon? How best to deal with the Hawai'ian provocation, of course. There've been attacks on megacorporate assets— personnel *and* materiel. An outrage like that can't go unanswered, you understand that. The Corporate Court is more or less split on what the response should be."

"What are the choices?" the ex-*Ali'i* asked.

"Again, what do you think? Diplomatic pressure on one hand—sanctions, embargoes, and such. More . . . *direct* . . . action on the other."

"Military?"

"The supporters of direct action are split on that question," Barnard allowed. "Some believe this nonsense with ALOHA has gone on long enough and should be settled once and for all. Others prefer 'executive action' against members of the government."

I glanced over at Ho and saw he'd gone pale. No wonder.

I'd heard the euphemism "executive action" before. It generally meant "assassination."

"And where do *you* stand, Jacques?" the young ex-king asked softly. "Where does Yamatetsu stand?"

"In the middle ground, where else?" Barnard said with a shrug. "A very *lonely* middle ground, as it turns out. A 'wait-and-see' attitude isn't particularly popular with the Court at the moment."

"What about Donald?" Ho asked suddenly.

"Your great-uncle is finding it especially uncomfortable," Barnard told him. "Zurich-Orbital doesn't give him much chance to avoid contact with the others."

I blinked at that. So Gordon had some relative up on Zurich-Orbital? I filed that little gem away for future consideration . . . assuming there *was* a future.

"How is the Court leaning?" Ho queried.

Barnard's smile faded. "The direct action proponents seem to be ascendant," he said quietly. "There will be a . . . a *message* sent. A demonstration." On the screen the corporator checked his watch. "At midnight, local Honolulu time. If that fails to bring the government to heel . . ." He shrugged eloquently.

"A demonstration," I echoed. The word had a frightening sound to it, a bitter taste. "What kind of demonstration, Barnard?"

"Thor," he said quietly.

22

We stood shoulder to shoulder, the ex-*Ali'i* and I, our noses millimeters from room 1905's picture window. None of the respectable media had said word one about the Corporate Court's scheduled demonstration, but the word had certainly gotten out nonetheless. Part of that was due to the fact that a media lockdown simply isn't possible when parties with a vested interest in getting the word out—in this case, the corporations—can beam their message directly down from the high ground of low Earth orbit. Ground-based pirate stations had done their part, too, gleefully reporting on the Hawai'ian government's attempts to muzzle the commercial media outlets. Back in the Dark Ages—the nineteen-eighties and nineteen-nineties, for example—it might have been possible to keep this kind of genie in the bottle. These days? No fragging way, *hoa*, as the government was finding out.

I knew the word had gotten out thanks to reports that filtered in to the *Ali'i* from his few trusted assets still on the streets. Even without that source of data, though, I'd have guessed that people were getting the message. Normally Kalakaua Avenue, stretches of which I could see from my window, was two ribbons of slowly moving car lights until two or three in the morning. Tonight, at a couple of minutes to midnight, Waikiki's main drag was next to deserted. Idly, I wondered where everyone was. Holing up, terrified that the sky was going to fall on their heads? Or doing what Gordon Ho and I were doing, finding a good vantage point from which to watch the show.

"Twenty-three fifty-eight," Pohaku announced quietly from behind us. As if driven by the same mental impulse, both Ho and I took one big step back from the transpex of the window.

It was a perfect night for it. Since sunset dark clouds had been piling up along the southeast horizon. Now they hung

heavy over the ocean, black on black, flickering with lightning bolts, a dozen klicks offshore. An impressive background for what would probably be a bloody impressive
show. Directly over Honolulu and Mamala Bay, the sky was
clear. A couple of stars burned against the blackness.

At a signal from Ho one of the bodyguards killed all the
lights in the apartment. Outside, along Kalakaua Avenue,
other people had gotten the same idea. All along the shoreline, lights were going out. I blinked a couple of times, to
help my eyes night-adapt faster.

"What's the reaction going to be?" Ho asked quietly. His
voice was so soft, I wasn't sure if he even knew he'd spoken.

The question was an important one in both our minds, of
course. The megacorporations' little demonstration was like
a cop's warning shot. As I'd been taught at the Lone Star
Academy, a warning shot's *always* going to provoke a reaction. Sometimes it's the one you want—abject surrender,
when the perp you're chasing realizes you could have put a
round into his ten-ring. Sometimes it's the exact opposite—
a kind of "Oh yeah? Well, frag *you*!" response that turns into
a blazing firefight. I couldn't shake the worry that the high
muckamucks of the Corporate Court hadn't given much
thought to the second possibility.

"Thirty seconds," Pohaku announced. I felt movement behind me as the bodyguards pressed as close as they dared to
their ex-sovereign's august presence, staking out their own
view-spots. Mentally, I counted down.

T-minus three, two, one, zero ... Nothing. *Plus one, plus
two, plus three* ...

I'd reached T-plus five when Gordon Ho gasped softly beside me and pointed toward the sky. A new star burned in
the heavens, harsh and brilliant. It flickered, it moved. For
an instant it had dimension, more than a perfect geometric
point ...

And then the Thor shots rained down, perfectly parallel
bars of light, lancing down from the zenith to the black
ocean a couple of klicks offshore. They were impossible to
count, they were there and gone so fast, an impression of un-
believable speed. Like a burst of tracer fire from God's own
machine gun, but faster than any tracer bullet I'd ever seen
... and immensely larger. There was a flash of light where
they hit, a single strobe pulse—like a secondary explosion,

but without the fireball. I think that was the most chilling part of the whole demonstration. There'd been nothing under those descending bars of light, nothing but water. Still, the impact from the Thor projectiles had been enough to *strike sparks off the ocean itself.*

It was over in less than a second. I let out the breath I didn't know I'd been holding. *My God,* I thought dully, *how fast did those things come down?* I ran a quick mental calculation. Assume they were traveling at orbital velocity when they hit the atmosphere. What would that be? Something like *35,000 kilometers per hour*—in other words, 10 klicks *per second* or thereabouts, maybe 10 times the speed of a rifle bullet. And Thor projectiles were a lot bigger than rifle bullets, of course. I'd heard them described as "smart crowbars." Assume each one massed a nominal one kilo. How much kinetic energy was contained in one kilo of mass traveling at 10,000 meters per second? If I remembered my high-school physics—and hadn't slipped a decimal place somewhere—that would be something like 100,000,000 joules of energy: *one hundred megajoules. Per crowbar.* And how many crowbars had been in the burst we'd just seen?

I felt cold. No wonder the Pacific fleet had turned back when the megacorps had fired a warning shot like that across their bows back in 2017.

I heard a sound behind me and turned in surprise. Pohaku was glaring out the window, lips drawn back from his teeth in a rictus of rage ... and he was *growling.* I shrugged. I suppose if this had been my country, I'd have been pretty torqued off about the whole thing, too.

"Lights, please," Gordon Ho said softly. As a bodyguard flicked the lights back on, the ex-*Ali'i* turned away from the window and slumped down in a chair. He picked up a whiskey glass from the table beside him—mine, as a matter of fact, but I wasn't going to give him grief about it, not now— and polished off the contents in one swallow.

"What's the reaction going to be?" he asked again, and this time I knew the question *was* directed at me.

I shrugged. "You know your people better than I do," I pointed out.

He smiled at that. "I thought I did," he amended quietly. He paused, then went on, "It depends on how well ALO-HA's managed to stir them up ... and how crazy ALOHA is, when you get right down to it.

"It's possible to pull it back," he continued with a sigh. "*Na Kama'aina* doesn't want war with the corps. If the government can keep ALOHA under control, if it can prevent any more provocations, it should be possible to get things back under control."

I nodded. It made sense, what Ho said, but it sounded too much like Barnard's comment a day or two before that "perhaps saner heads would prevail," or whatever. They obviously hadn't prevailed yet. Was that going to change?

I turned back to the window. Now that the demonstration was over, there were cars on the streets again. Not as many as usual, but at least Waikiki didn't look like a ghost town anymore. From somewhere to the west—Sand Island? I wondered idly—a small constellation of lights was approaching, burning bright against the darkness of the sky. Choppers—two or three of them. Corp shuttles, maybe, coming downtown to pick up VIP vacationers and take them to the airport for a suborbital off-island? I didn't know, and I didn't really care at the moment. I started to turn away.

I didn't see it happen straight on, just in my peripheral vision. Without warning something flashed upward from somewhere to my left, almost like a Thor shot in reverse. The lance of fiery light transfixed one of the helicopters, blotting it from the sky in a dirty orange-black puffball. The surviving choppers broke formation, diving for the deck, killing their anticollision lights as they did so. In a second or two they were lost to sight.

I flattened my nose against the window, watching in shocked horror as burning wreckage plunged to the street or smashed down on top of buildings.

Gordon Ho hadn't seen it, but he knew *something* had happened. He gaped at me. "What was it?"

I didn't answer right away. Instead, I came over and fragging near collapsed into an armchair. Finally, I said, "It doesn't look like it's a good season for saner heads."

The downed chopper was a corp bird, Gordon Ho's informants confirmed an hour or so later. (I'd guessed as much earlier, but this wasn't a time when I felt good about being proven right.) The lance of fiery light I'd seen had been a Parsifal man-pack SAM, an obsolete Saeder-Krupp design. Ironic, since the chopper that ate the missile was a Saeder-Krupp bird.

Gordon Ho and I were shoulder to shoulder again, looking silently out the window of room 1905. The streets below us were empty now, except for the occasional corporate security vehicle screaming by, light-bars ablaze. There were more choppers in the air—angular, brutal-looking gunships now, instead of the more streamlined unarmed transports—buzzing around like angered hornets. Most of them were maneuvering radically in case there was another missile team out there somewhere, jinking back and forth, up and down, randomly. Some were dropping flares just in case, sun-bright points of light. I couldn't make out colors or insignias so I didn't know whose the choppers were, but it was easy to figure out they were from different corps. It was also easy enough to figure out that said corps weren't talking to one another efficiently; in a fifteen-minute span, I saw half a dozen near misses when choppers fragging near slammed into one another. Every now and then I could hear the rip of autofire, muffled somewhat by the double-glazed window. Were ALOHA assault teams actually engaging the corp forces, or were the corp sec-guards shooting at one another—a ground-based version of the chaotic gavotte in the skies? It was impossible to tell.

Finally, the ex-*Ali'i* turned away from the window and returned to the couch. After a few moments I joined him. Pohaku still looked as though he wanted an excuse to rip somebody's lungs out—*anybody's*—but at least he still had the presence of mind to freshen our Scotches.

Ho stretched, working his neck and shoulders. He looked like he'd aged a decade in the past couple of hours, I noticed suddenly. Well, I guess getting deposed, then seeing your country stumbling toward the brink of war might do that to you.

"What now?" I asked.

Ho looked over at me and smiled. (I *think* that's what the expression was supposed to be, at least. It looked more like the facial reaction of a torture victim.) "I've given up on the oracle business," he said. Then his smile faded, and his eyes seemed to grow even more haunted.

"The government doesn't have much choice," he went on quietly. "They've got to act fast, before the Corporate Court does. Which means they can't do much about ALOHA."

I nodded. That made grim and nasty sense. Hunting down and neutralizing a militant policlub—a terrorist group by another name, when you think about it—is never a short-term solution. It takes resources and it takes time. The *Na Kama'aina*-dominated Hawai'ian government might have the former, but Ho obviously didn't think the corps would give it the latter . . . and I had to agree. Hell, when you came right down to it, stamping out a militant policlub wasn't necessarily possible even in the long term. Ask the FBI teams tasked with eliminating Humanis and Alamos 20K. "So what are the options?" I asked.

Gordon Ho shrugged. "Few." He sighed. "Negotiation—but that requires the corps to be interested in listening, which isn't a certainty at this point.

"Or a counterthreat," he went on, his voice bleak. "The corps have a gun to the government's head, Thor. The government has to draw its own gun." He shrugged again. "Mexican standoff. But at least it gives both sides a little more time to negotiate before the killing begins."

I raised an eyebrow at that. "Bluff, you mean?"

"Bluff wouldn't work. The counterthreat has to be substantive."

"Yeah, *right*," I snorted. "Threatening the corps?" The idea was so ludicrous I almost laughed out loud.

But Ho obviously didn't think it funny. "You'd be surprised, Dirk," he said darkly.

I *did* laugh out loud now . . . and then shut up so abruptly I almost swallowed my tongue. Suddenly, I'd remembered some of the weird things Scott had rattled on about during our first breakfast together, about the freaky drek that had gone down around Secession Day. Frag, now that I let myself realize it, there'd been some major questions rolling around in my head about the Secession.

For one, how come the U. S. had let Hawai'i go so easily? (Okay, the feds *had* tried to clamp down . . . *once*. But after the warning Thor shots on the naval task force, they'd basically rolled over and played dead. No attempts to take back their military bases.) For another, how had the equivalent of a civilian militia been able to defeat the Civil Defense Force—full-on military? The only answer that made any sense whatsoever was some kind of big stick with which to threaten the good ol' US of A.

I turned to Gordon Ho. "Spill it," I said quietly.

"Magic, of course," he answered at once. "*Nui* magic. *Big* magic."

In the back of my mind I heard a kind of almost subliminal *click*. "Sites of power," I said.

The ex-king nodded. "Of course," he confirmed. "Hawai'i has some major ones."

I felt a cold wind blow through my soul. "You've got some kind of project going, haven't you? Since before Secession, you've had it going."

"Of course," he said again. "We're a small nation. We need an equalizer."

"Tell me about it."

Ho shrugged. "It was my father's idea, I think. He and his *kahuna*—his shamanic advisor—they came up with the details. They'd heard about the Great Ghost Dance in the States, of course," he explained softly. "The federal government wanted to suppress details, but news always leaks out. When my father and his advisors learned that another group of aboriginals, the Amerindians, had developed large-scale magic as a military tool, they figured if it could work on the Great Plains, why not on the islands?"

"You did your own Great Ghost Dance," I said wonderingly.

Ho nodded. "In essence, yes. The details were different, of course. Hawai'ian traditions are very different from those that Daniel Howling Coyote used. But the principles were the same: massed shamans—*kahunas*—using their own life-force to power a great ritual.

"We had a major advantage that Howling Coyote didn't, however," the *Ali'i* continued. "We had those sites of power you mentioned. The *kahunas* were able to draw a large measure of the mana they needed directly from the land, rather than from their own life-force. Some died anyway, of course, but the cost was much less for us than for Howling Coyote."

I shivered. It was chilling, the almost casual way Ho was talking about this. The kind of rituals he was describing were "blood-magic." I'd read somewhere that the "cost" of the Great Ghost Dance was measured in dozens, maybe hundreds, of shamans who'd given their lives to power it. The same in Hawai'i, apparently: "True believers" had effectively suicided to give the islands their independence.

"Where did this happen?" I asked. "Puowaina?"

"The Hill of Sacrifice?" Ho's eyebrow quirked. "It would have been appropriate, wouldn't it? But no, the volcanic crater of Haleakala was chosen because it had a higher magical background count, which made the ritual easier."

Something else went click in the back of my mind. It was like I'd been struggling vainly with a jigsaw puzzle for the last couple of days, and suddenly somebody had started handing me the pieces I needed, one by one. "It's still going on, isn't it?"

"The Dance?" Ho shook his head. "No," he said firmly. Then, "Not as such."

I looked into his eyes and saw him trying to decide what to tell me and what to keep hidden. "Spill it, *e ku'u lani*," I said again.

He hesitated for a long moment, then I saw him come to his decision. "The Dance ended with Secession," he said firmly, "but there were some interesting consequences. For some reason, the background count in the Haleakala crater was higher after the Dance than it was before. Considerably higher, in fact. We wanted to know why, of course. And we also wanted to learn how to use the additional power. My father established a research station on the crater rim. He code-named the program Sunfire. A staff of *kahunas* were assigned to Project Sunfire to figure out what had happened to the background count . . ."

"And how to use it," I completed.

Ho nodded uncomfortably. "Yes," he acknowledged. "Initially. When I took the throne, though, I decided to back off from that side of things."

"Why, for frag's sake?" I wanted to know.

The ex-*Ali'i* looked even more uncomfortable. "*She* convinced me," he said, inclining his head toward Akaku'akanene who was in full lotus again, staring into space and listening to geese.

"Her?"

"She virtually raised me, Dirk," he said, almost apologetically. "Of course I listened to her when she warned me about something."

"Why?" I pressed again. "What was the fragging problem?"

He glanced away, apparently unable to meet my gaze. "She didn't know," he admitted, "not really. She just had a feeling. A premonition, you might call it." He shrugged once more. "That was good enough for me, Dirk," he said earnestly. "I knew her, you see. I knew what her premonitions were like. If she sensed that something was dangerous . . . well, that was good enough for me," he repeated.

Another faint *click.* "That changed, didn't it?"

"Against my wishes, yes," Ho acknowledged. "Six years ago, the *Na Kama'aina* faction in the legislature finally accrued enough influence to basically take over Project Sunfire. They switched the emphasis of the research from simple understanding back to exploitation. They thought the kingdom might someday need the power that Haleakala represented.

"Maybe they were right," he added with a wry glance out of the window at the flying circus of choppers over the city.

And then came the last mental *click.* Suddenly I felt really cold, as though somebody had hooked the room's ventilation up to an industrial freezer. "That's the big stick, isn't it?" Ho blinked in confusion, so I elaborated. "That's *Na Kama'aina*'s counterthreat to use against the corps. They want to draw power from Haleakala."

"Of course," he said simply.

Oh, drek . . . That *had* to be what bug-boy was talking about, didn't it?

The horrible realization must have shown on my face, because Ho asked, "What's the matter, Dirk?"

"We've got to stop Project Sunfire, *e ku'u lani*," I told him. "We've got to stop it *right fragging now.*"

23

Gordon Ho blinked. Behind him, I saw Pohaku glaring at me.

"Stop it?" Ho echoed. "Stop Project Sunfire? Why? I admit, I *did* consider it dangerous. But there's danger and then there's danger, if you take my meaning." He gestured out the window toward the corp gunships hanging against the sky.

I sighed. "Maybe I should have told you about this earlier," I said, then summarized, as succinctly as I could, what bug-boy had told me.

Ho held his peace throughout my spiel, not even asking any questions. He understood what I was telling him, though, I could see that in the way his eyes narrowed and his face hardened. Finally, after maybe five minutes of talking, I concluded, "The way I scan it, your Project Sunfire *kahunas* are going to get a frag of a lot more than they bargained for."

The erstwhile King Kamehameha V nodded thoughtfully. "*If* you believe an Insect shaman is telling you the truth," he said slowly.

I shrugged uncomfortably. That was the fragging point, wasn't it? Did I believe bug-boy? "It's not like I've really got much choice."

Ho glanced away, as if not wanting to meet my gaze. I knew what was coming. "I understand, Dirk," he said quietly. "I do. But . . ."

"She's not your sister," I said, my voice cold and bleak in my own ears.

The ex-king shrugged. "I understand your concern," he went on, still not meeting my gaze. "But I have to consider more than just one person. The entire nation—"

"Will get drek-kicked by these 'entities'," I broke in sharply. "*If* bug-boy's telling the truth. Hell, maybe he's lying through his fragging teeth. But *I* don't know, and neither do you." I leaned forward intently. "You're right, you've got to think about your people—*all* your people. Are you willing to put them at this kind of risk?"

Ho fixed me with his gaze then, and again I felt the immense force of will, of personality, I'd experienced when I'd first met him in the Iolani Palace throne room. "You make a good case, Dirk," he said calmly. "But am I willing to put them at risk from the corporations? I *know* that risk exists. What you're talking about—"

"It's not immediate, that's true," I said. "Frag, it might not even be real. But there's a big fragging difference, *e ku'u lani*. You can negotiate with megacorporations . . ."

Ho had to smile. ". . . And not with malignant 'entities.' Granted." He sighed. "If anyone ever tells you they'd like to be a head of state . . ."

"I'll tell them they don't know what the frag they're talking about," I finished. I paused. "So what's it going to be, *e ku'u lani*?" My chest was tight, as if a cold fist were reaching down my throat and trying to turn my lungs inside out. I was afraid I knew which way he was going to jump. Frag, it was the way I'd probably decide if I were in his position. Which threat would any reasonable person consider the most important? One that anyone with a pair of eyes could recognize? Or one based entirely on the testimony of a soul-sucking Insect shaman?

Yes, I thought I knew how Gordon Ho would have to decide. And then what the frag would *I* do?

I jumped fragging near out of my chair as another voice broke into my thoughts. "The Insect *kahuna* was telling the truth."

Like two puppets on the same strings, Ho and I pivoted our heads to stare at Akaku'akanene. The bird-boned woman was still sitting in full lotus, staring off into space. For all the reaction she'd shown—or showed now, for that matter—I'd have sworn she was so wrapped up in speaking to geese that she hadn't heard a word we said.

Gordon Ho leaned forward, his gaze drilling into her. "Say that again," he instructed. His voice was soft, but it was an order nonetheless.

Finally, Akaku'akanene focused her eyes and turned to look at her sovereign. "The Insect *kahuna* was telling the truth," she repeated calmly. "To the best of his understanding."

" 'To the best of his understanding'?" Ho echoed. "What's that supposed to mean?"

The Nene shaman shrugged her scrawny shoulders. "He spoke the truth as he believed it to be," she elaborated, almost casually. "There was no prevarication in what he said. He spoke the truth to the best of his understanding. Nene tells me so."

"But he could be wrong," Ho pressed.

"Of course," Akaku'akanene agreed easily. "But *he* didn't think so."

The ex-king fell silent, and I could almost hear his brain working. Unbidden, my memory brought back an image of Theresa—of her glassy, unblinking eyes. It was all I could do not to speak out, not to throw every argument I could think of behind Akaku'akanene's take on things. But I knew that was the worst thing I could do at the moment. Ho had to come to his own conclusion. It was one of the hardest things I've ever done, but somehow I managed to keep my yap shut.

"What do *you* think, *makuahine*?" he asked after what seemed like forever.

"You know what I think, *e ku'u lani*," the old shaman said with another shrug. "What I always thought, what I always told you. Forgotten, have you?"

Gordon Ho smiled wryly. "No, *makuahine*, I haven't forgotten." He turned to me. "What do you want to do about this, Dirk?"

I wanted to slump back into my chair and just enjoy the relief that washed over me. But I'd have time for that later. "Shut down Project Sunfire," I said flatly.

To my right I heard an exclamation, quickly muffled, from Pohaku. Ho turned to the bodyguard, one eyebrow raised in query. "You have something to say, Pohaku?" he asked dryly.

The hard-man swallowed visibly. "No *e ku'u lani*," he said firmly. "I . . . No. *Kala mai ia'u*, forgive my rudeness."

I shot the bodyguard a sharp look. *Like frag you've got nothing to say,* I thought.

The ex-*Ali'i* was speaking again, and I turned away from Pohaku. "Shut down Project Sunfire," Ho echoed with a crooked smile. "It sounds so simple. But how, Dirk? I'm no longer *Ali'i*, remember. And the faction of the government with direct control over Project Sunfire is the same faction that arranged to pry me out. Somehow I don't think they're going to listen to a decree to close down the project, do you?"

"Don't just tell them. *Do* it."

"And how do you propose I manage that?"

I swallowed hard. We all knew it was going to come down to this, didn't we? "Send me," I told him. "By all the fragging spirits, *I'll* shut it down."

He fixed me with those sharp, dark eyes. "How, Dirk?"

"It doesn't matter, does it?" I shot back gruffly. (Translation—*I haven't got a fragging clue* ...) "Just give me some assets and some gear, and get me there. I'll do the rest."

Ho's gaze didn't shift, and I felt as though his eyes were burning their way deep into my brain. "You have your reasons for this ..." he said slowly.

"So do you, *e ku'u lani,*" Akaku'akanene put in.

The moment stretched out until I was fragging near ready to scream. But then the ex-*Ali'i* nodded once. He seemed to shrink in on himself, as though—just for an instant—he was just plain Gordon Ho instead of King Kamehameha V. "You know, Dirk," he said quietly, "apart from Akaku'akanene, you're the only one I know who treats me as a *person,* not as a king. You tell me what you think, and you don't care if I agree with you or not. Do you have any idea how refreshing that is?"

He sighed, and his face changed. King Kamehameha V replaced Gordon Ho once more. "What do you need?" he asked me.

If Ho's capabilities were limited by being booted off his throne, I'm not sure I wanted to know how all-encompassing they'd been beforehand. With the sole exception of Jacques Barnard, I'd never dealt with anyone who could whistle up a military transport, personal gear, and personnel with a single phone call. (It was funny—Ho was fragging apologetic that he could supply only one military transport, and that the personnel he could offer were limited to Louis Pohaku, Alana Kono, Akaku'akanene ... and a SWAT-style Quick Response fireteam. *Only!* Cut me loose, here.)

Down in the elevator we went—me, Pohaku, and Akaku'akanene. Another call from the ex-*Ali'i* had arranged for a car—a Toyota Elite, as it turned out, gleaming like brushed stainless steel under the lights of the underground parkade. My little entourage piled in—Alana Kono was waiting for us inside—and we were off, howling westward along the semideserted streets.

It wasn't what you'd call a comradely ride. Akaku'akanene was talking to geese again, staring off into space like a chiphead. Alana Kono looked like she *might* be up for friendly conversation ... if her boss, Pohaku, hadn't been doing his best imitation of a slotted-off statue. So I sighed and settled back in the upholstery, trying to relax ... and trying to figure out just what the frag I'd gotten myself in to.

Out onto the Kamehameha Highway we hurtled, me wondering idly what it would be like being descended from someone they named fragging *highways* for—and westward toward the airport.

And past the airport. Lord knows, I was no expert at Honolulu geography, but I could recognize an airport when I saw it flashing by at 200 kilometers per hour. I leaned forward and rapped hard on the kevlarplex partition. "Hey, slot!" I yelled at the driver. "You missed the fragging turn"—I hesitated—"didn't you?"

Pohaku's iron-hard hand on my shoulder pulled me back. He sneered at me and pointed out, "You think we're going to the civilian field ... e *ku'u haku*?" His tone of voice turned the term of respect into the foulest of epithets.

"Where, then?" I shot back, loading my response with as much sarcasm as I could generate on the spur of the moment.

Pohaku didn't even bother to answer. Instead he just turned away, and pointedly stared at nothing out the Elite's window.

Alana Kono touched my arm, and she shot me a slightly embarrassed grin. Apparently, she'd finally decided that her job description might just include acting like a human being after all. "Kaiao Field, Mr. Dirk," she explained softly. "Used to be Hickham Air Force Base."

I sat back and tried to pretend I was as unconcerned as Akaku'akanene. But it wasn't easy. Jam or no jam, did Gordon Ho really think he still had any influence over the military?

Within a matter of minutes the Elite slowed, and we took a long sweeping left onto a minor connecting road. A few hundred meters to our right, I could see the floodlights and warning signs of a military compound. Ahead of us was ...

Well, nothing that I could see. It was pitch black . . . apparently all the way to the horizon. The only illumination came from the headlights of the Toyota limo.

Finally, after a minute more, those lights fell on a heavy-duty chain-link fence topped with hair-thin lines of refracted light that I identified as monowire. A sign on the fence read, "Lahui Mea Ki'ai o Hawai'i." Basically meaningless, until I saw the translation in small letters underneath: "Hawai'i National Guard."

The Elite sighed to a stop in front of a reinforced gate. Uniformed guards double-timed it toward the limo from an armored guard post, then suddenly snapped salutes to the car—or anything else that happened to be in their field of vision—and double-timed it right back to the guard post. The gate rolled back silently, and the Elite accelerated through.

Out onto the apron of a small airbase we drove, hanging a sharp left and finally to a stop in front of what looked like an administration building. A uniformed NCO—a troll, looking entirely too spit-polished—opened the door of the limo and snapped me a textbook-perfect salute as I climbed out. "Welcome, sir!" he damn near bellowed. "If you'll come this way . . . ?"

Believe me—I've never been one of these hard-case slots who thinks that happiness is a warm gun, but . . .

By Ghu, it felt good to wrap my hands around something with a little more authority than a pistol, let me tell you that, chummer. The spit-polished troll presided over a load-out that would have left an NRA nut juicing his jeans. Basically, I'd been given my choice of any personal arms and armor I wanted from the Hawai'i National Guard's extensive collection. Full-on battle armor? What's your size, *hoa*? Panther assault cannon? Would you like that with or without a smartlink, sir?

Don't get me wrong—I didn't go overboard. There are people out there who think they're innately capable of handing top-drawer military hardware. Active battlesuits? Man-pack miniguns? Bring'em on!

Not me. Frag, I remember how much it affected my balance the first time I tried on a suit of heavy security armor during my Lone Star Academy training. I fragging near did a face-plant when I tried to get up off the bench. Any sales slot who tells you "Anyone can wear any kind of armor, right off the shelf" is giving you the major song and dance, trust me.

So I crammed my fears way down deep into the back of my brain, and I kept tight rein on my impulses. No heavy security armor or miniguns for this kid. I picked out a nice, familiar set of Level 3 form-fitting body armor, and—okay, maybe I overreached myself on this one—an Ares high-velocity assault fire. As an afterthought, I picked myself out a nice assault vest—basically, a harness with the sole purpose of carrying an obscene number of spare ammo clips—and I was ready.

When I came out of the armory, my "troops" were waiting for me: Pohaku, Kono, and eight hoop-kicking military types.

Well, okay, apparently they weren't *my* troops. When I stumbled out, weighed down with lethal ordnance and feeling like a cheap knockoff of Slade the Sniper, they didn't spare me so much as a glance. Instead, their attention seemed focused entirely on Pohaku. For a moment I considered bitching about it, but then my better judgment overrode the testosterone overload the armory seemed to have caused. What the frag did I know about leading troops? Sweet frag all, that's what. Much better to leave it to someone who at least *thought* he was qualified.

Pohaku's expression told me he shared my viewpoint. He spared the time to shoot me a nasty sneer, then turned to my "troops" and snapped, *"E hele!"* The fire-team took off at double-time, with Pohaku picking up the rear. Kono was there, too, and she gave me what could have been a smile of sympathy. But then she was double-timing it after the combat troops as well.

Akaku'akanene was still hanging back, waiting for me. The shaman hadn't slapped on any armor or picked up any weaponry; apparently, she was content with her shapeless sack of a dress. She turned to me and gave me a gap-toothed smile.

Wonderful. Moral support from someone who talked to geese. I turned and jogged after the receding backs of the military types.

Out onto the apron we went, and I saw my contingent piling aboard a Merlin, a tilt-winged VTOL built along the same lines as a Federated-Boeing Commuter, but much smaller. I glanced back over my shoulder. Akaku'akanene was bringing up the rear, but at her own casual pace. The Merlin was already spooling up its engines, and I considered yelling something to hurry the old scag up . . .

And that's when I froze in my tracks. Not my idea—every goddamn muscle in my body seized up on me at once. I teetered for a moment on one foot, then started to overbalance as the vulcanized composite of the apron began to swing up toward my face.

In that instant my muscles unlocked again, and I did the kind of broad, lurching recovery that you expect from circus clowns. Cursing under my breath, I looked around me, knowing what I'd see.

There he was, just as I expected. Quinn Harlech, or whatever the frag his name was. He was cloaked in shadow . . . even though the section of the apron he stood on was well lit. He was wearing some kind of military uniform, but a couple of decades out of date. If his grin had been any broader he'd have swallowed his pointy ears as he swaggered up to me.

I glanced back over my shoulder. Akaku'akanene was a few meters behind me, looking madder than a wet cat. She was frozen in midstride, precariously balanced on the toe of one foot and the heel of another. She could still breathe, but she didn't have any fine muscular control of her throat or mouth—I knew that because her attempts to curse and bitch came out like, "Aaaaargh, *aaaargh!*"

Quinn Harlech took a step toward me, and instinctively I tried to bring my shiny spanking new Ares HVAR to bear. No luck. I could still breathe—thank the spirits for major favors—and I could still keep my balance, but I *couldn't* zero the assault rifle on the elf's chest. Momentarily, I considered butt-stroking him across the face with the rifle stock . . . and instantly the muscles I'd need for that move seized up on me, too.

"All right, already," I snarled. *"What?"*

Harlech smiled, but it wasn't the self-confident expression I remembered from our last encounter. If anything, he looked like some teenager trying to explain to his dad how he'd "creased" the family 3220 ZX. *"Gerelan-o témakkalos-ha, goro,"* he said. "Forgive my stupidity, Mr. Montgomery." He shook his head. "I misunderstood. It's been long"—he frowned—*"very* long, since I mistook matters so badly."

Again I tried to bring my rifle into line. Not so much because I wanted to cut him down, but just to see if I could. I couldn't.

"What the frag are you talking about, you slot?" I demanded.

Harlech shrugged uncomfortably. "I misjudged you, Mr. Montgomery," he said. "I thought you were a destabilizing influence. Instead, you were striving to *stabilize* the situation. I misinterpreted your place in the *zarien*. Do you understand?"

"Actually ... *no*," I told him.

"I was striving to eliminate a force that supported the *se-curo ja-riné*" he said earnestly. "The Chaos. That's what I thought you were. In fact, my actions might well have precipitated the *se-curo ja* I was trying to prevent. Will you forgive me, *goro*?"

I shook my head slowly. "Maybe," I said. "If I ever understand what the fragging hell you're talking about."

"Let me help put things right." Harlech reached out toward me, a gesture of pleading. "I can, you know. Let me come with you."

And that's when I laughed. "You've got to be farcing me."

His monoblade-sharp blue eyes flashed. "I know things you'll never know, Mr. Montgomery," he said softly, insinuatingly. "Do things you'll never be able to do. Things you can't succeed without."

"Then I'm fragged, aren't I?" I shot back, my voice harsh. "I'd rather French-kiss a fragging juggernaut than trust you, *slot*."

I could feel the elf's sudden anger, like a static charge in the air around me. But then I felt him willfully suppress it. "At least let me accompany you," he said reasonably, gesturing toward the Merlin.

"Frag you," I told him. "You try to get on that bird, I'll have you cut down in your tracks."

Harlech lowered his head, glaring up at me from beneath his dark brows. In that moment I felt real fear. "Do you really think you can do that?" he whispered.

From the corner of my eye I saw Akaku'akanene, still struggling against the magical control immobilizing her. "Maybe not, Quinn," I said conversationally. "But what do you want to bet? Are you willing to bet your life that you can control me *and* the soldier-boys on that bird ... and keep *her* from tearing your liver out?" I gestured with my chin toward the Nene shaman. "Do you want to bet on that, Quinn?"

I watched as the elf's eyes narrowed, and my gut churned with the conviction that he *could* manage it. But then his frown eased, and he shrugged lightly. "A point to you, my friend," he said. "But you *will* find it difficult to keep me away from Haleakala, you know. I *will* be seeing you again."

Harlech turned away, his old-style camouflage coat flaring behind him like an abbreviated cloak. Again—out of a sense of completion, if nothing else—I tried to bring my assault rifle to bear.

My muscles worked this time, for a wonder. My finger touched the trigger, the sighting laser burned, a ruby firefly tracked across to rest on Harlech's spine ...

And in that instant he changed, momentarily shifting into an extended prismatic after-image. An instant later, he was gone as if he'd never been.

With an effort I backed off on the trigger, a gram or two before it broke. Something told me that hosing down a Hawai'i National Guard base in the middle of the night wouldn't be the smartest thing I'd ever done.

24

Pohaku, Kono, and the military team were looking a tad edgy by the time I climbed aboard the Merlin, but I wasn't about to explain to them what had kept me. For that matter, Akaku'akanene was acting a mite testy, too, but I wasn't really in the mood to talk to her either.

The Merlin was set up as your standard troop carrier, with basic sling seats bolted to the fuselage on both sides, facing inward. Clambering up the ladder, I saw one empty seat up forward—beside Alana Kono, as a bonus—so I excused my way past the troops and slumped down into the kevlar fabric. I buckled up the four-point harness and then stashed the assault rifle under my feet, hooking its sling onto a retention bolt. In my peripheral vision I saw Akaku'akanene giving me a solid dose of stink-eye as she buckled in toward the tail of the plane, but I made sure not to make eye contact.

Someone outside folded up the ladder, before slamming and locking the hatch. The engines ran up, a howling turbine shriek that came right through the fuselage and drove into my ears like icepicks. The Merlin bobbled and shook, and then lifted up, up and away.

I'd ridden in Merlins and their ilk before, of course; who hasn't? So I wasn't expecting any problems with motion sickness. Of course, what I was familiar with was the civilian configuration of the tilt-wing bird, with comfortable, forward-facing seats and lots of windows. The military configuration? It sported the most uncomfortable seats I've ever gone a long way to avoid, and no windows whatsoever.

No windows. Ever think about what that means? A tilt-wing VTOL like a Federated-Boeing Commuter or a Merlin takes off and climbs like a helicopter . . . which means that it generally takes a serious nose-down pitch when it's climbing out. So how does the old sensorium interpret that? The floor's horizontal, chummer—that's what the eyes and the brain say, because floors are always horizontal. But the inner ear says the floor's at least 20 degrees *off* horizontal. It's that mismatch between what your brain knows and what your inner ear's saying that causes serious motion sickness. Typically the cure is to look out the window and get a reality check from the horizon ...

No windows in a military transport, chummer. I was starting to feel real green around the gills when Alana Kono came to my rescue. At first I thought she was just massaging the base of my skull behind my ear, but then she removed her finger and I realized she'd slapped one of those neoscopolamine narco-patches onto my scalp over a major artery. I turned to thank her ... and the neoscope in the patch had already kicked in enough to turn my grateful smile into a bedroom leer. The female gillette had the courtesy to blush and turn away.

I was *really* glad for the narco-patch as the Merlin pivoted its wings to shift from VTOL to forward flight. The turbulence was bad enough; even worse, though, was the knowledge that tilt-wings like Merlins are very vulnerable to engine cutout during the pivot process. If the engines stall out then, there's nothing to save you. Not gliding—there's no lift from the wing in the transition aspect—and not autorotation—ditto for the rotors/airscrews. Apparently, though, my narco-patch was dosed up with so much don't-worry juice that I could observe the tilt-transition as "just one of those things."

Suddenly I realized something and turned to Alana Kono. "You know," I said somewhat sheepishly, "I don't have a fragging clue where Haleakala is."

That earned me a sneer from Pohaku—no fragging surprise there—and another grin from Kono. From inside her armored jacket she pulled out a palmtop, flipped open the screen, and worked for a moment with the stylus. Then she handed it over to me. "Here," she said, pointing to the map.

Okay, there was the Hawai'ian island chain, traced out in plasma-red on the flatscreen. Not that it helped me much. "And Honolulu is ...?" I mumbled.

"Here." She touched the map, and one of the islands—the second major island from the northwest end of the chain—burned brighter. "That's Oahu. And this"—another touch with the stylus, and an island that looked something like an asymmetrical dumbbell glowed in double intensity—"is

Maui, see? Haleakala's here." She stabbed at the center of
the larger, lower "lobe" of the island.

"And that's . . . about how far?"

She shrugged. "Two hundred klicks, maybe?" She nudged
me gently with an elbow. "Not long."

I nodded glumly. Neoscope or not, my guts would be glad
to get out of this bird, but my mind would have been a *lot*
happier to know what was waiting for us when we got there.

Through the thin skin of the fuselage, I could hear the
Merlin's twin engines straining. We still seemed to be
climbing—at least, my inner ears were convinced we still
had a slight nose-up pitch—but the engines didn't seem to
like it in the slightest. Why? I wondered grimly. Headwinds?
There'd been clouds building up to the southeast when I'd
last looked out the window at New Foster Tower, hadn't
there? And according to Kono's map, that was the direction
we were heading. Into the teeth of a storm? I closed my eyes
and tried to hear if there was rain hitting the airframe, but
the tortured howling of the engines made it impossible.

Just fragging great, I thought. *Couldn't King Kam have
gotten us a bird with two good engines?* Then I remembered
something I'd scanned on the flight over to the islands, oh
so long ago now. Haleakala was a big fragger of a mountain,
wasn't it? Three thousand meters or something like that. No
wonder the Merlin didn't sound too happy. It was intended
for low-altitude short hops, or so somebody had told me
once. It must be a cast-iron bitch for the little bird to claw
its way up to this kind of altitude. No wonder the engines
sounded like souls in torment. I sat back and sighed. I
wasn't really sure whether that made me feel any better or
not.

I tried to disconnect my brain, then, to give it something
else to think about, *anything,* so it couldn't worry about the
engines and the storm. Haleakala, I thought. "House of the
Sun." I remembered that's what the name meant from my
database scan during the flight to Hawai'i. *Hale*—"house."
A—"of." *Ka*—"the." *La*—"sun." Simple, *neh*?

Interesting, too. It had stuck in my mind, like so many little bits of irrelevant trivia, because it had prompted a question when I'd first noted it. The Hawai'ian word for sun was
La. And wasn't the ancient Egyptian word for sun *Ra*?
La—Ra. Pretty fragging similar, particularly if you included
the possibility of "phonetic drift." Was it just coincidence?

After all, there weren't that many fragging single-syllable words that the human throat could pronounce, were there? Or was there more to it than that?

I wondered suddenly if Chantal Monot could answer that one. Chantal, with her whacked-out ideas about Lemuria and sunken continents, and her Andrew Annen-something paintings. (Now that I thought about it, didn't some of them have pyramids in them? Pyramids on the floor of a tropical ocean . . .)

With a snort I shook my head and forced away all those flaky imaginings. Sometimes letting your mind wander is worse than obsessing about what's scaring the drek out of you.

We'd been underway for nearly an hour when the turbulence began in earnest, and I started to appreciate anew the limitations of neoscopolamine. The Merlin started surging up and down in hundred-meter bounds like some kind of chipped-up roller coaster, and if I'd thought the engines had been straining before, I hadn't heard anything yet. Over the mechanical screaming, now I *could* hear the rattle of the rain against the airframe, driven by mighty gusts of wind. (Or frag, maybe it was hail. Whatever, it sounded like rock salt shot from a Roomsweeper.)

The troopers in their military gear weren't enjoying themselves. They wouldn't admit it to a civilian *haole* puke like me, of course—frag, they probably wouldn't admit it to each other—but I could see the way the muscles of their jaws were standing out. They were biting back on complaints, or maybe doing the iron-jaw trip to stop themselves from spewing their midnight snacks. Even Pohaku was starting to look a mite queasy. My own discomfort was almost a reasonable price to pay to see proof that he was actually as human as the rest of us. Beside me, Alana Kono was looking decidedly pale. In my peripheral vision, I saw her pull out another neoscope patch and slap it onto her own neck. I shot her what I intended to be a reassuring grin, but judging by the look in her eyes, I didn't quite make it.

And that's when the bottom dropped out. For a second or two we seemed to be in free fall. Kono yelped, and one of the troopers grunted in alarm. The only reason I didn't yell out loud was that I was too busy biting my tongue hard enough to taste salty blood. The engines wailed like banshees as the Merlin's dive bottomed out. We jolted hard a couple of times, almost as though we were taking fire from somewhere ahead of us.

Frag it, I couldn't just sit there. I reached down to unbuckle my four-point. Kono grabbed my hand and shook her head—apparently she didn't trust herself to speak—but I gently pushed her hand away and gave another try at the reassuring grin. This time I apparently did a better job, because she nodded and closed her eyes again.

I clambered to my feet, grabbing at whatever came to hand to keep from pitching onto my hoop—the back of my chair, the helmet of a green-gilled trooper . . . I managed to keep my feet somehow, and—getting a good two-handed grip on an overhead rack—I dragged myself forward. A light sliding door was all that separated the troop compartment from the flight deck, so I slid it back.

The flight deck was in total darkness. (I guess I should have expected it, but it still jolted me. Didn't you need some kind of instruments to do that pilot drek?) For an instant I couldn't make out squat, then my eyes adapted and I could see two silhouettes—deeper black against the black outside the cockpit—in front of me. "What the frag's going on?" I demanded.

The silhouette in the right-hand seat turned its head, and I saw two faint pinpoints of red light where there should be eyes.

Okay, that freaked me for a moment, too, before I realized the points of light were the copilot's cybereyes. Stray light from his active IR system, or some such technodrek. "*Hele 'ela!*" the copilot snarled at me. "Get the frag out of here, *le!*"

I ignored him and grabbed the shoulder of the figure in the left seat. (That had to be the pilot, right?) "What the hell's going on?" I demanded. And, as an afterthought, "How about lighting this crap up?"

For a moment I thought the pilot was going to tell me frag off, too, but then he nodded once. The control consoles came live with lights, data displays, radar images, and all the other junk that (meta)humans need to play bird. In the bright plasma light I saw the fiber-optic lines connecting pilot and copilot to the panels.

"So what the hell's going on?" I asked again.

"*Ino,*" the pilot snapped. "Storm. *Big* fragging storm. What the hell you think?"

As if to emphasize what the pilot was saying, the Merlin did another one of those roller coaster plunges, fragging near bounding me off the overhead. Neither pilot nor copilot moved; they kept their arms loosely crossed over their chests. But, from the sudden tightening of their muscles in their jaws and around their eyes, I knew they were working as hard mentally as if they were hauling back on physical control yokes.

"Do you usually get storms this bad?" I asked as soon as my heart had cleared my airway again.

"No way, brah." It was the copilot who answered me this time. "Never bad as this, yah?"

"So what the frag's happening, then?" I pressed even though I was afraid I knew the answer.

"Something fragged," the pilot responded. "Up ahead."

"Where are we, anyway?"

"Passing over Kihei, altitude twenty-nine-fifty meters. Airspeed two hundred, ground speed closer to fifty."

That little gem of information didn't make my gut feel any better. Airspeed 200, ground speed 50—that meant the little Merlin was fighting a headwind of 150 kilometers per hour.

I tried a quick glance out through the canopy. Nothing— quite literally squat. Rain was hitting the windscreen faster than the wipers could clear it, almost as if it was being flung from buckets or sprayed from a fire hose. Beyond that was just blackness. No ground, no horizon, no stars. Nothing.

I gestured to the canopy. "Have you got some instrument that can see through this drek?" I asked.

Nobody answered aloud, but the display on one of the console's screens changed. In computer-enhanced false color, I could see the towering slopes of a huge mountain. Haleakala, it had to be, rearing up ahead of us.

The colors on the display were wrong, but the contrast and contours were off, too. It took me a moment to understand. I wasn't looking at the mountain via visible light. This display had to be generated by some kind of FLIR pod— Forward-Looking InfraRed—slung under the Merlin's belly. I was seeing by heat, basically.

Which added a threatening significance to the glow that seemed to be emanating from the top of the mountain. On the FLIR screen, an amorphous plume of pale light sprouted from the top of Haleakala, silhouetted against the blackness of the sky. It shifted and shimmered like Global Geographic trideos of the aurora borealis.

"What the frag's *that*?" I demanded, stabbing a finger at the display. "I thought Haleakala was a dormant volcano."

"It is, brah," the copilot said shortly, "since twenty eighteen. Don't know *what* that is." He turned to me, his cybereyes glowing like sullen embers. "Mo' bettah we head back, yah?" he asked hopefully.

Good fragging idea. But, "You've got your orders," I told him.

He turned away, muttering something in Hawai'ian under his breath. I didn't need a translator to get the drift: Mo'bettah the *haole* have himself a brain aneurysm . . . *right fragging now*!

The Merlin jolted again, seeming to stagger in the air. I grabbed onto the backs of the crew's seats, bracing myself with legs widespread. Either the neoscope in the narco-patch was wearing off, or the fear was really starting to cut through the chemical well-being. I didn't like where I was, chummer, not one little bit.

Again the tilt-wing staggered, left wingtip dipping sickeningly before the pilot could recover. In that instant something slapped against the canopy—a solid sheet of water, it sounded like, not discrete drops anymore. The engines wailed.

And I saw something that shouldn't—couldn't—have been there. A *face*, chummer. A face, pressed against the transpex canopy. There for an instant, and then gone, staring into the flight-deck with eyes that weren't quite human, grinning with a kind of unholy glee.

"And just what the frag was *that*?" I yelped.

For an instant I thought—I hoped—the crew hadn't seen anything, that my imagination was running away with me. But then that hope died as the copilot turned to me, his face suddenly ashen in the plasma-light. "*Uhane, hoa,*" he gasped. "Spirit. Storm spirit."

Oh, just fragging peachy. I turned—almost pitching to the deck as the Merlin jolted yet again—and bellowed back through the door into the passenger compartment. "Akaku'akanene! Get your feathered hoop up here, *now*!"

It didn't take the goose shaman more than fifteen seconds

to join me on the flight deck, but that was still enough time for the Merlin to jolt and jar another couple of dozen times. In the plasma-light of the displays, her eyes glinted coldly like glass beads. She didn't speak, but her body language perfectly communicated the peevish question, *"What?"*

I grabbed the copilot's shoulder. "Tell her," I instructed.

The man gabbled quickly in Hawai'ian. I picked out a couple of words here and there—*uhane, haole,* and *lolo* among them—but that was it. When he was done, the bird-boned *kahuna* nodded.

"Nene signs of danger," she said to me. "Much power ahead."

Well, no drek, Sherlock, I managed *not* to say. "What about the spirits?" I demanded.

"I feel their presence." Her voice was calm, fragging near conversational.

"Well, bully for you!" I snapped. "Can you feel a way of getting rid of them?"

She shrugged her scrawny shoulders. "They stand guard," she pointed out.

"I'd kinda guessed that," I said dryly. "Can you persuade them to go guard somewhere else?"

"They guard the fabric," the *kahuna* shot back, her voice suddenly sharp. "They guard the pattern."

I blinked at that. What the frag was she talking about? Unless . . . "They think we're part of *that* drek?" I pointed again at the ghostly plume of light on the FLIR display. "Is that it? Christ, then tell 'em we want to *stop* it, for frag's sake!"

Akaku'akanene shrugged again. "They don't believe me."

I ground my teeth together so hard that pain shot through my jaw muscle. "Then be more persuasive," I grated.

The Nene shaman nodded and closed her eyes. The Merlin still jolted and jostled, but somehow she kept her balance perfectly—almost as if she could anticipate every movement of the small craft and adapt to it.

I didn't know if it was my imagination, or whether the *kahuna* had somehow gotten her message through, but after a few moments it felt as though the buffeting had diminished. The airframe still vibrated, the engines still complained, but at least the carnival-ride whoop-de-doos seemed to be under control. "Better?" I asked the pilot.

He nodded. "Altitude thirty-one hundred. Airspeed, two-ten. Ground speed one hundred. Ten klicks out." He glanced back at me over his shoulder. "Any instructions for the approach?"

I gave him my best pirate's smile. "Whatever'll get us there in one piece."

"Echo that, bruddah. Nine klicks."

On the FLIR display the volcano was looming large. The periphery of the giant heat plume was still amorphous, fuzzy. But for the first time I thought I could make out some kind of internal structure to it. There seemed to be semicircular wave-fronts propagating through it, like ripples spreading across a smooth pond from a dropped stone. *Something* bizarre was going on down in the crater, that was for fragging sure.

I turned back to the door into the passenger compartment. "We're about eight klicks out," I told "my" fireteam. For an instant I felt like I was in the middle of some ancient flatfilm about Vietnam. "I think this is going to be what they call a 'hot LZ'," I added dryly.

The plane echoed with metallic castanet-clatter as the squad locked and loaded. I thought about my own weapon, that ever-so-wiz assault rifle, on the floor under my vacant seat. Having something lethal to cling to like a security blanket would have made me feel a touch better about the whole thing, but it would have meant sacrificing one of the two hand-holds that was keeping me from measuring my length on the cabin floor. All in all, on balance, I figured I'd pick up my playtoy later.

When I turned back to the control console, the pilot had killed the FLIR display to replace it with a complex hashwork of approach vectors, wind axes, and all that other pilot drek. I didn't begrudge it to him. On reflection, I'd much rather he knew what was going on than me.

Beside me Akaku'akanene was still doing her balancing act, maintaining her equilibrium better than I was despite the fact she wasn't holding onto anything. Her eyes were still closed, and in the instrument lights I could see a bead of sweat tracing its way down her temple. *God,* suddenly I wished I knew what she was doing ... so I could understand, of course, but also so I could help. Judging by the motions of the Merlin, she'd persuaded at least some of the storm spirits—or whatever the frag they were—than we weren't a threat to the "fabric" or "pattern." If the addition of my concentration could help her convince the rest—or stop the ones she'd already convinced from changing their insubstantial minds—then I'd gladly give it my all.

The blackness was still unbroken outside the rain-blasted canopy. We were still in the middle of the stormclouds I'd seen gathering a few hours earlier. Mentally, I thanked whatever gods there be that there wasn't any lightning.

I almost pitched backward as the Merlin took on a steep nose-up pitch. From behind and to both sides I heard the scream of the engines change pitch. A computer schematic on the control console confirmed what I'd already guessed: The wings were pivoting again, from forward flight to V/STOL mode. We were on our way in. I drew breath to yell word back to the troopers ...

And fragging near swallowed my own tongue. Without warning the Merlin cleared the clouds, popping down out of a ceiling of roiling blackness. For the first time I could see the peak and crater of Haleakala volcano with my own eyes, without the need for FLIR intermediaries.

First impression: Spirits, what a blasted hellhole of a wasteland. Nothing grew; nothing lived—nothing seemed to *ever* have lived here. Just barren rock—rough, scattered scree slopes. Cinder cones. Outwellings of solidified magma. Precipitous slopes, vertical cliffs ... klicks upon klicks of lunar landscape. For an instant I didn't know where the image of the lunar surface had come from, but then I remembered. Back almost a century ago, when NASA was trying out their Lunar Rover designs, they'd picked the Haleakala crater for the tests, because it was the closest to the rugged emptiness of the moon that could be found on this planet.

Second impression: Holy fragging drek, I could *see* those klicks upon klicks of lunar landscape ... and I *shouldn't* have been able to. We were on top of a fragging mountain, three thousand meters up, and the cloud deck was so solid there was no chance for a single photon of moonlight to make it through. Yet the whole blasted prospect was illuminated—not as bright as day, by any means, but about like twilight.

It was a strange illumination, too: cold, sourceless, shifting, ebbing and flowing. I could see the source, roughly ahead of us—an area of what looked like absolute chaos. Light bubbled and roiled in the depths of the crater as though it were a physical fluid. Spreading up into the sky, in an ethereal fan-shape, the air itself seemed to glow with a pearly radiance. This had to be the visual equivalent of the heat-plume the FLIR had shown me, I realized instantly.

In the midst of the rolling, churning light were motionless points of brilliance, much brighter than the shifting illumination surrounding them ... but somehow sterile, dead. It took me a moment to understand those points were artificial lights, arc lamps set out by the *kahunas* of Project Sunfire so they could prepare the process that now seemed well advanced.

Something flashed by the Merlin's canopy, going like a bat out of hell. A well-chosen simile, since it seemed to be a mass of pure liquid fire about the size of a man's head. It was past and gone before I could make out any details, leaving a blue-green streak of afterimage across my visual field. As if my vision had suddenly become attuned, I saw there were *many* ... things ... flitting and hurtling around the central mass of light. Balls of fire, sheets of heat lightning, unidentifiable shapes moving so fast my mind couldn't make sense of them. They seemed to be orbiting that central light, like chipped-up moths dancing around a porch light. And that, too, seemed to be a well-chosen simile. I couldn't be sure, but neither could I shake the feeling I was seeing a kind of approach-avoidance behavior going on. The *things*— whatever they were—were both repelled and attracted by the drek going down in the center of the crater.

The *magic* drek going down. Deep in my gut where the truth lives, I *knew* it was magic, seconds before my intellect caught up and figured it out logically. I could feel the magic, deep in what I laughingly call my soul—like I'd felt it when Scott's fetish had cut loose, the instant before he blew Tokudaiji-*san*'s skull to fragments. It was like vertigo, like that flip-flop your stomach does when a super-express elevator momentarily goes into free fall. It was *like* that, except it wasn't my stomach doing flip-flops but ... *something else*. It was like I'd suddenly, momentarily discovered new senses, and the information those senses were feeding me prompted a reaction from a part of my body I previously didn't know existed.

It was over in an instant as if it had never happened, as if I'd never recapture that sudden broadening of perspective ...

For *me*, it was over in an instant. Not so for Akaku'akanene.

Which made sense if you think about it. If the level of magical activity down in the crater was enough to twist the guts of a mundane like me, what would it do to somebody who actually savvied that mana drek? Beside me, Akaku'akanene's eyes snapped open in a face suddenly pasty white. She opened her mouth to groan, and then she was lurching across the flight deck, her extraordinary stability suddenly gone. I grabbed her shoulder and dragged her upright an instant before she would have pitched over into the pilot's lap. (Vehicle control rig or no, I couldn't help but think an unannounced visitation to his groin by a little old lady would have messed up his control of the plane, at least a little.)

Akaku'akanene's wide eyes fixed on my face, and I could feel her fear and horror. She croaked something in Hawai'ian. I'd never heard the phrase before, but her tone of voice made the translation a no-brainer: "Oh, holy fragging *crap* . . . !"

I knew we were in even deeper drek before it happened. If Akaku'akanene was talking to me, it meant she *wasn't* talking to the spirits or whatever that apparently wanted to geek us. The Merlin staggered in the air as *something* slammed into its right wing. The right engine screamed like a speared devil rat, and then *something* blew up. In my peripheral vision I saw the flash of flame to my right, then shrapnel tore into the fuselage. Aft, I heard someone shriek in agony.

The right wingtip dropped instantly, and this time I couldn't hold my balance. I slammed into the right wall of the flight deck, and I howled as something went *gruntch* in my right shoulder. The impact was enough to defocus my vision and knot my guts with nausea. I could have let consciousness slip away right then, but somehow I clung to it, holding back the darkness. Frag, if these were going to be my last moments alive, I wanted to be awake for them.

We were in serious drek, I knew that even through the throbbing disorientation in my head. The Merlin was going down, and it was going down fast. Somehow the pilot had managed to get the right wingtip back up, but there was no way he'd be able to keep the crippled bird in the air much longer.

For the last time the copilot glared at me with his glowing eyes, and ordered, "Get back there! Strap in!"

This time I didn't feel any urge to argue with him. I struggled to my feet, dragging the almost inconsequential weight of Akaku'akanene with me. Back through the door into the passenger compartment I lurched. I pushed the old woman down into my old seat, the one beside Alana Kono. "Strap her in," I told the gillette.

The Merlin lurched, and I knew I wasn't going to make it to a seat myself, not in time. The seat Akaku'akanene had vacated was way aft toward the rear of the fuselage. With the bird pitching and rolling the way it was, there was precisely zero chance I'd be able to negotiate the legs and gear blocking the way and strap myself into the four-point before we slammed down. Instinctively, I glanced back over my shoulder. Through the flight-deck canopy, I could see the broken, rocky ground rushing up toward us. Frag, I had even less time than I thought . . .

Somebody else recognized it, too—one of the young, spit-and-polish troopers, the guy sitting next to Louis Pohaku. With a fist he pounded the quick-release on his four-point harness and was on his feet in an instant. "Sit!" he yelled at me, then reinforced the word by literally flinging me into the canvas sling chair. My fingers fumbled with the straps and buckles, trying to lock the harness closed across my shoulders and chest. Firm hands pushed mine away and finished the procedure much faster than I could ever have done it. In the dim light I looked up into the trooper's face. Just a kid, he was, maybe twenty at the outside. Keen and eager. He smiled as I tried to thank him.

And then we hit.

25

I don't know how long I was unconscious. A couple of seconds, maybe as long as five. The back of my head felt pulped where it had slammed against the fuselage, and the four-point was applying agonizing pressure to my injured shoulder. Still, I was alive, that was what mattered. My benefactor, the fresh-faced trooper . . .

Well, he *wasn't* alive. With nothing to brace him he'd been flung forward when we hit, smashing against the bulkhead. He lay like a broken doll, his back bent the wrong way, blood masking his face. I looked away, swallowing bile.

The pilot and copilot hadn't fared any better, I saw. The Merlin's nose had slammed into a house-sized boulder and crumpled on impact. The flight deck looked like a scene out of *Splatterpunk VI,* the crewmen splashed out of all human shape.

Toward the back of the fuselage one of the troopers seemed to have gotten himself under control. An older man, he looked, on his feet with weapon in hand, yelling at his charges. (A sergeant? Or did some other rank run squads in the Hawai'ian military?) *"E hele!"* he bellowed. "Go, go, go!"

Around me I could see military training kicking in. The young troopers must have been almost as shaken up as I was, but when a ranking officer yells at you, it doesn't take much intellectual skull-sweat to obey. Ingrained reflexes take over. Troopers were punching themselves free of their harnesses, leaping to their feet, and checking their weapons. Pohaku and Kono, too. The only people not responding were me, Akaku'akanene, and the dead trooper crumpled against the bunkhead. The sergeant bellowed again . . .

And my own training kicked in, coming out of the past like a ghost. Not military, Lone Star, but the next best thing.

I popped my own harness and my reflexes fired me to my feet. I looked around for the exit. There was just the single door in the side of the fuselage, the one we'd boarded through. That didn't make a frag of a lot of sense, did it? How were you supposed to debark combat troops—possibly under fire—when all you had was one piddling little hatch?

A concussion I felt through my feet and in my chest answered that question. I hadn't paid much attention to the rear of the cabin. I'd noticed the metal floor angled up at about 45 degrees immediately behind the last seats, but I'd written that off as a consequence of the fuselage design and given it no more thought. Now I understood. The up-sloping metal wall had become a down-sloping metal ramp, blown free from the remainder of the fuselage by explosive bolts. Before the echoes had even faded, the troopers were double-timing it down that ramp, boots pounding on the metal plate. Pohaku and Kono were on their heels, the woman stopping just long enough to shoot me a "today, today" look over the shoulder.

Across the fuselage Akaku'akanene was struggling to extricate herself from her four-point. With a sigh I crouched down and helped her unlock the harness and pull the straps clear of her narrow shoulders. *"E hele,"* I told her, and she nodded. As she hurried aft toward the ramp, I retrieved my Ares HVAR from under the seat. I started to follow her, but another thought struck me.

The troopers had loaded out with their own assault rifles, but many of them packed other weaponry as well. Considering that things had just gotten a little nastier up here in the House of the Sun, didn't it make sense to pack along anything that might even up the score for me?

It was tough to overcome my queasiness, but I managed to force myself close enough to the broken-backed trooper to see what he was packing. Lots of hand grenades, I noticed, but I left those well alone. (I'd never been trained in their use, and to tell the truth, "personal explosives" scared the living drek out of me. I found it much too easy to imagine pulling the pin and then panicking ... and throwing *the pin* instead of the grenade. *Boom.*)

There *was* something that looked more my speed, however. In a specialized holster on his right side, he was packing something that looked like the world's biggest-bore pistol. I pulled it out and turned it over and over in my hands. It was a grenade-launcher pistol; what the frag else *could* it be? Behind the pistol grip was a magazine, and the digital display on the weapon's mainframe told me I had six rounds ready to fire. Wiz. I made *damn* sure the safety was on, before cramming it under a strap of my assault vest. I picked up another magazine of grenades and shoved that deep into a pocket. Then I jogged down the ramp after Akaku'akanene . . .

And out into the middle of some beetle-head's worst chip-trip. Above me the black clouds roiled like liquid, churned by a hot, dry wind that tugged at my hair and clothing like invisible hands. Shattered rock shifted and rolled under my feet as I tried to keep my balance. The entire volcano seemed to *thrum* with a deep, almost subliminal vibration. My bowels cramped, and it was all I could do not to drek myself. Not from fear—frag, sure I was afraid, but that wasn't it; it was like the sound itself was churning my guts into a pit of diarrhea.

The Merlin had bellied in under the skirts of a hundred-meter-tall cinder cone. Boulders ranging from dishwasher-size to bigger than houses dotted the sloping ground. The shifting light that *was* Project Sunfire was *down there*—maybe half a klick away, down a steep scree slope, in the blackened and charred bottom of a secondary crater. The great fan of light—the nimbus of glowing air—towered up above me, reflecting off the underside of the rolling clouds. At its base amongst the lifeless points of arc light, I could see figures moving.

Half a klick—that's 500 meters, a long way to make out details. But maybe there was something in the air up here—magical or mundane, I couldn't know—that added clarity. The moving figures were tiny, but still I could make out some features. They were dancing, for one thing, an even dozen of them, stamping and gyrating, as they pranced in a great circle around the center of that unnatural, liquid light. They were fragging near naked, men and women alike wearing nothing but loincloths and headpieces of woven grass on their brows. The *kahunas* of Project Sunfire.

A dozen meters to my right, Pohaku and Kono were standing like statues, staring down at the spectacle in dumbstruck amazement. I started over toward them, picking up my pace when I saw the sergeant approach Pohaku. I made it over there in time to hear the sergeant ask, "What are our orders?"

"Stop *that*," I fragging near yelled, pointing down the slope toward the dance and the light. "I don't care how the frag you do it, but *do* it, *karimasu-ka*?"

The sergeant's face became a stone mask, and he turned toward Pohaku, as if I didn't even exist.

I grabbed him by the shoulder and dragged him back to face me, using my *left* hand, the cyberarm with the enhanced strength. Hardened soldier or not, by God he *turned*. "Listen to me, slot!" I screamed in his face. "Your orders are to *stop* ... *that*! Orders from the fucking *Ali'i*, do you hear me?" I fumbled in my pocket and hauled out the deputy's badge Ho had given me at our first meeting. "See this?" I bellowed, holding it up so close to his face that his eyes crossed. "From the fucking *Ali'i*, yah? Now, *do* it!"

The sergeant did what just about every military type *ever* does if someone screams at him loud enough and with enough confidence. He saluted me, right out of the textbook. He spun on his heel and dog-trotted off, yelling orders in Hawai'ian to his troops.

I could feel the hatred coming off Pohaku in fragging waves, but at the moment I couldn't have cared less about his bruised ego. I turned my back on him and ran over to where Akaku'akanene was staring down into the secondary crater. "What's happening down there?" I demanded. "What the hell are they doing?"

Under the weird witch-light in the air, her face looked like a corpse. "They're weakening the veil," she told me, her voice a ghastly whisper. "Preparing to draw it back."

"How long? How far along are they?"

"Far," she answered simply.

"Then we'd better be fragging moving, hadn't we?" I started jogging down that scree slope, starting the 500-meter trek to where the Dance was going on. (*What the frag are you going to do when you get there?* part of my brain asked. *Shut the frag up!* another part explained politely.) Around me, I could see the troopers heading down the hill, too. Kono and Akaku'akanene were starting down after me. Pohaku was still standing in the shadow of the downed Merlin, frozen in indecision. Well, fuck him if he couldn't take a joke. I ran on, quickly losing ground to the trained and fit troopers.

That's when the spirits hit us again—maybe the same ones that had downed the Merlin, maybe a different bunch. They hurtled down on us from above, like Thor shots—fire, and wind, and water, and Christ-knows-what-else. They hit the troopers first, the young, hardened men and women who'd easily opened the distance between themselves and the wheezing, out-of-shape erstwhile PI who was trying to keep up with them. Some of the soldiers saw the spirits coming, had enough time to get their weapons up and fire them. Most didn't. Not that it made any difference at all. Bursts of tracer fire, grenades, whatever—everything just went straight through the attacking spirits as if they weren't even there. And then the spirits were among the troopers, and the carnage began.

I turned back and screamed over my shoulder, "Akaku'akanene! *Stop* them!"

The bird-boned shaman stopped in her tracks, closed her eyes and began to sing. But it was too late for the troopers. They were all dead, or the next worst thing to it, before she even got the first notes of her croaking song out of her throat. Below me some of the spirits were still disporting themselves with the bodies of their victims—rending them into little pieces, carrying them high into the air and dropping them onto the rocks below, or scouring them with fire and cooking off their ammunition. As I watched, frozen in horror, some of the spirits seemed to notice me and the others for the first time. Breaking off from their diversions with the corpses, they hurtled up the scree slope toward us.

I had my own assault rifle off my shoulder as they came, but I didn't even bother touching the trigger. I was dead when those spirits reached me.

They didn't reach me, of course. They broke off their direct trajectories, soaring up into the sky like planes pulling out of power dives at the last instant before slamming into a previously unseen obstacle. My ears were filled with inhuman screams and howls—the spirits' anger and frustration at being blocked from their prey. Behind me I saw that Kono and Pohaku were moving in nice and close to Akaku'akanene, and I figured that they had the right idea. Whatever the Nene shaman was doing, I didn't want to test its range.

Overhead, the spirits were plunging down from the sky again, but before they could reach us they pulled out of their dives once more. Within seconds, we had a dozen of more of the fragging things swirling and orbiting around us, filling the air with their shrieks. At no point did they come closer than about fifteen meters from Akaku'akanene, and I belatedly realized they were displaying the same sort of approach-avoidance reaction as the spirits I'd seen circling the distant Dance.

"What the frag *are* they?" I asked Akaku'akanene in a husky whisper.

If the *kahuna* hadn't answered me, I'd have understood. Hell, curiosity always took backseat to survival in my book. She didn't open her eyes, but she did stop her song long enough to tell me, "Guardian spirits."

"Storm spirits? Volcano spirits? What?" I pressed.

"Both. Neither. *Guardian* spirits." She went back to her song, and I left her to it.

Now what the frag was I supposed to do? Akaku'akanene was the only thing keeping the "guardian" spirits off our collective ass. Somehow, I couldn't see her extending that protection to me as I jogged the half klick across the volcanic wasteland to get to the Dancers. (*And what the frag will you do when you get there?* part of my mind asked. *Shut the frag up!* another part responded.) Likewise, I couldn't see her keeping the shield (or whatever it was) up while she jogged along with me. Maybe she could walk and still keep the spirits at bay ... but would we be able to get to the Dancers in time?

"*Frag!*" I yelled in frustration. "They're *gaurdians*, right? Can't you just tell them to leave us alone?" I gestured wildly in the direction of the Dance. "We're trying to *stop* this thing. I thought that was what *they* wanted too. Don't they get that?"

Akaku'akanene nodded and broke off her song just long enough to say, "Yes. They want to preserve the pattern."

"Then why'd they want to scrag *us?*"

"I don't know." And again she returned to her harsh song.

Great. The only thing that could make things worse would be if ...

And, as if in response to my thought, there he was. Quinn Harlech, appearing maybe fifteen meters downslope from me, materializing out of a prismatic shimmer of light. Even at that distance I could feel those lasers he called eyes burning holes in me. His lips twisted in a scornful grin, and he drew breath to make a (doubtless scathing) remark.

Before he could get a single word out, I saw his eyes go wide, and he looked up. He threw up his arms in a sweeping gesture, and the air directly above his head flickered as if with heat lightning.

Not an instant too soon. The guardian spirit that was making a high-speed pass at the elf's cranium slammed into Quinn's magical shield, deflecting off like a basketball hurled at a concrete wall. The elf made another, more casual gesture, and with a despairing shriek the spirit was torn apart as if by invisible claws.

It had taken him less than a second to dispatch the attacking spirit, but that was long enough for the other guardians—the ones swarming around Akaku'akanene's arcane shield—to notice his existence. And, to judge from their actions, to decide that he was more of a threat to their precious pattern than we were. Of the dozen or so spirits swirling around us, all but a couple broke off and bee-lined it for Quinn Harlech.

I heard the elf curse in some fluid, complex tongue. He reached out toward the approaching spirits with a hand twisted into a claw. Half of them burst asunder, spattering the rocks below with the spirit equivalent of guts and gore. (Ectoplasm, maybe . . .?) The others, totally undismayed by the geekage of their colleagues, hurtled on, screaming like chipped-up banshees. Quinn frowned. He gestured again, and another half dozen spirits exploded.

That should have put paid to all of them, yet still the air around the elf was filled with ever more screaming, circling spirits. Where the frag were they coming from?

It took me a moment to understand. The elf's presence was siphoning off spirits from the vicinity of the Dance itself. As I watched, a constant stream of gibbering guardians was peeling away from the vicinity of the Dance, flooding over toward Quinn.

He fought well, that beleaguered elf. I don't know how many guardian spirits he blew to ectoplasmic tatters, or turned inside out, or transformed into clouds of ashes or drifting puffs of smoke or rains of frogs. Dozens. But for each one he geeked, two more joined the fray. Within half a minute the guardian spirits were so numerous I couldn't even see the elf anymore.

Finally, from within the tumult of spirits, I heard a sharp, "Frag!" Then came a brilliant flicker of prismatic light, partially occulted by the swarming guardians, and I knew Quinn had made his departure.

Once he was gone, I expected the spirits to turn their attentions back to us.

And, to be honest, I expected to die. There were so many of the fragging things—so many that even Quinn Harlech had decided discretion was the better part of valor. If the elf couldn't take them on, how could Akaku'akanene shield us from them?

But they didn't come. Still they churned through the air, swirling and hurtling around where the elf had stood, as if searching for some trace of him. I looked about me. There were *no* spirits paying any attention to us anymore—none at all. And frag it, there went my last excuse.

Suddenly, I laughed. On the runway back on Oahu, Quinn Harlech had told me he could do things I'd never be able to, hadn't he? Things I'd never succeed without? Well, he'd just proven it, hadn't he? He'd drawn away the spirits that were standing between me and my objective ...

Before I could have second thoughts, I gripped my assault rifle, and I started running down the scree slope toward the Dance below.

26

Running full-tilt down the slope, I suddenly pulled up short as I heard a scream from behind me. I turned.

Pohaku had Akaku'akanene locked in a kind of sleeper hold, her stringy throat gripped in the crook of his left elbow. In his right hand was a small pistol, a hold-out, its muzzle held firmly to the Nene shaman's temple.

"Turn into ice, *haole*," the bodyguard spat.

I froze. Alana Kono had her own gun out, the ruby dot of its laser sight settled firmly on her erstwhile partner's forehead.

"*Don't!*" Pohaku snapped at the woman. He glanced pointedly at the hold-out pistol. "Two-way trigger, *hoa*, okay? I squeeze, it fires. I release, it fires. Got me?"

Ah, drek. I'd read about guns with that kind of rig. At the time I couldn't understand why anyone would want a two-way trigger. The only possible application I could think of was ... well, *this*. A Mexican standoff where you need the ultimate dead-man trigger. Where regardless of what reflex action you take when you catch a bullet, you *know* your own gun's going to go off. Great.

I looked into Akaku'akanene's face from a distance of maybe ten meters. Her dark, beady eyes were calm, accepting. She had to know the thoughts that were going through my head.

Too bad, old lady, you've got a lot of jam. But there's more at stake here than one woman's life. May Goose have mercy on your soul ... I shifted my grip on the assault rifle. One quick burst into Pohaku's head and trust the impact of the rounds will knock his gun hand off-line before the pistol splatters the *kahuna's* brains ...

"Don't even *think* it, Montgomery!" Pohaku growled. "Look!"

I looked.

And started to sweat again. Most of the guardian spirits were still flailing about where Quinn had vanished. But two of them—big, nasty, fiery ones—had turned their attention back to us and were orbiting us slowly at a distance of fifteen meters from Akaku'akanene. *Drek!*

"Don't do it, Montgomery," Pohaku repeated, vocalizing the thoughts that were running through my own mind. "You shoot me, I geek her, and those things have you for dinner. You try to get down there, they'll rip you apart. You saw what they did to the troopers."

I saw, all right. I ground my teeth, and lowered my weapon.

"Put it down," Pohaku ordered. "Both of you, weapons on the ground."

Kono and I exchanged helpless glances. Neither one of us knew what the frag to do. Slowly we crouched to set our weapons down on the broken volcanic rock. "What now?" I asked.

Pohaku grinned, possibly the first time I'd seen any expression other than anger, hatred, or scorn on his face. "Now we wait, and we watch. It should be an interesting show."

No drek. I looked downhill toward the shifting, churning light. The intensity of the Dance seemed to have increased. The fan of witch-light was brighter, and the wave-fronts propagating through it seemed sharper-edged. Static discharges licked along the lower margin of the cloud-deck, strobe-lighting the scene below. In the flashes some of the boulders dotting the scree slope seemed to be moving—slowly, like cautious animals. My feverish imagination, of course.

There had to be some way out of this stand off. I just needed time to think of it. "You're *Na Kama'aina,* aren't you?" I said, turning back to Pohaku, more to keep him talking than because I really wanted to know the answer.

He snorted his derision. "*Na Kama'aina?* Pigeon-livered cowards, all of them."

"ALOHA, then," I suggested.

"Of course. Just like Ka-wena-'ula-a-Hi'iaka-i-ka-poli-o-Pele-ka-wahine-'ai-ho-nua."

For a moment I thought he'd lost it for some reason and had just started babbling. But then a couple of the fluid syllables clicked with something in my memory. That was Scott's name, wasn't it? The name that Scott, the chauffeur/

assassin, had told me his mother had given him. (Like drek, I thought suddenly. He'd *taken* that name himself, just like Marky "Te Purewa" Harrop, hadn't he?)

"ALOHA, then," I echoed in agreement. I paused, my mind whirring. "So I guess you've finally convinced *Na Kama'aina* to go along with your anticorp plan, haven't you?" I said at last, glancing pointedly down-slope toward the Dance.

Pohaku laughed harshly. "It took them fragging long enough, too, *haole*. But now we're going to see some *real* action."

I nodded slowly. "You *know* I'm trying to figure a way out of this," I said after a long moment. "Why don't you just cack me now and get it over with?"

He snorted. "I take my gun off-line and *she* drops me." He inclined his head toward Kono.

And vice versa, I thought grimly. The only one with any real freedom of action was Akaku'akanene herself. So why wasn't the shaman doing something? Couldn't she cast some kind of spell, blow the gun out of his hand, and drop the fragger in his tracks?

Then, *no,* I realized. He had to have some kind of magical protection, some antispell barrier or *something*—maybe spell-locked to him, or even Quickened so it was part of his aura. So Akaku'akanene was as immobilized in all of this as we were.

Downslope, I could feel the waves of magic spun off by the Dance. My stomach knotted and churned; my bowels felt like they were full of ice water. Frag it, I had to do *something*. I had to gamble. Maybe if I dropped Pohaku—and managed not to get Akaku'akanene geeked in the process— the shaman *could* shield me from the guardian spirits while I made a run for the Dancers . . . I took a deep, energizing breath, locating my assault rifle *precisely* in my peripheral vision. I wouldn't have much time to do it right. I tensed . . .

And that's when *it* hurtled into my field of view. A *nene*—a fragging goose. Honking and flapping, it soared in from Akaku'akanene's right, seemingly straight for her head.

Pohaku reacted instinctively, bringing up an elbow to protect his face. His *right* elbow, the elbow of his gun hand. The hold-out pistol came off-line.

Time seemed to flick into slow-motion mode. As I dived for my assault rifle, I saw the goose as it hurtled in.

Pohaku's reaction was an instant late, and the big bird's clawed feet tore at his face. He yelled in pain and alarm, rearing back from the threat to his eyes.

And then everything seemed to happen at once. The instant the barrel of Pohaku's hold-out was away from Akaku'akanene's head, the shaman drove an elbow up and back. The bony joint sank deep into the bodyguard's throat, knocking him back and off balance. Almost simultaneously a single shot rang out as Kono—who'd had the same idea as me—drilled a round into Pohaku's ten-ring. And then the Ares HVAR was in my hands, barrel coming up, laser sighting dot tracking onto the stumbling Pohaku's torso. I clamped down on the trigger; the rifle didn't so much stutter as *scream* on autofire. The stream of bullets did Pohaku like a chain-saw.

And then it was over. Of the three of us, only Akaku'akanene seemed unshaken by what had just happened. She brushed at her baggy clothing as if to rid it of some offending dust. Then she looked at me with those dark, glittering eyes and said quietly, "Go."

Like frag I'll go, I almost said. Then I saw the two guardian spirits that had been circling us. They were hurtling in, almost like the goose that had already vanished back into the shadows that spawned it. Akaku'akanene must have dropped her magical shield in the excitement. Instinct brought up the assault rifle again, even though intellect told me it was useless.

Akaku'akanene had seen the spirits, too . . . and she was smiling. One of them shot by me so close I could feel the heat of its passage. The other made an equally close approach to Kono, who flinched away and almost capped off a reflex round into it. Both totally ignored us as they fell on the mangled body of Pohaku, gleefully completing the dismemberment my long autofire burst had begun.

As time snapped back to normal, realization went *click* in the back of my brain. Okay, so that was why the guardian spirits didn't leave us alone even after Akaku'akanene had told them we wanted to *stop* the Dance. They'd sensed that somebody in the group had wanted to *protect* the Dance— Pohaku, to be precise. Maybe the spirits couldn't identify just which one of us was the enemy of the pattern (perhaps the antispell barrier that had protected the gilette had confused them). Or maybe the conflict between Akaku'akanene's reassurances and their own perceptions had decided them not to take any chances and geek us all, just in case. Whatever the case, I seemed to be in the clear.

In a manner of speaking, of course.

Again, I acted before I had a chance to paralyze myself with second thoughts. I flashed Alana Kono my best frag-the-world smile, and I took off down that scree slope at a dead run, toward the Dance half a klick away.

Bad move, chummer, *real* bad move. I'd made it maybe 100 of those 500 meters when I put a foot wrong, turned an ankle, and did a classic one-and-a-half-gainer to land on my neck and shoulder. My *injured* shoulder, of course. I did what anyone would do in that situation—I screamed bloody blue murder, as I did this graceful skidding roll down the loose scree slope. After what seemed like a frag of a long time, I came to rest upside down against a car-sized boulder.

Well, okay, maybe it turned out not to be such a bad move after all. Apparently what gods there be look out for babies, drunks, and overconfident drekheads. An instant after I fetched up against the backside of that boulder, fire washed over it from the front in a great roaring, flickering sheet. I tried to curl up so tight I vanished into my own belly button as the heat-pulse washed over me, crisping my hair and tightening my skin.

It was over in less than a second, almost like the wash of a single fireball. I popped up and risked a look over the top of my smoking boulder.

I must have attracted the attention of at least one of the Dancers, that was for fragging sure. The Dance continued, but one of the loincloth-clad *kahunas* had pulled out and was glaring out toward me over the intervening territory. Obviously, he'd cut loose with some nasty fireball-like spell. (An unpleasant thought struck me then: Were the Dancers able to draw energy from the site of power that was Haleakala? If so, all the guidelines I'd learned about the limits on just how much juice a mage can cast without keeling over had just gone right out the window.)

Well, frag it, now he'd attracted *my* attention, too. I brought the HVAR to bear and hosed off a short ripping burst. (Burning the entire clip in the progress. *Man,* that puppy fired fast!) I didn't think I'd hit him—he probably had some kind of magical barrier up—but reflex made him hunker down ... which is the purpose of suppression fire anyway. I ducked down into the blast-shadow of my boulder again.

Again, not a moment too soon. Something—some *things,* to be precise—spattered off the other side of the boulder. The impacts were hard enough to be bullets, but the sound they made weren't quite right. Shrapnel of some kind cascaded over the top and down my side of the boulder, and some went down my collar. Cold, wet . . . ice chips. The fragger was firing high-velocity icicles at me, or some damn thing. Then and there I decided that yes, maybe I *was* a magophobe after all.

This was *not* going to be easy. I looked back upslope for Alana Kono. A second gun would make all the difference down here. Maybe we could each take turns giving covering fire while the other leapfrogged forward.

No luck on that score, I saw immediately. I'd been shielded from the super-fireball by my boulder. Kono hadn't been so lucky. She was down in a huddled heap, unmoving. Sullen flames licked over her body, sending a twisted totem of greasy smoke up toward the clouds. Frag it to hell . . .

The almost subliminal vibration—the low, cosmic *thrumming*—I'd felt from the rock underfoot (now underass) changed its timbre, almost as though its frequency had been kicked up an octave. My bowels knotted again, and my vision blurred as the vibration conducted through my hoop, up my spine, and into my skull. Once more I could *feel* the magic that was being worked 400 meters away from my boulder, *sense* the almost limitless power that was being harnessed. Not so many minutes ago Akaku'akanene had told me the Dancers were far along with their ritual. Now, I didn't need any shaman to tell me that the ritual was approaching its climax.

I had to do something, and I had to do it *right fragging now*! What was it both Akaku'akanene and bug-boy had told me? That I was woven into this all-fired important pattern they were yammering about? And that I had influence, that events would revolve around me (or some such drek)? Well, now was the time to check out if they were telling the truth or feeding me a line of *kanike.*

Crouching there, with my back against a fire-scorched and ice-spattered boulder, I took the HVAR in my left hand, settling the stock up against my ribs under my arm. In my right, I took the grenade-pistol I'd requisitioned from my dead benefactor aboard the Merlin. (*Daisho,* I thought, suddenly recalling my friend Argent. He'd have approved of my weapon load-out, I realized. Put the autofire weapon—the one that can hose down an area in a hurry—in the off hand, the one with which you have less accuracy. Let the enhanced strength of the cyberlimb handle the recoil. Put the single-shot weapon in the hand I normally shoot with.)

I forced those thoughts aside. They were just ways my brain was trying to put off the moment when it might get itself blown to bits. I made sure both weapons were loaded and locked, safeties off. And I burst from cover like a pop-up target on a combat range.

The *kahuna* was waiting for me. The moment I came up and around my rock, he started a kind of shuffling dance, and I could see a nimbus of power building up around him. With the same supernatural clarity of vision I'd enjoyed earlier, I saw him smile nastily, baring his teeth.

Well, let him chew on *this.* I cut loose with a grenade from the pistol launcher, shooting from the hip. The recoil was grotesque, and the thing that had already gone *gruntch* in my shoulder definitely made its presence known. Even with that much kick the minigrenade flew slowly enough that I could track its trajectory, could see it arcing down under the effects of gravity. The shot was going to fall short, but the concussion and splinters might still give the shaman something to think about other than geeking me.

The grenade *did* fall short. Or, at least, it would have if it hadn't struck some invisible barrier between me and the shaman, about five meters in front of my loinclothed antagonist. The grenade detonated, filling the area with a cloud of thick, viscous smoke. *Ah, frag* ... I almost threw the launcher aside in terminal frustration. I'd picked up a weapon loaded with a full clip of fragging *smoke grenades*! If I thought I was going to live more than a few seconds more, I'd probably have felt humiliation for my stupidity. I hadn't even checked the fragging load!

What was that old joke? *Death's better than failure, because you have to live with failure.* Odds were, I wouldn't be having that problem. I cut loose with a short burst from the HVAR as I sprinted forward, knowing the bullets would deflect off the same invisible barrier that had stopped the grenade. But what other fragging choice did I have? Just stand there and wait for the shaman's spell to lash out through the thick cloud of smoke and smite me dead?

Wait one fragging tick ... *Through* the thick cloud of smoke?

That's when it hit me. I *couldn't see the shaman* for the smoke. And if I couldn't see him, *he couldn't see me.* And—last step in the logical progression that might just save my sorry hoop—*magic works on line-of-sight. You can't zap what you can't see* ...

I think I whooped with a terrible kind of glee as I brought the grenade-pistol up again and continued pumping round after round into the invisible barrier in front of the *kahuna* until the weapon clicked empty. The shaman caught on quickly to what I was doing. A witch-wind whipped up out of nowhere, lashing across the jagged rocks. But smoke grenades don't just burst in a cloud of smoke and that's it. No, they continue to pour the stuff out for some few seconds after they've detonated. The shaman's tame wind might blow away the smoke that was already there, but half a dozen grenades were lying on the ground between him and me, still gouting great viscous clouds of the stuff.

While I was pumping the grenade-pistol empty, I was still making my best time across the open space, my long legs eating up the distance. I kept my main focus on the smoke cloud—and, indirectly, the doubtless-pissed *kahuna* behind it—but I couldn't help but notice what was going on around me.

Which was, to my unschooled mind, a close approximation of Hell preparing to break loose in a big way. The tempo of the Dance had picked up, from that of a stately gavotte to something that looked like a chip-head jiving to shag rock while suffering from Saint Vitus' dance. The Dancers were moving counterclockwise in a circle twenty meters in diameter. Around them the air shimmered with power, as though each molecule burned with its own faint witch-light.

As I ran, still I managed to note for the first time that the pyrotechnic effects *weren't* centered on the Dancers' circle, as I'd assumed. No, not by a good margin. The fire-fan—the plume of light and infrared I'd first spotted on the Merlin's FLIR display—originated from a spot offset from the Dance's center by a good fifty meters. *There* was the real center of the power. The Dancers were within the margins of its nimbus, but the real ground zero (as it were) was *outside* the circle.

It was there—at that "ground zero"—that the really freaky things were happening. There, the air glowed with such intensity—not brilliance, as such, but intensity . . . and there *is* a difference—that it could almost have been solid: gases chilled to the point where they crystallized, and then the resulting crystal lit from within. Above ground zero the roiling, turbulent cloud deck bulged downward, as though the center of the glow were a partial vacuum, drawing air and clouds into itself. Static discharges lashed from point to point within the cloud deck, and from the clouds to the ground. They flashed through and among the dozens of guardian spirits that still swirled in their approach-avoidance display around the Dance and around ground zero itself. My ears were filled with the howling and wailing and gibbering of those spirits, with the titanic whipcracks of the static discharges, with the low-pitched, fundamental *thrumming* that conducted itself as well through the rocks as it did through the air.

Bright though the light ahead was, the static discharges were infinitely brighter still. Each time they flashed, they froze movement in the crater like the strobe light of a photographer. They froze my limbs, they froze the pattern of the drifting smoke, they froze the motions of the Dancers . . .

And they froze the motions of the boulders around me. For the boulders *were* moving—slowly, lumberingly. I couldn't spare them any attention, but my peripheral vision *did* pick up details. They *had* been boulders, I knew that. But—and here was one detail—they didn't look like inanimate rocks anymore. No, they looked like great beasts—like titanic hounds, crossed with the rocks of the earth in some kind of unholy breeding experiment. I could feel their eyes on me sometimes, and I felt the intensity of their hatred. Yet I could also feel that the hatred wasn't directed at *me*. I was irrelevant to them, I knew, just another feature of their environment, like the crashed Merlin or the clouds overhead. All of their attention was focused on the Dance, and on the crystal-fire air at ground zero. Slowly, they moved, but inexorably. They'd reach their goal sometime—I knew that, deep in my gut. What would they do when they got there? You got me, chummer.

And would they make it in time?

Time was again flowing like summer-weight oil in a deep freeze. I was hauling hoop over the broken rock. I'd already covered more than four hundred meters, leaving me maybe fifty more before I hit the smoke cloud. I was running as fast as I'd ever run in my life.

But I still had time and attention to spare to see that something had changed at ground zero. Something was there, in the midst of the crystal-fire air.

Or, more precisely, something *wasn't* there. If the crystal-fire air were a cloud deck, I'd say the clouds had parted to show the black sky beyond, dotted with stars. Except that the lights I could see, there in the center of the crystal-fire air, weren't stars—stars don't shift and blink like that. And the darkness—it had the infinite sense of depth that you see in the night sky, but I knew, *knew,* it was bounded with the crystal-fire. Maybe I *was* looking into the infinite depths of a sky, I thought suddenly.

But it wasn't the sky of *this* world. And there were *things* moving in it.

I thought I was going mad.

My time sense pulled another shift on me, and suddenly I was plunging at full sprint through the thinning smoke cloud. I kept my legs driving, but I brought up the barrel of the HVAR.

There was the shaman, right in front of me. He'd moved forward since I'd last seen him, right up to the edge of his magical antiprojectile barrier. Bad move. A freak gust of wind had blown the smoke back toward him, engulfing him. In the instant before I plowed full-on into him, I saw his eyes—puffy, red, watering—bug wide open. He opened his mouth—maybe to cast a spell, maybe to yell "fuck," I'd never know.

My shoulder went into his lower chest—my injured shoulder, frag it all—and I bowled him clean off his feet. As he went over backward, I stroked him reflexively across the side of the headbone with the empty grenade-pistol. And then—insult to injury—I blew his guts wide open with a burst from the HVAR as I staggered on.

The circling, churning mass of guardian spirits was behind me. That meant I was inside the magical barrier that was keeping them from getting to the Dancers. I was also through the antiprojectile barrier the downed *kahuna* had put up to protect himself. That meant . . .

I think I grinned as I slapped new magazines into both the HVAR and the grenade-pistol.

There were the Dancers, twenty-five meters away from me, no more. If they even knew I was there, they couldn't divert one iota of attention from what they were doing. For the first time I saw the patterns traced out on the ground—sketched with ash or flour, and with white rocks arranged in complex shapes, dotted throughout with wood, bone, and feather fetishers—and I understood a little better what was going on.

The Dancers themselves were within something that had to be a protective pattern of some kind, a circle twenty-five meters in diameter circumscribing their movements. And then, offset from the Dance, was another protective circle—smaller, but much more complex . . . and, I sensed somehow, much more *powerful*. The crystal-fire air, the region of darkness, the "stars," the *things*—they were all within that second circle.

So what did that mean? Circles can keep things in, or they can keep things out—that's about the extent of my understanding of conjuring. The smaller, more complex circle had to be intended to bind bug-boy's "entities" when they came through what I'd started thinking of as the "gate"—the rent the Dance had made in reality. (And, if I was to take bug-boy's and Akaku'akanene's warnings at face value, it wouldn't be enough to do the job.)

What of the circle around the Dancers, then? There was nothing to keep in, so it must serve to keep something *out*. A kind of magical bullet-proof vest—coverage for the shamans, in case the entities that came through managed to defeat the circle intended to constrain them.

Well, fuck that noise, that's what I say.

The entities weren't coming through the rip in reality, but they *would* come. I was convinced of that. The Dancers had opened a portal, a fistula, between our world and *another*. The damage was done. Any moment, one or more of bug-boy's entities—my "cosmic nasties"—would slither or leap or bound through that gap, and then the drek would drop into the pot. The islands of Hawai'i would suffer the torments of hell . . .

So were the Dancers—the slots who'd brought this whole drekky situation about—going to get away unscathed? Were they going to stay, safe and secure, inside their protective circle, while the cosmic nasties headed off on their rampage?

Not if *I* had anything to fragging say about it, chummer, let me tell you *that*.

I felt my lips pull back from my teeth in a terrible smile as I brought up both my weapons, bringing them to bear on the Dancers. Grenade first, just to let them know that hell was coming for them. My right finger tightened on the trigger ...

And every fragging muscle in my body froze. Every one. My breath was stilled, I think my heart stopped. Just as before, on the tarmac at Kaiao Field, I was magically paralyzed.

God damn you, Harlech! I tried to scream, but the words were confined to my own mind.

At my left side a figure appeared. Just *appeared*—one moment nothing, the next moment there, *blink*, just like that. Not Quinn Harlech. A Polynesian man, wearing the same uniform as the other Dancers—loincloth, woven-grass headdress, and that was it. Except for a nasty smile.

I *knew* him, the fragger. I'd seen him before, wearing more or less the same retro-drek. Standing at the left hand of King Kamehameha V in the throne room of the Iolani Palace. I knew that scrawny, withered, nut-brown body, now glistening with sweat. King Kamehameha's *kahuna*, his magical advisor. Did Gordon Ho know how close to him the treachery had been? Well, if he didn't, it was a fragging cinch *I* wouldn't be telling him.

The world was already starting to tunnel down around me as my brain cried out for the oxygen my heart wasn't sending it. What a fragging lousy way to go: *this* close, and then stopped in my tracks by an old rat-frag of a shaman, who just hung out invisibly until I wandered into his little ambush. What a drekky way out, asphyxiating with all my muscles frozen ...

Muscles? How did this magic drek work, anyway? Did it block the motor nerves, or did it freeze the muscles themselves? Only one way to find out. And hell, it had worked in an ancient book I'd read once ...

With my left arm—my cybernetic replacement arm—I lashed out with all the boosted strength of pseudomyomer fibers, servo-motors, and cyber-actuators. Not a muscle moved—just the technological *replacement* for muscles.

My left hand, and the assault rifle it was holding, moved so quickly it was blur. The barrel smashed into the old *kahuna*'s throat with a horrible crunching sound, still accelerating out and up. And fragged if it didn't tear his goddamned head clean off! The *kahuna*'s body went one way, his head went another, and my own body went a third, flung off its feet by the violence of my motion. I hit the ground hard, driving from my lungs what little stale air they still contained. I gasped in an agonizing breath . . .

Repeat that. I *gasped in agonizing breath!* The pain I felt was like a benediction. *Only living men feel pain.*

As the *kahuna* had died, so had his spell. I was free again. I could breathe, I could move.

For a few long seconds I lay there, relishing—*wallowing* in—the sensations of breathing. Then a sudden change in the vibration humming through the ground reminded me that my only chance of *continuing* to breathe—and slim chance it was—lay in my own hands. With a snarl, I forced myself up to my hands and knees, then to an unsteady crouch.

The Dance had reached its frenetic crescendo. Two of the Dancers seemed to be down—fainted or dead, I had no way of telling—but the others were still leaping around as if they were having convulsions. Fifty meters away, at ground zero, the rent in the fabric of . . . well, of *everything* . . . had opened wider. I could feel cold radiating onto my face. (Okay, I *know* cold doesn't radiate. But frag it, that's precisely how it felt . . .) Something filled the gate, started to emerge through it. Something . . .

I forced myself to look away. *My God* . . . My brain couldn't comprehend what my eyes had seen . . . not *quite.* I was right on the terrible brink of comprehension, and I had the unshakable conviction that if I ever *did* comprehend, then in that instant I'd go incurably insane.

I didn't have to look at ground zero, anyway. My real targets were much closer than that.

I brought the grenade-pistol to bear, aiming carefully over the open sights. The circle surrounding the Dancers was divided into quadrants by small but elaborate cairns built out of white stones, carved wooden sculptures, and chunks of bone. The nearest of the four cairns was less than thirty meters away from me. I checked my aim and squeezed the trigger.

The grenade hit it dead center and detonated. No pussy

smoke this time; the second magazine I'd grabbed were frags. I heard the almost subliminal whisper of splinters cutting through the air around me. The cairn was already blown to drek, but what the hell? I had five more grenades. I pumped another one into the wreckage just for good measure.

I'd breached the Dancers' protective circle. Somehow I *knew* that, I could *feel* it. And they knew it, too. They stopped in midconvulsion and they stared—some at me, most at the gate, but all with the same expression of mindnumbed terror. They stared.

Until I cut them down with a single long, hosing burst from my HVAR. They went down like tenpins, sprawling, slumping, spraying blood and tissue. I laughed then, an irrational, insane sound in my own ears. *Well, that's* one *way to tell the dancers from the dance* ...

My job wasn't done yet. I turned toward the gate, keeping my eyes averted from the rent in space, and I pumped out the four grenades remaining in the magazine. As before, I was aiming not at what was inside the protective circle, but at the circle itself. The minigrenades exploded among the white stones, ash, flour, and carved and feathered fetishes, blowing them to hell.

Something slammed into my back, driving me to the ground. Sharp lava rock slashed my face and hands. I raised my head, blood already running into my eyes and blurring my vision.

It was one of those big rock hound-things that had knocked me down. It hadn't stopped to so much as sniff me or lift a leg on me. It and a dozen or more of its fellows were hightailing it toward the gate. If before they'd moved about as nippily as a glacier, now they were making up for it. Huge, bounding strides ate up the distance.

On their heels, quite literally, came the wild tumult of guardian spirits that had been kept out by the Dancers' magical barriers. Like a wailing, screaming pack of lost souls, they flooded in above me. Not toward the gate, I saw quickly—toward what was left of the *kahunas* I'd cut down. As the hounds (or whatever they were) loped on toward the gate, the guardian spirits fell on the corpses and not-quitecorpses and tore them to bloody shreds, gibbering and yelping with unholy glee.

Hounds were converging on the gate from all directions.

For the first time I heard the sound they made—a hideous, unnatural baying that pierced my ears and turned my blood to ice. Onward, inward they charged. Their bulk hid from me the horror of the *thing* that was emerging from the gate.

I thought they'd hurl themselves headlong at the *thing*, like attack dogs going for an intruder's throat. No way, chummer, that would have been too predictable. They skidded to a stop, all of them, forming a solid ring around the gate. Shoulder to stone shoulder they crouched. Then, simultaneously, they raised their blocky muzzles to the sky and they *howled*.

It cut through me, that sound, reached deep down into my soul and touched every remnant of despair, loneliness, and abandonment I've ever felt—touched them and roused them to life again. I would have cried—would have burst into tears, never to stop again—but my soul hurt so much I *couldn't* cry. I thought I was dying, then. How could a pitiful human feel so much desperation and *not* die?

Yet somehow I didn't. Somehow, my heart kept pumping, my blood kept flowing. I lay there on the rocky ground, watching as the great hounds howled at the gate.

And it changed, the gate did. It shivered and shimmered, losing resolution. Lightning flashed and cracked, but now *within* the infinite depth of the gate. Actinic light strobed, throwing the hounds into sharp contrast, black on blinding white. From within the gate, *something* screamed, adding its own cry of despair to the howling of the hounds.

With a final sky-splitting crash, the gate collapsed in upon itself. The crystal-fire air shimmered, and I saw a shock wave—a perfectly hemispherical wave-front—spreading out from the center. As in all those old flatfilms of nuke tests, the shock wave expanded toward me, the air before it compressed to such density that it was opaque.

The shock wave touched me, and everything stopped.

Epilogue

And, yet again, I came back to what we laughingly call consciousness in a hospital bed, staring blankly at a featureless white ceiling. The same damn thing over and over again ...

I took a breath and moaned aloud at the pain it caused me. I felt as if a troll with combat boots had stomped—with precise and loving care—on every important part of my anatomy, *and* several parts I wouldn't previously have classed as important. I *hurt*. All of me, all over. Deep down, and out the other side. (Except for my left arm, of course, but even it sent my brain its own weird analog of "pain" signals.)

Only living men feel pain, I tried reassuring myself. It didn't work worth squat. Lying there hurting, I couldn't help but envy the dead.

I guess I drifted off then for a while, because the next time I was aware of my own existence the ceiling lights were out. The only illumination came from the direction of the foot of my bed. A cold, blue-white wash of light. Moonlight?

I tried sitting up, quickly giving up on that as a bad job. Instead, I had to satisfy myself with rolling my head on the pillow so I could cast a corner-eyed look down the length of my body.

Yep, moonlight. Somebody had neglected to close the shutters over my window, and I could see straight out into the night. The full moon rode high among the clouds, like a ghostly galleon sailing through an archipelago of surrealistic islands.

Full moon? I tried to remember what phase the moon had been when Gordon Ho and I had stood watching the Thor attack from the window of New Foster Tower. I found I couldn't recall details—of that night, or of just about anything else, for that matter. Some part of me knew that this *should* disturb me, but at the moment I didn't have the en-

ergy to give a frag. I was pretty sure the moon had been new
or close to it even though I couldn't pin it down exactly.

Which meant I'd been out of it for *two weeks*? Remembering the last time I'd woken up in a hospital after a protracted unconsciousness, I quickly ran a kind of mental
inventory of my body. Did anything feel strange, numb or—
worse—absent?

No, I realized after a nasty moment, letting myself relax
back into the bed with relief. Everything felt just about right
. . . which meant it hurt like frag. If I *had* lost something and
the docs had replaced it with chrome—as had happened to
me the last time—they wouldn't have gone to the effort of
perfectly replicating posttrauma pain, would they?

I rolled my head again for another look at the moon. Good
old moon, I thought foggily. Thank whatever gods there be
that *you* remain unchanged, at least. We can frag up our own
world all we want, but at least we can't jack with *you* . . . not
bad enough that we can notice it, at least.

I closed my eyes, and for some unmeasured time I listened to the soft soughing of the air-conditioning. When I
opened my eyes again, it was day. I blinked, and it was night
again. Like my blurring of memory, I knew that *should* have
worried me, but again I couldn't generate a sense of outrage
or concern. All in its own good time, thank you very much.

Again the man in the moon did his Peeping-Tom act in
my window, and I listened to the sighing of the ventilation.
That was all I could hear—artificial wind inside, real wind
stirring the palm trees outside. No explosions, no gunfire, no
screams. The gate had to be closed, then. I couldn't imagine
that any night could be this peaceful if that rent in reality
hadn't been sewn back up.

"The gate *is* closed."

The soft voice from somewhere to my right fragging near
stopped my heart then and there. I let out a yelp and jumped
like someone had jolted me with a cattle prod. When I'd gotten my heart rate back under the five hundred mark, I turned
my head to the right and scowled at the silhouette—black on
deeper black—of a seated figure. "I didn't think I spoke
aloud," I said accusingly.

I heard Akaku'akanene's smile, rather than saw it. "You
should continue to surprise yourself, maybe, as you do others."

For a moment I mentally chewed on the twisted grammar of that statement, then I gave up. "How?" I asked.

"How much do you know of the workings of magic?" the old woman began elliptically.

I couldn't help but smile. "Do you have any elven blood?" I asked wryly.

Again I heard her smile broaden. "Why, because I answer a question with a question?"

I sighed. "Word games later," I told her. And I repeated, "How?"

"Guardians," she said simply. I waited for her to amplify, but she didn't.

"The spirits, you mean?"

"Yes, the spirits. And other guardians as well. Guardians of Haleakala, guardians of the pattern."

She had to mean the rock dogs, didn't she? I nodded. "Go on," I suggested.

"The *kahunas,* they had to keep the guardians out to unravel the pattern."

Again I waited; again, I had to prompt, "And . . . ?"

I saw the silhouette shrug, as if to say, "That's it!"

And I guess it was. I'd wrecked the Dancers' protective circles, which let the "guardians of the pattern" in to do their thing. Simple.

"Okay," I admitted, "I scan it. But"—I gestured at my body, the bed, the hospital room—"what's wrong with me? I feel drek-kicked."

Silence for a moment, then Akaku'akanene said softly, "Do you understand the powers you were close to?"

Something in her voice made my skin crawl, but I pressed on anyway. "The Dancers were closer than I was," I pointed out.

"Yes. Shielded by protective wards. Skilled in the working of magic. You?" She snorted. "You are lucky Nene watches over you."

"What would it have done to me?" I didn't really want to know, but I had to ask. "Killed me?"

"Worse," she said, her voice a chill whisper. "Much worse."

I lay back and stared at the ceiling. I blinked. After a few moments a memory jarred me. "Hey," I said, "what was that drek with Pohaku—that goose *ex machina*?"

I didn't look at her, but still I felt her smile. "When the

spirit sings, the shaman answers," she said softly. "But sometimes it is the *shaman* who sings."

Typical spiritual mumbo jumbo, is what I didn't say. I blinked . . .

And it was day again, and Akaku'akanene was gone. I never saw the old goose again.

Maybe it was the old shaman's visit, or maybe it was my own indomitable strength of will (yeah, right). But after that my rate of improvement increased drastically. Within two days of Akaku'akanene's nocturnal admissions, I was on my feet and taking mild exercise, and two days after that I was rolling toward the main door of the hospital—the Kuakini Central, I'd learned its name was—in a powered wheelchair. (Why do hospitals, even in this day and age, insist that patients can't leave the premises under their own power? In case other prospective "clients" think they're actually cured . . .?) My escort—the practical nurse assigned to my rehabilitation, a big, jovial ork called Mary Ann—pressed the Door Open button for me and stood clear as I rolled out into the sunshine. She bent down and planted a wet, tusked kiss on the top of my head. (We'd gotten along just fine, me and Mary Ann—when she wasn't threatening me into one more rep on some exercise-torture machine, that was.)

"So, what now?" I asked her. "And can I finally get out of this thing?"

Mary Ann gave me one of her best child-terrifying grins. "You're through the doors," she pointed out. "Now give us our fragging wheelchair back, *hoa.*"

I chuckled as I extricated myself from the depths of the powered chair. I drew breath to repeat the first part of my question.

But she cut me off with an inclination of her head. "You're expected," she said quietly.

I looked where she indicated. A limousine—not a Phaeton, not this time—had pulled up at the curb, the rear door opening with a hydraulic hiss. "No space for me at your house?" I asked the ork mock-hopefully.

"Always, lover," she purred. "But my husband, see, he's kinda touchy about these things."

I laughed freely. It felt good. "Well, far be it from me to jack with your marital bliss." And then I let my face grow serious for a moment. "Thanks, Mary Ann. I mean it."

She hugged me. And if you've never been hugged by an ork who's been trained as a practical nurse . . . bruddah, you ain't never been hugged.

When I could breathe again, I gave her a last smile and went slowly down the stairs toward the limo.

All the windows were tinted and polarized. The driver could as well have been that *thing* that had tried to come through the gate, for all I could see. I sighed. Well, if anyone out there in the big, wide world wanted me dead, they wouldn't have had to pay for a limo to arrange it. I climbed inside and closed the door after me.

The kevlarplex screen between the passenger and driver compartments was in place—no surprise there—and it was also fully polarized. I couldn't see so much as a silhouette of the driver's head. I sat back as the limo accelerated away from the curb, and I waited.

Nothing, so I waited some more. Still nothing. So this time I rapped on the divider with a knuckle. "So what gives, huh, brah?" I asked the kevlarplex.

More nothing. I was winding up for another, harder rap when the telecom screen in the limo's entertainment/commo suite lit up and filled with a familiar face.

"I'm glad to see you've made it in one piece, Mr. Montgomery," Jacques Barnard said.

I sat back in the sumptuous upholstery and scrutinized the corporator's on-screen image. He was in a new office, I saw. The background was a simple wall, not an out-of-focus view of a garden and statues. "More or less," I admitted. And then I waited. I could tell from the suit's expression that this was definitely *not* a social call.

Barnard nodded then, apparently satisfied that I'd caught the tenor of this "virtual meeting". "Well, Mr. Montgomery," he said lightly, "you'll be glad to know that the . . . *confusion* . . . of the past month has come to a satisfactory conclusion. Satisfactory to all concerned, I'm pleased to say."

I nodded. "Uh-huh."

He hesitated slightly, put off stride for a moment. "You'll also be glad to know that King Kamehameha has staged a"—he paused, theatrically searching for the correct word—"a *countercoup*. The *Ali'i* is back on his throne. The *Na Kama'aina* faction in the government has been humbled. And, as far as I can tell, ALOHA has been nearly eliminated." He smiled magnanimously. "And much of the credit must be accorded to you, Mr. Montgomery."

I nodded. "Uh-huh." Barnard didn't seem to have anything else to say, so after a long, uncomfortable pause, I said, "So, business as usual, *neh*?"

He shrugged. "More or less. Again, thanks to you, Mr. Montgomery."

"Uh-huh." I paused again. "And how far do those thanks extend, Mr. Barnard?"

He gestured broadly, his telecom image seeming to encompass the entire limo. "*This* far, to begin," he said. "The charges for your hospital stay have, of course, been absorbed. And there is a room in your name at the Diamond Head Hotel for one week."

"Uh-huh. And transportation back to the mainland?"

"When you wish to leave, contact one of my people," Barnard said. "The driver will give you a datachip when he drops you off at the hotel. The contact information is on it . . . along with data on an account at the Zurich-Orbital Gemeinschaft Bank."

"Uh-huh." And again, I paused. "And future contact, Mr. Barnard? Future work?"

Jacques Barnard gave me one of his best plastic corporator smiles. "If the need arises, one of my people will contact you, Mr. Montgomery. Count on it." And with that the screen went blank.

Uh-huh. Translation: *Don't call us, we'll call you.*

So, what about Barnard's protestations of respect, back when he was recruiting me for this job? Of affection, for frag's sake?

Everybody lies.

Back in the Diamond Head Hotel. A different room, but the only way you could tell the difference was by looking at the number on the door. I dumped what few things I'd taken with me from the hospital—my toothbrush, basically, and not much else—into the corner. Then I sat on the bed and stared at the datachip in its carrier that the chauffeur had given me when dropping me off. A couple of times I glanced at the room's sophisticated telecom, but I simply couldn't get up the energy to slot the chip and check it out.

So it was over. The gate closed, the corps satisfied. *Na Kama'aina* out, Gordon Ho back on the throne . . .

Well, hell, let's admit it: I tried to phone him. Gordon Ho, King Kamehameha V, *Ali'i* of the Kingdom of Hawai'i. I checked my wallet, and I found the mylar card he'd given me in his office at the Iolani Palace was still there. I called the number.

Unlike the last time Ho himself picked up the phone. When he saw who it was, he smiled. And then, an instant later, that smile was extinguished by an emotionless, politican's expression. "Mr. Montgomery," he said coolly.

Okay, I knew where this conversation was going, so I didn't belabor the point. All that *kanike* about "keeping in touch?" Just that, chummer—bulldrek, pure and simple. Politically, he couldn't afford to be friends with some low-life *haole* shadowrunner. He had to cut loose from me, past protestations of friendship notwithstanding.

Everybody lies.

And what the frag, since I had my momentum up, I phoned the LTG number bug-boy had given me on that strip of pocket 'puter thermal printer paper. A voice mail box—predictable, of course. I left a message, requesting—well, maybe *demanding*—a meeting later that afternoon, down at the east end of Waikiki Beach, in front of a statue of some slag with a surfboard I'd spotted on my first day in the islands.

I was at the site fifteen minutes early—I didn't have what it took to wait any longer—but bug-boy had beaten me to it. The Insect shaman was sitting on a wooden bench in the shadow of the statue, gazing out over the surf with his glassy eyes. I don't think he could have heard me coming, and I knew he couldn't have seen me unless he had a third glassy eye in the back of his skull. Yet he turned when I was still fifteen meters away, and watched as I slowly walked over.

He stood as I approached, and again I was glad that he didn't offer me his hand.

"We had a deal," I said flatly.

He inclined his head—agreement, admixed with regret. Just as with the *Ali'i*, I knew where this conversation was going. "Yes," he said.

"Well? Where's my sister?"

The Insect shaman shrugged almost apologetically. "Gone," he said simply.

"You can't bring her back." My voice sounded soulless in my own ears. "You never could, could you?"

The nondescript man shook his head. And then he turned his back on me and started to walk away.

I wanted to scream. I wanted to chase after him and smash his head to pulp. I wanted to pull out the pistol I was packing and empty the clip into his back. I wanted to turn that same pistol on my own head and pull the trigger. Instead, I said to him, honestly, "Thank you for coming alone."

He hesitated for a moment. He didn't look back, for which I'd be eternally grateful. Then he nodded once, and he walked on, westward, toward the sinking sun.

Everybody lies.

It was like I was back in the hospital. One moment I was sitting on a wooden bench, watching bug-boy walk away across the sand toward the setting sun. I blinked, and the sky was dark. Lights burned in the hotels along the curve of Waikiki Beach. Behind me, on the street, cars cruised by, their stereos playing Hawai'ian music.

A taxi stopped for a few moments a dozen yards away, its windows down, stereo blaring. I recognized the song— "Hawai'i, My Home," by that group Scott had played for me my first full day in the islands. *Kani*-something. All dead, now. Appropriate, somehow.

I felt a presence beside me. I turned.

It was the elf. Quentin Harlech, or whatever his real name was. An arm's length away, he was staring out over the night black ocean.

"How long have *you* been here?" I asked. Then, "Skip it," I told him.

Hotel lights glinted off his teeth as he smiled. "Long enough," he answered the question I'd just canceled. Then he waited—to see if I'd speak again, to see if I'd try to geek him . . . I don't know which. I didn't do either; I just looked out toward the pink-tinged horizon.

Finally, I saw the silhouette of his head nod. "You don't know what you did, do you?" the elf asked quietly. "You don't know the importance, you don't know why it mattered. But you did it anyway."

I didn't look his way, but I could feel his eyes on me. I knew the question he was asking—the question he couldn't bring himself to voice. But I didn't know the answer. I shrugged.

"I thought so," he said, responding to the answer I hadn't given him. "I think I knew you before, Derek," he went on quietly a moment later. "Perhaps we fought alongside each other once before."

Now I turned to him. "Chummer," I said, "you're up the pole. I never set eyes on you before Puowaina."

"Not *those* eyes, no," he agreed . . . if it was agreement. "But I know you, Derek. You face overwhelming odds. And you vanquish them . . . merely because you don't know it to be impossible." He smiled—sadly, I thought suddenly. "You remind me of . . ." His voice trailed off, and he looked out to sea again. "Long ago," he whispered, almost inaudibly. Or maybe it wasn't him at all, but a breath of night breeze.

"Question," I said, after a long silence. "You were trying to close the gate, right?"

Quinn shrugged. "Rather, to prevent it from ever opening."

"Then why did the guardian spirits attack you?" My gaze fixed on his face. "*Why,* Harlech?"

To my utter shock and amazement the elf seemed unable to meet my gaze. "History," he said quietly. "I have . . ." He stopped and tried again. "I have . . . *touched* . . . this danger before," he went on. "The guardian spirits sense its taint on me." His lips quirked in a smile. "I wonder how they would react to *you,* Derek, should you go back there a second time?"

"No danger of that."

Quinn laughed softly. "I think I rather like you, Derek," he said. "Some of my contemporaries would laugh if they could hear me say this, but . . . I feel that you might just be a kindred spirit. Do you realize how rare that is?"

Now he *did* meet my gaze. I saw . . . *something* . . . in his eyes. If I hadn't known better, I'd have thought it was envy, or maybe even longing. Longing for something that had been lost, a long, long time ago. Stupid, of course.

I snorted, and I turned away. "Frag off, Harlech," I said. Then I yelled it, still not looking at him: "*Frag off!* Okay? Just get the fuck out of here."

I couldn't bring myself to turn around and look at him. I didn't dare—I was afraid of what I might see in his eyes.

I felt him stand up and hesitate a moment. Then I felt him stride away from me into the darkness.

"I don't need you!" I yelled after him without turning my head. "I don't need *anybody*!"

Everybody lies.

Even me.

NEVER DEAL WITH A DRAGON

Secrets of Power Vol. 1
by Robert N. Charrette

Where Man Meets Magic and Machine

The year is 2050. The power of magic and the creatures it brings have returned to the earth, and many of the ancient races have re-emerged. Elves, Orks, Mages and lethal Dragons find a home in a world where technology and human flesh have melded into deadly urban predators. And the multinational mega-corporations hoard the only thing of real value—information.

For Sam Verner, living in the womb of the Renraku conglomerate was easy, until his sister disappeared and the facade of the corporate reality began to disintegrate. Now Sam wants out, but to "extract" himself he has to slide like a whisper through the deadly shadows the corporations cast, through a world where his first wrong move may be his last ... the world of Shadowrun.

▼ 2 ▼
CHOSE YOUR
ENEMIES CAREFULLY
Secrets of Power Vol. 2
by Robert N. Charrette

When Magic Returns to the Earth

its power calls Sam Verner. As Sam searches for his sister through the slick and scary streets of 2050, his quest leads him across the ocean to England, where druids rule the streets . . . and the throne. But all is not what it seems, and Sam and his new shadow friends are plunged into a maze of madness on the trail of destruction.

Only when Sam accepts his destiny as a shaman can he embrace the power he needs. But what waits for him in the final confrontation of technology and human flesh is a secret much darker than anything he knew lay waiting in the shadows. . . .

▼ 3 ▼
FIND YOUR OWN TRUTH
Secrets of Power Vol. 3
by Robert N. Charrette

Find the Magic!

He was only a "beginner" shaman, but Sam Verner had to find a cure to ward off the curse on his sister. Only something of great magic would do the trick. It was this quest that took him to a mystical citadel in Australia, where, with the aid of his shadow-runner friends, he recovered the strange artifact he hoped would prove helpful. But instead of anything that even remotely resembled help, an unexpected and ancient terror was released—a terror that erupted into a shadow war for dominion over an awakened earth. And while the evil kept growing, inexorably drawing him into battle, the curse's power over his sister was also growing, bringing her closer and closer to death. Soon a truly desperate Sam realized that the last and only hope for saving his sister was to find the greatest shaman of the Sixth World, former leader of the Great Ghost Dance—a man who may no longer exist. . . .

▼ 4 ▼
2XS
Secrets of Power Vol. 4
by Nigel Findley

2XS, The Hallucinogenic Chip of Choice

To Excess, that's how they say it on the streets, before it destroys their minds. Dirk Montgomery thinks he knows those streets. He's watched it change with the world, as the power of magic grew and altered the balances of power. He thinks he understands even the deepest shadows and the darkest of hearts. He is wrong.

Now there's something out there beyond his understanding. Something foul and alien. Something that will consume even the most wary soul.

Like Dirk's.

▼ 5 ▼
CHANGELING
by Chris Kubasik

The Magic Is Back

By 2053, the return of magic to the world has filled the streets of Chicago with beings and creatures from mythology. For those in the politically dominant mega-corporations, the underworld, and everywhere in between, it is a time of chaos and wonder, and opportunities ripe for the taking.

For fifteen-year-old Peter Clarris transformed by his Awakened genes from a human to a troll, the forces of magic are a curse to be combated with science. Torn from the comfortable biotech fast-track of his childhood, he becomes an outcast, shunned by friends and strangers alike. Now, living among the outcasts—the underclass of orks and trolls, the criminal societies of gangsters and shadowrunners—he grows up, pursuing the elusive means of controlling his own genes, and ultimately his own destiny. . . .

▼ **6** ▼

NEVER TRUST AN ELF

by Robert N. Charrette

Who Understands the Ways of Elves and Dragons?

Some say that the dragons are the most powerful beings on Earth. Certain elves disagree with that belief in the strongest, most violent terms.

An ork of the Seattle ghetto, Kham usually worries about more mundane problems. Day-to-day existence in the now magically active world of 2053 is tough enough. But all that is about to change.

Drawn into a dangerous game of political and magical confrontation, Kham not only learns to never deal with a dragon—he also discovers that trusting an elf may leave you dead. . . .

INTO THE
SHADOWS
by Jordan K. Weisman

Mercs, Magic, and Murder—

In the world of the future, reality has shifted. It is a time where supercorporations are the true rulers, and their corporate wards, power games, and espionage missions all too often rampage out of control. The nation is divided into megaplexes, sprawling urban centers peopled by everything from true humans to elves, dwarves, orks, trolls, werefolk, mages, and the occasional upwardly mobile dragon.

In this world where magic and technology coexist, and where both become far too advanced for comfort, the shadowrunners survive by the quickness of their wits, the sharpness of their fangs and blades, and their skill at riding the computer Matrix. And if the price is right, or the need is great enough, they'll sell their services to any bidder. These are their stories.

▼ 8 ▼
STREETS OF BLOOD
by Carl Sargent

Razors in the Fog

London, 2054. Shadows dance in every fog-bound lane and alley of the historic city—shadows that hide a sadistic murderer, somehow summoned from Victoria's reign to kill once more.

An uncertain alliance of shadowrunners is thrown together by violent death and corporate intrigue. Geraint, noble lord from the Principality of Wales; Adept, politician, bon vivant. Serrin, renegade Elf mage from Seattle, in search of vengeance or forgetfulness. Francesca, high-class decker for hire, haunted by blood-drenched nightmares. Rani, Punjabi Ork street samurai, a true shadow-dweller from the lowest level of British society.

All are drawn into a web of death and deceit; a conspiracy which reaches to the highest powers of the land; an intrigue built upon murder and manipulation.

When death stalks the dark streets of London, no one will be safe from the razor's kiss.

▼ 9 ▼
SHADOWPLAY
by Nigel Findley

Sly is a veteran. She's run more shadows than she cares to remember, and has the physical and emotional scars to prove it. But no matter how violent it became, it had always been business as usual. Until now.

Falcon is a kid. He thinks he hears the call of magic, and the voice of one of the Great Spirits seems to whisper in his ears. He's gone to Seattle, to the urban jungle, to seek his calling.

Thrown together, veteran and novice, Sly and Falcon find themselves embroiled in a deadly confrontation between the world's most powerful corporations. If this confrontation is not stopped, it could turn to all-out warfare, spilling out of the shadows and onto the streets themselves.

▼ 10 ▼
NIGHT'S PAWN
by Tom Dowd

For years Jason Chase was the head of the pack, shadowrunning with the best in the business. When time dulled his flesh and cybernetic edge, he knew it was time to get out, or get dead.

Now his past has come back to haunt him. To protect a young girl from the terrorists who want her dead, Chase must rely on his years of experience, and whatever his body has left to give. And everything he's got, he'll need as he comes face to face with a part of his life he thought he'd left behind, and an enemy left for dead.

▼ 11 ▼
STRIPER ASSASSIN
by Nyx Smith

Prey for the Hunter

For the world of humans, she is Striper, the deadly Asian assassin and kick-artist. She has come to the City of Brotherly Love seeking revenge and made it her killing ground. But she is not the only predator stalking the dark underbelly of the Philadelphia metroplex. There are other hunters prowling the night, and some possess a power even greater than hers.

Some may even want her dead.

When the moon rises full and brilliant into the dark pall of the night, the bestial side of her nature battles for dominion, demanding vengeance and death.

Who will survive?

Who dares to hunt the hunter?

LONE WOLF
by Nigel Findley

Blood and Magic ...

... rage in the streets of Seattle. The shifting of turf by a few blocks costs lives, innocent and guilty, silenced forever and then forgotten in the city's deepest shadows. Lone Star, Seattle's contracted police force, fights a losing battle against Seattle's newest conquerors—the gangs. From his years of undercover work for Lone Star, Rick Larson thinks he knows the score. The gangs rule their territories by guns and spells, force and intimidation, and it's the most capricious of balances that keeps things from exploding into all-out warfare. Inside the Cutter, one of the city's most dangerous gangs, Larson is in a prime position to watch the balance, react to it, and report to his superiors. But when the balance begins to shift unexpectedly, Larson finds himself not only on the wrong side of the fight but on the wrong side of the law as well.

▼ 13 ▼
FADE TO BLACK
by Nyx Smith

Honor, Loyalty, Rep

In 2055, Newark is an over-crowded urban nightmare populated by hordes of SIN-less indigents. Millions live in abject poverty. Violence is rampant. Brutal gangs and vicious criminals control many sections of the city like feudal lords. Amid this harrowing landscape Rico gathers his team: Shank, Thorvin, Piper, and the eccentric shaman known as Bandit. The job is to free a man from a corporate contract that is the moral equivalent of slavery, but that is only the beginning. The runners' diverse skills and talents are swiftly put to the test. Rico's challenge is to keep the team alive as they sort through a maze of corporate intrigue and misdirection, but without discarding honor, for without honor a man is nothing. Honor alone distinguishes a man from the ravaging dogs that fill the streets, and as the runners soon learn, the price of honor is high.

▼ 14 ▼
NOSFERATU
by Carl Sargent and Marc Gasoigne

Nowhere to Hide

Serrin Shamander, rootless mage and part-time shadowrunner, is on the run. First he flees New York, hoping to find refuge in Europe. But somebody is determined to corner him—he doesn't know who or why. On the run with Serrin is a brilliant decker named Michael and a burned-out troll samurai named Tom. Behind them is Kristen, a street kid from Capetown with a list of names . . . or victims, if you will. Now Serrin and his friends are driven by mounting panic. Everywhere they go they feel evil eyes, elven eyes, watching them. Gradually they learn of their enemy's plan to wipe humanity from the face of the earth, and they are desperate to confront him. Their enemy, however, is in no such hurry. Why should he be? Restless, powerful, demonic, hasn't he already been waiting for more than three hundred years . . . ?

▼ 15 ▼
BURNING BRIGHT
by Tom Dowd

Spare No Expense

Missing: Mitch Truman, heir apparent to an entertainment megacorporation. He may have fled his parents for the sake of love, but if magic is involved the reason could be darker. . . .

Wealthy: Dan Truman, CEO of media giant Truman Technologies, doesn't care how much it costs—he wants his son back. He'll hire the best to find his heir, even if their motives are suspect. . . .

Experienced: Kyle Teller's done this job before. He knows the tricks of the trade, and not only because he's a mage. He think finding the missing boy will be easy. Why shouldn't it be?

But will money and experience be enough to defeat the terrible power growing beneath the city of Chicago?

▼ 16 ▼
WHO HUNTS THE HUNTER
by Nyx Smith

Hunter and Hunted

From the distant forests of Maine comes the deadly Weretiger known as Striper, seeking nature's own special justice.

From the shadowed heart of the south Bronx comes the shaman called Bandit, interested only in the pursuit of his arcane arts, and the reconciliation with nature that Raccoon demands.

From the nightmare streets of Newark come Monk and Minx, seeking life itself.

Who is predator and who is prey? The assassin? The shaman? The kids with the red flashing eyes? The Director of Resource for the Hurley-Cooper Labs, or HCL's dedicated scientist? Or is it the elves? Or the mystery man from the Department of Water and Wastewater Management with a technical rating higher than God's?

Before they are done, a killer will learn the meaning of mercy, and one who has honored life will discover the necessity of ruthless destruction. . . .

"TERMINATE YOUR INVOLVEMENT.

"Get out of it, Mr. Montgomery. *Right* out."

"I would if I had the opportunity," I told him honestly.

"Then *make* the opportunity."

"Who the frag are you anyway?"

"As I said, a friend," the man repeated softly.

"And you're telling me you know what's going down?" He nodded. "Yeah, right," I snorted. "*Prove* it, if you want me to pay any attention to you." It was only after the words were out of my mouth that I remembered that last "proof" anyone had provided me. Out of reflex, I glanced at the bullet hole in the window.

By the time my eyes were back on the screen, the man's outlines were flowing, shifting—*morphing*. Any hotshot with a Cray-Amiga submicro could produce this, but deep down, I *knew* what I was watching wasn't any kind of special effect.

The man's skull expanded, elongated. Those icy eyes swelled, shifting apart, migrating toward the sides of the skull. His mouth opened, showing dagger teeth. Beyond the serried rows of teeth, something moved—a black tongue, forked like a snake's.

"Is this sufficient proof?" asked the dragon.

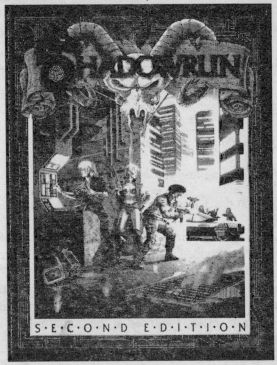